Destined For More

Julie DeFisher

Spears
PUBLISHING

E-Book Edition, October 2022
Hardcover Edition, November 2022
Softcover Edition, November 2022

ISBN 978-1-959816-01-0

Visit traespears.com

There are so many people I want to thank for this. In the end, I did this for my son. To show years from now that Mommy was different too. She didn't let that stop her and neither should he.
~Love you, my little Monkey.

Chapter 1

As the afternoon sun shows through the window of the second-floor bathroom, Rose sits on the toilet staring at the piece of plastic in her hands. Two pink lines staring back at her like two hot daggers to the stomach. Something told her to take that test that afternoon, but how could she have known this would be the results. How could this have happened? How was she going to tell her parents? What would be her fate now?

Her parents were Gammas. Third in command among the Hollows pack. Rose's mother, Kate, was a daughter of an Alpha and ended up mated to a Gamma. Kate's twin sister, Eva, Rose's Aunt, ended up with a Beta of the Harvest Moon pack. Kate was always jealous due to the lack of power and position that the Moon Goddess saw fit to give her, and this would be just one more thing that Kate would blame on her misfortune.

Therefore, this development would shame and cause scandal for the family along with her pack. Not sure of what to really do, Rose walks out of the bathroom and into her bedroom. She hides the box in there to be less likely to be found there since she is the only one that goes in there. After disposing of the box and trying to warn off the wave of nausea, Rose lays on her bed with her eyes closed.

Her phone had been ringing off the hook all morning and most of the afternoon. As she looks down at the caller ID, Rose shakes her head. DALLAS in bright bold letters shines back. **Not now. I can't deal with his BS right now...** she thinks to herself as she reaches for the phone and debates on whether to answer or turn it off.

Dallas, the Beta's Son, and best friend to the soon to be Alpha, has been sniffing around for months. His cropped black hair and honey brown eyes made every girl, wolf or otherwise, swoon over him. His tall muscular stature gave him that dark and dangerous feel. Everyone wanted him and the Alpha's son Asher as friends or at the very least allies. After all, they were the next in line to run this pack.

Rose found it funny that one day while working on her 69' Oldsmobile Cutlass in the yard of her house, the boys stopped by for a chat. Rose was always working on something, but the classics were where her passion really came alive. Rose was an excellent student and even top of her class. It surprised her deeply that the pack "bad boys" would be stopping by on that day. The topic was always about cars and the fact that girls couldn't fix them the way a man could. Rose would always laugh off such nonsense, but that's where it all started.

Rose was seventeen and a few months off her eighteenth birthday. A special time in a young wolf's life is when they find their mate. Long red hair, always neatly braided, hung to her waist. Her semi-tall stature standing at 5'8" and long legs made almost every male stop and look. Her emerald-green eyes enchanted onlookers even though she was never really interested in anything but her cars, education, and three best friends. Rose had no trouble fitting in with the pack. She was a fighter and was quicker than most men in her age group. The word around the pack was that she was going to be named the top female warrior and leader of patrols.

Dallas, already nineteen, had become extremely interested in Rose over the last three months. Dallas was following her every move and even came off almost more like a stalker. Rose began to believe in some ways maybe she was Dallas's mate with the way he was acting. He had already been of age. Therefore, he should have known one way or the other. Maybe he was just waiting to come out about being her mate until she was of age and they both felt the mate bond.

All these thoughts flashed like a neon sign in her head as her phone kept going off over and over again. Rose sighs and finally answers the phone with a silent plea.

"Yellow" Rose rubs her temples.

"Well, she lives." Dallas's overly happy voice booms out the speakers.

"Yeah, shits been a little crazy." Rose says, eyeing the box in the trash along with the test sitting on her nightstand.

"Well, I missed hearing your honey voice." You could hear the charm dripping off each and every word Dallas spoke.

"Really?... Look, we really need to talk. Can you come by?" Rose taps her fingers on the pregnancy test and then lays it back on the nightstand.

"Sure can. Be there in like ten."

"Cool. See you then." Rose, hanging up the phone, taking a deep breath and dropping the phone to the bed for a moment.

Rose knew she would have to prepare herself for what was about to go down. She grabbed the test, her phone, and a few of her knives. Gathering all her courage and wit, Rose went downstairs to wait for the person; that she hoped could give her the answers she desperately needed.

Rose had to think hard about the situation she happens to find herself in currently. She knows the *who*, by the current actions, but not the *when* this could have happened. ***Think Babygirl think….*** It was the only thought Rose could keep in her head as she heard her wolf start howling and snarling in her mind.

Snow, Rose's wolf, typically showed this sign of distaste for anyone she didn't like or trust when they were near. As Rose looked out at the driveway, threw the living room windows, sure enough Dallas, in his silver mustang, was coming down the driveway. ***Remain*** *calm. You got this*. It was all that Rose could say to herself as she heard the car come to a stop and Dallas opened his door. Just a few seconds later, the doorbell rings and it is now the ultimate moment of truth.

Opening the door, there stood Dallas in all his glory. A white t-shirt, black jeans, and black boots were Dallas's everyday go to wear. His hair slicked back and would normally make any girl's mouth water. His hands propped on the door frame waiting to be invited into the house. Under normal circumstances, this would be a welcome visit, but Rose was not ready for the conversation that needed to take place right now.

Rose nods and turns her back to Dallas as she walks into the kitchen. Dallas, taking this as his invitation, follows her into the house, closing the door behind him. Dallas couldn't keep his hands to himself and kept trying to snake his arms around Rose. Rose, wanting to keep a level head about all this, pulls away. Why was he always trying to cloud her judgment? Rose, trying to keep her senses sharp, nods to a stool on one side of the bar and quickly moves to the other side across from him. For some reason, Rose desperately needed to look him in the eye for this.

"So, you just can't stay away, huh?" Dallas started off smugly.

"We have a lot to discuss… and it's best to do this without prying eyes and big ears" Rose said with a big deep breath.

"What do we have to discuss?" He says while trying to reach across the bar and grab Rose's hand.

She slides the piece of plastic across to him with a blank face. He laughs when he picks it up and turns it over in his hand. At first, Dallas looks confused and then starts belting out laughter. He is laughing like this is the biggest joke he has ever heard.

"This has to be some kind of joke," Dallas says, still wailing from laughter.

"This isn't some joke. I took that about 30 minutes ago" Rose says, becoming increasingly angry and fire starts rising in her body and blood.

"And what do you want me to do about it? I only slept with you one time. How do I know that you haven't been whoring around with every guy in the pack?" Dallas stops laughing and looks at her with defiance and anger in his eyes.

"Because I was a virgin before I ever had any kind of dealings with you!!!!" Rose said with her face as red as the blood moon.

Dallas, laughing again, replies "Well, I guess that LycanBerry did the trick then."

Rose's look of confusion flashes back to the night two weeks ago when she was asked out to a party with the guys. Her realization of waking up the next morning barely remembers anything from the night before. Rose only knew she was sore and there was blood on her panties. Her eyes went from emerald to bright red. Her wolf growled in her head and tried to tear her way to the surface. A low growl coming out of Rose caught Dallas's attention.

"Look here, little wolf… You can't take me. I will kill you!" Dallas said, trying to make a domineering move and make her submit.

Unfortunately for him, before Dallas could make it over the top of the bar to stand face to face with Rose, she already had both her knives out and ready to play. Rose had one at his throat and the other at his balls, begging him to just breathe wrong. He wasn't going to get away with this even if she had to neuter him.

"You think you can just do this and get away with it?" Dallas's words were just barely an audible whisper.

"You attacked me, remember? Now I have some questions. I'm going to walk you back to your seat and you're going to answer them, or so, help me by the Goddess, I will leave you to bleed out on this floor." Rose backed him back around the bar and he sat back down on the stool.

"What do you want?" Dallas's eyes seething into Rose's but never taking one eye off the knives. He almost looked like he was trying to control his wolf but knew in the back of his mind she would fulfill the promise she made.

"Did you drug me?"

"I guess you could say that."

"Are you my Mate?"

"Oh, Goddess No! You were merely just the little princess that everyone wanted. I figured I could keep you around until I found my mate. Maybe even after." Dallas said more to add more fuel to the fire.

"So, what are WE going to do about this?" Rose said through gritted teeth.

Dallas's laughter hit an all-time high, which further enraged Rose. "WE aren't going to do shit. YOU are the one that is knocked up, not me. That's not my pup!"

Snow wanted to rip his throat out as the river of tears ran freely down her human's face. How could someone say one thing and do another? Had she been so blinded by the possibility of love and thought that this boy would do the right thing by her?

As Dallas stood up from the stool, puffing his chest out and spoke, "I will say one thing and leave. This never happened. That's not my pup and I have never laid a hand on you in any way, shape, or form. And as long as you don't want your precious reputation destroyed by being labeled a "whore", I'd keep your trap shut." Dallas practically ran for the door, knowing that he had a very small chance of making it out without being stabbed.

As he got to the front door, he turned and said, "I, Dallas Ellis, future Beta of the Hollow pack do hear by reject you and anything to do with you Rose Wells."

"I, Rose Wells, do hereby accept your rejection. And I hope the Goddess has a better plan for me and mine. You will never look for me or the child I choose to bring into this world." Fire flamed with eyes staring holes through the piece of trash in front of her.

With one nod, Dallas ran through the door and to his car. Once the engine roared to life, Dallas wasted no time tearing out of her driveway. She closed the door, finally letting her guard down for the first time since she came face to face with that slimeball. Rose fell to her knees, crying out to the Goddess "Oh Goddess, what is your plan for me?"

Clearing her eyes from the hot tears, Rose looked up at the clock. 3:45pm... Her mother would be home soon. How in the name of the Goddess was she going to tell her that this had happened? She knew that her mother would be completely enraged and feel betrayed by the situation. Rose wasn't stupid enough to expect compassion from her mother, but maybe a little understanding and loyalty for her daughter would not be overreaching at this point.

Chapter 2

At 4:00pm on a Saturday afternoon, Rose's mom, Kate, returns home from her Gamma female duties with Luna Zara. In just two short weeks, the seniors will be graduating. This was always a huge time for the packs.

This being the biggest graduating class in the last few years was always something to celebrate. With the Alpha's son and the Beta's son being part of this graduating class, it was an even bigger celebration than normal. Asher and Dallas, being next in line, would take over the pack in just two short years upon their 21st birthdays. Therefore, everyone was buzzing with party planning.

Rose was lying on her bed. The realization that this was the first time in the last few weeks that her phone wasn't going off like a late alarm clock. Rose was overly aware when her mother's car pulled up the driveway and even cringed when she heard her come through the door. Rose's crying left her with little to no strength to go downstairs to deal with her mother. Rose had no idea how she was going to tell her mother what had happened to her. Would Kate stand by her daughter and make the boy pay for the damage he caused or blame Rose for the shame she had brought on the family name?

Kate was a very conservative but also extremely materialistic person. Standing at 5'7", roughly 130lbs, and with shoulder-length strawberry blonde hair, Kate was a beauty in her own right. Kate was also about standing and position. Kate, in so many ways, hated that she wasn't mated to an Alpha, being an Alpha's daughter and all. She has always played her part, especially with her daughter. Rose's older brother Delli was mated to a lovely woman, Lily. Lily is the only child of her Alpha father. Which made Delli an Alpha by default. Kate was extremely proud of her son's match.

While Rose was a beauty. She was a bit more Tom-boyish. Books, cars, and sitting in the background. While others were out running in the woods and causing trouble, Rose was busy figuring out her end game. How she was going to better her life. This is what made Rose happy. Her mother wanted a social butterfly and ended up with a grease monkey with more of a wallflower tendency.

"Rose… Rose…" Kate called out to her daughter. "Are you home?"

"Yeah, Mom. I'm here." Rose said, trying to cover up the subsiding sobs and sadness in her voice.

"Can you come down here please." Rose could hear the chipperness in her mother's voice.

"Coming." Rose yells back, taking a steading breath.

Rose looked at herself in the mirror, trying to erase the signs she had been crying. She didn't want her mother asking questions just yet. Rose didn't know how her mother was going to react to this news, but she had an idea though.

Rose came down the stairs and her mother was standing at the bar in the kitchen drinking a soda. Kate had her hair pulled up into a bun but with her strawberry blonde hair catching the afternoon light. Kate looked agitated and Rose knew something was up.

"Hey Mom." Rose greeted her and came to give her mother a kiss on the cheek.

"What's wrong with you?" Kate saw the red rings under her daughter's eyes.

"Oh nothing. I just smashed my hand working on my car today. Don't worry, it's all better now", Rose said, thinking quickly on her feet and trying to cover it up.

"Okay." Kate eyed Rose suspiciously. "So… Are you going out tonight?"

"Nope." Rose was short, sweet and to the point in her response to her mother.

"Dallas not coming by? I think he is a lovely boy. I think he could be so good for you." Kate said, holding hope that her daughter would fall in with the right crowd.

"No, I don't believe we will be seeing him around anytime soon." Rose was hoping that just saying this would drop him from the conversation and from being brought back up. No such luck…

"Oh really? Did y'all have a fight?" Kate was prying.

"Kind of. He's moving on with his life and trying to find his mate." Rose felt the heat rise back up through her blood replaying the events over and over in her head.

Kate stood there and looked closely at her daughter before slamming her drink down on the counter. Rose didn't even flinch. Kate was fuming for what possible reason no one knows. Kate would go off at the drop of a hat, and all because things wouldn't be the way she wanted them.

"You can't hold on to a man at all, can you?" Kate began the attack on her daughter.

"Really Mom? Really?" Rose looked at her mother in disbelief.

"Really ROSE! That was your best chance to be someone in this pack. You just threw it away like you have so many other options?" Kate began seething at her daughter through gritted teeth.

Rose, feeling so much more than hurt, gets ready to furiously unload on her mother. Rose balls up her fists and slams them on the counter. Which catches Kate off guard. Rose's eyes turned from emerald to blood red, showing her lack of control over her wolf at that moment.

"Oh, My Goddess Mom! Fucking Really? Do you have any idea? A fathom of an idea of what the hell I've been through today?" Rose looked straight into her mother's eyes, trying to gain some sort of control of her emotions and Snow.

"What could you have possibly gone through today?" Kate pops her hand on her hip in a condescending stance.

Without thinking, Rose threw the pregnancy test out on the counter. Kate picked it up and turned it over, revealing the two pink lines staring back. When the realization came to light, Kate walked over and smacked Rose across the face. Fire burning in both their eyes facing off mother against daughter.

"You FUCKING WHORE!" Kate screamed at the top of her lungs.

"You don't even want to know what happened?" Rose touched the burning handprint on her cheek.

"You're pregnant, that's all I need to know. How could you do this to me! To your father! To our pack!" Kate paces around the kitchen.

"I did nothing wrong here but get taken advantage of and you're making this about you! I have no idea why I thought it would be any different." Rose stood there more in defiance than in the shame that her mother thought she should have. After all, Rose was drugged.

"I swear if it wouldn't cause a scandal I would have you out of this house tonight! BUT I would have to answer too many questions." Kate paces around the kitchen for a few more minutes, dramatically rubbing her temples.

Kate must figure out how to handle this situation quickly and quietly. She needs to think of a way that would be the least amount of scandal and embarrassment to her and the family. Finally, she stops and looks at Rose, still holding the cheek that she had belted with her hand. Kate knew that she couldn't do anything until graduation and, thankfully, that was merely two weeks away, well a week from Friday.

"Go to your room! I can't bear the sight of your face." Kate yells at her daughter.

Rose, with less emotion on her face than what was going on in her body, did as she was told and went back up the stairs to her room. Slamming the door when she is safely inside, Rose holds her stomach and slides to the floor, finally allowing the tears to flow. This has definitely been the single worst day of Rose's life.

After Kate hears the door slam, she grabs up her cellphone to call the one person she believed owed her a favor… Her sister. Even though they haven't talked in years, Kate believes that Eva, with absolute certainty, will help in this delicate matter, family honor and all. And if, by chance, she couldn't or absolutely wouldn't, Kate knew of some bones believed not to be wanted out of the dark grave they rested in. Kate always believed holding on to such little secrets was always eventually needed as a bargaining chip.

The phone didn't even ring twice. When Kate was met with the cheery voice of Eva on the other end of the phone. Kate merely rolled her eyes. There was a deep loathing in Kate and Eva's relationship with each other.

"Well, Hello Kate, as I live and breathe. How are you?" Eva was as surprised as ever to not only see her sister's name on the caller ID but to be actually talking to her.

"Hello, Eva." Kate was short and emotionless. "I have a problem and I'm afraid you are the only one that can help."

"Everything alright? Rose, Okay?" Eva spoke with concern in her voice.

It didn't escape Kate's attention that only her daughter and not her husband were mentioned in the concern. This would fuel a fire for a fight for another time, but at this moment she needed Eva's cooperation. Kate hated to ask, more like demand, anything from her sister, but desperate times called for desperate measures.

"You always seem to jump to the right person right off the bat." Kate said, drumming her nails on the counter.

"So, something is wrong with Rose? What happened? Is she hurt?" Rising panic in Eva's voice let Kate know she had taken the bait.

"Look, I'm not going to explain too much over the phone. There could be ears listening in to this conversation. I need her out of here. Embarrassing herself is enough, but when it affects her father and myself, that won't be tolerated. I will not have her tear down our good name along with our rank in this pack for her mistakes." Kate spat out with the venom and distaste she has for her daughter at the moment.

"I will have to inform my Alpha and Luna of her arrival. When should I be expecting her?" Eva spoke without any question or hesitation.

"I will be sending her on her way a week from Friday. She graduates that day, and it will be easy to explain her leaving right after that." Kate smiles evilly, knowing the situation will be taken care of soon enough.

"We are supposed to be having dinner at the packhouse tonight. I will talk to my Alpha and Luna then. Will there be a return date, or will I find out more when she gets here?" Eva knew that her sister would do anything to save and keep her "good name" intact.

"When she gets there. I think I will head Kyle off before he gets home and put things in motion on my end." Kate said, feeling pretty proud of herself getting her sister to do what she wanted.

"Fine. I will call you tomorrow with the details." Eva hoped that her niece would be safe until she could get her in possession.

"That will be fine. Till tomorrow." Kate hung up the phone. No goodbye, love you, miss you or anything.

Eva just looked at her phone, floored and in complete disbelief of the conversation they had just had. She knew Rose to be an extremely bright, caring, and beautiful young woman. What could she have possibly gotten herself into that would warrant a phone call and banishment from her mother. Eva really didn't care about the situation. She had been trying to get her hands on Rose since she was a baby. Even more just a few short years ago when the problems started between Eva and her sister. She would finally have her chance.

Chapter 3

Kate calls her husband to see can head him off before leaving the training grounds. If he came home, he would more than likely want to talk to Rose and right now Kate can't have the cat coming out of the bag right now. Therefore, a little game of keep away was in order for the time being.

"Hello, my love" Kyle answered on the first ring.

"Hey darling. I was wondering if we could possibly have dinner at the packhouse tonight?" Kate said, trying to sound nonchalant.

"That sounds fine. Is Rose not going to be home?" Kyle inquires about his daughter's plans for the evening.

"No, she is home. Rose has finals starting Monday that she has to study for and just needs quiet." Kate hoped that he would take the blatant lie as fact.

"Okay then. I will meet you there. No sense in coming all the way back to the house to end up right back here." Kyle said not knowing how pleased this made his wife. Kate wanted to lay her plan in motion without her husband being none the wiser.

"I'll see you there then." Kate smiled.

"Love you!" Kyle says and hangs up the phone.

Kate stomps up to Rose's room. She straightened herself up and felt pretty proud of herself. Just a two-week time frame of having to play this all off and then no more stress. No one would know anything, just what she chose for people to know. Kate thought, *See Goddess I have all the traits for a good Luna and yet you disgrace me like this.*

Rose was still curled up in a ball on the floor when she heard the footsteps heading toward her room. She sits up with her back against the bed, knowing at any second her mother would be busting through the door. Rose knows that she will now be faced with receiving the brunt end of her rage until she gets out of this house.

Her door flings open with her mother now standing in her doorway. Anger still painted on her face but something else was there as well. Kate almost looked like she was pleased with herself. This was an odd combination for a woman that was just screaming at her daughter less than thirty or so minutes ago.

"I have come to a decision. I will talk to the Alpha and Luna tonight. Your father and I will be having dinner tonight at the packhouse. I will tell them that you have been accepted into a school near the Harvest Moon pack. Eva, your aunt, will be talking to her Alpha and Luna. As you will be sent to her. My sister will be making arrangements on her end to have you set up once you are there with her. Once the bastard you carry is born, you will be putting it up for adoption. You will come back here and marry whomever I see fit. That man like your father will never know about any of this. Do you understand me?" Kate says while walking about Rose's room spitting out orders and demands.

"When do I leave?" Rose says calmly.

"After your graduation, a week from Friday. Until then you will stay in this room and go to school. No one will know anything. Maybe we will be able to save face as long as no one knows." Kate says while looking at her daughter as if she was trash.

Rose simply nodded her head at her mother. She had her own plans and by the Goddess they had nothing to do with her mother, father, or their standing in this Goddess forsaken pack. She just wasn't going to let anyone in on it. This was her life after all, and she was never going to bow before anyone no matter the circumstances.

"Now I'm going to get ready to meet your father for dinner. Don't you dare leave this room!" Kate walked out of Rose's room slamming the door. Kate felt pleased with herself while she headed down the hall to get ready for dinner.

Kate arrived at the packhouse a little before 7pm. She parked her car and headed into the massively large building. Floor to ceiling-stained glass windows depicting the great battle that told the story of the pack's history illuminated the entryway. Kate could see Omegas hurrying about getting all sorts of food and tables ready for dinner. Kate casually walked into the dining room looking about the room for her usual group.

Kate's husband Kyle was standing by the main table with a drink in his hand. Kate walks to his side and snakes her arm around his massive waist. At six foot even, Kyle wasn't the tallest of his comrades but what he lacked in height he made up for in speed, agility, and strength. With his dark red hair and bright green eyes, Kyle knew how to direct attention without having to put in much effort.

Kate, on the other hand, with her strawberry blonde hair and slender stature commanded attention from everyone male or female in the room. She wanted to be noticed when she entered the room. Some would say she almost needed it. Kate always aimed too high. She had the point of view that you are what you make yourself to be. If you seek a higher rank, then by the Goddess, you represented yourself as such until you had gotten where you needed to be. It only took time to get what you wanted in Kate's eyes.

"Hello Gamma Kate. So nice to see you for dinner tonight." Alpha Kent spoke with such sweetness.

"Well, I figured it had been too long since we all shared a meal, or even just sat and chatted." Kate spoke, setting up her plan.

Kyle pulled out his wife's chair and sat beside her at the big circular table. He was a bit curious about the change in plans of eating at the packhouse instead of just ordering in which is what they normally did at home. It wasn't unusual when Rose was out on a date or social event, but Rose was at home studying to his understanding. Kyle would just wait to ask questions until later in the evening after his wife had a little more relaxed tongue from drinking.

"So, graduation is only two weeks away. Does Rose have any plans for after High School?" Luna Zara says while slipping in to sit next to Alpha Kent.

"Actually, that was one of my reasons for coming here tonight. I needed to have a word with both of you and it couldn't very well wait till morning." Kate smiles brightly not to show any hint of the actual problem.

"Go on." Alpha Kent says sitting up in his chair to show he is giving the Gamma his complete attention.

"Well, my extremely bright daughter got into college. She got the letter today. But that would put her leaving for summer semester right after graduation. She would be near my sister, Eva's pack. I have been in contact with her to get permission on their end. I know she would need permission on this end to leave without being considered a rouge." Kate spun her lies with so much carefulness that it actually sounded true even to her ears. She was very good at making people believe exactly what she wanted when she wanted.

"Well, that is amazing. I'm so happy for Rose. I see no problem in granting her time to continue schooling." Alpha Kent with such pride that one of his pack members would be bettering themselves and in turn the pack when it was all said and done.

"Oh, I completely agree. I mean it is so hard to get any of these pups to think past the next party let alone their future. There is always a problem with them tearing things up and not even wanting to take the responsibility for their own actions. It is really refreshing to see a young woman taking charge." Luna Zara said understanding the challenges she currently faces with her own child.

"So glad you two see it that way. I know she is going to be so much better after this experience." Kate says, hiding her evil grin behind her glass as she takes a drink. She knew her plan was coming together with little to no effort.

"Maybe we should have some sort of party for the graduates and a sendoff for Rose?" Luna Zara said to the people sitting around the table.

Gamma Kyle was sitting there looking at his wife wondering what was really going on. She could never hide things very well from him. He also knew if Rose had gotten this kind of news today, he would have been the first to get a phone call. He also knew that sharing news like this with her mother would have ended in a giant fight. Was this the real reason that Kate wanted to go to the packhouse for dinner instead of being at home?

Gamma Kyle always knew that his wife was never happy simply being a Gamma. She wanted elevation but she couldn't do that on her own. He knew she would have no problems using her children to accomplish that. While Delli had no problem going along with the program, Rose very much minded someone butting into her life. Rose lived up to her name being full of thorns like the flower he named her after.

Gamma Kyle gathering all the information that he would use in his questioning later also took note that Kate talked to her sister. Something was definitely not right here. She despised her sister since Eva was a rank higher than her, even if she was the Beta Female of another pack the fact remained, Eva was a Beta. Eva used to call and write often especially after Rose was born. About 10 years or so ago, Kate and Eva had a falling out in a very big and semipublic way. Though no one talks about it, they all know that Kate would rather eat a silver bullet then call on Eva.

"That is extremely gracious, but I don't believe Rose will want to attend. She has made it very clear that she will be leaving right after the ceremony. I believe for the others that sounds like an amazing course of action. After all, it is tradition for the Alpha and Luna to host that celebration." Kate tried not to come off as rude but definitely spin it the way she needed it to go.

"Alright then we should set up an appointment for some time later this week to get papers in order for her pass. After a call to Alpha Jax to make sure he has everything in order for Rose to cross into the Harvest Moon territory." Luna Zara said, looking at Alpha Kent to confirm the correct course of action.

"Wednesday, work for her at about 3:30?" Alpha Kent said, looking to Kate for an answer.

"That will be fine. I will let her know." Kate looking like an overstuffed Cheshire cat settled back into her chair waving down an Omega for another Jack and Coke.

The rest of the dinner went well. With polite conversation about training and patrols, shop talk for the men. Beta Knox and his mate female Beta Haven came by the table and had a drink with the group. They struck up a conversation about the graduation party. Everything had settled into its normal rhythm.

As things began to wrap up and disperse, a young fighter ran in and drew the men away from the table. Some raised voices and angry growls from the corner of the room where the men were now standing caught everyone's attention. All anyone could hear was there was something about a fire in the woods.

Alpha Kent waved his hand and sent the young man on his way. Looking completely exacerbated with the situation, Alpha Kent with the other men went back to the table to explain to the others what was going on. Such a quiet evening ruined by the events that just came to light.

"Well, it would seem that the boys decided to have a party in the woods this evening. They were drinking and the fire they lit got out of hand." Shrieks about the room caused everyone to stop and listen to the Alpha.

"It is under control now, but they are all being brought to my office. So, they can be dealt with accordingly. The problem at hand is the fact that 3 of these boys were supposed to be on patrol. I'm so sorry Gamma Kyle, I need you to go out and handle it while I deal with the boys." Alpha Kent looked so apologetic.

"Of course, Alpha." Gamma Kyle said kissing his wife goodbye and heading out to check where he was needed.

Alpha Kent and Beta Knox headed to the office to deal with the drunk and reckless teenagers that were being brought in. Luna Zara stayed behind for a moment. Her presence would be needed at some point to keep the Alpha from going off the deep end, but for now she would let the boys sweat it out.

"I bet you're glad you have a responsible daughter instead of these crazy boys right now." Luna Zara said looking up as she could hear the Alpha's voice boom through the inside of the packhouse.

"Oh, it is just kids being kids. I bet the young Alpha and Beta-to-be were just doing what boys do." Kate said with the understanding that boys will be boys.

"Well, I better get up there before he brings the roof down on their heads." Luna Zara excused herself and Beta Haven followed.

After their backs were turned to Kate she sneered after them. She could have lived here but Gamma Kyle wanted a private setting to raise a family. So, the Delta Rhett and his mate Nala took the Gamma floor. Kate would never let him forget they could have had it better.

With Rose's father having to be on patrol, Kate rushed back to the house to tell Rose of the plan and all the arrangements that she had made. Rose's mistake would not come back on Kate or the family. She would see to that. What no one would be the wiser about, made it easy to get away with. Rose would still serve her purpose if Kate had anything to do with it.

Chapter 4

Eva wakes up thinking about the phone call from her sister the day before. Eva knows it has to be something big that is going on with Rose. After all, she has not heard a word from her sister in 10 years. Some would say that Eva had the beauty, grace, and kindheartedness of the sisters. It was hard to even believe that they were twins with them being more like night and day in not only their appearances but in their whole outlook.

Eva stood 5'10" and roughly 175lbs of muscle and long legs. Her waist length blonde hair always braided back. Her honey brown eyes would always be filled with understanding and care. She was more in between a lady and tomboy with not only how she acted but her appearance as well. Pulling off whatever look she needed when the time came for it.

While she was supposed to talk to Alpha Jax and Luna Hazel last night, there was a border patrol breach and dinner was cut very short. However, Eva was able to make an early appointment to speak with both of them this morning. It wasn't often the Alpha and Luna took an audience with anyone on Sunday mornings.

Sunday morning meetings were reserved for very important business or matters that absolutely couldn't wait for Mondays. Eva believed that this was one of those circumstances. Eva, not knowing the trouble that could potentially be following her niece, believes this would be as good a time as any. She hadn't even talked to her husband yet, as he was called away from dinner with Alpha Jax to handle the patrol problems.

She rises from her bed to get a shower and get ready for her meeting. As she grabs her clothes and heads to the bathroom, she hears the front door open. Eva knows there is only one person that should be coming through that door, but she freezes and calls out.

"Tony, hunny, is that you?" Eva is ready for anyone to call out.

"Yeah, baby it's me." Tony walks into the bedroom and flops down on the bed exhausted and completely over the night that had unfolded.

"Oh sweetie. You look so tired." Eva goes over to the bed where her mate lay in just a pair of running shorts.

"Damn rouges had us running all night. We finally caught up to them. It was nothing major, just some young wolves trying to find their way in the dark. Kinda funny that they gave Old Paul quite the scare though." Tony props himself up on his elbows to see Eva holding her things for her morning shower and gathering the rest of her essentials.

Eva, realizing she is being observed, gathers more things that she might need in the bathroom. She looks back at her mate with a raised eyebrow. While she wanted to discuss the situation at hand, she was worried that he would either fall asleep or blow it completely out of proportion. Mainly since he never liked Kate or her attitude toward her sister.

"What are you staring at?" Eva finally gives in and sparks the conversation.

"Why are you up so early?" Tony noticed it was only 7am on a Sunday morning. Normally, they didn't get up til 9. Then Eva and Tony would head for a late breakfast and morning meeting at the packhouse.

"I have a meeting with Alpha Jax and Luna Hazel this morning." Eva says like it was any other day.

"This early?" Tony cocks an eyebrow at his mate.

"Well, it's the only time they had to meet in private." Eva wanted to tell her loving mate what was actually weighing on her mind.

"Well as your Beta and your mate, don't you think I should know what my mate needs to talk to Alpha and Luna about?" Tony pushed looking at her confused. Tony now positioning himself from propped elbows to a sitting position.

Eva sighs heavily. She decides this will probably be the best time to just lay it out there. She prays that he understands that this is not for Kate but for Rose. She would protect that girl with or without his help at this point.

"Okay… but just hear me out completely before you say a word. Agreed?" Eva looked sternly at her mate knowing that she would have to lay down the law or he would just pop off.

"Agreed." Tony sat up straight, waiting for the bombshell that Eva was going to drop.

"I got a call yesterday from my sister Kate." Eva held her hands up when she saw Tony's jawline visibly tense and tighten. "It wasn't a long conversation. Lasted maybe a whole 5 minutes. The just of it is Rose is in some kind of trouble. Kate is sending her away. For how long? I do not know. Why? I do not know. All I do know is that if Kate is sending Rose away; this means something big is or has happened. Her only tell was she wasn't going to let her mistake black mark the family name."

Tony sat there on the bed listening to all the information. He knew that Eva loved her niece more than anything in the world. He also knew that he would protect Rose no matter what trouble followed her. So as any good husband would, he dragged his butt off the bed and started finding clean and respectable clothes. Afterall, this wasn't the normal Sunday brunch among the leaders; this was much more serious.

"What are you doing?" Eva asked in amusement as her extremely tired mate went sifting through laundry to find something to wear.

"I'm getting ready to jump into the shower with you. So, we can go talk to Alpha and Luna together." Tony says while looking at Eva like it should be completely obvious what was going on.

"You're not going to say anything?" Eva knows his distaste for her sister and would expect something to be said.

"What is there to say? Rose is family. She is in some sort of trouble. Obviously, Kate doesn't want it getting out destroying her image in some way, shape or form. And what does she do when shit gets tough? She cuts it off. Somehow Rose has been caught in a crossfire. She needs help and here we are." Tony standing there making sure he got all of the facts out there and in the correct order before looking at Eva. "Like what else is there? Did I miss something?"

Eva teary eyed runs to her mate and gives him the biggest kiss ever. This among other things is why she loved this man. 20 years they had been together, seems like just yesterday they had shown up at the same Blue Moon ball. BAM that was all she wrote. Though the Moon Goddess had not blessed them with their own children as of yet, they were content being the Aunt and Uncle that spoiled every pup in the pack.

In 20 years, he hadn't changed in the least. He was still tall, dark, and massively handsome. Standing at 6'6" and all of 275lbs with muscles for days and shoulder length black hair with hazel green eyes, Tony was perfect. Even if the Goddess had not given him to Eva, they would have still ended up together. They were perfectly matched in every way.

"Well, the meeting is at 7:45, so we better get a move on." Eva says, grabbing her clothes and walking to the bathroom. Tony quickly followed in tow.

By 7:30am, Eva and Tony were properly dressed and headed out of the house and toward the packhouse. While most packs would have Alpha and Luna along with the Betas, Gammas, and even Deltas all under the same roof; the Harvest Moon packhouse was more of a meeting place. A common ground, if you will, to show every member the same respect and courtesy. The Alpha and Luna do live in the packhouse, but the rest of the members have their own private homes.

The packhouse has always been a welcoming environment and if anyone chooses to, they could stay there. It was more like a hotel for when meetings were held from neighboring packs. Parties and celebrations were held at the packhouse. With most of the higher ups being only a ten- or so-minute walk away. No one really minded it. It's just the way it was in this pack.

The massive wooden cabins gave all the feel and warmth of how close the pack really was with one another. One would swear that this was a hotel or a resort to the looks of the surrounding buildings.

The houses blended perfectly into the backdrop of the foothills of the mountain. Large and spacious walkways gave the illusion of something far more fancy in the mountains of Montana.

Walking through the front door of the packhouse, you could hear the Omegas busy in the kitchen and running about making the dining room ready for the typical Sunday brunch. The early morning patrols would have eaten and gone already, and the next crowd wouldn't be along for at least another hour or so.

"Good morning, Beta Tony, Beta Eva." A lovely young girl responded when she saw them standing in observance.

"Good morning, Sky. How are you this morning?" Eva's always cheery voice rang out over the hustle and bustle.

"Oh wonderful. If you are looking for Alpha Jax and Luna Hazel, they are upstairs in the office." Sky pointed an elbow at the stairs as her hands were full with a tray full of glasses.

"Thank you, Sky. Have they sent down for coffee yet?" Tony asked in desperate need of caffeine.

"Why yes, they have. The kitchen Omegas just brought up the tray." Sky smiled in response.

After saying their goodbyes, they proceeded to walk up the three flights of stairs. Down the right wing of the house were the living quarters and to the left were the Alpha and Luna's offices. Tony and Eva walked to the Alpha's office and taking a slightly deep breath, they knocked on the office door.

Chapter 5

After just a few short minutes, footsteps could be heard making their way to the door to open it. Luna Hazel answered the door in a perfectly designed sweater and pants combination. Warm and comfortable was their normal weekend attire around the packhouse, but Monday thru Friday was all business.

"Come in Beta Tony, Beta Eva." Luna Hazel says with her pleasant and sing-song voice.

"Right on time as always." Alpha Jax stands from behind his desk and shakes his Beta's hand.

"Would you like some coffee?" Luna Hazel motions to the tray with the coffee and cups.

"Oh, Thank you. We would love some." Eva speaks up for her and Tony knowing it's only a matter of time before he falls out on his feet.

Luna Hazel smiles and walks over to start preparing the cups. As the coffee was poured and handed out, everyone took their seats. It was time to get down to the business at hand. Alpha Jax settled into his chair and looked attentively at the two Betas sitting across from him not knowing what to expect.

"Well first off I would like to Thank you both for having this meeting not only on such short notice but so early in the morning." Eva began.

"Oh, it's nothing Beta Eva. We are always here for our pack no matter what the situation might be." Alpha Jax spoke with such calmness.

"Well, there is no other way to put this… so I'm going to just lay it out on the line." Eva looked at Tony and smiled. Taking strength with the fact that he was right there beside her no matter what. She was a very lucky woman, and with a deep breath she began.

"My sister called me last night. Well late afternoon actually and said that she is sending my niece, Rose, away. I wasn't given any real details except that she is in some kind of trouble. Knowing my sister, it's gotta be something big. Something that she doesn't want to get out among her pack. Something that, in her eyes, would cause people to look at the "family" in a different light. I'm not sure what she happens to be telling everyone back there, but I'm sure whatever it is it wouldn't reflect badly on her or her mate." Eva said with a heavy heart for her niece.

Alpha Jax and Luna Hazel sat and listened in a bit of shock. First, this was not the kind of news that they had mentally braced themselves for. Secondly, how could a mother turn her back on their own child? It seemed unfathomable. Especially for the sake of image among the pack. They both knew so many were about good standings and being placed in good favor among their pack. It was just beyond comprehension that this was happening in this day and age.

"So, more than likely we should be hearing from their Alpha sometime this week?" Alpha Jax said with his hands folded around his coffee cup looking very interested.

"She was supposed to talk to their Alpha and Luna last night. I was supposed to discuss this with you all last night and see if we could allow her a pass to come here. She will be calling me this afternoon to find out the yes or no's."

Alpha Jax sitting at this desk thinking. He had no real problem with another coming into his lands and even took great pride in the fact that he was being asked in this manner. It showed that his pack respected him not only as the Alpha of the Harvest Moon but as a friend they could come to in this time of need.

Alpha Jax was a young Alpha and took over when his father died just 3 short years ago. He took his father's Beta, Tony, as his own. Therefore, the fact he was being shown this kind of respect was amazing and showed he was doing something right not only in his eyes but in the eyes of the pack.

"Well, I don't see a problem with this. I will want to have a formal sit down with everyone when she arrives. Mainly to get the facts and to find out what we might be up against as a pack with whatever problems she might be being sent away from." Alpha Jax said, finally relaxing his hands, setting his coffee down, and looking to his Luna for agreement.

"I would like to say something. And I mean no disrespect. I think it's just a shame that so many people would rather sweep things under the rug instead of facing them head on. Especially, for the sake of image among their circles. We will do what we can for your kin to keep her safe. As if she were our own." Luna Hazel spoke her peace.

"She graduates in two weeks from what my sister says. Well, a week from Friday. My sister said she will be sending her off right after." Eva said in such disdain.

"So, the Saturday after next?" Alpha Jax said, looking at the calendar.

"No Alpha Jax. She is going to be leaving right after the ceremony as on that Friday." Eva corrected.

"Do what? She has parties to be at for the pack or don't they do that there?" Alpha Jax said, with a little more force than was entirely necessary or intended.

"Oh, they do, but her mother wants her gone now. If it wasn't for the sake of finals and graduation being in two weeks… she can't just make her poof. It would cause too many questions for my sister to have to answer." Eva was ashamed of the fact that her own sister was being like this and there wasn't more she could do for Rose right this second.

"So, if she leaves out Friday afternoon, she should be here Saturday morning or so… Where is she coming from exactly?" Luna Hazel said, trying to rain in the anger she could feel coming off her mate.

"Colorado. The Hollows pack." Beta Tony, who had been completely silent drinking his coffee finally spoke up. Everyone had almost forgotten he was sitting there. But when he spoke everyone seemed to look at him like when did you come in.

"Awe yes, the Hollows pack. Alpha Kent and Luna Zara. They have that wild boy Asher, right?" Alpha Jax spoke up, bringing their attention back to him.

Alpha Jax didn't have much use for packs like theirs. They were more about looking the part than being the part. While they were a rich pack, they were poor in the ways of true defense. Most of the warriors were more for show than for actual defense purposes. They believed they could buy their way out. At the very least intimate others into believing they could really do something.

"Yes, sir. I believe that would be the one." Beta Tony nearly had coffee come out his nose.

"Now this has me very interested. Beta Eva, you said you were going to talk to your sister this afternoon, correct?" Alpha Jax straightened up in his chair.

"Yes, sir." Eva responded

"Okay which means they will probably have the meeting with her on Wednesday or Thursday. I should be getting a call on Thursday or Friday." Alpha Jax was trying to play the details out like a well-oiled machine.

"Sounds about right." Beta Tony said.

"Well then everything seems to be in order for the moment. We shall convene back here Friday evening and discuss plans on behalf of your niece. Her name is Rose?" Luna Hazel said believing they all knew their game plan.

As Beta Tony and Eva rose, they said. "Yes, Luna. Her name is Rose. And thank you so much for being so understanding. Alpha Jax, we truly do appreciate it."

Alpha Jax shook both their hands and came around the desk to walk them to the door. Something didn't seem right here. An Alpha always knows it deep in their gut. He didn't believe that the Betas were untrustworthy, but the other pack was not one to just will someone away. Was their Alpha being told the truth? Was there a scandal that involved the higher ranks? Or was this just one selfish mother playing games with her child's life just because she didn't like her choices? Currently there were too many questions and only time would tell the answers.

Chapter 6

By 5:00pm, Kate's phone is ringing off the hook. Kate finally picks it up after what seems like forever to hear it ring from Rose's bedroom. Rose hasn't seen or heard from her mother all day. Even though she knew she was home and loose somewhere in the house.

The last contact she had with her, unfortunately, was at about 10 pm the night before. She came through the door looking like she was on cloud nine. Rose didn't say a word to her and was just in the kitchen getting a bottle of water. Kate was skipping around like a schoolgirl that just got asked to the spring formal.

"Everything is set. You will see Alpha Kent and Luna Zara on Wednesday at 3:30. Remember you got into college and you will be leaving as soon as graduation is over for summer classes. No one will know anything about your unfortunate mistake or anything else. Not even your father! Am I understood, Rose?" Kate said checking her nails like she just pulled off the greatest plan of the century.

Rose merely nodded at her mother and walked back upstairs to her room. While she wanted to say something, Rose thought it best to just walk away. Kate was always one for the physical attacks and Rose would not give her the satisfaction. She wanted to break down and ball her eyes out. A release from all the pain and hurt. She wouldn't give them the satisfaction there either. She would not be broken from this.

From what she could hear, her mother was pleased with whoever it was on the phone. She seemed by the tone of her voice extra pleased by the conversation. After about 20 minutes, Kate hung up the call and proceeded to stomp up the stairs to Rose's room.

Rose was sitting at her desk reviewing notes for the math final the next morning, when Kate walked in almost skipping. Rose knew this wasn't going to be good for her. She tried to ignore her mother but alas no such luck when it came to Kate. She was going to make you listen whether you liked it or not.

"Well guess who I just got off the phone with?" Kate pranced around the room.

"Your shrink?" Rose said nonchalantly, never taking her eyes off her notes and flashcards.

"Watch your mouth, you filthy whore. I won't take shit like that from the likes of you." Kate's good mood quickly dissipates as she turns on her daughter.

"What the hell ever. What do you want? I'm trying to study. You want me gone don't you. I have a test to pass to make that dream come true for you." Rose spat daggers at her mother.

"Well thankfully you will not only be gone but long gone. Far away from here. No one will know a damn thing thankfully. And you will be all the way in Montana. You're going to see your Aunt Eva at the Harvest Moon pack. Go ahead and milk her like you try to do me. Just two more weeks and it's going to be Rose Who? Then I will have my way when you do come crawling back here. You better not come back fat either. I don't think I could stand to look at you let alone get someone else to. It's already going to be hard to get someone to marry a whore. A fat whore would be worse." Kate went on and on for 45 minutes. The only thing that finally shut her up was seeing Kyle's truck pull up and hearing him come through the door. Rose had never been so happy for her father to FINALLY be walking through the door.

Kate walked out of Rose's room smug, feeling very pleased with herself, and seeing the love of her life, was a bonus. He looked tired from patrol last night, having to be the leader of training today, all because two of the leaders were still hung over from the night before. She felt he needed a night out just the two of them.

"How's my love?" Kate cooed at him.

"Extremely tired. I can't believe half of those guys are still hung over from last night." Kyle said slumping on the couch. Kyle started looking around the room. "Where is Rose?"

"She has a math final tomorrow. So, she is in her room trying to make sure she is fully ready." Kate always has an answer for her daughter not being within arms length.

"Well I haven't seen her in days. Maybe I should go upstairs and check in with her." Kyle says getting ready to climb off the couch and up the stairs.

"Oh no, don't bother her. She is really just going to yell about everyone distracting her. You know how she gets." Kate says, trying to run interference and keep her husband from going up to Rose's room.

Kate didn't trust her daughter to keep her mouth shut. She figured that she would play on the "Daddy's Girl" thing. She would spill the beans before it's time to do so. Not that Kate had any intentions of telling her husband anything.

Rose would do as she was told and give the mutt up for adoption. She would stay long enough to lose the weight and at least give a good show at the "appearance" of her attending college. Then Kate would marry her off to some unsuspecting person. Someone of an elevated rank would play well into Kate's plan.

Kate had it all carefully planned out. No one needed to know and maybe she would get some sick satisfaction in making her perfect sister do some of the dirty work for a change. Eva always got everything and Kate thought it was her turn to start cashing in on that.

Kate breaks the silence in the room. "What would you like for dinner, my love?"

"Not really sure. It's been a long day. Maybe just some burgers or what do you think about pizza?" Kyle says, looking around knowing something was majorly off about the situation at hand.

Kyle figured that maybe it was Kate and Rose fighting. The closer Rose gets to graduation the more tension is in the house. Kate always wanted Rose to be more than she intended to be. She was an amazing girl, but she wasn't the center of the room. The "Look at me kind of girl" is what Kate wanted. She got the "Damn. How do you not know how to change a tire?" kind of girl.

Kyle also figured if he could get his wife to go get dinner he would find out from Rose what was actually going on. Kate, on the other hand, wasn't going to let up on him not going up stairs. Therefore, Kate switched tactics.

"Well how about we go to that little place around the corner? We can always bring Rose something back." Kate cooed at Kyle while wrapping her arms around his neck and pressing herself up against him.

"That sounds fine." With one look up the stairs, Kyle figured maybe she really was studying.

Kate grabbed her purse and they headed for the car. Kyle looked to his daughter's window before climbing in the driver's seat. He could see her light was on and her back was to the window. He could see her sitting at her desk more than likely studying.

Rose waited till she heard the car pull out of the driveway before she flung herself onto the bed. She knew she had barely two weeks before she was out of here. Only thing was Rose had no intention whatsoever in doing what her mother planned. Rose knew that if she could play her cards right she could hopefully convince her Aunt to help her stay there.

Waves of nausea hit Rose like a ton of bricks. Trying to explain this tomorrow was going to be fun, was all Rose could think to herself. She knew this was going to be slightly tricky but she had pulled off worse in better timing.

"Oh my Goddess! Tomorrow is Monday! I have school. I'm going to have to see that piece of shit. How? How am I going to do this?" was the last thing Rose thought out loud before realizing that she was just going to have to deal with it until she could get out of here. Just Flippin Perfect!

Chapter 7

Staring at the ceiling while waiting for the alarm clock, Rose believes being up all night puking her guts up gave her the necessary time to think. Not really, but it did make her have to address the situation at hand. Rose had come up with a plan for the day. Dallas, in so many ways, gave her the answer. She wouldn't forget or just pretend the last few months didn't happen though. She just wasn't going to give him the satisfaction. She couldn't do that to herself. She was going to hold her head high.

The first alarm goes off "**buzz buzz buzz**" like a bumble bee. Rose swings her legs over the side of the bed. She needed to take this one final at a time and she would make it out with what little bit of her sanity she had left. Starting the countdown to her leaving this place, her mother, and all the complications that came with the child she carried behind her.

If everything worked out with scheduling, finals would be over on Friday. By the following Friday she would be on track for the nine-hour drive to her Aunt Eva's house. She would then have time to piece back together her new life with just her child and herself.

Rose reminded herself to make a checklist some time today. That way she was prepared for the events yet to unfold. She also knew it was safer to make the list at school due to her mother not being able to discover it.

Rose knew most of the things she needed. She thought while picking out her outfit for the day. She would need her paperwork. That she would have to sneak around to collect. She didn't want to stir suspicion before she could haul her ass out of the countryside. The last thing she needed was Kate getting wind of something.

Looking through her clothes, she decided on a loose-fitting green button-up with a black tank under her shirt. Her black jeans and black leather boots always rounded out the unique style. A quick brush through the hair, and Rose was good to walk out of the house for school.

One last look in the mirror before grabbing her keys, bag and cellphone while walking out the door. Her beautiful dark blue 69' Cutlass sat perfectly off to one side of the driveway. She always did a quick walk around the car before she got in and headed out. All because one time Kate stuck a screwdriver in her back tire. She didn't even make it down the driveway. Rose got in her car, put the key in and the little princess roared to life.

Ru The amazing dark blue 69' Cutlass gleamed in the sunlight. Little princess was her baby. Everyone could look but no one could touch her. The 442 under the hood could blow anything off the road and often did. With this new change in her life, she would do her best not to get rid of her.

Pulling up at the school only ten minutes from the house, Rose finds a parking spot. As she sits in the parked car staring at the big building, she knows she has to get started. Therefore, Rose drops her sunglasses on the seat and exits the car headed toward the main building. The marble stone columns always seemed to tell the story of this high school. It had been burnt down three times but the pack rebuilt it back every time. A little of the black smoke stained the pillars that were never cleaned properly.

Rose smiled, thinking not too much longer, and she passed under that spot and aways from this school forever. Rose headed to her locker and then to math her first final. With the "**Let's just get this done.**" attitude, she enters the room and finds her seat. So it begins.

Class after class, Rose makes it through her day with minimal distractions. Asher and Dallas were being pains in the butt as per usual, but hey, it was a somewhat normal day. Sometimes a false normal is better than no normal at all. After all, neither boy said a word to her and in some ways that was just the way she wanted it.

Three finals down, as Rose headed to the lunch room. She finds a seat with her Coke and a slice of pizza at a table in the corner. With her back against the wall, Rose began to eat, keeping her eyes out for any kind of activity she would have to avoid.

Taking out her notebook from her bag, she reviews the list she started working on in her free period. She had planned on stopping by the bank after school. Rose also planned on talking to a few guys that owed her some money for work she had done on their trucks. Rose would also have to stop by the shop she worked at and pick up her last check and say her goodbyes there as well. Rose also knew that she would have to plan and rehearse what she was going to say to Alpha Kent and Luna Zara. Nothing could be left to chance in any way and Rose knew that with every fiber of her being.

While deep in thought, Rose had the feeling she was being watched. When she looked up, she locked eyes with Dallas from a couple of tables over. Saying nothing with a look of disgust, Rose put everything in her bag and got up to throw her trash away.

Feeling that she had to get out of there before anything was said set her on edge. Rose didn't let that stop her from walking out calmly and with her shoulders squared up and head held high. She headed to the bathroom after leaving the cafeteria. Mainly to make sure that she could keep her resolve in place and to make sure she wasn't followed out of there as well. Rose always had to appear to be rock steady as she headed down the hall.

Looking in the mirror once, she was in the bathroom. Rose's eyes seemed to glow. She knew this was her wolf trying to break free. Even though she was just merely agitated, not in any real stress, this puzzled Rose a little bit.

"What's wrong, Snow?" Rose said, trying to talk her wolf down for the moment.

"We need to hurry up and get the hell out of here." Snow's voice growled in her head.

"What's fixing to happen?" Rose knew from the time her wolf, Snow, came to her at 13. She was special. Snow could see ten steps ahead of anyone and anything. The only time they were both thrown for a loop was when Rose was slipped the LycanBerry.

"Nothing that I can see right now. I just can't stand the way that asshole looks at us." Snow says with a deep growl.

"Few more days, Snow. We will be on our way to Aunt Eva's. How is my pup?" Rose asked, knowing full well that one of the reasons Snow was completely on edge was the pup they carried.

"Fine." That was Snow's last response before she faded back to that one corner of Rose's mind.

Rose thought to herself. *Crazy, she doesn't speak to me often, but when she does it's always important. What isn't she currently telling me?*

When Rose got to her next class, she found that it had been canceled due to exams. It seemed like all her afternoon classes had been canceled for exams. Two of which, Rose, wasn't scheduled to take until tomorrow or at least that's what the note on the doors said. Therefore, it was time for Rose to put her plan into action.

Stopping by her locker to place the afternoon class books inside, Rose could feel eyes on her once again. This time when she looked around, Rose saw three girls come walking down the hall. All the seniors found out that afternoon classes had been canceled for most of them.

"I can't believe that Dallas asked you to the graduation party." Bethany said with a high giggle.

"I know. I thought he was seeing someone else. What's her name? The Gamma's daughter?" Abby asks, slightly puzzled about not being able to remember her name.

"Rose. No, apparently they broke it off because she is going to college and doesn't want to have any kind of distractions." Lizzy said, playing with what looked like Dallas's chain around her neck.

"Well, I heard that she didn't want to lead anyone on since she was holding out for her true mate." Bethany said matter-of-factly.

"I think that's wise. I mean you wouldn't want to get tangled in that kind of mess and then later find your mate and have to explain it to them." Abby says, looking at her nails.

"I heard another rumor… but of course I know that can't possibly be true. Rose is too much of a good person for it to be that." Lizzy said, trying to whisper, but in an empty hallway everything echoed.

"What?" Both Bethany and Abby chimed in.

"Well, I heard that she got caught with a boy. Not Dallas. And when her mother found out that it was an Omega, she flipped out on Rose and is making her leave until she finds her mate or someone more worthy." Lizzy seemed to have all the good gossip.

"No. That can't be true. We have never seen her with anyone but Dallas and, as stated, she broke it off with him to not lead him on. I swear people will say anything to try to ruin someone else's good name." Abby shook her head, not letting that rumor go anywhere.

"True. Plus, let's face it, she is a tomboy, a great fighter, a bookworm even. She helps everyone. Maybe it is as it looks. Rose is leaving to get her education under her belt." Bethany said.

Standing with her face practically in her looker, Rose was extremely happy to hear that Dallas was not trying to destroy her at that moment. She could care less what people thought of her. Rose could always hold her own, but when shit hit the fan, she wouldn't be there to defend her name or deny the allegations against her.

The three girls turned to go into the bathroom and Rose headed for the parking lot. Finding solace in her car, Rose took a minute to breathe in deeply. She figured the rumor mill would eventually fire up and her name would have others' tongues wagging. She also figured that things would get messier as the week went on. The once highly esteemed girl. Rose knew how fast the word whore would come out of their mouths. Rose was thankful Dallas took the threat seriously enough to keep her good name in check for the moment.

Rose started the car and pulled out of the parking lot. No one would be expecting her home for hours. So, it was time to put the plan in place and start collecting her things. If Rose was right, she would have more than enough to start over and keep her and her pup until she figured out her next step. First stop, the bank….

Chapter 8

Rose pulled into the bank ten minutes after leaving school. It had been six years when she opened the account that right now held her life savings. She prayed that it would be enough to start over. She was always very careful with her money.

Mrs. Bell, an aging woman with blondish red hair and blue eyes, sat behind the counter. Rose always chatted her up when she went into the bank. Rose would be here every week as clockwork to handle her weekly deposits. Rose found it fitting she would be the one to help her close the account she worked so hard to grow.

"Afternoon, Rose. How are you today?" Mrs. Bell said with a smile on her face and a cheery tone in her voice.

"Oh, can't complain. How are you today?" Rose, making her usual small talk.

"Oh, very well. Heard you got into college. That is so grand." Mrs. Bell beamed.

"Yes, I did. That's actually why I'm here." Rose said, lowering her voice.

"Oh, really?" Mrs. Bell said, looking a little confused.

"Yes. I'm leaving right after graduation. So, I'm just getting everything in order." Rose said, hoping that she would get an understanding of the information.

"Oh, well, we are really going to miss you." Mrs. Bell said, starting to tear slightly.

"I'm going to miss you as well. I need to get everything out of my account and safety deposit box." Rose said, trying to remain like this was just any other transaction.

"Oh, of course dear." Mrs. Bell punched in some numbers on the keyboard and almost looked shocked.

"What is it?" Rose started to panic a little bit. No one was supposed to have access to her account. She was sure of that.

"Oh, nothing dear. I just never realized how much you had saved here with interest and all." Mrs. Bell's eyes were as round as saucers while staring at the screen.

"That sounds about right. A penny saved is a penny earned." Rose said. Which so happened to be what Mrs. Bell would say to her every Thursday when she would come in to deposit her check every week.

"That's right. I'm glad someone listened to the advice." Mrs. Bell said so proudly.

"Well, if it wasn't for not wanting to take out loans and such, I would just leave it be. I want to be able to take care of whatever comes along when I get there." Rose said, hoping that Mrs. Bell would understand.

"Such a responsible young woman." Mrs. Bell commented on seeing that Rose was always one to plan ahead when others left everything to chance.

Rose knew, on the other hand, that this wasn't all her money. So, while Mrs. Bell was getting the account closed and cashed out, Rose went to her safety deposit box. Rose knew, if, by chance, her mother ever got her hands on the account information, she would never be able to get her hands on the box. That needed a key and password that anyone besides Rose would need to access it.

Mr. Jones, a round and Santa Clause-looking man with a long white beard, guarded the back. Mind you that this is a werewolf bank. No one in their right mind would dare think of robbing this place. For appearance's sake only, the bank had guards. The area did have humans that traveled through from time to time along with some that lived in the neighboring areas.

"713, please Mr. Jones." Rose smiles at the man that she had seen every week.

"Why, of course, Ms. Rose. By the way, congratulations on getting into college. We are all so proud of you." He said, walking over to a keypad and punching in the code.

"Thank you so much. That truly means a lot." Rose said, looking back at the old man she would crack jokes with every week. There was so much she was going to miss but knowing this was for the best.

"I figured we would see you soon. So much to do in so little time." Mr. Jones said, always one for small talk.

"Isn't that the truth? I have to gather everything so I can be fully prepared when graduation hits next Friday." Rose said, completely confident.

The box came down the conveyor and he knew it was time to leave the room. Rose took the key out of her pocket and opened the heavy footlocker-looking box. All Rose's important things were kept there. The title to her car, birth certificate, more money, and gold bricks that she had invested in. She shoved everything into her bookbag and looked back at the door. Mr. Jones had his back to it. Rose knew she was okay. She couldn't shake the uneasy feeling but knew that everything would be fine. It always was.

Rose knocked on the door and Mr. Jones turned around to let her out. Rose smiled at him. As another gentleman walked, Mr. Jones simply nodded his head to Rose. Mr. Jones began another conversation with this man. One would think his day was simply filled with random conversations one right after the other. Rose just smiled at the thought and headed her way back up front to Mrs. Bell.

"Okay sweetheart, I just need to get you to follow me into the office to sign these papers." Mrs. Bell ushered Rose into the open door of the average-sized office. Dark wood was everywhere. Rose swore it looked more like a principal's office instead of the inside of the bank. Not that she would know. Rose had never been in trouble a day in her life.

Mrs. Bell put the cash onto the desk in front of her. As all the money ran through the counter, Rose could see all 20 thousand was accounted for. Mrs. Bell then put the papers on the desk that would close out her account.

"Okay, Rose, sign here." Mrs. Bell showed her every line to sign on.

"Thank you so much for all your help, Mrs. Bell. By the way, Mr. Jones was busy with another person, so I wasn't able to give him the key." Rose said, taking the bank zipped bag that Mrs. Bell handed her and handed her the key to the box.

"It has always been a pleasure. Is there anything else I can help you with?" Mrs. Bell said, trying not to tear up.

"Yes, just one thing. I mean if you can. If you could keep the fact that I have been here and closed everything out under raps? You know how my mother is, and I wouldn't want to be broke and to leave with nothing." Rose said, through pleading eyes to Mrs. Bell.

"Oh of course, Rose. I remember why you started that account all those years ago. I will pass the word to Mr. Jones as well. No one knows anything!" Mrs. Bells gave Rose a big hug and showed her to the door.

Rose walked over to the trunk of her car and popped the trunk. She placed all the items in there for safe keeping. Rose knew that she needed to be quick with the next few stops. Rose started back down her to-do list and drove to her next stop. Three guys owed her money and, unfortunately, she was going to have to collect all the debts today.

Just a quick little hop skip and a jump from the bank, Rose pulls up at Mike's house. She noticed Mike and Nathan's trucks were parked outside the garage. *Two birds with one stone.* Rose thought to herself as she pulled her car in behind the two jacked-up old GMCs. Rose fondly remembers single-handedly rebuilding both those engines from the ground up just two months ago.

Rose walked up past the trucks to the side door where loud blaring music bellowed out. Rose looked in to find both boys sitting on an old oil-stained couch just unwinding. Rose was always going to remember these times. These boys aren't just people that come to her to fix things. These were two of the trio that were her small group of best friends.

"Ello." Rose calls into the garage over the loud music. Nathan looks up and smacks Mike in the arm. Mike, getting a little irritated at his friend, finally looks up to see Rose standing in the doorway and turns the music down.

"Hey Rose. Haven't seen you all afternoon." Mike says, throwing a can of coke that she catches in mid air.

"Canceled my afternoon classes due to exams. Plus, I had other things to attend to." Rose said, popping the can open and taking a drink.

"Lucky ass. We had Mr. Wilson's shop class. He never lets us out early." Nathan said while reaching for his drink.

"I had him in the 2nd period. By the way, the final is a breeze." Rose said, taking a seat on an old five gallon bucket sitting by the couch.

"So I heard you aren't sticking around for the summer." Mike looked at Nathan to chime in with his thoughts.

"Something about college... or a broken heart?" Nathan, taking his queue to pipe up and Rose, caught off guard, had coke come burning out of her nose.

"Do what?" Rose began horsley. She tried to gain her breath but wasn't quick to do so.

"Oh we heard that the asshole broke your heart." Nathan and Mike both over dramatize with hands on their foreheads and over their hearts.

"That would be a NO. And for the record, I broke it off with him. No reason to play fool when we both knew I wasn't his mate. Besides, I got into college and he..." Rose trailed off in thought on just how to word it. "He wants what every Beta's son wants. To be the Beta. No other thought in his head or plans for the future. Just Asher and him running the show."

"See, I told you our little Rose wouldn't be the typical girl." Mike said, reaching over to punch Nathanin the arm as payback from earlier.

"I knew it was a lie, but let's face it. Your leaving has caused the rumor mill to start over time." Nathan said, wagging his eyebrows up and down at Rose.

"Well, let's not get carried away, boys. Roses have thorns and not many people can deal with that. I have never been boy crazy and I'm looking out for my future. This college has the best automotive department in the country." Rose said, trying very hard to over sell the reason for her going away.

"Well, I guess we should feel privileged to get a face-to-face goodbye." Nathan said, looking at Rose with such admiration that she could do anything.

"Not goodbye. Just see you later. You have both been great friends. I know the Moon Goddess will bless you both with fantastic mates. You will never think of the girl that rebuilt both those heeps into the mean ass trucks you see today." Rose, playing on the drama in the room, felt proud of herself.

"You're such a liar. But damn, we will always love you." Both boys stood to come over to her and give her a big hug. They were two of the three boys that, when shit really hit the fan, they were there. No matter what, Rose knew the boys well enough if she would have told them what had happened. They would not only have believed her, but they would potentially have had blood on their hands.

"Another reason I'm here. You guys happen to have the money for the work on the trucks? I hate to ask, but until I get settled I'm trying to work with what I have." Rose said, asking in the best way she knew how for the overdue money owed.

"Yep, sure do. When we heard through the grapevine about you leaving we figured it was time to pay off." Nathan said, grabbing two envelopes from behind the radio and walking it over to Rose.

"Thanks guys." Rose gave one last hug to each of the boys. After putting the envelopes in her back pocket, she took her leave. Time was running a little thin and she knew that this was not the only hard stop she had to make today.

Walking back out to her car, Rose got in and put both envelopes in the glove box. Rose knew there was no need to count the money. The boys have never stiffed her on a payment. Rose wished to the Goddess that they would only find happiness. Taking one last look at the garage, Rose decided that it was time to head to the next spot on her list.

The last guy on her list that she had to meet up with was Chris. The last of the trio of boys that she hung out with. Rose knew again she could kill two birds with one stone. Seeing and collecting from Chris and her last paycheck. This would be the last stop before having to head home.

About 20 minutes later, Rose pulls up outside the garage. Rose saw the old rusted sign of Carl's Auto Shop and smiled. This was her favorite place in the world. Old junk cars came in on one side and the baddest hot rods on the street came rolling out the other. Carl was one man that took a chance on Rose. She rebuilt her car for months in bay six, which at the time was just storage.

So many good memories here, Rose was truly going to miss coming here every day. Chris's El Camino was sitting on the side of the building. Rose knew he was there. She walked up to the office door and pulled the heavy metal door open to step inside.

"Hey Carl." Rose greeted the older man behind the desk.

"Well, if it isn't my little college girl," Carl beamed back at Rose.

"Yep yep." Rose said, thinking **Damn news travels fast!**

"So, I guess this is you telling me you quit?" Carl said, taking his hands off the keyboard and putting them on the desk.

"Unfortunately, yes. Not that I wanted to, but I know if I don't go up for summer classes it's not going to be great. I'll never get settled. Plus, I have to meet with my Aunt Eva's pack. It's just a whole big thing right now." Rose tried hard to keep up with the lie she had been telling all day.

"Oh believe me, I understand." Carl reaches over and grabs an envelope. "I figured cash would be better. Figured you already handled the bank." Carl says while handing Rose the envelope.

"Thanks Carl. I'm really going to miss you." Rose said, knowing that it was the complete truth.

"Well, I put a little extra in there. For graduation and all." Rose walks over and hugs him.

"Thank you so much. Chris in the bays?" Rose said, looking toward the sliding doors that led into the main part of the shop.

"Yep. He should be finishing up that old vet as we speak." Carl said, trying to hide his emotions about losing one of the best mechanics he ever had.

"Okay. I got to settle up with everyone. So, I'll go find him." Rose said, walking through the heavy metal doors that led to the bays.

The sound of what would pass for today's heavy metal came screaming out of bay 3. No more war of music, and Carl screaming at the two of them to "just pick something" would be heard anymore. As Rose walked over, Chris was screaming along with the music and it was bad. Like baying at the moon because your ears were bleeding kind of badly.

Rose walked right up behind Chris and jabbed him hard in the sides. Chris jumped a good four feet in the air. Rose couldn't stop laughing at his reaction. Chris looked at her and shook his head. Chris then walked over and turned down the music.

"Where the hell have you been?" Chris scolded.

"I guess you haven't heard." Rose was surprised that only one person might not know what was going on.

"Oh no, I heard. You're leaving and I don't even get to hear it from you?" Chris looked at her slightly hurt. He went over and leaned on the hood of the vet.

"Oh my Goddess. Drama Queen much?" Rose teased him.

"Am not!" Chris crossed his arms over his chest and began to sulk.

"Are so!" Rose looked at the pouting Chris. She knew that he was always sulky when everyone else knew more than he did.

"You could have called or texted and said something." Chris said, trying to put out the option that he didn't have to be the last to know.

"Look, I came to see you. I came to say goodbye before shit gets out of control with graduation and parties. I'm leaving right after the ceremony. Mom is seeing to that. You know how she is." Rose said, sitting on the workbench.

"It's just not fair. Yes, we all know your mother is the extra of extra, but damn." Chris looked up, trying to read Rose's face for any clue of something else.

"Didn't know you cared so much." Rose teased him only in a way that friends that have known each other for their entire lives could do.

"You have always been a constant in my life. Since we were 13 and would come hang out here. When mom died, we sat on the roof and drank dad's beer and got so sick." Chris sat there thinking of all the good, bad, and ugly times they had been through.

"I know, but it's time to do what's best on both ends. You'll find your mate soon and BAM it'll be like Rose who?" Rose said, trying to cheer Chris up.

"Whatever!" Chris said, throwing the oil rag that he had been absently rubbing his hands on at Rose's head.

"Look, you got my number. That's not going to change. I'll always be here for you. Just not right here in this place." Rose said, starting to feel the guilt from lying to everyone all day. She knew she had to lie to him. He was as short tempered as they came. Her one shot at this was to play it out to make sure no one got hurt and everything remained civil.

"You happen to have that 500, I borrowed to you?" Rose said, being the first to break the silence.

"Yes, I do." Chris took out his wallet and handed it to her.

"Thanks buddy. I'm trying to get everything together so mom doesn't know anything." Rose, playing on the fact that everyone considered her mother a golddigger.

"I know. Bet you'll feel great when you get out of here." Chris said, trying to keep his chin up.

"It'll definitely be different," Rose said, looking around the shop one last time.

"Well, I gotta get back to work. You take good care of yourself, Little Rosebud." Chris snaked an arm around Rose and pulled her in for a hug.

Rose didn't let the tears fall but she wanted to. That scared her most of all. She wasn't the overly emotional type of girl. The hormones were what was getting to her. And she didn't like it one damn bit! Rose now knew this was going to be harder than it looked.

Rose left through the open bay door. She hadn't realized the money was still in her hand. She was normally very careful to put everything up. Rose took the money and put it in with her last paycheck. When she got in the car, she put the envelope in the glove box. Rose knew she would have to find time to count it all up to see what she was going to have to start over with. Rose knew there was only way forward and make no mistakes. She had a plan for her and her child's future.

With one last look at the old garage, Rose looked down at her watch. It was nearly 4pm. Her mother would be home soon and the Goddess knew she would be watching her every move. Therefore, it was time for Rose to get back to the house and plan for the next thing to come.

Chapter 9

One never seems to know how slow and fast time goes by. Days bleeding one into another. Nights of begging the Goddess for clarity and understanding. The whole time wondering why was this happening? Rose always dreamed of being free. No mother hanging her expectations like stones around her neck.

Rose would have to take this next path and hold her head high. She did nothing wrong. Even though plenty of wrong had been done to her. Even within her own family, Rose now felt like an outcast and her mother was seeing to that. She was being kept very isolated from everyone.

Tuesday was another short day with just three more finals and another afternoon free. Therefore, Rose decided to make the most of it. She began packing up the extra contents of her locker. One last thing not to have to deal with later. Old pictures, notes and mementos of the years now off the side of the metal locker.

Shoving things into her backpack, her hair on the back of her neck began to stand up again. It seemed to be a regular occurance as of late. Rose knowing she was being watched, She finished up the packing, closed her locker door, and began to walk away and ran face first into something hard.

There stood Dallas in all his glory. Rose straightened up and looked him dead in the eyes with her eyes now glowing in anger and frustration. What could he possibly have to say to her? Was he just keeping up appearances?

"Sorry I didn't see you there." Rose said sweetly. Rose believed in putting on a good show for any onlookers.

"So, I hear you're leaving." Dallas says trying to block Rose's exit to the door.

"Sure am. Got into college and I'm going to go and do something with my life." Rose said, trying to find an easier way around him.

"I bet. So, what will you be back in a few months with your tail between your legs?" Dallas snorts out at Rose.

While this infuriated Rose, she kept her cool. "I highly doubt that but hey who really knows. As it stands though, I have things to do. So if you don't want me to make good on that promise from a few days ago…" Rose paused, pulling the knife she always kept in her leather jacket.

"I think it's time for you to let me pass. I say nothing and you say nothing but the fact is simple if you plan to still have your balls intact when I'm done. Make no mistake Dallas, I will cut you nine ways to Sunday and walk past your bleeding body." Rose lowered her voice into a growl while keeping a distasteful smile on her face.

Dallas, choosing to be smart, moved out of the way. Glaring daggers into the back of her head as she walked out of the building and toward her car. Rose kept her pace as normal as possible but did not breathe an easy breath until she was safe in her car. She knew that there would be a showdown eventually. Dallas was always the one for the cat and mouse games.

Seeing it was nearly noon, She knew she had a good four hours that could be utilized before having to deal with her mother or before her father came home from the training field. Rose drove to the store and picked up just the basics to organize everything. She stopped by the gas station and grabbed a drink before heading home.

Looking around the yard and the house, Rose thanked the Goddess that no one was home. Rose still parked behind the garage. She didn't want people to see her car and either decided to stop by and talk or radio back and tell her mother she was home. She was basically talked out for the most part.

Rose first popped her trunk and took inventory of her assets. Making sure everything was filed together and began counting her money. Her life savings amounted to 40 thousand and 12 gold bricks. While for a soon to be 18 year old, that was a good chunk of change. Rose knew in the end that would only hold her a little while with the pup on the way.

Rose's phone vibrated and scared her back to the present. As she reached down to look it was the school text alert. "No Finals Tomorrow! If you are not taking a final you are excused for the day."

While normally Rose would have been over the moon. She knew that meant she would have her last to finals on Thursday. She just kept telling herself she would be out of here soon. Rose could also get some things she didn't dare try to leave behind packed and ready to go.

After everything was safely put in her trunk she went into the house and up to her room. Rose was not allowed in the main part of the house due to her being grounded until she left for her Aunt Eva. Rose also didn't want to be anywhere near her mother. By chance, Kate happened to come home early from the park house and her duties there. Rose was going to make herself scarce.

Rose laid on her bed staring at the ceiling when she heard a car drive up. Looking at the clock, Rose knew it was too early for her mother. So Rose took a peek out the window, and was relieved to see her father's old mustang sitting in the driveway. She then heard the front door open and close a few minutes later.

"Rose, You home?" Her father called up the stairs.

"Yep, I'm up here." Rose yelled back running to her desk to at least make it look like she was studying.

Rose hadn't spoken to her father in almost five days, and if her mother had anything to do with it, it would have been the day she graduated before she was allowed to say a word to him. When he climbed the stairs and knocked on the door her heart nearly leaped out of her chest. Rose's heart was starting to thump so hard she was afraid it would give her away. She had to play it cool, mainly because she wasn't going to deal with her mother over this also.

Kyle knocked on his daughter's door. She had been acting slightly strange as of late. He didn't know why. He knew this was a difficult time in anyone's life. So many changes with so little time to fully understand and adapt to them.

"Come in." Rose said sweetly.

"Hey little bud." Kyle said to his daughter

"Hey pops."

"Can I come in for a minute?" Kyle said seeing if there was anything off about the way she presented herself.

"Of course." Rose said, spinning around in her desk chair.

"Thanks. I know it's been a while since we have had a minute to talk and I thought I'd touch base with you." Kyle said going to sit on her bed.

"Everything is good here." Rose kept it short but not too short as to think she was being rude.

"Well how are you feeling about the whole college thing? I know it was kind of sudden to just find out and now poof you're leaving." Klye said, looking at his daughter.

"Not too bad. I thought I didn't get in so there was no reason in mentioning I applied. Then when I found out I did in fact get in it was just like Wow. I think it's something I have to do and that I really need to do. More importantly I think I just need to get away from here for a while and concentrate on my future." Rose said, trying to play to the story her mother had been telling everyone.

"Well I know things have been moving really fast and I'm just making sure this is what you really want." Kyle said, looking for any sign that something was off with his daughter. If this was really her idea or something she is being made to do.

"No, I swear I'm fine. Mom seems to be completely over the moon about me leaving for college. So it seems everything is good right now. All's right with the world." Rose tried to brush off the conversation and put her father's mind to rest even though she hated lying to him.

"Yeah, she is. Almost like when your brother found out he was going to be an Alpha..." Kyle paused for a moment. "Just know I love you. No matter what."

"I know daddy. Plus who knows. I might even find my mate and that will put her in an even better place. Knowing her children are happily placed in their own lives." The bile started to rise in her throat knowing she was flat out lying to her father.

"Well, I came home early to see if I could get a word with you. Since you have been so busy with the end of the year things. I don't think I have seen you since Friday?"

"Yep, I believe it was Friday. I was supposed to go on a patrol but you let me stay home because I didn't feel well." Rose is now thinking of the real reason she wasn't feeling well.

"Glad to see you feeling better now."

"Yeah, I mean I think it was just my nerves with all the pressure from finals and everything else just hit me like a ton of bricks." Rose knew that this was going to be the last time she could talk to her father like this without prying ears. She wanted to tell him everything but that wasn't going to be possible.

Rose heard car breaks screaming to a halt and knowing without even looking who it was. She heard the front door open and slam shut. An extremely angry and panicked Kate came running through the house.

"Kyle? Rose?" Kate's voice screamed.

Kyle walked out of his daughter's room and yelled, "Up here."

Kate scrambled up the steps so fast, throwing her arms around her husband's neck. Kate shot a look at Rose that if looks could kill, Rose would be dead. She let go of her husband and shot a warning smile glare at her daughter.

"How was your day, honey? You seem to be home early and in such a rush." Kyle knew his wife was acting strange even for her.

"Well when I went by the training grounds to share some news with you they said you were gone for the day. Then when I went by the school, they said that afternoon classes were canceled and then I came by the house to see both your cars home." Kate tried to sound like she was just excited about some news. Rose knew for a fact that this had nothing to do with the news and everything to do with the fact they were together. She knew what was sending her mother into a panic attack.

"Okay then what's the news?" Kyle said, trying to hurry his wife along here.

"There is going to be a ball two days after graduation. And you will never guess who will be in attendance. The Four Lycan Kings… The Four Lycan Kings will be attending to bless the new Alpha and Beta. Isn't this just amazing?" Kate puffed out her chest practically jumping up and down like an unmated shewolf in flipping heat.

"I thought they only did that at the changing of the Alpha's?" Kyle said, slightly confused by these news of events.

"Oh apparently they are doing it at the graduation ball because the Alpha's son won't be taking over for some time and there are other pressing matters they always have to attend to. Therefore, the Kings want to just get it out of the way in case anything does happen and they are unable to return back here." Kate said strutting around like a Benny roster.

"Well that means more patrols. I guess I'll have to head back to the packhouse to discuss the protocol. It's been many years since the Kings have made their way here for a visit." Kyle says walking over and kissing his daughter's forehead. Walking up to Kate before leaving, Klye gives her a kiss and runs out the door.

As soon as Kate heard Kyle's car fire up and leave the driveway, Kate turned on her daughter so fast one would think she had rabies. Almost snarling and snapping at Rose, Kate's eyes were rimmed in red. Rose knew this wasn't going to be good.

"What in the hell do you think you were doing?" Kate snapped at Rose.

"Talking with my father. What did it look like mother?" Rose was going to rise to the occasion. She couldn't do much but her wit would always be there.

"So help me if your father finds out about this problem you got yourself into." Kate started pacing around the room.

"You'll what mother? You will do what?" Rose mouthed back. Before Rose could brace herself Kate's hand came down hard across Rose's face. Before Rose could utter another word, Kate had a back hand to follow up with the slap.

"Well let's just say it's a long drive to your Aunt Eva's house. I can definitely make sure you never make it there alive!" Kate spat at her daughter, taking her fist to Rose's face. Rose instinctively went to cover her belly as her mother went on the attack between knees and punches.

Rose had had enough and began to reach for her knives, when Rose heard her mother's phone start to ringing. She controlled the tears and the rage inside her as her wolf tried desperately to come to the surface. Rose knew her mother's day would come and may the goddess have mercy on her soul. Days that is all she had left in this hell. Rose wouldn't have to take this shit anymore.

Rose heard her mother answer her phone with a couple of Yes Luna, Of Course Luna, before hanging up the call. Kate waked over to the mirror and fixed her hair and make up while Rose remained laying still in a ball on the floor.

"I have to go back to the packhouse. We have a ball to plan for after all. By the way you have a meeting with Alpha Kent and Luna Zara tomorrow at 3:30. You better do what you are told. Because if one word is mentioned out of line, I will make sure whoever I get to take your sorry ass makes sure you wish you had never been born. Do you hear me?" Kate punched her daughter one more time in the face to get her point across then left her room.

Kate proceeded down the stairs, and back out to her car. Where she left the house once again. Kate was feeling powerful. Her problem would be out of her hair soon and that would be that.

Rose could only thank the Goddess for giving her a strong wolf and making her strong in the process. Rose knew that Snow would possibly have her healed in just a few hours. She knew she would have to endure this just a little bit longer. She needed the papers to cross the borders.

When Rose finally had the strength to pull herself up into a sitting position, She thought long and hard about not waiting for graduation. She could have the diploma mailed to her for all she cared. Rose was merely keeping this up for her father. She knew that the school would have Final Grades by Monday or Tuesday at the very latest. She would have to get a hold of her Aunt Eva's number and just see if it was possible to come a day or two early.

Rose heard her wolf start stirring again and she knew Snow was itching for blood. They both knew they couldn't shift because of the pup. They had heard terrible stories of pups being badly hurt if their mother shifted while pregnant. That didn't stop them from wanting to. Rose knew she would have to calm not only herself but Snow down and just ride it out.

Chapter 10

Rose, not having classes this morning, thought sleeping in would be a good thing. No such luck. After she heard both her parents leave, she knew this would be the best time to get up. She began to start gathering her clothes and important things she wouldn't dare to try to leave behind. She started packing everything in boxes and suitcases, leaving just enough clothes for her to make it look good to anyone that might start poking around.

When she was packed up, Rose grabbed some clothes and headed for the shower. Looking at her body in the mirror, Rose's bruises from the night before were faded and almost gone. Rose believed it was the pregnancy that was keeping her from healing quickly. Normally, within a few hours, she would have been fully healed.

After the shower, Rose headed down stairs and into the kitchen to hopefully find something edible in the fridge. The only thing Rose found was what looked like take-out from a few nights ago. On further investigation, Rose decided against it. Rose, shaking her head, grabbed her keys and leather jacket. After doing a once over check of the phone, keys, and wallet, Rose headed out the door.

Rose knew that the dark purple spaghetti strap top and tight black jeans would be enough in this weather. Rose, no matter what the weather, never left the house without her leather jacket and black boots. This was her look: part goth and part biker, but all wolf.

Ten minutes down the road was Rocky's dinner. Pack's favorite for just about anything anyone would want to eat. Rose pulls up and sees her boys at their normal booth. Chris, Nathan, and Mike all started waving when they saw Rose. As she walked into the restaurant, the boys waved her over.

"Well, look at what the cat dragged in." Nathan said with a slight punch to Mike's arm.

"Well, she still knows where Rocky's is?" Mike picked at her.

Chris sat in silence for a moment. "What have you been up to?"

She noticed he decided not to tease her like the other two bone-headed friends. Rose was really going to miss these guys. That, along with the other things, made her so badly sick to her stomach. Rose knew she was going to have to eat soon or she was going to be sick.

"It's only been two whole days. Which I will agree seems like an eternity with how things have been at my house. So, how have things been?" Rose said, settling in next to Chris which was the only seat left in the booth.

"Well, nothing much has been going on. You hear the Four Lycan Kings are coming to bless the pack?" Nathan said, looking at Rose for confirmation.

"From what mom said to dad, they are coming to bless Asher and Dallas. Something about them might not be able to be here in a few years to hand the blessing over then. So they are doing it at the ball after graduation." Rose was the go-to-with her parents being Gammas about any kind of information. When Rose spoke about this though, it was as if it was like everyone should already know this.

A pretty waitress appeared at the table to take orders. She batted her eyes at the guys when she spoke. "What can I get for y'all?"

"Burger, fries, cherry coke." Mike ordered.

"Same" Nathan sounded off.

"Patty melt, onion rings, coke." Chris ordered.

"Okay, guess it's my turn. I need a double cheeseburger with everything, cheese fries, and a chocolate ice cream soda." Rose said with the boy's jaws dropping, and staring at her. Normally, Rose had coffee and maybe a slice of pie for breakfast. It was easier to say she didn't eat breakfast.

The waitress just nodded and walked away. The boys sat there wide-eyed for a few more minutes before Rose had to just look them in the eye and say, "What?"

"Something you want to share with the group?" Mike piped up and looked at his two other friends for back up.

"Yeah, Katie is trying to cook again." Rose blurted out and the whole table erupted in laughter. Kate was known for a lot of things. Her cooking was not one of them.

"Oh you poor thing. Is that why she and Gamma Kyle are seen at the packhouse every night?" Chris said. Carl and Chris ate at the packhouse once or twice a week to keep up appearances.

"Yep. She leaves me with the hazardous waste and they go eat real food." Rose said, hoping they would buy into the lie.

They talked for a while about everything from upcoming plans to why Mike should not get a mohawk. Mike and Chris were being trained as warriors. Nathan was in the line to become Delta in the pack. Of course, he didn't want that. He wanted to be a warrior like the others.

Nathan had a head for business and was great at diplomacy when it came to conflicts. He knew that being lumped into the same situation as Asher and Dallas would just cause more problems in the future. They were high ups and Nathan came from an Omega family. Delta's were high ups but at the same time they were still working class. They were still a step above the regular wolves and the bottom rung in the pecking order of the hierarchy.

Nathan knew if he took this opportunity that it would lead to disaster. He would be constantly cleaning up Asher and Dallas's messes with no credit for doing so. On top of that fact, he never really fit into that world. He was content being a protector.

"Oh you'll be fine." Rose told Nathan.

"You know I can't stand those guys. It's going to end up being like high school all over again. The top dogs and the rest of us are just lowly servants. I'll be surprised if they don't run the pack into the ground in five years." Nathan said, popping another fry into his mouth.

"Well, I guess I'll just have to pray for the Goddess to keep your butts out of trouble while I'm away." Rose said, keeping up the act that one day she would return.

"You always get to go and have adventures. While the rest of us have to stay and do the real work." Chris said, poking fun at the fact he was really going to miss her.

"Oh you know I'll still be around, so to speak. Even though I won't physically be here." Rose said, trying not to feel guilty for not telling the boys the truth.

The pretty waitress appeared and started passing out the food. Rose tried to eat normally, but everything smelt so good that she just dug in and once again the boys were just staring at Rose. Trying to ignore them, Rose popped a very cheesy fry into her mouth. She was starving and by the Goddess she was going to eat.

"It's not polite to stare!" Rose finally said.

"It's just weird seeing you actually eat something for breakfast." Mike said, amazed that she was eating like a normal person.

"Well, technically it's 10, so mid-morning brunch." Rose corrected.

"Same difference." Mike rolled his eyes, which earned him a kick under the table.

"Yeah, Babygirl. What's the deal?" Chris said, starting to be concerned.

"Kate decided that I should either eat what she believes to be food or nothing at all. So, I haven't been eating anything for going on three days now." Rose lied, but in all actuality it really wasn't. Kate grounded her to her room, banning her from anything in the house.

"Damn. She's going that far again?" The boys said in unison. It wasn't uncommon for her to do that. Rose would normally eat at school and stop by one of their houses for dinner when things got really rough. But with Rose being watched like a hawk, it doesn't work like that right now.

Rose dropped her head, not wanting to admit the problems of the past were looming over their heads once again. She was strong and determined to just push through. She tries not to have to rely on anyone else. This way, no one gets hurt because of her. After all, once she leaves, it's going to be all on her anyway.

"I can handle her. After all, it's just barely one more week until I leave." Rose tried to play it off with the same toughness as she always did.

"You need anything and I mean anything you call us." Nathan spoke up and then looked at the other two guys to confirm. They were all in agreement.

"I got you." Rose said, deflecting as usual. She was good at that. Not letting people see when she didn't want them to see was her way of truly dealing with the bullshit.

They sat and talked as the time passed. The funny, the sad, and the hopefully happy days to come. These were her boys. Each memory is clear in her mind. The cars they built and the money they made off stupid buttheads that wanted to race. Awe the good ole days were soon to be over forever locked in their memories.

Time flew and before they knew it, they were about 5 cokes in and it was nearly 2:30pm. When Rose looked up at the clock, she started to scramble and get the waitress's attention to pay her bill. The boys were looking worried. Not 20 minutes ago, they were all cutting up and now Rose looked like she had seen a ghost.

"What's wrong?" Mike sounded off first.

"I have an appointment at the packhouse in an hour. I have to get going." Rose replied, still trying to wavy the young lady down.

"It's cool. It's on us." Chris said, hoping that Rose would calm down.

"Are you sure?" Rose looked bewildered.

"Yeah, I'm sure we owe you a meal or something by now. Who do you have to see?" Nathan chimed in.

"Alpha Kent and Luna Zara. They have to sign off on me leaving the territory." Rose relaxed slightly.

"Okay. You go and meet with them and let's just plan to meet back at Mike's house for dinner?" Chris pops off.

"You think your mom will mind?" Rose came off, not wanting to impose.

"You know momma. She's always the more the merrier. Well except that one time, but we didn't tell her that 30 people would be showing up at the house. And she wasn't mad, just thought people would look at her badly because nothing was prepared." Mike said. His mother was the pack cook. Well morning cook.

"Okay meet y'all there." Rose hugged Mike and ran out the door.

Rose fired up her car and practically broke the sound barrier to get there on time. Rose arrived at the packhouse 20 minutes early. She hoped this would be an in and out situation. She knew exactly what to say for this to go smoothly. Rose just hoped that she wouldn't have to deal with her mother or the rest of the counsel.

Chapter 11

Rose looks at herself in the rear-view mirror. Making sure her eyes were clear. Taking a steading breath, Rose got out of the car. She straightened her clothes and walked toward the packhouse's front door. *You got this!* *Was all Snow piped up and said.*

Rose walks through the door and hopes she doesn't run into her mother. She needed a level head walking into this meeting. Kate needed this to go well too. So, she wouldn't have to deal with Rose any longer.

Rose stood in the foyer looking around for a moment. One could hear the busy kitchen Omegas working to get dinner ready. The normal busy workers zoom through keeping everything clean and cared for. She actually hadn't been here in so long that the place looked so different. Almost like walking into a foreign land.

Rose, trying to stay under the radar, found her way to the stairs and went up to the Alpha's office. *No reason to prolong this any further.* Rose thought to herself. The quicker this was handled the quicker Rose could start to put her plans into action.

She just prayed that it would be a private meeting. Most times when someone wanted to leave it would be more of a council meeting. Rose didn't think that she could handle dealing with her mother and father along with the whole upper class sitting in on the conversation.

Rose reached the door of Alpha Kent's office and taking one more steading breath she knocked on the door. Rose could hear footsteps before she saw the doorknob move. Luna Zara with her stunning smiling face waved her inside.

"Good afternoon, Rose." Luna Zara reached out and shook her hand.

"Good afternoon, Luna Zara." Rose greeted back.

"Come and sit down. Alpha Kent will be along at any moment. That man is never on time." Luna Zara teased.

"That's fine. I believe I'm actually a little bit early." Rose tried hard to keep up the small talk. Rose wasn't great at small talk but she would do her best.

"Only ten minutes or so. But it's good to be early. It shows that you have respect for your time and others. May I offer you something to drink?" Luna Zara motioned to the pitcher of water and tea along with some homemade cookies.

"Tea please. And are those chocolate chip cookies?" Rose said, trying to remain casual.

"Why yes they are. Baked just this afternoon. Would you like some?" Luna Zara said, taking a small saucer up for the cookies.

"Yes, thank you." Rose took the glass of iced tea and the small plate of cookies.

"So, you got into college? That is an exciting time in any young person's life. What will you be studying? Or have you not thought that far ahead?" Luna Zara figured they would just start the meeting without Alpha Kent.

"Yes, it is very exciting. Honestly, I didn't think I would get in. I mean my grades are top notch but this program is very competitive. I was very surprised when I got my letter. I will be studying Automotive design and engine repair. Minoring hopefully in business." Rose played the script just as she wrote it down. Every possible question and answer was studied over and over again.

"That is very practical since you already do so much with cars. Weren't you working at Carl's shop?" Luna Zara said, dunking her cookie in some hot tea.

"Yes, I was until Monday. I left the shop. Carl understands that with the finals and leaving it was best for all involved. I think he's really going to miss me. I kept everything organized there." Rose slightly giggled to herself.

"I bet he will. From what I gathered talking to so many people about you. You are very well liked, great student, an amazing warrior, and a good mechanic. I feel you will do well with whatever you choose to do." Luna Zara smiled at Rose.

Just as Rose was beginning to respond, Alpha Kent entered the room red faced and trying to fix his tie. This was a funny sight mainly because Alpha Kent rarely wore ties. Rose guessed he was trying to look respectable for this meeting.

Both ladies rose to great Alpha Kent. Alpha Kent looked at his watch and then to Luna Zara slightly embarrassed. Rose kept her gaze down and tried not to laugh. Alpha Kent looked like the kid that was late for class but thought he could just slip in without being noticed.

"I'm so sorry I'm late. There was a situation that needed my attention. I thought I had enough time to shower and get her before the meeting." Alpha Kent explained while going over to kiss Luna Zara on the cheek.

"Situation? Anything I need to handle?" Luna Zara looked concerned.

"No, just a problem on the training field with Asher and Dallas." Alpha Kent responded.

"Boys causing trouble again?" Luna Zara was quick to respond.

"Unfortunately. That and having a meeting about the four Lycan Kings, Patrol schedules for the next week while they are here. I mean we barely have a week until they arrive. And I'm waiting for their people to get back to me on the exact day they will be here." Alpha Kent said, pouring a glass of tea and taking a seat next to Luna Zara in the sitting area of his office.

"Sounds like a lot to deal with. So, I hope I'm not taking up too much of your time." Rose said, trying to hurry this along.

"Oh no we always have time for our pack members." Luna Zara said, kind of cutting her eyes at the Alpha for always being late.

"Absolutely. Especially the Gamma's daughter. It's so amazing to have one of our own wanting to do something with their future." Alpha Kent said, settling into his chair next to Luna Zara.

"So, as you were saying. You're going to be studying Automotive design with engine repair with a minor in business." Luna Zara recapped so Rose didn't have to for Alpha Kent.

"Well, that seems to be right up your alley. And you will be leaving for summer classes?" Alpha Kent relaying the information that he was given by Gamma Kate.

"Yes, Alpha Kent. I want to get some of the easier classes knocked out before Fall semester." Rose said, putting down her drink on the small coffee table.

"Well, that sounds very responsible, good planning, and extremely smart. So you will be in the Harvest Moon's territory?" Luna Zara inquired.

"Yes, Ma'am. My aunt Eva's pack. She has graciously offered me to stay with her until I can get settled on campus. The college is only located about 20 minutes from their home." Rose said, selling it as her life depended on it.

"Well, I see no reason not to grant your pass. We will still have to call the Harvest Moon and let them know." Alpha Kent said looking at his watch.

It was nearly 4:30pm and most packs were run like businesses. Alpha Kent thought what was the harm in just making the phone call now instead of waiting till morning. All the paperwork could be in order and it would be one more thing off his plate for the moment.

"Rose, do you have a few minutes to stick around?" That way I can go ahead and call the Harvest Moon's Alpha and get the ball on the roll for you." Alpha Kent said getting up and moving to his desk.

"I don't have anything going on right now. I cleared my afternoon to make sure I could give this all my attention." Rose said, trying to sound casual.

"Good you can sit over here with me. After Alpha Kent gets all the formalities done we can go ahead and issue your papers. That way you don't have to make another trip. I'm sure you have a busy schedule with all the upcoming plans." Luna Zara said, offering Rose another cookie from the plate.

"Oh yes. Between finals and packing, I don't think I have found one free moment to just breathe." Rose said, trying to control her breathing at this point. Everything was moving so quickly and she was very happy about that.

Alpha Kent went to his desk to look for the information on the Harvest Moon pack and the contact phone number. Within minutes, he was picking up the phone and dialing the number. He was hoping to speak to Alpha Jax today if he was still in the office.

"Good Afternoon, Harvest Moon. How may I direct your call?" A lovely sounding young lady answered.

"Yes, ma'am Alpha Kent of the Hollows pack for Alpha Jax please. If he is still available?" Alpha Kent spoke as he turned his chair around to gain a little privacy.

"Oh yes, Alpha Kent. Alpha Jax has been expecting your call. One moment please." The young lady said, putting Alpha Kent on a brief hold.

A booming voice came back on the other end. "Alpha Kent of Hollows, So good to hear from you." Alpha Jax said, coming on the line.

"I hope it's not too late for my call but we have so much going on down here. I figured I would just get this out of the way." Alpha Kent explained.

"Oh nonsense. We always have time for other packs. What can I help you with?" Alpha Jax responded waiting to see if he was going to get any new information.

"Rose Wells, Gamma's daughter and niece to your Beta Eva, wishes a pass to leave our territory and enter yours for college." Alpha Kent giving all the information in one sentence.

"Well of course that should be fine. Beta Eva had indicated that she will be staying with her until a spot opens up on campus. But still remaining in the territory. I see no problem granting her stay." Alpha Jax said, trying to read between the lines and see if he happened to know anything else.

"Well that's wonderful. I'll have the paperwork handled after the call and fax a copy to you after. Is that good for you?" Alpha Kent said, turning his chair back around.

"That will be fine. Is there anything else I can do to help you with Alpha Kent?" Alpha Jax says realizing he wasn't going to get any new information.

"No, that was it. Thank you again for taking my call." Alpha Kent knowing that showing respect among other Alphas was how they brokered alleys.

"Not a problem. Do you know when we should be expecting her? That way I can inform my patrols and such." Alpha Jax inquired to see if anything had changed from the original information.

"Well it was supposed to be after graduation next Friday. Unfortunately, we are afraid that we are going to have to move up graduation. We are having visitors coming and while the parties are not moving the ceremony is having to." Alpha Kent said, Looking over at Luna Zara and Rose sitting on the couch.

Rose wasn't surprised by this. Though she knew this probably had something to do with a suggestion from her mother. That it would give everyone time to handle both events without one being overshadowed. This also put Rose out of the picture way faster and much sooner than expected. Rose was completely fine with that.

"So when will graduation be?" Alpha Jax inquired curiously. He had the feeling like he was dragging information out of him.

"Saturday." was all Alpha Kent would say.

"They will be announcing it at school tomorrow." Luna Zara said, looking at Rose.

"Well then it looks like I have so much to do before then." Rose said, running the list of what she could possibly have left to do.

"That'll be fine. I believe if there is nothing else, I have to go see to some of our graduation prep plans as well." Alpha Jax said, trying not to come off rude but knowing they would have to end the call with no new information other than the moved date of graduation.

"Pleasure, Alpha Jax." Alpha Kent said.

"As always." Alpha Jax said, hanging up the phone.

Alpha Kent hung up the phone and hit a button on his desk. The Alpha's secretary came in and handed him the papers that were already prepared. Rose knew she would just have to keep her cool for just a few more minutes and everything would be in place.

Alpha Kent looked over the papers and signed in all the correct spots. Then passed the papers to Luna Zara, which had gotten up and had walked over to his desk, to sign off. The papers were handed back to the secretary and she left the room with them.

"Okay, Rose. When the papers come back you will be free to go. I hope that you do well in your future and we will see you when it's all over." Alpha Kent said as the lady reappeared and handed the papers back to Alpha Kent.

"Here you go. I know you will do great things in college." Luna Zara said, holding out the papers to Rose.

"I thank you both for allowing me this opportunity." Rose said, taking the papers and walking out of the office.

Rose made it all the way out of the packhouse before she saw her mother and father headed up the walk. Rose simply smiled and tried to keep walking. She knew that there was little to no chance if she got caught up talking that she would get away.

"Rose." Kyle called out to his daughter.

"Hey, Dad." Rose said, thinking that there was no such luck.

"How was your meeting with Alpha Kent and Luna Zara?" Kate was quick to get to the point.

"Went very well. I have my papers. Alpha Jax will be expecting me after graduation. Which I just found out was moved to Saturday because of the four Lycan Kings visit." Rose said, trying to remain neutral with both her parents standing there.

For a moment, Kate looked pleased with herself. Not only did the Alpha and Luna take her suggestion in moving graduation so it could be a week-long party but also she got Rose out of her hair a whole week early. Kate couldn't seem too eager about the news but inside she was over the moon about it.

"Well that doesn't give you much time to pack your stuff up." Kate said, faking concern in front of her husband.

"I'll manage. Are you eating here tonight?" Rose more addressed her father at this point.

"Yes, we will be." Kyle spoke up, still noticing his wife's ever curious growing behavior.

"Okay. Well, I'm headed to Mike's. He and the guys invited me over for dinner."

"Well don't you think your time would be better spent getting your things together and studying?" Kate now throws looks that could kill at Rose.

"Now now. She doesn't have long left with her friends. Go ahead Rose. Don't stay out too late though. Okay?" Kyle said overruling his wife and letting his daughter go.

"I'll get everything done when I get out of school tomorrow. Thanks Dad. Don't worry I won't stay out too late." Rose said, and then turned her back before anything else could be said to her. After all, now there were only two full days left and she was going to make the most of it.

Rose climbed into her car and left for Mike's house. Rose knew that once she was gone from this place she would never turn back. No more dealing with the hell she has had to endure over the last week. No more boys trying to pursue what they only wanted to play with and discard like trash. The next steps were within her grasp.

Chapter 12

Alpha Jax hung up the phone and was very puzzled by the conversation. He knew that only the basic information had been given to Alpha Kent. At this point, there wasn't much more than he himself had. The only thing new was the fact that they were moving up graduation. But why? It couldn't just be because it was more covenant.

Taking out his cell phone, Alpha Jax quickly sent a text to Luna Hazel and his Betas, Tony and Eva. While mind linking would have been faster, he just wanted this between a short group and sometimes it didn't work like that. It occasionally went skew and more people got the "memo" than was supposed to. After all, Alpha Jax had only been an Alpha for a few short years and he was still trying to figure it all out.

Within minutes, Luna Hazel walked into his office. Beta Tony and Eva showed up within minutes after her. Once everyone was set inside the office, the door was closed and Alpha Jax looked around at the people in front of him. Where to begin?

"Alpha Jax, What's going on? Is everything okay?" Beta Eva finally spoke to break the defining silence.

"Well, I got the call from Alpha Kent over your niece. Something is either very off about the situation or that man is easily played. Have you heard anything more from your sister?" Alpha Jax questioned.

"No, not since Sunday afternoon. Why?" Beta Eva said, puzzled with worry rising in her heart.

"Well, apparently the Four Lycan Kings are coming for a visit. In the process, they moved up to graduation. Graduation is now on Saturday." Alpha Jax relaying the information.

"Now something is very odd about that. I mean the graduation being moved up for what reason? Are the parties and festivities being moved up as well?" Luna Hazel said propping on the Alpha's desk.

"Nope, they just moved graduation up. They are holding a bigger celebration because the four Lycan Kings are coming." Alpha Jax said, trying to see what he was currently missing. Sometimes laying all these pieces of a puzzle out makes it easier to solve.

The four of them sat there racking their brains. They knew that Kate had to have something to do with the abrupt move of graduation, but with her only being a Gamma, how would she have that kind of power? It would have to be a suggestion that would easily make sense to them, so that's what they would have to go with.

"Wait, isn't one of the Lycan Kings a seer?" Beta Tony said, trying to remember. It was like the "ah ha" moment going off in his head.

"I believe the Lycan King of the West. Why?" Alpha Jax said, trying to see what the realization was with this information. Why did he always feel like he was missing something?

"Anything that Kate would try to hide when it came to Rose would be seen. If Rose was still there. The seer can only put both halves of the puzzle together if they are both in front of him. He would be able to tell that something was off with Kate and that she was currently hiding something. But without the other piece, Rose, to confirm suspicions, he couldn't make a formal claim and, so to speak out her. Therefore, she would have to be gone to keep whatever under wraps. That's the only problem with the seer's powers. Everything has to be in place for the current to see the future. And Kate is VERY gifted at hiding her past." Beta Tony said, looking over at Eva with a major sense of clarity.

"Well, Damn. Beta Tony, I would never have thought of that. But you're absolutely right. You are closer to the situation with this being your sister-in-law. Would you happen to know if she is capable of this? I mean it seems like a reach for a Gamma to openly suggest and actually be taken seriously. I mean from what I gather, she isn't the most liked but is the most feared." Alpha Jax said, knowing more than ever that he made the right decision keeping Tony as his Beta.

"But wouldn't they still be able to see through Kate even without Rose being there? I mean you would really have to be doing something to keep a natural born seer from that kind of information?" Luna Hazel said, now slightly puzzled.

"No, because Kate is a very cunning liar. Why won't they be able to see through her? A seer has to have proof when he names anyone of wrongdoing. So, without Rose, they have no way of actually calling her out on anything she has done. They can suspect all day long but without Rose standing before them there is no proof. There is nothing more than just that suspicion. Kate would be just cunning enough to use every flawless attribute to keep them off her tail." Beta Eva said, seeing her husband's train of thought and knowing this had to be right.

"So what do we do now?" Luna Hazel came to the same realization as everyone else in the room.

"We prepare for her arrival and hope that nothing bad happens to her along the way. We have our own graduation ceremony to prepare for." Alpha Jax said, as there was nothing more to do until Rose arrived and they could put the rest of the puzzle pieces together.

Beeping sounds came from the fax machine behind the Alpha's desk. Eight pieces of paper came rolling out one by one. Everyone's attention stopped and they looked at the machine. Alpha Jax got up and went over to retrieve the papers. He held in his hand the pass for Rose Wells to leave and enter the territory.

"Here's the papers. So now it won't be long." Alpha Jax said, reviewing the papers one time to see if anything was out of place. There wasn't, unfortunately.

"Well, this still seems like the only course of action. I will have a word with the patrols to make sure she passes in without any problems. I will also make a call, if that is okay, down to the other packs along the way to make sure if they see her to make sure nothing happens." Beta Tony piped up, knowing his sister-in-law had no problems with causing accidents to happen.

"Agreed." They all chimed in at once.

"So Sunday we shall have an early meeting with Rose." Alpha Jax said.

Everyone nodded and knew their assignments. In all actuality, all they could do is wait and put certain precautions in place. They knew that the offense on her name couldn't be as bad as everyone was thinking. But with so much trouble to keep everything hidden, Rose was the only one to know at that point. Alpha Jax was suspicious at the fact that Alpha Kent was fed the same lines as Beta Eva. Rose would hopefully give everything more light on her arrival.

Chapter 13

The annoying buzzing of the alarm clock woke Rose out of her awful dreams. She couldn't tell what was worse, the dreams or the reality it was based off of. Rose knew that it would all be over in two days' time.

Rose put her feet on the floor and began to gather her thoughts. Looking into the mirror, the black eye was faded but not gone. She knew there was going to be trouble when she returned home last night. Kate was not happy about being shown up in front of Rose's father.

Rose hoped that they would not be home when she arrived at 10pm. One car was there but not her dad's mustang. She honestly hoped that they had taken the mustang to the packhouse. Rose got out of her car and when she entered the house it was silent as a grave. She couldn't hear anything that would set off alarm bells.

Rose went to her room, silently creeping up the stairs to make sure no one could hear her. As she entered and turned on the light, she saw stars. Kate was standing behind the door with a right hook ready to do damage. Kate managed to mask herself so as to not be noticed. Rose never saw it coming. Through the yelling and beating, Rose kept her stomach covered and protected.

Rose knew that the only thing that kept Kate from doing more damage from all the punching, kicking, and clawing was the fact that Kyle, Rose's father, had come home. Rose guesses he was earlier than expected because Kate rushed out and into the bathroom to keep from being discovered. Kyle, smelling the blood, rushed upstairs.

Rose had to drag herself from the floor and pretend to be asleep when her father entered her room. Trying hard to disguise the smell of the blood with her blankets. He didn't go over to her to thank the Goddess. He would have seen what was done to her and Rose would have had a hard time explaining. Rose knew she just had to endure it a little bit longer.

Kyle smelt more blood coming from the bathroom, which led his attention away from Rose's room. When he got there, he found his wife already in the shower. Kyle was very confused. What was going on right under his nose? Was he too blind to see?

"Everything okay in here?" Kyle asked through the shower curtain.

"Everything is fine. Why?" Kate said, trying to think on her feet.

"I smell blood. I thought it was coming from Rose's room. While there is a smell there, it's also coming from here." Kyle said, trying to see if something had happened before he returned home.

"I cut myself on some broken glass in Rose's room. One of her picture frames had fallen off the wall and busted." Kate showed her hand to her husband and saw the superficial wounds on her hand.

While Kyle didn't believe that was the whole truth. He had nothing else to go on. Kate was acting weirder than normal and extremely aggressive towards Rose. Everytime he questioned anything Kate would play it off. Rose would deflect and change the subject. With nothing currently going on, he dropped it for now. Kyle left the bathroom and headed for bed.

After getting out of the shower, Kate knew there was nothing more she could do because her husband was home. She knew it was just a matter of time before he was going to find out what was really going on. Kate would not have it.

Kate thought to herself that this would be the perfect time for another special drinks to keep her husband from looking too hard into this matter. Without any further thought, she headed to the kitchen to make her husband a nightcap before he went to bed. When Kate felt Kyle slipping out of her grasp one of her special drinks always did the trick to keep him in line.

Rose broke out of the memory of the night before and began to ready herself for what was going to be her last day of high school. Rose took out what little bit of makeup she actually owned and began to cover what should have been healed by now. Rose wore dark eyeliner to make her eyes pop in color. Simple light pink lipstick completed her look as she got dressed. Blacked out from head to toe, Rose wore a black tank top, black button-up, black jeans, and, of course, her black boots.

Rose looked in the mirror one more time and decided to just get going. Grabbing her bag and leather, she knew there were only two exams today. That was it. She would be done with High School.

Rose was now more on guard than ever. She had her knife out as soon as she left her room. Thankfully, this time no one was home. She knew that she was going to be packing up the rest of her room and starting to move it to her car after school.

Rose walked out of the house, got in the car, and drove to school. After she arrived and parked, she headed to the first of her last two classes. Rose found her seat and waited for the test to be passed out so she could begin.

Within three hours, Rose had both tests completed and was now sitting in the office. Rose was waiting to have her last talk with the counselor. Why? Rose had no idea. Rose knew that the counselor requested to have a meeting before she left the grounds today.

"Ms. Wells. Mrs. Dole will see you now." The teacher's assistant said, showing her to the door.

"Oh, Ms. Wells. Thank you so much for stopping by." Mrs. Dole said, standing to shake Rose's hand.

"Not a problem. How can I help you?" Rose said, trying to get to the point.

"Well, I have some news and I thought I would give it to you personally." Mrs. Dole beamed.

"Okay." Rose said, looking very sheepishly.

"Okay. I will get right to it then. Your grades are in. You have a 4.9 GPA. You have been named Valedictorian." Mrs. Dole beamed brighter. This woman would give the sun a run for its money.

"Are you sure? I mean my last final didn't feel like I did too well with it." Rose said, thinking that there must be some mistake.

"But you made a 100% on it." Mrs. Dole said.

"Well, I guess I was worried about nothing. But while I am grateful for the honor, I would really rather you pick someone else for it." Rose said, understanding that this was a great honor. One that she had been working for a really long time. In some respects, it was a bigger deal when it came to the pack. During the celebrations, she would be honored and she wouldn't be there to have that happen for her. In a lot of ways, this saddened her, but it is what it is.

"Are you sure? This is an amazing achievement." Mrs. Dole asked, perplexed that Rose was turning this down.

"Yes, ma'am, it is. But I'm leaving right after graduation. And in that process, that honor comes with certain pack responsibilities that I won't be here to fulfill." Rose pleaded with Mrs. Dole.

"Oh, I see. So, are the rumors true about you leaving for college?" Mrs. Dole asked.

"Yes, ma'am." Rose confirmed.

"Then that explains it. You will still be listed on the paper from the school, but we will name another in your place." Mrs. Dole seemed more than just a little upset about this.

"Thank you so much. I just know that someone else will be able to handle that honor better." Rose said humbly.

"I understand. Well, I wish you the best of luck with your future Rose. You have always been an extremely bright girl and I know you will do amazing things." Mrs. Dole said.

"Thank you so much. Mrs. Dole." Rose stood to shake her hand and walked out of the office.

Rose avoided all contact with everyone till she got to her car. Rose drew in several deep breaths. For some reason, Rose didn't feel the calming effect she would normally have come over her. She thought she would feel happy that it was all over. Maybe it was because she had one full day to get through before she was on the road.

It was 1pm when she arrived back in the driveway. Rose made sure that no one was there. There were no cars in the driveway. So,

Rose went into the house to pack the rest of her things. She needed to get this done now.

Rose already had half of her room packed. Her one big duffle bag held all the clothes that she was using to get through till she left. It didn't take her more than an hour to pack everything in boxes and suitcases.

Just a little over an hour after she was done packing, Rose's car was packed with all her things. She then moved her car to the back so no one could see that she was already ready to go. Her duffle bag was the only thing left in her room of her personal items.

It was just about 4pm and Rose knew it was time to deal with the wicked witch. Why would she have to endure more? Rose reminded herself that just one more day. It did, however, take everything she had not to just jump in her car and start driving. She knew she couldn't do that to her father.

Chapter 14

Rose woke to a quiet house. She had been up most of the night on guard. Kate wasn't going to get the jump on her two days in a row. After packing up her car and going back up to her room, Rose locked the door and sat at the ready for whatever was going to happen.

While there was a lot of shouting through the door, Kate couldn't physically get through the door. By the time she tried to break down the door, Kyle had come home once again foiling Kate's plans. Kate had to cover up the situation and, in the process, drag Kyle off for dinner.

With graduation tomorrow, she knew she was as safe as anytime. If she showed up with a mark on her, Kate would be found out and her plans would be ruined. Rose was going to use this to her advantage.

She suspected that they stayed at the packhouse due to the text Rose received from her father. It had stated that he was proud of her and they would be out most of the night. Even with this information, Rose didn't let down her guard and unlocked the bedroom door.

Rose still didn't go to bed till nearly 2am. So when she woke to a quiet house it scared her a little bit. Rose slept with her knives and finally took them out of her hand when she confirmed that the house was empty. Rose went to the kitchen in search of coffee. Her phone rang and it startled the hell out of her till she saw it was Mike on the caller ID.

"Ello?" Rose answered, trying to control her breathing.

"Hey Rosebud." Mike sounded more chipper than normal.

"What's up?" Rose was a little annoyed.

"We have a plan for the day. Are you interested?" Mike sounded a little more like the partner in crime then usual.

"Is coffee included? Cause I really just got up. It was a very late night on my end." Rose would take the bait. After all, they used to do this to each other all the time.

"Of course."

"Everyone coming?"

"Yep."

"Can someone pick me up? My car is already packed up."

"I can come get you."

"10 minutes?"

"Bet." And just like that, the phone call ended and the plans were made.

Rose went to take a quick shower. After coming out of the hot water, she looked in the mirror. Rose had noticed that her burses had now completely faded. Rose was extremely happy about this. She didn't like wearing makeup.

Rose wrapped a towel around her body and began to walk into her room to get ready for the day. Within a few minutes, Rose was dressed out in a blue button up, black tank top, and black jeans with her boots. She pulled her hair back in a bun and grabbed her keys and wallet.

As she was headed out of her room and towards the door, Rose could hear the sound of Mike's GMC and that made her smile. She went out to meet her friend. No matter what, this is what she was going to miss. Last minute calls to go and meet up with friends to just blow off steam.

As Rose climbed in the truck, she could see there were two baskets sitting in the floorboard. No doubt, Mike's mother would have to be thanked there. She was always worried about us eating nothing but junk food.

"Hey Mike." Rose beamed.

"Hey Rosebud!" Mike was so happy to see his friend.

"Mom?" Rose said pointing down at the baskets.

"Yep. She sends her own version of a graduation feast for you. She is so pissed at your mother right now that she can't even begin to see straight. Gamma Kate has been put in charge of the menu for all the celebrations to calibrate with my mom. When mom was beginning to find out which special desserts for each of the graduates. She found out you weren't kidding about leaving the moment they say congrats "Class of 2010". So, you know mom. She got on the horn with all the boys and the mothers of the pack with little to no effort. With all being told, your mother is to know nothing. "You will have what you have earned" as momma said." Mike said, relaying the message from his mother.

"Well that is amazing but she didn't have to do that. I do appreciate it but really she didn't have to." Rose had given up all hope of having her graduation be anything more than just the end of an era.

"Nope. Mom wasn't taking no for an answer. While everyone is setting up for tomorrow mom thought this would be the perfect time to pull this off. Basically a bait and switch with everyone having to be somewhere else setting up. She knows that Gamma Kate has been to overly happy about you leaving. She wanted you to know, more than ever, not everyone felt that way about you leaving." Mike said looking at the shock on Rose's face.

"I really don't know what to say?" Rose began to tear up a little bit.

"You don't have to say anything, just know that we boys had to have our own send off with you." Mike said putting the truck in drive and pulling away from the house.

"You guys really are the best friends a girl could ever ask for. I don't know what I will do without you." Rose said, trying to hold it together.

"Well as you said there is always the phone and email. It's not like we won't keep in touch. Oh and by the way this is kind of supposed to be a surprise. So be surprised." Mike said, laughing his ass off.

Mike could only keep a secret if it was 100% necessary. Otherwise, It wasn't going to happen. But he would always say you still gotta act surprised. Christmas was always fun because two weeks before he would tell us all what he got us. You couldn't help but just shake your head.

"So where are we headed?" Rose knew that Mike wouldn't be able to keep that to himself.

"To the lake house property. Carl said if he heard of anyone heading our way. He would give us a call. Plus they would have to come past the shop first. That way we can have a completely relaxing day." Mike said pretty proud of himself.

"Well it's not only my day. After all, we all walk tomorrow. Graduation is for all of us." Rose said not really liking things being made all about her.

"But you're the only one leaving us tomorrow. You're the one that doesn't get to have the fun that comes with graduation. So, no this is your day. And from all of us, we hope you enjoy it!" Mike said with that wicked little gleam in his eye.

"I'm sure I will." Rose said just sitting back and enjoying the ride.

After about 20 minutes or so, they took the lake side cut off. Carl kept a huge place down here by the lake. Mostly for fishing but when his wife, Chris's mother, was alive they all spent so much time down here. Rose couldn't remember one year that Chris hadn't had a birthday party, their first runs after shifting, or even their first camp outs right here at the lake house.

Most werewolves, when they lose their mates, go crazy. Like a blood lust that would drive them insane. Carl on the other hand kept it together for Chris. He drank himself into a hole for a while, but with the help of Chris and a few close friends, he was able to get out of it again. Some say it was Rose showing up at the shop and him being reminded the world didn't stop spinning because of a broken heart.

As they pulled up, Rose could see all the trucks and car waiting for them. The guys were all unloading various plates and presents. Rose was overjoyed to have friends like this. Her friend's moms were no doubt the reason behind this and just being there for her was like a dream come true.

They parked by the side of the old pale blue house that overlooked the water. This was the only house out here and really the only house for miles. This is where the four swore a blood oath to always be there for each other under their first full moon. Through thick and thin they would always stand by one another.

Nathan and Chris rushed the truck yelling "SURPRISE!!!"

"Oh guys you shouldn't have." Rose gushed as she looked around at all the decorations.

"Well you don't think we could just let you go off without a proper party could you?" Nathan said, helping Rose out of the truck while Chris grabbed the baskets.

"Plus you know the moms and dads wanted to do something and with you leaving. Let's face it with your mom being a bitch.This was the best they could do on such short notice." Chris said, knowing that it was just the gesture that made Rose feel special in this time where she was being treated as anything but.

"While most had to keep up appearances in town, they did send their love and support. Getting this all done without Gamma Kate finding out was a task though. Don't worry she and Gamma Kyle will be kept busy all day." Nathan and the other boys boosted with their evil smiles.

Rose knew that this was no easy feet. The three boys and their families had pulled off the biggest whammy of the year. So, why not enjoy it. The four headed into the house where there were pictures of them everywhere. They had been friends so long it was like they were more siblings than best friends. It was always the four. Even as they grew up. They might have all done their own things, but they always had time for each other.

The room was decorated in streamers and balloons. Graduation banners and a table with all kinds of gifts and food. They already had the T.V. set up and it would be their last movie marathon. This made Rose a little sad even though she wouldn't show it now.

"Oh guys. You really shouldn't have. And a movie day too! We haven't done that since we were kids." Rose began to gush again.

"Well should we do presents first then dig in?" Chris said, setting up the first flick of the day.

"Sure. why not." Rose said, with the biggest smile plastered on her face.

There were dozens of gifts. Everything from new towels and bedding to gift cards and cash. New cook sets, storage bowls, dishes and silverware. She really was set for anything now. She knew when they finally did make it back to the house everything would go safely in her car.

After hours of pigging out and watching one movie after the other, Rose was exhausted. They had told so many stories, thrown popcorn at each other, and just laughed until it seemed like the wide open room was laughing with them. Rose didn't want this to end. She wanted to lock up this memory forever. Alas, they couldn't hide here forever. They weren't children anymore. They would have to do what needed to be done.

"I think we should start cleaning up." Rose said, knowing she would have to be the party pooper.

"Oh just one more movie." Nathan and Chris chimed in.

"Maybe for you guys but I'm exhausted. I need to get home and get ready for tomorrow. WE all do." Rose said, looking at their disappointed faces and smiled, this was a classic. Rose stuck to her guns, putting her hands on her hips and just giving them the stern look.

"She's right, guys. Mom will be expecting us for dinner soon anyway." Mike said, looking at the guys in a way that they knew it was time.

"Yep. Dad is probably going to be calling any time to tell us we are being looked for." Chris said looking at his friends.

With that one realization, they had one last group hug. They started cleaning up and packing presents out to Mike's truck. They knew this was the last hora. They came from different directions and in different vehicles so no one would get wise and try to alert Gamma Kate. Not that many people fell in that category, but they left nothing to chance.

Everyone knew that Gamma Kate was completely against anything for Rose. The ones that were closest to Rose made sure she did have something. That's why everyone had eyes on Gamma Kate. If she had made one move through the day that would make anyone think that they found out the alarms would have already been sounded. Precautions were always put into place though.

With one last hug and wave, they all set off in their own directions. Mike took Rose back to the house. He knew deep down there was more to the story. Rose was good at keeping things out of sight and playing it close to the vest. So, he knew not to press her but wanted to make sure she knew no matter what, they were there for her.

They made sure the coast was completely clear. Mike even called his mother before they had pulled up at the house. Mike pulled up behind Rose's car. Which was still behind the house. They quickly unloaded all the things from his truck into her car. They made it look like nothing new had been added to her effects so any onlooker wouldn't know the difference.

After the last item was put in the trunk, Mike closed it and now they just looked like two friends having a chat. Appearances were everything. Rose and Mike were cutting up and just playing back and forth like this was any other day.

"I want to say something, Rose. I don't need a response. I just want you to know. I know there is more to this. I know that Gamma Kate is already too happy about you leaving. So you know if you wanted to tell us anything at all... We'll take it to the grave." Mike said looking deep into Rose's eyes trying to drive the point home.

"How about this? In one month I will call you. You need to gather the guys and go fishing. If you all still feel the same way. I will give you some information then. Agreed?" Rose said as Mike's cell phone rang and it was Nathan.

"Agreed." Mike said, grabbing his cell phone and making his way to his truck. He knew he had to make an appearance at the packhouse to help his mother. So with one last look, Mike fired up his truck and backed out of her driveway.

Rose went to go get washed up and get ready for what she hoped to be a peaceful night. She was still going to barricade herself in her room. She wasn't scared. Rose just knew that the hours counted down. She did have a crazy thought about just leaving. Getting in her car right then and there and driving away.

Rose wasn't going out like that. She would not be seen as a coward. She would walk the stage tomorrow and that was that. She would handle her business with grace and fire. She had nothing to lose and was going to prove it.

Chapter 15

7am and the buzzing of the alarm clock was almost so loud that Rose wanted to knock it into the middle of next week. As her eyes open and her foggy brain comes into focus, she realizes this is the day. Everything came down to the next few hours.

No noise in the house again startles her. No happy graduation day screamed at her. No celebration of her and the fact this was another chapter closed in her life. Rose honestly didn't expect anything different. She knew better.

Gamma Kyle and Kate were busy with the set up for graduation. So they didn't come home last night. Rose finally had a good night's sleep. Something she had been in desperate of for the last week.

Buzz Buzz Buzz went Rose's phone. Rose was sure that she turned off the alarm clock on her phone. She thought maybe she just hit snooze instead. When she reached over and picked up her phone she saw it was texts from her boys.

"Hey Rosebud. Good Morning! HAPPY GRADUATION DAY! A better life awaits you!" Mike wrote.

"Hey Babygirl! I know you will be gone in a few hours but I wanted you to know you're my best friend. I love you! Safe travels and text us along the way so we know you are safe." Nathan wrote. He was always the sappy of the three.

"Good Morning Little Bud. You will always be my most treasured friend. My ride or die. Let's go out with a BANG today!" Chris wrote.

Rose smiled. The only people she was going to truly miss were these three and the people that came with them, parents and such. Rose quickly had a plan pop into her head and she figured why the hell not. She sent a group text hoping the boys would agree.

"ROCKY'S 15 MINUTES" was all it said. Rose knew that's all it had to say.

"BET" was all that they replied.

Rose went and got dressed. Looking around her room for anything that she might have left behind. It was all thrown in her duffel bag. This was it. The last bag to be packed into her already stuffed car.

While the dress code for graduation was a dress for girls and suit and tie for boys. Rose had her own plans for that. Rose wore no makeup. Not even her black eyeliner. She wore a black tank top, Black jeans, and her black boots. Her hair was neatly braided back.

The worst they could do is not let her walk in graduation and in such she would be on her way earlier than expected. She was going out her way. With her shades on her head and the duffle bag slung on her back, she walked out of her room for the last time.

As she walked down the stairs and through the kitchen, Rose noticed a note on the kitchen counter. When she picked it up she immediately recognized her mother's handwriting. This must have been left here last night, because it wasn't there when she got home from being with the boys.

It simply read: **Don't embarrass me today. All the information you need is in the envelope with a letter for your Aunt Eva. You know what to do so do it. One miss step and you'll wish you had never been born. Xoxo ~Mom**

Rose opened the envelope. It had the letter for her Aunt Eva. All of her Aunts Eva's contact information with phone number and address. Also what looked like the number to two adoption agencies. Well she was pushing the issue. Wasn't she?

Rose wasn't going to let this spoil her mood. She would never see this place after today. She would no longer play along. She was going to show out like there was no tomorrow today. And the first order to that fact was Rocky's.

Rose walked out of the house and saw the beautiful day the Goddess had given. She walked over to her car and gave it the once over. Tires looked good. Nothing looked out of place. Rose even popped the trunk to make sure all her stuff was as she left it. Nothing could be left to chance.

Money, clothes, personal effects and all the gifts that had made it her way were accounted for. She loaded her duffel bag and got in the car. She started up and got away from that house as quickly as possible.

She made it to Rocky's and the boys were already there. Normally seeing them like this was like any other Saturday. Rose pulled up next to Chris's El Camino. She got out and looked through the window. Rose was happy to see them.

She walked in and the place was actually quiet except for the three boys sitting in the booth. No doubt because everyone would be at the packhouse. She walked up and everyone fell silent for a moment.

"You gonna make room?" Rose picked at Chris, who always sat on the one side by himself.

"Yeah. I guess." He smiled so big sliding over into the booth.

"So, what's the meaning of this emergency meeting?" Nathan is always the card.

"Yeah. You know mom's gonna kill us for not being at the packhouse for the graduation breakfast." Mike chimed in trying to be serious.

No one could hold it in and burst at the seams laughing. They knew that if it was something to do with Rose then all bets were off.

Mike's mom loved her. Chris's dad, Carl, loved her. Nathan's mom wanted to swap her for Nathan. Which always made everyone laugh.

"No Offense to Momma Kay, Mike, but I just can't deal with the packhouse right this second. I know we have to go and graduate but I want one last time with Y'all." Rose said so heartfeltly.

"You know momma won't care. When she asked where I was headed and said to meet with you and the boys at Rocky's, she just smiled. She did, however, send a message of her being so proud of you." Mike said.

"Well, tell her thank you… for everything really. I just don't want to spend anymore time with people that don't matter to me. You guys have always been my boys." Rose said getting a little more sentimental than she wanted to.

While she wanted to break down right then and there, and spill her guts about everything. She knew it would cause hell. She wouldn't leave her friends to clean up the mess. She wasn't that girl! She cleaned up everyone else's messes, though. She was good at that.

The waitress came by the table. "What can I get started for the graduates today?"

"Cheeseburger, onion rings, and a Cherry Coke." Nathan piped up first.

"Same." Mike repeated.

"Patty melt and fries with a Root beer float." Chris said.

"Cheese Fries and a Dr. Pepper." Rose ordered.

The guys started laughing hysterically. Rose looked as lost as a goose in a hail storm. What were their problems? Rose looked at them like they had officially lost their minds.

"WHAT?" Rose finally said.

"You're back to normal." Nathan said, trying to control his giggles.

"Oh, shut up." Rose said, throwing a straw paper at him.

It was always the funny stories of why they all worked well together. The reason that whoever ordered first between Mike and Nathan the other one would have to order the same thing. Which all started with a bet in this very booth when they were all 13. Now five years later, they are still holding true to it.

The waitress returned quickly with their drinks and they sat there picking on one another like it was any other Saturday. Rose needed this. Normal in an abnormal situation. This was what she would hold on to when things got bad. This is what she would always hold on to.

"So did you tell them yet?" Rose looked at Mike.

"Not yet. I was going to wait till after you left." Mike said while Chris and Nathan were busy trying to get the old jukebox to play.

"Good. No reason to have to answer so many questions today. I just need to get through this." Rose said, not really wanting to answer the whys right now.

"You know that no matter what we got you. Nothing is going to change with that. We've been through some major shit, Rose. We held it together because of you. You wouldn't let us fall apart." Mike said, reaching over the table to touch Rose's hand.

"I know. But I won't have y'all cleaning up the bomb without me here. Just remember one month from today, call me from the lake house." Rose said, looking so serious.

They shook on it. As they looked at their friends, Rose laughed and went over to help them. Only one person could make that old jukebox run and that was Rose. One little hip bump in just the right spot brought it to life.

Rose giggled as Chris and Nathan just stared at her. Rose walked over and put on E12 "I Stand Alone." Her anthem when she was fixing to do something majorly crazy and foolish. The boys understood and merely smiled. This was going to be the day.

Chapter 16

Rose, Chris, Mike, and Nathan played around at Rocky's for nearly two hours. They would have still been there if Mike's mom didn't call telling them all loudly that they needed to get to the training field. Apparently that's where the Alpha decided to hold such a large group for graduation.

As They went to pay their tab, Rocky, himself came out from the kitchen and said not today. As his best customers, it was on the house. A graduation gift from the place they always came to. They did, however, leave the waitress a very nice tip.

They all loaded up in their vehicles and headed toward the training field. Rose stopped first at the gas station her parents had an account at. This tank of gas would be on them. Also she wouldn't have to stop for at least three hundred miles.

Rose made sure when they got there to park close to the end of the line. She was going to be the first one out. So, she needed a smooth getaway spot. Chris, Nathan, and Mike all parked side by side just a little up from Rose's car. They all walked back to get her so they could all walk in together.

The four got more looks than Asher and Dallas as they walked into the staging area. They each collected their cap and gown. Then they proceeded to get a once over by Mike's mother. Momma Kay giggled at the fact Rose didn't conform to the dress code. She knew she was leaving straight after and it would be impractical for Rose to wear anything but jeans. She also noticed that her son and his friend also followed the same suit.

"Okay, you four stand still so I can get a picture. I know I won't get one after." Momma Kay said, holding up her camera.

They did as they were told, Mike on the end followed by Nathan, Rose, and Chris. Then the three boys stood behind Rose and they took another. Rose then proceeded to take one picture by herself and then one with each boy individually. When Momma Kay was sure she had all the pictures, she pulled Rose to the side.

"Hey Babygirl." Momma Kay said, giving Rose a big hug.

"Momma Kay, I thank you so much for everything. You really made these last few days ones to remember." Rose said, trying to hold in her emotions.

"Oh, think nothing of it. You're one of my pups too. But I have one more thing for you. And of course I can't give it to you here. Is your car unlocked?" Momma Kay inquired.

"Yes ma'am. It's parked at the end of the third row. So I don't have to fight to get out of here in just a bit." Rose said, pointing at the car.

Momma Kay just winked at her and set off through the crowd of graduates. What could that woman have done now? She had already done so much for Rose. Rose thought it was only right to start making her appearances.

She left the tented area that was set up for the graduates. She was immediately swarmed by other parents and congratulations. After about 15 minutes, Rose broke away from the pack of "Well wishers" and found some air. This was another reason she was happy she turned down the Valedictorian spot.

Before she could get a breather, she heard the voice of a demon. Rose tried to control her eyes and her wolf inside her head. She knew that this was going to happen. Rose just had to deal with him.

"Don't you look pretty." Dallas said, trying to play the part. After all, there were people around.

"Why thank you. I wish I could say the same, but it seems like someone sprayed too much cologne." Rose said, bluntly. She smiled but the daggers coming out of her eyes gave a warning shot.

"Now now. Is that anyway to talk to your Future Beta? Show some respect whore." His low growl didn't catch any attention.

Rose picking him up off the ground while kneeing him in the nuts did, however. She couldn't believe it was just a week ago that she thought she had feelings for this boy. After everything he had done to her, he deserved that and more. Rose had nothing but blind hatred for the asshole in front of her.

"Oh, Dallas. Are you okay? Did you take a trip?" Rose said sweetly.

Dallas red faced had a hard time straightening up. But when he finally found his way to an upright position she whispered in his ear. "You wish not to play this game with me. I will cut your balls off and leave you to bleed out in front of this whole pack."

"Oh there you go. Just breathe now. You have to watch where you're walking." Rose said over-selling the fact that she was trying to help him.

As she walked away, it was out of the frying pan and into the fire as Gamma Kyle and Kate came up. They happened to be on the other side of the crowd that seemed to be forming around Dallas. Rose knew she would now have to deal with her mother. Public was the best place for that. She could put on a show but couldn't lay a hand on Rose.

"What's going on over there with Dallas?" Kate is always to the point.

"He fell into the table. Clumsy boy needs to watch where he walking." Rose said, smiling smugly.

"Oh really now?" Kate eyed Rose suspiciously.

"Yep. Ran right into the table and fell into the grass. I did help him up but he looks like he is having trouble catching his breath." Rose said, looking back at the group babying him currently.

"Kate, why don't you go and check on him and see if the table needs to be moved." Gamma Kyle said as he got Kate to walk away from Rose.

"Thanks, Dad." Rose said, looking at her father. She didn't know when she would see him again. Rose only knew she had right this second.

"It's cool. So we haven't had much time to talk. I know your mother has you leaving right after. I just want you to know I'm proud of you. I love you, Rose." Kyle said to his daughter.

"Dad, can I ask you something? I mean something personal." Rose figured now would be as good of a time as any to get a small answer.

"Sure sweety. What do you want to know?" Kyle said, intrigued by this from his daughter.

"Why do you put up with mom's shit? I mean all her craziness and underhanded shit. Why do you put up with it? With her?" Rose looked sincerely at her father for answers.

"Well that's a long conversation, we don't have time for right now. But I guess the simple answer is you'll understand when you find your mate." Kyle said as Alpha Kent keyed up the microphone calling for all graduates to line up in the tent.

"Well that's my cue. I have to go. I love you, Dad." Rose said, giving him one last hug as they parted ways.

"Wait." Kyle said, handing his daughter an envelope. "Don't let your mother see it. She wouldn't let me do anything for your graduation."

Rose stuck the envelope in her back pocket and winked at her father. Rose went into the tent and got in line. Rose was happy her last name was Wells. She was in the back with only two people behind her.

As the ceremony began, everyone walked out and was seated. Alpha Kent and Luna Zara both made speeches about the pride they had for the graduating class. The Valedictorian stood and made her way to the microphone. She gave an epic speech on how this was our time to make something of ourselves.

Rose sat there making faces at Mike and Chris. Which were the closest to her. Nathan was in the second row. No one could get to him. After the speeches were made, the principal came forward to start handing out the diplomas.

With what seemed like forever to Rose, the principal finally said her name. She walked defiantly across the stage, her head held high.

Her friends erupted in cheers. Rose shook the hands of the principal, Alpha Kent, and Luna Zara. Then Rose received the leather bond diploma.

Rose was overjoyed when she returned to her seat. When she looked inside to see her diploma, Rose discovered there were envelops from other pack members tucked inside As the ceremony came to an end the principal said, "I now present the Class of 2010"

Cheers erupted from everywhere. Growls and howls from the patrols of the wolves on guard added into the almost deafening sound. Thank the Goddess that they were outside. If they were in a building everyone's ears would have been ringing for a week.

Momma Kay was the first to hug Rose. Followed by Nathan's mom and dad. Carl came over to send her off with "well wishes". Kyle finally found his daughter through all the sea of people.

"I'm so proud of you, Rose." Kyle said, trying not to tear up.

"Thank you, Dad." Rose hugged her father.

"Shouldn't you be getting on the road? You know traffic is going to be a nightmare." Kate said, trying to lean in for a hug to make it look good.

Rose wasn't playing along, not today at least, and immediately shifted to the side. As Kate stumbled, she shot daggers at her daughter. Rose just merely stood her ground. Rose looked at her mother and silently challenged her to do something.

"Well, I should be heading out." Rose said and turned on her heels to walk toward her car. Mike, Chris, and Nathan broke away from the crowd when they noticed Rose was leaving and being followed by an angry Kate. No one else seemed to notice. What was going on. Klye was quickly called toward the stage as Rose walked toward the parking lot and her car.

Kate fuming grabbed Rose's arm. Rose just shook her off and kept walking. Kate managed to get her hands on Rose's arm again and when she tried to pull her. Rose rounded on her with a fist to the face knocking Kate to the ground.

The boys stood there in shock that Rose finally did something. Rose didn't miss a beat and turned on her heels and finished walking to her car. When Rose made it to her car. She took off the cap and gown and got in. Starting the engine, Rose rolled down her windows and put the car in reverse.

Kate was just picking herself up off the ground when Rose's car came to life. Rose put on "Blue on Black". As the music came pouring out, she lit the tires and spun off with her middle finger in the air

Chapter 17

Rose never looked back. She was sure the shocked looks on her friends' faces were priceless, but before she tore her mother a new one in front of the Goddess and all. She got out of there. Rose would just have to live with the memory of belting Kate in the face.

Three hours into a 9hr ride, Rose thought it would be a good time to pull off and top off the tank. She hated for her car to get below a half tank. She wasn't close. Rose also knew she didn't want to stop anymore than she currently had too.

The adrenaline was still kicking through her veins. She didn't know if it was because she had already graduated, laying her mother out, or her personal favorite, kneeing Dallas in the balls. So much had already happened that day, Rose was just elated.

Rose had set off on the complete unknown with just her and the pup she carried. Snow would chime in every once in a while with a pur on how proud she was. Seeing an exit for gas ahead, Rose pulled off the highway.

As she pulled up at the pump, Rose noticed the car getting a lot of attention. When she stood up out of the car, everyone's eyes bugged out. This made Rose giggle. Where she was from she was average. Out here on the other hand, she looked anything but average.

She went in to prepay for gas. Rose went to the case and grabbed her a drink. Walking back up to the counter, the guys all looked her up and down. She waited in line putting thirty dollars on the pump and paying for her drink before starting back toward her car.

After putting gas in and getting a lot of compliments about her ride, Rose climbed back in. She took a survey of what she had on her. Momma Kay put a basket in the floor board with all kinds of road snacks and sandwiches. Rose smiled. Momma Kay would know that she wouldn't stop for anything but gas. She would make sure that Rose had food.

Rose also finally looked into the envelope that her father gave her. A letter which she would read later, and three thousand dollars. Kyle would make sure in his own way that Rose had what she needed on the trip. Kyle was a good father but he let too many things go when it came to things being done by his wife and mate.

Rose vowed that she would always put her child first. Mate or otherwise would always come second. She made that decision the moment she realized no one was going to be there for her or this baby. Rose might not have known what was going to happen but she knew she was going to do her best.

Rose thought that this would also be a good time to call her Aunt Eva and let her know she was on the way. Rose didn't remember her Aunt Eva very well. Rose desperately hoped that she was nothing like her mother.

Picking up her phone and ignoring the 50 text messages, Rose placed the call to Aunt Eva.

Three rings later. "Hello?"

"Aunt Eva?" Rose questioned the number on the paper.

"Rose?" Eva's voice had a panic in it.

"Yes, It's me." Rose replied relieved that she had the right number.

"Oh, Thank the Goddess. Are you alright?" Eva seemed to let out a breath she didn't know she was holding.

"Yes. I'm fine. I just wanted to make sure I had the right number for you. I have been on the road for about three hours. I just stopped for gas. GPS says I should be there at about 8 or so." Rose said, trying to be polite and give all the information.

"Okay sweetie. Please be careful and call if you need anything. Your Uncle Tony has informed all the packs along the route to be on the lookout in case something happens. Is there something special you want for dinner?" Eva finally finds some relief hearing Rose's voice.

"Tell Uncle Tony thank you. And I have no idea. One of my friend's moms packed me some road snacks. So, I have no idea about dinner." Rose said trying not to be rude or a problem.

"Okay. That's fine. We will figure it out when you get here. Please be careful." Eva said a silent prayer that Rose would make it safe.

"I will. I'm going to get back on the road. So, I will talk to you in a few hours." Rose said, hanging up the phone.

Aunt Eva seemed nothing like her mother. Rose knew she would be able to tell more when she got face to face with her. Rose knew as of now though she needed to get on down the road. The more miles Rose put between her and Hollows, the better she felt.

Jamming along to the music, eating one of Momma Kay's homemade cookies, Rose noticed the GPS saying she was only about 45 minutes away. Rose looks for one more exit to top her tank off before making the last bit of the trip.

The sun was starting to go down, Rose grabbed her leather and put it on at the gas station. It was a pretty area. Lots of wooded areas and the mountains with their snow covered peaks, made it look like something out of Hallmark.

Rose paid for her gas and went out to pump it. As she was leaving the inside of the store, she noticed two guys by her car.

Hand on her knife, Rose walked over like nothing was wrong. Rose was on her guard more since she was out in the open.

As she started pumping the one guy started to speak to her. "Nice car."

"Thanks, took me a while to get her this nice." Rose tried to keep her tone light.

"Where are you headed?" The second guys piped up.

"About 45 minutes north." Rose gripped the pump in one hand and her knife in her jacket in the other.

"Harvest Moon?" The first guy said.

"Maybe." Rose had the knife open in her pocket.

Rose could smell that they were werewolves. That didn't put her at ease at all. Kate had said that she could have an accident out on the road. Rose wasn't taking any chances.

They could tell they were making her uneasy. So, they showed their hands and backed up. Rose didn't let up on the grip of her knife. They both looked at each other and showed their throats. A sign in the werewolf world of submission.

"What do you want?" Rose straightened her shoulders and prepared for a fight. The pump clicking off barely caught her attention.

"Are you, Rose Wells?" A tall man that seemed to come out of nowhere stood to the side of the two guys.

"All depends on who's asking." Rose had the knife out and at the ready. It might be three on one but she was going to give them the fight of their lives.

"Whoa... Whoa... I'm Keven. These two numbskulls are Brent and Tyler." All three are now holding hands out and trying to calm the situation.

"And that is supposed to mean what to me?" Rose didn't relax with the knife still in plain view.

"We are warriors from the Harvest Moon pack." Keven said, trying to gauge the situation.

Keven was about 6 foot, dark brown hair, and bright blue eyes. Brent was a bit taller than Tyler at maybe 5'11". Brent had black hair and green eyes. Tyler was about 5'8" with blonde hair and smoke gray eyes. To any onlooker, they looked slightly thuggish. Blacked out in a t-shirt, jeans, and looked like jump boots, the three gave the vibe of "Don't start nothing and there won't be nothing."

Rose finally took a steadying breath and relaxed. She closed the knife and put it back in her jacket pocket. She hung the pump up and went to stand by the front of her car. The three took a cautious step toward her.

"Beta Tony sent us." Keven spoke hoping to further lessen the tension that was so thick around them.

"Oh okay. What no one thinks I can handle myself? And by the way next time lead off with that. I wouldn't have pulled the knife." Rose said, slightly annoyed and upset.

"Our apologies and nothing of the sort. We were sent to make sure you make it into the territory without any problems." Tyler said, looking at the others.

"Oh believe me, we have a very good idea that you know how to handle yourself. Beta Eva made Beta Tony send us out to make sure everything went smoothly on the crossing over. You're about 10 miles from entering Harvest Moon territory. Think of us more as escorts." Brent said knowing he would have probably been bleeding out if Keven hadn't stept in.

"We didn't have a description of you or your car. We just figured this is the last gas station for miles. You would have to stop here and fill up before finishing your way." Keven said, trying to clear up the misunderstanding.

"So how did you know it was me then?" Rose said, cracking a smile and the boys finally relaxed along with her.

"We could smell you're a wolf. But we had to confirm you were the right wolf." Keven popped off.

"Okay." Rose chuckled. "Well I would love to stay and chat But I have somewhere to be." Rose started back towards her driver's door. She smiled back at the three guys.

"Keep up if you can." Rose flipped her hair back, jumping in the driver's seat, and letting her car come to life once again.

Chapter 18

At 8pm on the dot, Rose pulled up at her Aunt Eva's house. The three guys were hot on her tail but they couldn't keep up with Rose's Cutlass. She meant it when she said keep up if you can. Rose felt alive, really alive in those moments. She hadn't opened Princess up like that since she dropped the engine in her.

As the three trucks passed her, Rose laughed. She had a feeling this wasn't going to be the last time she would have dealings with these guys. Uncle Tony would no doubt hear about this. Rose figured that she would have to answer some questions later.

She walked up to the door not knowing what to expect. Rose squared herself up and braced for the unknown. What seemed like a second later, Aunt Eva with her blonde hair in a messy bun answered the door.

Eva looked worried and relieved to see Rose standing there. She started crying and Rose didn't know why. Eva then threw her arms around her niece and gave her the warmest hug ever. Rose didn't know how to take this at all.

"Aunt Eva, are you alright?" Rose said, trying to comfort the woman.

"Oh, yes sweety. Let's not just stand here in the doorway. Come in." Eva said moving out of the way to let her niece in the house.

"Oh, before I forget I was told to give you this. Personally I would burn it but that would be up to you." Rose said, handing her a letter that her mother had left with the information.

"Well, I'll just look at it later. Come sit down. I know it's been a long drive. Do you need something to drink? Eat?" Eva was running around trying to be a good hostess.

"Aunt Eva, could you just sit down for a moment? I swear I don't need anything. Well actually maybe the bathroom." Rose said, trying to calm her own nerves but Eva wasn't helping with that.

"Oh, right over here the second door on the left is the downstairs bathroom." Eva said.

Rose excused herself and went to freshen up. After Rose was in the bathroom with the door closed she looked into the mirror. She looked tired. It had been a really long day. She was proud of herself. She had made it through and was safe 9 hours away from the hell she'd been in.

She pulled her phone out which she had been avoiding for the last 9 hours. Hundreds of text messages from Kate, Kyle, Mike, Nathan and Chris. Two death threats from Dallas, which rounded out the overloaded messages. She wasn't going to deal with it right now.

She did however send a group text to the boys: **Hey guys! Sorry I ghosted for the last 9. I was driving. I made it here safe, sound, and all in one piece. I will call you guys tomorrow afternoon. After, I have had time to rest. So meet up somewhere so I can talk to you all at once. Be safe. Xoxo ~Rose.**

Rose didn't wait for a response and did the best thing she could do. She turned off her phone and thought no more tonight. After relieving her bladder and washing her hands, Rose walked out of the bathroom. Rose needed one night even if it was just the one not to have to think.

Eva was sitting on the couch with the letter in her hand. Rose swears she saw steam rolling out of her ears. She was mumbling something under her breath and it sounded like a curse. Rose was a little worried because this sweet woman looked like she had just turned.

"Aunt Eva?" Rose proceeded with caution Eva turned around her eyes were red and Rose knew she was trying to control her wolf. What was in that letter, and was that look because of her or Kate? Eva quickly regained her composure and the tears wouldn't stop flowing.

"Are you alright? Did I do something?" Rose asked, keeping a clear line of sight to the door to make sure she had an exit plan.

"Oh sweety. My sweet Rose. No this has nothing to do with you. Well it does but not in that way. Please sit down." Eva did anything to make her feel at home. This was her home for however long she wished to stay.

"I want to thank you for letting me come. I know that this isn't your problem, but I thank you for the help." Rose said, trying to show respect.

"Rose, you are my family. I would walk through fire to make sure you stayed safe. But we really need to have this conversation. I was hoping that we could wait but we really need to have it now instead of later. I wasn't going to rush it but it seems like you got something you want to say. We got nothing but time. Your Uncle Tony is out with the patrol tonight. He won't be home for hours. So it's just you and me. Something tells me you would rather say it to me alone." Eva said, trying to put Rose at ease. Eva braced herself to hear her niece out.

Rose sat there and debated with herself for a few minutes before Snow came forward to talk.

"This is a safe place." Snow said.

"I don't know. What if it's just like at home?" Rose said, thinking hard.

"I promise you it's not that way. You can trust her." Snow cooed to try and calm Rose.

"Swear it."

"I swear to you." Snow said, and faded back into the corner one again.

Rose trusted Snow. She had always been there when push came to shove and had been a real comfort this last week. She might not have said much, but just knowing she was there was enough for Rose right now.

"I do have a lot to say, but I need to know what I tell you won't leave this room. I have to tell my own story and if I don't wish people to know every detail then I need you to respect that." Rose pleaded with her Aunt.

"That is completely understandable. You have my word. No one will know anything if you don't want it known." Eva said with the most sincerity she had ever seen in anyone's eyes.

"Okay…" Rose began.

"Wait first would you like to get more comfortable? Would you like something to drink?" Eva said knowing that this was going to take a while and needed to be completely prepared.

"Sure. I will just have to get my bag out of the car." Rose got up and walked out to her car. She retrieved the duffel bag and then went back into the house.

When Rose returned back inside she was met by Eva showing her to her room. Rose placed her bag on the bed and began to rummage through the bag for some sweats. After changing her clothes, Rose returned to the living room. She had seen Eva put out two glasses of iced tea, a tray of cookies, and a box of tissues out on the living room table.

Rose settled onto one side of the couch Eva was on the other facing each other. They both seemed to mirror each other sitting cross legged within arms length of anything on the table. They both took long steadying breaths.

"Okay, now that we are all comfortable let's start at the beginning." Eva said, full attention to Rose.

"Well it all started about three months ago. Asher and Dallas, the Alpha and Beta's sons, came by the house while I was working on my car. They struck up a conversation. And we talked for a while. After that it was hanging out at lunch, after work, after training. You know how it goes. Well three weeks ago, Dallas, the Beta's son, asked me out to a party. He had been almost stalking me for weeks. So, I thought maybe he knew something I didn't.

I said yes. Honestly, I don't remember much from that night. I woke up at home with blood on my panties and I was sore all over. I didn't think to ask any questions then. It all didn't seem real. Like just a horrible dream that I had woken up from. It wasn't until I was sick for a solid week that I thought about a pregnancy test. Last Saturday I took one and it came back positive. I confronted Dallas. And let's just say if I had opened my mouth about what had happened. I would be known as the Pack whore.

He formally rejected me. No he wasn't my mate but I guess he thought he would add insult to injury. I accepted his rejections. Stupidly, I thought Kate would have my back. You know, being my mother and all. That was again the wrong move. When I tell you that was the longest week of my life. I'm not joking. She put me through hell." Rose said as Eva just sat there and listened.

Eva was stoned faced at first. She was more in shock. She had questions, so many questions. Eva also knew that asking everything now would probably be better to get things rolling. Though her mind was making list after list of things needed and to be done.

"Okay sweetie." Eva started. "I need to ask you some questions. To make sure I understand everything along with your wants and needs right now."

"Shoot." Rose sat there ready for it all.

"Okay. So you're about 3 weeks or so along?"

"As far as I know."

"Do you happened to know what you were drugged with?"

"Lycan Berry."

"Do you want to keep this pup?" This was the hardest question Eva had to ask.

"Of course. I understand that this isn't the best situation but this pup is half me." Rose said, wrapping her arms around her belly.

"Do you plan on returning to the Hollows pack?"

"Not if I can help it. I will not deal with that woman again."

"Okay sweetie. Well first we will have to see Alpha Jax and Luna Hazel tomorrow. They will want to sit down and you can tell them whatever you wish. Uncle Tony and I will be right there. Next we will have to get you an appointment at the pack doctor and see how far you are. Also to make sure everything is okay with the pup. Have you been having any problems?" Eva looked at her with more concern.

"Other than not healing as quickly as normal, not really. The usual nausea and tiredness from what I have been told about pregnancy." Rose said, trying to think of what would be normal or not at this point.

"What do you mean?" Eva said with a raised eyebrow.

"Kate beat me up pretty bad off and on over the last week. It would take me a full day for me to heal up from the bruises." Rose said with Eva's eyes now going wide.

Eva was cursing her sister a thousand times over. She would have her head, make no mistake about that. How could she have done that? Yes, the situation isn't great, but this was her daughter.

"One more thing… Who all knows about you being pregnant?"

"Me, Dallas, Mom, and You."

"Kyle doesn't know?" Eva inquired.

"Nope, Kate saw to it. He wasn't even allowed to talk to me without her being right there. And not really even that." Rose indicated.

"It's going to be fine, Rose." Eva said, trying to reassure her niece that this was a safe place.

Rose began to cry. Tears she hadn't realized she was still holding back let loose like a flood. Eva went to her and wrapped her arms around Rose. She held her while she sobbed. She let her just cry until there were no more tears and nothing left to let out.

Rose was laying in Eva's lap. Eva was just petting her hair until she had fallen asleep. Eva vowed to the Goddess that she would protect Rose at all cost. The way she should have done ten years ago.

Chapter 19

It was early in the morning when Tony came through the door. He went to say something about the car in the driveway but stopped short when he saw Eva with, who he suspected to be, Rose in her lap. Eva looked up, putting her figures to her lips to hush him before he woke her.

Eva slipped from under Rose's head and walked to her husband. Leading him upstairs to their room, Tony followed without saying one word. Looking back at the young girl sleeping on the couch, he knew she was emotionally spent.

After they were quietly behind closed doors, Eva gave her husband not only the biggest hug but the biggest kiss ever. She needed his touch right now. It was going to be the only thing that would calm her. Too much had happened and she honestly didn't know what to do.

"So, that's Rose?" Tony said, keeping his voice down. Unfortunately, he had never met his niece. Eva would make it a point to go alone when going to see them all those years ago. Tony, who had a disdain for his sister-in-law, made sure to stay home.

"Yep. That's my little Rosebud." Eva said, trying to hold back tears.

"Nice car she has."

"I wouldn't know. I didn't go out there when she showed up."

"So, What are we looking at here?" Tony said, hoping to get the reader's digest version before the meeting in just a few hours.

"I can only tell you a little bit. I swore that her story is her story." Eva said, driving the point home that he would have to find out like everyone else.

"Okay." Tony stood there waiting.

"She's pregnant."

"By her mate?" Tony was slightly confused and starting to get angry.

"Nope. She was drugged. And with what it was it put her with the ability to become this way by sending her into heat." Eva saw the furry in her husband's eyes.

"Your sister had her as a breeder?" Tony jumped to the only logical conclusion that his brain could come up with so early in the morning.

"No! Kate would have never allowed that. It doesn't benefit her. She was drugged by a boy that took advantage."

"Did she name who?" Tony began pacing around the room.

"Yes. But I can't."

"So, your sister decides that the best course of action is to just hide her away?"

"Yes. But Rose has other plans."

"That is?" Tony praying to the Goddess it's not what he thinks it's going to be.

"To raise her pup on her own."

Tony smiled. He didn't know his niece but already had massive respect for her. He always wanted a daughter. The Goddess didn't see fit to bless them with children. Some couples are just like that. Both are healthy and strong but in the end it just doesn't happen for them.

"We have a few hours before we have to be at the packhouse. Why don't we lay down?" Tony said, knowing his wife would need the comfort right now.

7am came faster than anyone expected. It almost scared Rose when she woke up in an unfamiliar environment. It took her a few minutes to realize where she was. The bright sun showed through the windows and into her eyes.

Rose began to stretch and loosen the tight muscles. A wave of nausea hit and she ran for the bathroom. She didn't know if it was from all the crying or the lack of anything real in her stomach, but she dry heaved for twenty minutes until the pain finally subsided.

Eva, hearing her from up stairs, ran down without a second thought. She knocked on the door but didn't get an answer right away. Eva knew this was the process for the first month or two.

"You okay, Rose?" Eva said concern in her voice.

"I'm fine." Rose answered back horsley.

"Can I get you anything?" Eva didn't know if Rose had any kind of medication for something to be able to stop it.

Eva knew with the current situation that was probably going to be a no. She still couldn't believe that Kate would do this. Eva wanted to believe the best about her sister but knew first hand that was never the case. Kate wouldn't risk anyone finding out that's why she sent her here.

"No, I'm okay. Normal morning for me." Rose said, coming out the bathroom door pale as a sheet.

"We need to get some actual food in you." Eva said, knowing that would make her feel better.

"I swear. I'll be fine. Just takes a minute to pass. Anyway, when are we supposed to be at the packhouse?" Rose said deflecting as usual. Rose didn't know if she would ever get used to someone trying to help her.

"In about half an hour. I have to wake your Uncle to see if he's going with us." Eva said, heading back to the stairs.

Rose went to the room that was given to her by her Aunt. She rummaged through the duffel bag to find something suitable to wear. She found her toiletry kit in the bottom of the bag. She dressed in a light blue button up, black tank top, and black jeans.

By the time she was done brushing her hair, teeth, and putting everything away, she took one last look at herself. Rose had gotten distracted hearing a man's voice coming from the kitchen. She walked around the corner and there stood the most handsome older man. Rose knew this would have to be her Uncle Tony.

"Well if it isn't my little Rosebud. Not so little anymore." Tony said adopting the nickname from Eva. He came closer to take a better look at his niece.

She was too thin in his opinion. Not just because she was pregnant, but in general. She was just too thin. He knew some fresh mountain air and the laid back atmosphere would have her right as rain in a few days.

"Uncle Tony." Rose said sheepishly.

Tony walked over and gave Rose a hug. He wouldn't have her scared of him. Rose giggled as he took great care in the act. She wasn't made of China, but he thought she would break just the same if not handled with care.

"Heard you gave my boys a run for their money last night." Tony said, while Rose died out in laughter.

"Look, I gave them the option and told them to keep up if they could." Rose said, trying to look anything but incent.

"What's under the hood?" Tony inquired.

"442" Rose evilly smiled.

"Very nice." Tony just laughed.

"Thank you. I built her myself. Painted it too." Rose was always super proud of her car.

"Okay, I'm ready." Eva said coming down the stairs.

Eva took a once over of the scene in front of her. Tony seemed to be bonding with Rose and this thrilled her more than ever. Tony would have been a great father if given the chance. Tony would have the chance now to watch over Rose.

They walked out the front door and Eva got the first look at Rose's car. The girl had taste that was a given. Eva melted over the midnight blue and paired with the black racing stripes. She knew she would have to get a closer look later.

"Wow." was all Eva could say. They knew they had to be somewhere so off they went. Rose was amazed at the openness of the area around the packhouse. Even with all the little houses placed around, things didn't look or seem cramped.

Even as the packhouse came into view it was like something out of a dream. The huge looking wooden resort type building was their packhouse. People passed and waved greeting Beta Tony and Eva. A lot took stock in the beautiful young woman that was walking rather closely to Eva's side.

There was no time for small talk today. The three went straight into the packhouse. They headed right over to the stairs and right up to Alpha Jax's office. They knew they were possible a few minutes late but it would be okay this one time.

Chapter 20

Eva knocked on the door. Luna Hazel answered in her usual sunny manor. When her eyes locked on Rose all decorum seemed to go out the window. Luna Hazel reached out and took Rose by the hand. She led Rose into the office.

Eva seemed to just giggle as Rose looked back at her with a plea for help. Tony just looked at his wife and headed inside the office. That was a little weird. Luna Hazel was usually so reserved with her attention.

After closing the door, Eva and Tony could see that Rose was being led to a couch and they were really paid no mind. Tony thought this was amusing because Luna Hazel was being the typical "mother hen". It was refreshing to say the least.

"Good morning, Beta Tony Beta Eva." Alpha Jax said, watching his mate with so much love in his eyes.

"Morning Alpha Jax." They said.

"Oh where are my manors? Good morning you two. I'm so sorry. I just got carried away." Luna Hazel said sheepishly.

"That's alright." They said, looking at Rose who seemed to have a look of panic on her face.

Luna Hazel stood and began to make cups of coffee for the group. After all the cups were passed out and everyone had settled into chairs in the large sitting area, it was time to get down to business. Rose looked to her Aunt Eva for strength through this.

"Well I suppose we should all get to know each other. Then we can get down to the business at hand." Alpha Jax spoke with regards to why they were all here this early in the morning.

Rose knew the rules. Not to speak unless addressed directly. So it took her a minute to open her mouth. She figured they could ride this out as long as needed. Rose knew what details she had planned to say and what she was going to choose to keep to herself.

Rose did, however, remember she had forgotten her paperwork for this meeting. They were in such a rush this morning that she left it in the car. She hoped this would not look poorly on her at this time.

"Okay." Alpha Jax noticed no one was saying a word. "I am Alpha Jax as you might have gathered.

"I am Luna Hazel." She tried to put Rose at ease.

"I am Rose Wells. Daughter of Gamma Kyle and Kate of the Hollows pack. Pleased to meet you." Rose said, trying to be as polite as possible.

"So, it has come to my understanding that you have just graduated." Alpha Jax doing anything to try to put her ease and loosen her tongue.

"Yes, sir. Just yesterday actually. 4.9 GPA." Rose answered.

"Wow. That is amazing. I don't think our top student has more than maybe a 4.5 GPA." Luna Hazel admired.

"So, what's your area of interest?" Alpha Jax figured this would spark a more than one sentence answer.

"Mainly cars. Classics to be exact. I worked at a shop run by one of my best friend's dad. Carl's Auto Repair." Rose said proudly.

"So you're a mechanic?" Luna Hazel chimed in.

"I do much more than fix them. I restore them. I bring them back to life. I'm decent with paint and body work also." Rose said, kind of trying to downplay her skills.

Tony saw right through that, but wasn't going to call her out on it. After all, he had seen the beauty sitting in his driveway. The way she lit up about doing all the work on it. Everyone could tell that the car was her baby.

"You seem to be a very sweet and skillful young woman. So, I guess it is time to get down to business." Alpha Jax spoke switching gears. He was a little confused about why she was sent away.

Rose squared up ready for whatever they seemed to want to ask her. Her life would be on display now and hoping that she could have some form of dignity and respect. Rose believed with everything she had been through this would not be too much to ask.

"So, what could you have possibly done that would warrant a banishment?" Alpha Jax got right to the point. He wasn't holding any punches.

"I found myself in a problematic situation that wouldn't look good on the family if it made its way to light. This is my mother's answer to said problem." Rose said, trying not to come off harsh or rude.

"And that situation is?" Alpha Jax said, trying to pry the information out. He felt like he was having to pull information with a rope out of her.

"I'm pregnant." Rose said with no shame whatsoever in her voice.

"You're WHAT?" Alpha Jax and Luna Hazel nearly both spit and dropped their coffee cups on the floor.

Rose took a steading breath. Rose knew that she was not going to be able to give small bits of information and hope they wouldn't ask for more. She was prepared for this though. She knew she was only going to give what she wished everyone, but Eva, of course, to know.

"Okay." Rose took a breath. "Let me start from the beginning. I found out last Saturday that I was pregnant." Rose began while everyone got quiet and listened intently.

"I confronted the boy that I suspected. He confirmed that we did indeed sleep together. He rejected me and the pup. No, HE is not my mate. I did ask that because he is of age to know but me being about now 6 to 7 weeks from my birthday. I did not.

I foolishly confided in my mother. That ended up with me not only dealing with the worst week of my life but also dealing with the situation by sending me here. Kate has reservations on how I will handle this and live my life after. I, on the other hand, have other plans." Rose said, holding her head high.

Luna Hazel sat there with her mouth wide open. She could see that as messed up as this situation was, Rose was a strong girl that would shoulder her responsibility. Luna Hazel respected that.

Beta Tony and Eva just sat there letting what needed to unfold happen. They were proud of Rose and the fact that she took a leap of faith in letting the truth be known. Tony wanted a name to see the end of that boy that did this. Rose would only tell Eva and that had to be good enough for him right now.

Alpha Jax was floored and fuming. More questions came to his mind than he was prepared for. This was serious and a complete break in the rules of the Goddess. A shewolf was only supposed to be able to get pregnant by their mate. Rose had indicated this boy was not her mate.

"I have some questions." Alpha Jax said, trying to hold in his anger for what was going on and what had been done.

"I understand. I do, however, want to make it known that I will not be answering the ones I do not see important to my current situation." Rose might not have had room to make any kind of demands on the information put to light but she still had her pride and her self respect. That she was going to hold on to no matter the cost.

"The boy in question… Did he rape you?" Alpha Jax tried to choose his question wisely.

"In a manner of speaking. Yes."

"Can you clarify that? You also indicated that you had to ask if you slept with him." Alpha Jax said, watching her closely.

"Yes, I had to ask because I had no memory of the act or most of the night that it had happened. I was slipped Lycan Berry." Rose's voice while clear held a venom that was undeniable.

Again the room fell silent with Rose's words hanging in the air. Alpha Jax and Beta Tony had the same thoughts of wanting this boy's head on a platter. Alpha Jax also knew that he would have to be careful, because she had already been through enough.

"The BASTARD'S name" Alpha Jax demanded.

Rose squared up and held her head high before answering. "Not important. This is my pup and I intend to bring them into this world alone." Rose replied this way more out of defiance than out of respect.

While this infuriated Alpha Jax, he had the most respect he had ever held for anyone in his life. Alpha Jax understood that she wouldn't want the mark left on her child. He tried desperately to control his anger and his wolf. At this moment, both wanted blood.

"So, what is your plan sweety?" Luna Hazel said, trying to continue making this about the delicate situation and not about who caused it.

"My plan is to take care of my pup. I'm a hard worker. I don't expect anything to be given. I have some savings to start putting a life together for my pup and myself. If I'm pointed in the direction of some housing and where I might be able to start looking for a job. That's all I currently need right now." Rose said, looking at the four people around her.

"Do you have intentions of returning to your pack?" Alpha Jax tried to control his tone.

"Not if I can help it. It has been indicated to me that I will not be welcomed back if I choose to keep my pup. My mother's wish is for me to give it up for adoption and come back. In which time, if I return, she will arrange for me to marry someone of her choosing. If my mate ever does find me I will have to reject them. I, on the other hand, have no willingness to do my mother's bidding." Rose became cold with this statement.

They all sat quiet for a moment. So much had come to light in such a short time. Alpha Jax was not pleased at this. He did have respect for the girl that sat in front of them. How could someone with so many short years be so wise in shouldering her responsibilities?

"Okay then. I will check into a few things and send word back through Beta Tony. As for now you will be given the same respect and courtesy as any other member of my pack. I hope you enjoy your stay here." Alpha Jax said standing and shaking Rose's hand.

They all took this as an indication that the meeting was over and it was time to leave. Beta Tony was the only one to stay behind, while Eva and Rose left the office. Alpha Jax was polite but extremely pissed off. Ending the meeting now would ensure that he didn't say anything that was out of line.

Chapter 21

After the door had closed with Eva and Rose departing, Alpha Jax just lost it. Throwing a coffee cut at the wall and growling loudly, Alpha Jax tried to relieve the anger that seemed to radiate from his core. Some would think that Rose was his own daughter or even sister with the way he was acting. After all, they were probably close enough in age to be siblings.

They thought hard why Rose didn't bring this to her own Alpha. Would she have been so easily dismissed over the situation? Would the boy in question have still gotten away with it? Alpha Jax supposed now he was her Alpha and as such he was extremely upset about what had been done. All he could see was red and that wasn't going to help anyone right now. This was against everything when dealing with the Goddess. He knew that there were real assholes playboy wanna bees out there but to just play with someone's life was just the beyond to him.

"Calm down, Jax. You need a level head for this one." Tony said hands up showing he was on his side. When he saw that Jax's eyes were bright red.

"Tony is right, Jax. You need to sit down and breathe. No sense in letting Edge out without reason." Luna Hazel said, knowing that he was barely holding a grip on his wolf. She went over to touch his face to try to calm him.

"Believe me. I'm trying. You heard her. Goddess knows what was done to her before she got here and now what?" Alpha Jax started pacing the room.

Alpha Jax's own sister had been in this situation when he was young. She didn't make it through the delivery of her child. Like Rose, his sister would never give up the name of the person that did this to her. All he knew was after her death, Jax had a very big soft spot for girls that had found their way into situations that weren't of their own making. He also had a rage for the boys that put them there.

"Believe me when I say that I feel the same way. The only person she has confided in is Eva. Even with Eva being my mate, Eva refuses to tell me the whole story concerning Rose. Rose wants it that way. It's her story to tell and if she doesn't want to say then we have no choice but to respect that." Tony, just as exasperated as Alpha Jax over the situation, said.

Alpha Jax stopped pacing the room. He had hoped if any of his members had ever come to him in this kind of situation; that he would handle it better than this. There would be a formal investigation and the guilty party would have been dealt with swiftly. No hiding or sweeping things under the rug.

Alpha Jax, finding some calm and resolution, went back to his desk and pulled a book out from the drawer. As he flipped through it, He noticed there were three cabins down by the lake that were open right now. It would be a private area for a young mother. He thought plenty of open space for a child to play.

The cabins were for the younger members of the pack to go and relax around the lake. Most of the older ones just went out there to fish and have a nice family day. They hadn't been used in a few seasons due to bad storms that came early a few years in a row. But if she wanted a place of her own this would be a good start.

"Does anyone know if she has seen a doctor?" Luna Hazel piped up as Alpha Jax seemed to be working on one problem by himself.

"I would suspect not. I do believe that Eva was going to call to see if she could get her in tomorrow." Tony said knowing his wife would be on top of this matter.

"Well then she will have to be checked out immediately. The first month in a pregnancy is vital for proper treatment. I'll just give Eva a hand and make a call." Luna Hazel said, pulling out her phone.

Luna Hazel called the pack doctor.

"Good morning Luna Hazel. Is everything alright?" Dr. Violet said, knowing she didn't normally get a call so early in the morning from the Luna.

"Yes, ma'am everything is fine. I need to know if you have an appointment open for tomorrow morning?" Luna Hazel began to pace the room.

"I believe so, but let me check." Dr. Violet said, grabbing for her appointment book. "Yes, I have an 8am open."

"Good. Have to have a full work up from head to toe and an ultrasound done." Luna Hazel said making sure that everything was requested ahead of time.

"Luna are you?" The doctor was cut off short.

"Oh, No. No. The Beta's niece has arrived and is believed to be with child. She has received no care and she is approximately..." Luna Hazel looks to Beta Tony for answers.

"I think about 3 weeks maybe a touch more or less." Tony said.

"Did you get that Dr. Violet?"

"Yes ma'am about or around 3 weeks. Okay have her here by 8am." Dr. Violet said and hung up the phone.

"Okay that's one thing checked off." Luna Hazel said going into problem solving mode.

"I don't know if she'll like it but I have 3 options for housing. The cabins down by the lake. It's only 15 minutes from you and Eva and 25 minutes from the packhouse. It's private, and the patrols still go through there. They haven't been used in a while. So they are going to have to be cleaned and possibly repaired." Alpha Jax said, regaining about 95% of his composure.

"I'll take her out there after the doctor's appointment tomorrow and see what she thinks. I believe she will be grateful for anything at this point. I was going to offer her to just stay with us but I think Rose is going to want that independence." Beta Tony said pleased that his Alpha was finally thinking rationally.

Alpha Jax checked off the list and thought of something that would kill two birds with one stone. "Tony didn't you say there have been some boys lately causing some trouble down at the training grounds? Been getting in trouble around town also?"

"About two or three of them." Tony looked a little confused

"Well we have the labor to get any and all repairs done to Rose's liking." Luna Hazel chimed in.

There were two things off the list. Rose would have somewhere to live and be seeing the doctor the next day. Now on to the last item of business. They all knew that she wouldn't accept a hand out. Why else would she have mentioned she had her life savings to start over with.

"After she is cleared by Dr. Violet we can set something up with the Housekeeper Omegas or even the kitchen. That way everyone can keep an eye on her." Alpha Jax said, realizing that she would need to be careful for this pregnancy.

"I know working in the laundry isn't ideal but I don't think going back to work on cars right now would be the safest option. We have seen how one wrong move can end a pregnancy." Beta Tony said, thinking about the only time Eva was ever pregnant. He wasn't taking anything away from his niece by any means he just knew that her safety was the number one priority.

"There will have to be talks about her joining this pack after the pup is born. If she truly doesn't want to go back to Hollows. Then an offer should be made for her to remain here. Of course that will be months down the road before we have to discuss that. From the looks of her pass from the Hollow. They have her written out for 4 years for college." Luna Hazel said to Alpha Jax looking at the paperwork that was faxed in that still was sitting on his desk from Wednesday.

"You're absolutely right. We have time. We just need to get these certain things in order for right now." Alpha Jax said finding pride that they had come together for this.

And just like that plans had not only been made but set in place. Rose would be protected and cared for along with her child. Alpha Jax believed there to be great strength in that girl and time would tell if that would end up being an asset to the pack.

Chapter 22

Eva and Rose went down to the dinning hall. Rose didn't know how to feel currently. She was very numb from the meeting. Had she said too much or too little? Was she perceived as rude? Rose had hoped not.

Eva could tell that there was a lot on her niece's mind. She wasn't sure of the protocol here. Eva just decided to treat her like her own pup, and be the mother she needed right now. Eva desperately wanted to comfort Rose.

Eva directed Rose to a table in the grand room. After they were seated, Eva tried to put Rose at ease. This would be a task and she knew it wasn't going to be easy. Rose had been through so much in the last little bit and today was just one more of those things.

"Okay little bud. What's wrong?" Eva finally began.

"Was I rude? I mean I thought I made it very clear to everyone that I would not give information that wasn't pertinent to my situation." Rose looked at her aunt.

"Oh, no sweetie. Alpha Jax is just very passionate. He's a young Alpha but he cares deeply." Eva explained.

"So, he's not mad at me?" Rose desperately wanted to make a positive impression. It would make everything a little less difficult.

Rose knew that she was strong willed and wouldn't change her mind on not telling them the name that sirered her child. It wasn't important. She wouldn't have her child tainted by the act that had them come into existence.

"Well we should get you something to eat. No telling when you last had a decent meal. Kate still can't cook as far as I know." Eva said to Rose while thinking about what would be on today's menu.

"Actually Friday. Momma Kay, Mike's mom, made a big feast for Mike, Chris, Nathan and myself. Her way of sending me off. She did pack me a basket for the road, but I mostly just nibbled on the cookies." Rose admitted.

A young girl, no more than 17, came by the table to take orders. Rose had gotten a BLT and a coke. While Eva got her usual pancakes. They tried to keep the conversation light while they waited. It wasn't long when the young lady returned with their drink orders.

Rose looked around the room and saw people coming and going. After about twenty or so minutes, Uncle Tony came into view. He scanned the room for the two before locking eyes on his mate and Rose. He walked over kissing Eva on the forehead and sitting next to her.

"Everything alright?" Eva asked Tony.

"It is now. Took me and Luna Hazel a minute to talk him down." Tony replied.

"I'm so sorry for causing trouble. Honestly I didn't think anyone would care about a person they just met." Rose said, hoping that she could just fade into the background after this was all said and done.

"Take it as a compliment that he reacted that way. He is very caring but at the same time he has no problem pulling the roof down on people's heads." Tony said to Rose trying to put her mind at rest.

"I ordered your breakfast. Didn't know how long you would be." Eva said, squeezing her mate's hand.

"Thank you, my love." Tony said, picking up her hand and kissing the back of her knuckles.

After the food arrived and they began eating, Alpha Jax and Luna Hazel had entered the room. Everyone took time to greet and speak to them. Rose sat back and observed. On the few occasions she was at the Hollow's packhouse, Rose always took stock in how everyone conducted themselves. This was much more relaxed.

Rose never really went to the Hollows packhouse. Special occasions that Kate would make her go. She always found it stuffy and full of people that were just lobbying for some kind of favor. Stuck up people with nothing better to do then show off what they had or lobby for what they wanted.

This was different. Everyone was welcomed here. The Omegas were shown respect not just ordered around like servants. Rose unexpectedly found peace sitting at the table watching the room and all the people in it just flowed like water. It was very refreshing.

Soon Alpha Jax and Luna Hazel had made it to their table. Luna Hazel smiled at Rose. Alpha Jax seemed to avoid eye contact. Rose didn't understand why but figured it for the best right now. Rose remembered he was pretty upset just a little while ago.

Small talk began with the four and then two others came to the table. A tall 6'2" man that had a lean muscular build, blonde hair and smoke gray eyes. The woman that accompanied was petite and standing at maybe 5'6". Strawberry blonde locks and blue eyes gave this woman more the look of an angel than a werewolf.

"I would like to introduce Gamma Otis and Ivy." Eva said to Rose.

"I am Rose Wells. Beta Tony and Eva's niece. How do you do?" Rose said politely, shaking hands.

"Well isn't she just a little doll." Ivy said.

"So young lady are you enjoying your time here?" Otis said to Rose.

"So far so good. I haven't been here a whole day yet. So it's hard to tell." Rose joked at the thought of everything that has happened in fourteen or so hours since her arrival.

"Really? When did you get in?" Otis asked curiously.

"8 last night." Rose said, wondering why he would be asking.

"Is this the girl that gave Keven and the boys a run for their money last night?" Otis looked at Tony half in shock.

"Yeah, she is the one." Tony laughed that the whole pack got to hear about her before ever meeting her.

"I told them to keep up." Rose said in her defense.

"Well anyone that can make Keven do his job and cuss about it all night is good in my book." Otis said, just rolling with laughter.

The now six of them chatted for a minute before the waitress came by to fill more cups and clear dishes. Rose wanted to leave because she had a few things to do and needed to get the ball rolling.

Eva sensed that Rose was getting bored and decided to excuse themselves. Tony stayed behind to listen to the meeting and the morning announcements. After walking outside, Rose let out a breath she didn't know she was holding.

Rose wasn't easily rattled. But for the last week, everything Rose had been through seemed to put her on guard. She knew it would take time to get used to a new place and people. The unknown was the biggest thing and she would face it head on.

Rose figured she would eventually find her new "normal". But for now, she would have to float around for a bit. Rose knew she would stick close to home as much as possible until she figured out the lay of the land.

"Everything okay?" Eva finally asked after they were about half way back to the house.

"Yea, just a new place and all. Things will even back out. They always do." Rose responded half to Eva and mostly to herself.

"You know if you need to talk about anything I'm here. Not just about the big things either. I'm here for the little things too." Eva reassured her.

"Why couldn't you have been my mom?" Rose joked but Eva froze for a minute.

"Well sweetie with the day you have had. That's a conversation for another time." Eva was serious but Rose took it as just a smart remark.

When they got back to the house, Rose went and got her phone off the charger. She turned it on to a few hundred texts coming in at once. Rose seemed to think her phone was possessed with all the dings, beeps, and buzzes.

Rose sent out a group text to the boys. "Where y'all at?"

Mike was quick to text back. "LAKE HOUSE!"

"Call in 5 minutes." Rose replied.

With her phone in hand, she walks into the living room where Eva is sitting. Eva looked like she was still processing everything even though she was holding it all together. Rose saw the letter was back in her hand. Eva finally just crumbled it up and threw it away.

"Aunt Eva?" Rose said, trying not to startle her.

"Yes, Rose?" Eva said, looking up to where she was standing behind the chair.

"I'm going to make a phone call. I have to let my buddies know I made it safely." Rose explained.

"That's fine. There is a nice patio set out back. If you need some privacy." Eva said, trying to turn her attention more to Rose than the distasteful letter her sister sent.

"Okay." Rose said and headed for the back door.

Eva and Tony had a very spacious backyard. A concrete pad that held the patio set was just to the left out the back door. Rose admired that this would be a great place to just sit and watch the sunset.

She got comfortable in one of the chairs and prepared herself to call the boys. Mike's phone didn't even seem like it rang before he answered. Mike sounded panicked and pissed at the same time.

"Rose?" Mike said loudly.

"Hey Mike." Rose was a little bit amused.

"Where the hell have you been? We have been worried sick. Carl let us stay out at the lake house to wait for your call." Mike said, trying to breathe.

"Sorry. I got in at 8pm and after everything I just couldn't deal anymore." Rose said apologetically.

"You could have texted along the way. Momma Kay was worried sick. Especially after what happened at graduation." Mike was damn near shouting.

"Well, let her know I'm fine." Rose hated worrying anyone but she felt worse that it was Momma Kay.

Chris and Nathan hearing Mike shouting ran from the inside of the house. You could hear them in the background asking what was wrong? They figured out what was up when they saw the phone in Mike's hand.

"That Rose?" Chris yelled.

"Put me on speaker, it'll be easier that way." Rose said, beginning to rub her temples.

"Hey Rosebud. What the hell happened to staying in contact through the drive?" Nathan started to scold right off the bat.

"Okay everyone knows I'm not on my cell while I'm driving. I only stopped twice. I was just trying to get here. I'm completely fine." Rose defended herself.

"But you're okay?" Nathan said and Rose could imagine the final calm that came over him.

"Yes. I swear I'm fine." Rose said one more time.

"Okay then let's get down to business then. What the hell happened at the end of graduation?" They all sounded off.

"What all did you see?" Rose was thinking back to yesterday and had tunnel vision. It was all a bit of a blur to her.

"You hitting Gamma Kate in the face. And peeling out like a bat outta hell." Mike said almost a sound of shock in his voice.

"I was done with her putting her hands on me." Rose said simply.

"Rumer also has it that you knead Dallas in the nuts before the ceremony." Nathan questioned.

"He should have kept his hands to himself." Rose said coolly.

The three started rolling. Rose had to pull the phone away from her ear. They were so loud someone might have thought they were right in the backyard with her. Why was it so funny? Cause everyone wanted to put Dallas in his place but no one ever did, till now.

"You are something else girl." Chris said, trying to regain his breath from the laughter.

"I try." Rose said, shining her knuckles on her shirt.

"So, are you still going to wait that month? We are all here right now." Mike said, bringing up the conversation from Rocky's.

"I want to wait but I know y'all wont let me. So let's do it this way. Only if you all swear to me it goes no further. You can't do anything about it. You can't ask questions about it. You just have to keep it to yourselves and be satisfied with knowing." Rose stressed the importance of what she was about to tell them.

"Damn Rose, did you kill someone?" Nathan popped off. You could hear the seriousness in his tone.

"No, But I think I would have been better off if I had." Rose said seriously.

"It can't be that serious, Rose." Chris said, sounding worried.

"Swear it on the box." Rose said and the three knew it was serious.

As they looked at each other, they knew what that meant. There was a box buried out at the lake house with things that no one wanted discovered. Each one of them hid something that only the others knew about. So to prove a point on how serious the situation was they would bring up the box.

"We swear." The three said at once.

Rose took a steadying breath. She knew that they boys would be there for her but was scared that there was a chance they would turn their backs. She knew there was only one way to find out. With a stealing breath, she let it out.

"Okay here goes nothing." Rose braced herself. "I'm... I'm..."

"Your what?" Mike said, trying to coax it out of her.

"I'm pregnant." It was barely audible but the boys heard her as if she shouted it from the top of her lungs.

The line was quiet for a few minutes. Rose thought at first they had hung up but saw the counter still moving on the phone. She could imagine them all standing around the phone floored. Like someone had punched them in the gut and stole all their air.

"Are you still there?" Rose finally said hoping that they would just say something.

"Yeah, we are still here." Chris said anger evident in his voice.

"We don't get to ask anything do we?" Nathan chimed in finally.

"No. I'm sorry but no. My job is to keep you safe. And even knowing that could put you all in major danger at this point." Rose said feeling guilty that she didn't give them this news face to face.

"Wait, did you find your mate?" Mike said, confused. He knew the laws of the moon like any other wolf.

"No. And that's the only question I can or will answer on this." Rose said knowing that if she didn't cut it off there it wouldn't stop.

"I understand that this is a lot to deal with but you have to trust me as I have each one of you. I need you to not breathe a word of this. Keep your ears open and tell me anything you might hear. Shut it down if possible." Rose pleaded with the boys.

"We have been through hell together, Rose. I understand that you can't or won't say anything else. But that doesn't change the fact you are our Rose." Chris said, trying to stay calm through the anger.

"A blood oath is a Blood OATH." Nathan said, still slightly hurt that Rose felt the need to hide this from them.

"Now I understand why you said a bomb going off. You have our loyalty and our silence But I want pictures." Mike said, cracking everyone up again.

"I love you, guys. I'll text you the address so you can write. I will text and call as much as I can." Rose said, knowing that her friends were always going to be there.

Chapter 23

The rest of the afternoon into the night went uneventful. Eva was trying to get Rose to eat every five minutes. When Tony got home from the packhouse he was just as bad. They knew that she hadn't been eating back home and now made it their mission to make sure she had gotten more than enough to eat.

Tony let Eva know that Luna Hazel had called the doctor on Rose's behalf. Alpha Jax had found some possible places for Rose to live. Tony thought, like Alpha Jax, that the cabins down by the lake would be perfect with plenty of room for a growing family. As for the job situation, Rose was to see the doctor and only if cleared would she interview with the housekeeper Omegas. Things were certainly moving fast but also falling right into place.

At 8am on Monday morning Tony, Eva and Rose sat in the waiting room of the pack hospital. Eva tried to insist that she could go with Rose alone, but Tony wasn't having it. He wanted his niece to know that he was just as much there for her as Eva was.

It was a bright white room that smelled of disinfected. Rose was getting nauseous from the smell and tried to put it out of her mind. She was scared that something might be wrong with the baby with all the trauma she had been through the last week.

After roughly ten minutes, a lovely nurse came out dressed in black scrubs. She looked to be about mid 20s with chestnut brown hair pulled up in a bun. She seemed to be of slender build. She had a sunny disposition and a calming nature about her.

"Rose?" She said looking at her clipboard.

"Yes." Rose stood up and walked toward her.

"I'm Angel. Dr. Violet's nurse. Let's go fill out some paperwork and draw some blood." Angel said, escorting Rose down the hall. Eva was right behind her.

They went through all the paperwork, allergies, blood type, and medical history information. When they got to the father part of the paperwork. Rose simply said unknown. While Angel wanted to say something and pressure Rose for the sake of the paperwork. Rose wouldn't budge.

When asked if she had been on any kind of drugs or medications before or during conception or pregnancy. She only replied that she had been slipped Lycan Berry at a party. She didn't do drugs or take any kind of medication.

The nurse began to first draw blood. Then she sent Rose to the bathroom for a urine sample. After that Rose was led to an exam room. Rose and Eva sat in silence for what seemed like forever.

"You know everything is going to be okay." Eva tried to calm Rose's nerves.

"I don't know. A lot has happened in the last week." Rose started rocking back and forth.

"No matter what happens, I am right here." Eva said brushing over her hair with her hand.

Before Rose could respond in walked Dr. Violet. "Hello, Rose. Beta Eva."

"Hello, Dr. Violet." Eva said.

"Okay... So we presume you to be at 3 weeks 2 days. Does that sound about right?" Dr. Violet said looking at the chart.

"Yes ma'am that sounds about right." Rose said, waiting for more questions.

"Okay we are going to do a physical exam and then an ultrasound." Dr. Violet explained.

She began noting that Rose was slightly showing but hadn't put on a lot of weight. She was thin for a shewolf that had been almost a month pregnant. She would have to put on some weight to make sure she remained healthy for the baby.

After checking all the parts, she concluded that she was healthy and should have no problems currently. She would have to put on some weight. And the blood work would determine any long term effects of the Lycan Berry. On the one other occasion she had seen anyone use Lycan Berry, it seemed to be out of their system as fast as it made its way into it. She hoped this was the same case with Rose.

"Alright as of right now going forward I want you to take a prenatal vitamin at night before bed. We also need to get a little more weight on you. Also plenty of water and cutting back on the sodas. We need to make sure that you don't develop gestational diabetes. Alright? I know this mostly happens in humans but it has happened in werewolves a few times. It's completely rare but it has happened. We just need to be completely safe going forward. Now Rose, We are going to do the ultrasound. This isn't going to hurt. We are going to have you lay back and lift up your shirt. I'm going to take this wand and use it to see the pup." Dr. Violet said, preparing Rose for the procedure.

"Do you want me to ask Uncle Tony to come in?" Eva asked Rose.

"Sure. I think he would like to see his great niece or nephew." Rose jokes.

Eva stuck her head out the door and waved down the hall at Tony, who was currently pacing the waiting room. Tony was sure that something was wrong and hurried over. When he saw Eva's smiling face, he relaxed a bit.

"What's up?" Tony asked.

"Ultrasound. You want in?" Eva smiled.

"Of course." Tony was overjoyed to be a part of this.

After everyone was settled into the room, the lights got turned off and the show began. It didn't take long for Dr. Violet to find the little one. But when she did she froze in her seat and looked at Rose then Eva and Tony.

"What's wrong?" Rose began freaking out, holding onto Eva's hand tightly.

"Well... The fact is nothing is really wrong." Dr. Violet just stared at the screen.

"Then why are you looking like that?" Rose was trying to control her breathing.

Dr. Violet turned the screen around for Rose and the others to see. They all sat in shock. Not one heartbeat but two.

"Sweetie you're having twins!!!" Dr. Violet said in disbelief.

"Twins?" The sound was barely audible coming out of Rose's mouth.

"Twins!" Eva hugged her niece so tight.

"I would say you're due somewhere around Halloween." Dr. Violet said.

Dr. Violet printed out the ultrasound pictures for Rose. She knew once the shock wore off she would be excited about them. Eva tried to just hold Rose. Rose was feeling extremely numb. The only thing that kept going through her mind was TWINS.

Chapter 24

The shock didn't wear off until they were back in the car. Rose sat there staring at the ultrasound photos like it was a window into her soul. Not one but two blessings. She knew that this was meant to be on so many levels.

Rose tried to call Snow from her place in the corner of her mind. "Snow."

"Yes, Rose." Snow came forward when she called this time.

"Why didn't you tell me?"

"It wasn't time. You had too much to deal with already. I didn't want to make it worse on you." Snow replied.

"We will have our work cut out for us now." With that remark Snow faded back once again.

Rose, now back in complete reality, took stock in what all she would need. This wasn't going to be easy, but it wasn't impossible either. Women had multiple babies everyday. Rose was capable of so many things. This would just have to be one of them.

"You okay little bud?" Tony said, looking in his rear view mirror.

"Yeah, it just took me by surprise. I mean what are the odds? Aren't twins rare?" Rose asks Eva who was a twin.

"They are. Especially two sets in the same blood line. You must be very special to the Goddess indeed." Eva remarked. She remembered the story of why twin wolves come.

It is said that the Goddess blesses the mother with twins when she has great power that can't be just carried by one pup. Rose didn't believe she had such a power. Rose thought she was like any other shewolf. Time would prove otherwise.

Tony drove for about 20 minutes before ending up at the lake side cut off. Taking the road to the left, he drove a little bit down before they came to the first cabin. They sat there for just a moment when they realized without getting out that this wouldn't do. Too small with Rose having twins. She would need something to grow with her.

Tony knew the second one, while a little bit bigger, wasn't going to be big enough as well. So, he headed right for the third cabin. It was on the other side of the lake with its own road that came in and out off the main road. You could drive completely around the lake and would still have to take a cut off to get to this cabin.

When they pulled up, Rose immediately got out and fell in love with the place. It had a garage off to the side of the house and a small barn behind it. The tall log cabin with its wrap around porch gave Rose all the feeling of home.

Tony unlocked the door and they went inside. The spacious living room and large kitchen was just awed over. There was one room off the living room and a half bath on the first floor. The second floor had two bedrooms and a full bathroom. There was also a small room tucked off to the side at the top of the stairs that Rose could use for an office of some sort.

Rose was already making plans in her head for things that would be needed. The fact she could turn the room down stairs into a playroom when they kids got older or a nursery right now. So she wouldn't be dragging two kids up and down the stairs at all hours of the day and night.

"What do you think?" Tony asks Rose.

"What's the rent?" Rose didn't want to get her hopes up.

"I'm pretty sure you could get it for a steal." Tony said.

"I need to know figures. So, I can budget with two on the way. I'm going to have to be really careful with my money." Rose said, going back outside to look around at the property.

It was huge. A massive front and backyard, she knew she would have to put a fence in because they were so close to the water. She would have to see what she was and wasn't allowed to do with the property and the house.

So many decisions to make and very little time to get it all done. She hadn't gone through the rest of her envelopes from graduation but knew she had 43 thousand or so. She knew that wasn't going to go far if she didn't pinch every penny.

"Well what do you think overall?" Eva said while Rose looked out over the water.

"I think it's great, but I only have a certain amount that I can play with. And it's going to need some work." Rose said, turning from the water and looking back at the house.

"We will figure out a way to make it work if this is what you want." Eva said, trying to reassure her.

"It is, but I have questions." Rose said, dreaming of the family that would live here soon.

"Well how about this. We will go back to the house, order some Chinese, and write down all the questions. We will send them with Uncle Tony when he goes back to the packhouse. By dinner we should be able to sit down and make an informed decision." Eva said knowing that it wasn't even noon yet and Rose already had the shock of her young life.

"Yeah. There is nothing else we can do here anyways until I have all the pieces to the puzzle." Rose said walking back to the house.

Eva took Rose's arm and they walked back up toward the house. Tony was standing on the front porch with a tape measure out. The two stopped and watched him measure the one side of the porch and then write down the measurements.

"What are you doing?" Eva said, looking amused at her husband.

"Don't we have a bench swing in the garage at home?" Tony asked Eva.

"The one your brother made that is way too big for anywhere to hang? Yeah, it's still in the garage." Eva teased. Her brother-in-law was awesome at making things but alas he never measured the space in which it was supposed to go. So everyone would end up with things that were always too big.

"Well, I think it will fit right here nicely. I believe there is a chain in the garage to hang it as well." Tony said, imagining playing out there with the kids and just swinging away.

"Well we are going to have to see what its cost is first before we go making those kinds of plans." Rose said amused.

They gathered back into the car and headed back towards the house. Rose knew that the cabin is where she wanted to raise her kids. She would just have to make sure expenses were taken care of. Rose believed she finally found somewhere she could find peace.

About 25 minutes later, they were composing a list for Tony to take to the Alpha. Rose needed every detail. The list included: monthly rent, do's and don'ts to the property, electricity, water, and lastly when she could meet with the housekeepers.

Dr. Violet had cleared Rose to work with the understanding not to overdo it. She also told Rose it would have to be light duty because of the twins. She would go back in a few weeks for another check up, a glucose test, and possibly find out what she is having.

Rose just laid on the couch. She was spent in so many ways. She thought about calling Mike and the boys but she hadn't fully processed it herself just yet. She knew that they would be again in shock but over the moon about being uncles.

Eva came into the living room with two heaping bags of food. Rose finally perked up with all the smells. Eva didn't know what Rose would like. So, she ordered more than enough of everything.

Rose snagged an eggroll and smiled. She wasn't allowed this at home. Rose happened to get whatever they thought to bring her back or she would go to Mike's house. There were so many happy moments with the guys.

"So…" Eva began. "I think we should wait to paint the kids room until we find out if they are boys or girls."

"Agreed. I don't know how I'm going to do all this." Rose admitted taking a bite of beef and broccoli.

"We will figure it out together. I meant what I said. I'm not going anywhere. I will be right here through all of this." Eva said, squeezing Rose's free hand.

"Uncle Tony is going to end up being over protective isn't he?" Rose asked, taking another bite.

"Oh, you can count on that. By the way don't you have a birthday coming up?" Eva asked, knowing it was soon.

"Yea. July 13th" Rose said, cringing at the fact.

"Well shouldn't we be planning for it?" Eva asked, hoping for some pointers.

"No need." Rose was short with her answer.

"Oh come on. We have to do something. You are turning 18." Eva said, understanding the significance of that day.

"No really. I haven't celebrated my birthday since I was 13. And the only reason I believe Kate did it then was because of the full moon was on my birthday. Twelve of us shifted that night. Mike, Chris and Nathan, which are my best friends, are just a little bit older than me. Mike and Chris were born at the beginning of May. Nathan was born in June. They waited till I turned 13 in July. So, we all could shift together." Rose remembered.

"Sounds like a great bunch of guys." Eva smiled.

"They certainly are!" Rose said as they finished up their lunch.

Rose drifted off to sleep not long after they got done eating. It had been a long morning, but there was a hope she carried inside her. Two precious jewels of her eye. That's what Rose thought about as she finally rested her eyes.

Chapter 25

It was well into the evening when Tony returned home from the packhouse. Rose was still asleep on the couch, no doubt still exhausted from what she had been through. Tony saw the light on in the kitchen and headed that way.

Eva was sitting at the counter with her notebook making lists as per usual. Luna Hazel always said how she admired Eva for always knowing exactly what needed to be done because she had her lists. Everything had a list and Eva stuck to them religiously. While it drove Tony absolutely crazy. He knew this was her process in dealing with everything around her. Everything had a place and would be in its place if she had anything to do with it.

"What's up, baby?" Tony said, wrapping his arms around Eva.

"Oh there is just so much to do." Eva began. "What did Alpha Jax say?"

"He wants Rose to handle the house before she meets with the housekeeper Omegas. As it stands, there is a position open in the laundry that they are holding for her. So, that's handled. As for the cabin, it hasn't been used in years. He doesn't care what she does to it as long as it's not trashed up. He knows it won't be. He has also declined payment for taking over the property. He knows she is having twins and due to that fact he says it wouldn't be right." Tony said feeling a little exasperated.

Tony tried to explain to the Alpha that Rose would rather pay her way than be handed anything. He knew Rose would see this as pity and refuse the help. Tony had gone back and forth with Alpha Jax for hours. When he tried to get Alpha Jax to understand, he simply shut down and refused any and all talks about payment.

"You know she isn't going to be happy about that." Eva said hoping that her niece would just accept the help and not look at it like charity.

"I know. Luna Hazel and I have come up with a plan on that behalf." Tony said feeling pretty proud of himself.

"And that is?" Eva looked curiously at her husband.

"We tell her she will pay 250 a month, but we take that money and put it in an account for emergencies. Something for the kids later if push comes to shove. All transactions will go through you so she doesn't suspect anything." Tony smiled, figuring it all out on his own.

"So you want me to lie to her?" Eva raised an eyebrow at him.

"For her own good. It's not a lie. It's letting her think what she needs to right now. We both know she got your stubbornness. So letting her believe she is doing it on her own is easier than arguing with her and Alpha Jax." Tony said, trying to get his wife on board.

"Okay I will help sell this idea but if she gets mad at me for this... You're sleeping outside for a month." Eva told Tony.

They both heard Rose stirring from the living room. Eva figured Rose was finally waking up. She grabbed a glass of tea and went to check on her. Eva thought to herself. *It was all going to be fine.*

"Rose, honey are you awake?" Eva came into the living room.

"Yes, I'm so sorry. I didn't mean to just pass out like that." Rose stretched.

"Oh nonsense. You needed the sleep and you got it. Get it while you can." Eva handed Rose the glass of tea.

"Hey Uncle Tony." Rose said, eyeing him as he came out of the kitchen.

"Hey bud. Well I have your answers." He smiled sheepishly.

"And that is?" Rose sat up bracing herself for whatever came next.

"The cabin is yours. You can do what you see fit. Alpha Jax and Luna Hazel believe a fence is a great idea and far overdue. Can't be too careful with little ones. He will rent it to you for 250 a month and that includes electricity and water. You can keep the furniture. If you don't like it we can find you something else. At the end of 5 years, if you are still residing there they will talk about terms of you buying the property with what you have already paid in rent to go as the down payment." Tony laid it all out on the line.

"I was figuring more but 250 is well within my price range. What about the beds?" Rose inquired.

"They are new. Well new three years ago. They haven't been slept in since they were brought into the house." Tony responded.

"Security deposit?" Rose asked Tony.

"Not necessary because you will already be cleaning and fixing up the place." Tony said

"Okay. How soon before I can meet for a job? Bills won't pay themselves" Rose remarked.

"Alpha Jax and Luna Hazel want you to deal with the cabin first. That will also be taken off your first month's rent since they can't get an Omega over to the cabin to clean it up right now. I told them you had no problem cleaning it up. Plus, on a brighter side you won't have to go to the packhouse to make your payments." Tony said spreading everything out like honey.

"Why not?" Rose asked curiously.

"Luna Hazel has said to give the money to Aunt Eva. She will hand it off for you." Tony said, looking to Eva to back him up now.

"Yes. I make all the bank deposits for the rental properties. Part of my duties as Beta female. So, I will be handling it." Eva said, knowing through all the questions that it was apparent that Rose wouldn't accept help willingly.

"Okay. Well how soon can I move in?" Rose said excited to get started setting up her home.

"You're ready to leave already?" Eva looked a little shocked.

"No but I know I will have to get the place ready for the babies. We don't have much time at all. Even though they won't be running around the backyard just yet. The fence needs to be put in soon. There will be cleaning that will need to be done and getting everything ready for them to arrive." Rose went into mommy mode a little easier than she thought was possible.

"And we will get it all handled. Breathe little bud." Tony said, walking over to calm Rose and to try to keep her from having a panic attack.

"We have some boys that have been getting into trouble around the training field. They have been put under your supervision to help with any and all work that needs to be done." Tony said continuing to try to talk her off the ledge that she keeps finding herself on.

"Okay. I just want to be able to have enough time to handle everything." Rose said. Her strong will not really letting her except help.

"Everything will be in order soon, Rose." Eva started. "Now let's not stress anymore than we have to. It's not good for you or the babies."

The topic of conversation changed quickly and before anyone knew it they were talking about dinner and possible baby names. They would end up ordering out due to the late hour. Eva just knew that she had to get Rose to calm down.

Rose sat there and thought about the babies. Praying to the Goddess they were more like her than him. They would be loved and adored for that she was completely thankful. Rose also knew that, whether they were boys or girls, Uncle Tony was going to be wrapped around some pinkies.

Chapter 26

The night before ended with the three eating pizza and just goofing off. Eva was trying to talk Rose out of her girls names. Tony would defend the names which would result in popcorn being thrown across the room at the other. Tony thought they were lovely names.

Rose kicked around names like Lily and Willow for a girl. Porter and Dylan were chosen for the boys' names. Tony liked the boys' names. They were strong names and for kids raised by a strong mother. He believed that would be important.

Rose woke the next morning with a note on the counter. Eva and Tony had duties to attend to at the packhouse. Tony left the key on the counter to the cabin. He knew that Rose was set on getting the place together.

Rose got ready for her day. She loaded up her bag from the house and proceeded to take it back to her car. As she walked out of the house and looked at her car, Rose knew that she would need something else.

Rose knew that her classic Cutlass was slightly impractical for a single mom with two kids on the way. She was set on never getting rid of her. She was just going to have to put her away for a while. For nights when she could just be kid free and blow off a little steam for a while.

She would have to get Eva or Tony to take her to look for a van. That was going to be a chunk of changes out of her budget, but she knew that was going to be needed at this time. Rose never thought she would ever be the one to drive a minivan but with two car seats it was a whole lot more practical.

Rose loaded up and headed toward the cabin. She would unload everything and take inventory of what was going to be needed. That way she could see what kind of budget she had to work with. She would also make sure she had a budget for regular household items. Rose knew that once she had everything on a schedule it would be fine.

A fifteen minute drive to the cabin, Rose parked right by the backdoor that led into the laundry room and pantry area. She began unloading everything. Once it was all in the kitchen of the house, Rose sat at the table and began to go through every bag, box, and envelope.

Thank the Goddess that a lot of her graduation gifts were actually practical and useful. She had all the basics for her kitchen, bedroom, and bathroom. She would need things for the kids' rooms and a desk for that little room. All in all she wasn't as bad off as she thought she was going to be.

At least she wasn't starting from complete scratch. Rose was really thankful for that. After everything was in at least the room it belonged in, Rose started making lists of cleaning supplies and just basic household items that she didn't have and might actually need right now.

Rose was lost in her thoughts when she heard a knock on the front door that made her jump. Rose immediately went for her knife. As she peeked around the wall that shielded her from view. She saw her Uncle Tony standing on the front porch.

Rose, feeling extremely foolish, put the knife down and walked over to open the door. She knew she couldn't be too careful but that might have been jumping to conclusions. She could see three boys with him, and died out laughing when she recognized them.

"Uncle Tony." Rose said, looking toward Keven, Brent, and Tyler.

"Hey Rose. I hope I'm not disturbing you." Tony said with a slightly evil grin on his face.

"Not at all just making a list of things I need to run to town for." Rose eyed suspiciously the boys standing with their heads down behind him.

"Okay well, I thought I would bring the boys by to get started." Tony giggled.

"These are the boys that have been causing trouble?" Rose smiled thinking back to a few days ago and them nearly getting hurt by her.

"Yep."

"These are the same boys you sent to up with meet me." Rose said, eyeing her Uncle.

"Yep and it seems they couldn't even do that right. Keven told me about the knife incident." Tony said looking back toward the three that knew the protocol when it came to escort. In turn if it wasn't for Keven they would have ended up at the hospital instead of back on patrol.

"Well then." Rose giggled a little. "Let's walk around back and start with the fence."

After it was mapped out just as she wanted it, Rose walked back around to the front of the house with Tony. They both had slightly evil smiles on their faces. While the boys sat there and mumbled under their breath, Tony just eyed them with a warning.

"Do you have to rush back to pack business?" Rose asked.

"No, I got a minute. What's up?" Tony said, taking a seat on the steps.

"Well I need to go look for a car. Van would probably be more practical. Something that gets better gas mileage and easier to get two car seats in and out." Rose said, looking toward her car.

"You're going to sell it?" Tony was a little shocked.

"No, not if I can help it. I figured I would clean up that barn and keep her there for now. Take her out on the rare occasion that I can find a babysitter and just need some me time." Rose pointed over at the little barn that was behind the garage off a little bit to the side of the property.

"Well go get what you need. I'll run you around town to see what we can find you." Tony said, feeling proud of the fact he was the one she asked.

"Okay. I'll be just a minute." Rose ran in and grabbed just the money that came out of her graduation envelopes. That alone, with the money from her dad, was five thousand.

Rose and Tony gathered up in the old Cougar, that was Tony's baby, and headed into town. Four car lots later, Rose finally found what she was looking for. A 2003 Dodge Caravan that was white with a steel gray interior. It had really low mileage and was only two thousand.

Rose talked the guy down to 1500 with tags, title, new tires, oil change, and the air conditioner being recharged. Tony was so impressed. Every time Tony would go to say something, Rose would just say she could handle it. Hince four lots later before she finally walked away with something, Rose wasn't going to let anyone take advantage of her.

Tony followed her around for a few hours. They picked up cleaning supplies, curtains, a desk, and even picked out patio furniture for the backyard. They picked out so many different things that would make the cabin into a home. Tony was thrilled that he got to be there to help her with all of it.

A lot of the big stuff was going to have to be delivered. Due to no room in the van to transport it. It was going to be the next day before it would be at the cabin. By the time it was 2pm, they were hungry and worn out.

Tony called Eva to see if she wanted to meet for a late lunch. They decided on a little sandwich shop. The Lunar Moon Cafe was the hidden jewel of Harvest Moon pack. It was a picturesque small light purple building with ivy all over it. It reminded Rose of a small doll house.

The weather was warm and right outside were little tables that people could sit and eat at. So after they had gotten their lunches that's where they ate. Eva was happy to see Rose settling into the new environment.

"So, what have you been up to today?" Eva asked Rose, who seemed to be in a great mood.

"Well, I took everything to the cabin and unloaded it. It's not all put away but it is in the room it belongs. I want to clean everything out before I set anything in place. Uncle Tony scared the hell out of me. The boys that are at the cabin? They are the ones that Uncle Tony sent to escort me Saturday night. They are currently putting up my fence." Rose said between bites.

"So, who's van with the temp tag is parked next to the Cougar?" Eva says, looking around to just a few people sitting outside.

"Mine." Rose said.

"YOU sold your car?" Eva's mouth just dropped open.

"NO." Rose looked a little shocked that everyone seemed to think she was going to sell her baby. Rose believed she would if she had to but right now it wasn't a have to moment. "I just figured this would be a little bit better and easier with two car seats."

"Oh okay." Eva was stunned for a minute.

"I have furniture being delivered tomorrow. Nothing fancy. Just a desk for that little room at the top of the stairs and some outside stuff. Uncle Tony was a big help today. I thought I was becoming a bit of a pain but I wasn't going to let anyone sell me something that was crap." Rose explained, looking over to Tony.

"Well she can sure handle herself when it comes to knowing what she wants. I did help pick out the pillows and curtains for the living room though." Tony said, laughing a bit.

"Well I figure after your next appointment, we would be good to start baby shopping. Also we will be able to pick out the paint colors for the two rooms." Eva said, going down the list of things that would be needed. Eva was also so in love with the fact that Tony was acting this way.

After they finished their lunch, Rose headed off back to the cabin. Tony and Eva went back to the packhouse to finish up the details for the pack graduation. They knew that it was only a few days away and with that final prep would have to be done before the ceremony on Saturday.

Two of the boys had seen Rose pull up in the driveway with the van. They walked over to give her a hand with the bags that seemed to cover the whole inside. Brent and Tyler unloaded bags not really letting Rose carry anything into the house. While Keven finished setting the last post for the fence in the backyard.

"Oh guys you don't have to do that." Rose tried to say, but that didn't stop them from carrying every bag into the house and setting them down by the table in the kitchen.

Rose had no idea that basically everyone knew she was pregnant. Tony had told the boys before they got out to the cabin, that if they saw her do anything they were to help. If he found out otherwise they would be on Midnight patrol for the next 6 months.

They were trying to win their way back into good graces not the fury that Tony could bring. They knew it was going to take a lot, but they knew Rose was the key to get Tony off of their backs. So they would do what they were told or seen that needed to be done.

"So, new van?" Keven said walking up out of the backyard.

"Yes. Not my style but it will serve its purpose." Rose said, looking back at the van.

"So, you getting rid of that one?" Keven pointed to the Cutlass and prayed she said she was.

"Not if I can help it. She is the one good thing that is my past and hopefully my future." Rose said looking at the car she built with her own two hands.

Chapter 27

"If you love life, don't waste time, for time is what life is made up of."

-Bruce Lee

There have been some hard weeks. Rose finally got the cabin ready, which was an obstacle inside itself. She would move things and then move them again. She didn't know if it was what they called nesting or what. After just a week and a half she finally had everything right where she wanted it.

Rose during that week however felt very guilty for not telling her father what was going on or why she asked him what she did at graduation. So, she wrote a letter to him. She set it up with Mike to give him the letter so Kate couldn't intercept it. Mike inturn would explain that he had no knowledge of the contents of said letter and walk away. Needless to say after he received it things didn't go well.

Kate's plans were fumbled and in such she wanted nothing more to do with her daughter. Which didn't bother Rose in the least. Her father, on the other hand, turned his back on Rose. Which, in so many ways, hurt like hell. Kyle screamed at his daughter for nearly an hour before Rose just hung up on him.

She knew she would have to give him some time to come to terms. That not only was he going to be a grandfather but she wasn't coming back to Hollows. Rose hoped by sending copies of the ultrasound pictures of the twins would ease the blow back. No such luck.

Rose had no doubt in her mind that people would still be led to believe otherwise. She would soldier on like any good momma would. She had gotten her job with the laundry and worked the night shift for now. She could handle doctors appointments with this schedule. She also started a bank account and began dealing with things in her own way.

Rose was excited on this day though. No black clouds were going to hang over her head today. She had an ultrasound and would be getting the results of her glucose test. Rose was finally going to see what the twins were today.

She was finally going to be able to pick a color for the playroom/ nursery down stairs and what would be their room later up stairs. Eva was going to meet her at the doctor. She really did mean it when she told Rose she wouldn't have to go through this alone. Eva was also absolutely furious when she found out what Kyle had done.

Rose walked in to see Eva sitting in the waiting room going through her famous notebook. All smiles and sunshine, Eva was as impatient as Rose to find out what the twins were. Eva had so many things picked out and wanted to start buying already.

"Rose" Angel called before Rose could even sit.

"Yes ma'am." Rose smiled.

As Rose returned to her feet, Eva stood to help her up. They followed Angel down the hall a little bit. Rose had been weighed and measured before being led into a room. While in the room they took the rest of Rose's vitals. They were all very pleased to see that she had gained 10 pounds since she was there last. Rose knew it was mostly the twins. She thought she looked like she swallowed a small watermelon.

"Are you ready to see what you are having?" Angel said, bubbling over. She was the first to come up with twins in a very long time.

"I'm about as ready as I can be." Rose said, knowing that she was really just busting at the seems to know.

"Okay. Let's get the lights. Lay down and we will see the pups." Angel said as Rose laid back on the bed. Eva got the lights.

Just a few seconds later, Rose was hearing the two heartbeats. This made her so happy to know that they were both fine. After just a few adjustments, Angel had turned the monitor around. Rose could see they were both mooning them.

"Well by the judge of it. You will have twin practical jokesters of the male variety." Angel laughed.

"It had to be boys." Eva laughed so hard.

"Well I kind of figured with how big I was getting and how fast it was going to be boys." Rose just chuckled at the screen.

Angel got them to shift just a little to see their little faces. Rose knew she was going to have her hands full. Boys were always getting into something. At least she knew she would have someone to hand down her love of cars too. Two little ones to be exact.

Angel printed off the next set of ultrasound pictures and handed them to Rose. Eva was texting Tony, which couldn't be there because of a problem at the northern border. She had a grin from ear to ear. Rose knew that going forward this was going to be something to see with Uncle Tony and the boys. He would no doubt be the positive male figure she would want in their lives.

Dr. Violet entered the room almost as soon as the lights came on. "So what are we having?"

"Boys." Rose smiled.

"Oh Goddess help us now. Do you want a standing prescription for headache medication now or are we going to play it by ear" Dr. Violet joked and everyone erupted into laughter.

"I know right." Eva said, chuckling.

"Okay. Let's get down to business. Your blood work is still a little off. While the Lycan Berry didn't have a lasting effect on you or the twins it did send your system into a spin. It can all be corrected so don't worry about that. I want you to eat plenty of green foods, calcium, and still try not to have but maybe one or two sodas a day. Plenty of water also. Your glucose test came back in the normal range so that is also positive news. Have you gotten over the morning sickness?" Dr. Violet responded.

"I guess so. There are still certain smells that cause me to go green but other than that I'm good." Rose said.

"Okay. Well that's completely normal. I want you to rest as much as possible and we should see you back in about 4 weeks. I want you to come in on Thursday next week to do another round of blood though." Dr. Violet says to Angel to make sure an appointment is made.

Rose got cleaned up and left the hospital with Eva. Eva could tell something was weighing heavily on her. So they did what they did every Thursday. They went to Lunar Moon Cafe for lunch.

It was warm out so they sat outside to enjoy the air. After a few minutes Rose decided to finally say something. She was still very excited about the day but other things weighed her down. Eva was prepared to be the shoulder she needed right now.

"You know you're all I have." Rose finally said to Eva, slightly tearing up.

"That conversation is still bothering you, babygirl?" Eva was still hot about it herself but that's not where her head needed to be right now.

"A little bit. I mean how do you go from I love you no matter what to I can't believe you did this to me? I mean I can understand this from Kate, but not him. I thought he would get pissed at her for doing all these hurtful things to me. Not the other way around." Rose was trying to understand what she knew to be a losing battle right now.

"Just give him some time. He'll either come around or not. Either way you will always have Uncle Tony and me. "Eva said, taking Rose's hand.

"Well you're right. Nothing I can do about it. Just gotta let it be. But anyway, what were your plans for the rest of the afternoon?" Rose said, trying to get her mind back on the task at hand.

"Nothing. I cleared this for you." Eva smiled.

"Well I think we have paint colors to look at and things to go buy." Rose said, eyeing her Aunt, who has talked about nothing else for weeks. This in so many ways would make both of them feel better.

"Well no time like the present." Eva said almost as giddy as a school girl.

And just like that all bad moments tabled for another day. They just jumped into the van and headed off to find damn near two of everything.

Chapter 28

Between doctors appointments, work, and trying to be prepared for her sons's arrival, Rose had lost any and all sense of time. It always took her days to catch up and take stock of what was going on around her. It was like she was going through the motions but that was truly it.

Therefore, when Luna Hazel sent her a personal invite for tea, Rose was taken off guard. Eva brought the invite to her personally. Rose was told that this would be a personal tea with Luna Hazel. Rose was also told Luna Hazel would not take a refusal this time.

So on the afternoon of her birthday, Rose showed up at the packhouse. It was quiet. Rose figured it would be when lunch was already over and dinner wasn't being prepared yet. Rose believed that's why she loved working nights. It was so quiet you could hear a pin drop.

The invite said the garden behind the packhouse. As soon as Rose went through the double doors, she heard everyone yelling "SURPRISE". Rose just froze. As she looked around all kinds of balloons and streamers hung everywhere.

The Lady's of the pack had thrown her a birthday/ Baby shower. Rose quickly scanned the area for her Aunt Eva. Eva was standing to the side of the door that Rose had just come out of. Rose was floored.

"Happy Birthday, Sweety." Eva said, putting a sash around her saying Birthday Momma To Be.

"I told you I didn't want a fuss. We were just supposed to just have dinner." Rose stood there looking at all the smiling women.

"We are. This first though."Eva said, escorting Rose to a big over pillowed chair.

"Well you were surprised. I was hoping no one would give it away." Luna Hazel came up and gave Rose a hug.

"No, I'm completely surprised." Rose said, hugging her back. Luna Hazel then took the seat right next to her. Eva on one side and Luna Hazel on the other.

Rose, while accepted from day one, never felt like she really belonged. She was given the option to participate in their graduation but declined. She said it wasn't fair to the current class. Then when the Lady's tea came up once a month, which was held by Luna Hazel, Rose was extended an invite to be welcomed into this pack. She again respectfully declined it. When Luna Hazel found out her due date and her birthday from Eva. They sent the invite to be accepted without refusal.

Rose didn't feel like she deserved any of the things that a normal pack member actually took for granted. Where she came from things like this was just for show. She wasn't an official member and wondered if she ever would be.

The party was amazing. Everyone brought gifts. The food was all baby themed. They really went all out. Rose was starting to actually feel the acceptance and love. She was taken in by this pack and began to really believe she belonged.

After games were played and the gifts were opened. Everyone came by Rose to say Congratulations. They spared no expense for gifts of toys, clothes, and furniture that somehow they knew Rose hadn't gotten yet. Rose thought she wouldn't have to buy anything really until the boys were closer to nine months old.

All the ladies were super supportive of Rose raising her babies on her own. They loved how strong she was. How they could tell immediately that she was going to be such a good mother.

There were many that had their own opinions on the boy that did this. They spit on his name. A boy that wouldn't shoulder his half of the responsibility in their eyes was a pup that needed to be taken on down to the woodshed. To reject a woman after leaving her in this state was cause for castration in their eyes. Boys needed to learn consequences for their actions, but too many got away with it. Under Alpha Jax, this would not be the case. Even if it happened in other packs it would not happen in this one.

Once the party drew to a close, Tony and the boys appeared to load up the van and Tony's Cougar. After what seemed like a dozen trips they finally had everything packed up. Rose was really happy to have so many people that carried about her and welcoming the new little ones into the world. Even if this was just a small gesture it meant the world to her.

"Okay. Why don't you give Keven your keys and the boys can go unload the van while we head out for your birthday celebration." Tony said, looking at the boys that were managing to finally get off Tony's shit list.

"Are you sure?" Rose said, looking to Keven, who was the only one she trusted to drive her van.

"Yea, we got it. Do you still need the cribs put up? I can do that when I get there." Keven said, taking Rose's keys.

"Yes. Unfortunately I tried to just move the box and well it's still in the kitchen." Rose said not liking the fact that with her already so big she couldn't do much.

"Okay not a problem I got it."

"Hey if you don't mind, can you look at the back door? I think it's stuck again." Rose said liking the fact that she had someone to fix things, but hating the fact she couldn't right now.

"Yea. Have you checked the air conditioner yet?" Keven knew she was getting too hot in the house.

"I can't get the stupid thing to turn on." Rose grumbled.

"Okay looks like we got a list." Keven just winked at Rose.

"Thank you, really." Rose just smiled.

"Not a problem." Keven said, doing a little salute.

As Rose turned around to walk away, Eva noticed Keven watching after her. She smiled and thought they would make a nice couple. Rose would be set against it but it would be nice to have a friend to talk to and confide in. All her friends were back in Hollows, and Eva knew she missed them terribly. She could put out some feelers to see what was what though.

"I think someone is sweet on you, Rose." Eva said, teasing her.

"Naw. He's just trying to get back on Uncle Tony's good side." Rose said, looking over her shoulder.

"You know he talks about you a lot at the training field." Tony pipes in.

"No. No. He's not my mate. I can't do that to somebody the way it was done to me." Rose said not wanting to get any males hopes up that they had a shot when they didn't.

Rose was very much set against having feelings for anyone. Her boys would have her heart and that was that. There would be no other man in her life and she would see to it. She would have to think about her kids and the kind of people she was going to let come around them. Hell even once her mate came along, who knows what will happen. She knew one thing for certain: she was a mother first.

They dropped the subject and headed out for the evening's plans. They took her to this little Italian place and Rose thought she had died and gone to heaven. Rose wasn't much into pasta before she had gotten pregnant but since she couldn't get enough. Chicken alfredo, bread sticks, and a salad for her something green.

They all laughed and talked about the boys. It was the perfect birthday for Rose. By the time they had gotten back to the house, everyone was fed and tired. Eva convinced Rose to just sleep there and she would drive her back in the morning.

Before going to sleep, Rose dwelled on the conversation from earlier. Keven popped into her mind. She knew he didn't like her like that. Or did he? What had he said at the training field that would warrant Tony and Eva to think that there might be something there.

Chapter 29

Time flew like the wind rushing through the trees to take all the leaves and pull them to the ground. Before anyone knew it Fall had come to the valley that the pack was in, leaves changed colors and the trees began the process of readying themselves for winter. Rose worked very hard readying herself for motherhood.

With every doctor's appointment, She would write not only to her boys but her parents. She would send pictures of the ultrasounds. Her parents would call after each letter. Which would end in Rose hanging up on them and ask why she was still putting herself through this.

She knew in the back of her mind that she should just cut her losses and move on. The only problem was something told her that if she did that she would regret it. So she endured the arguments about once every few weeks.

Dr. Violet hoped that the twins would come a few days or even a week early. So it wouldn't be so much on Rose's body. Alas the twins were stubborn and were just fine being where they were. Rose had to cut her hours at the laundry and spend more time off her feet.

As Halloween night approached, Rose knew this was going to have to be her last shift until the babies came. Everyone begged her to take it off or even take a short shift. They knew Rose wouldn't listen though. She figured that there was no sign of the pups coming on their due date. So, she thought it best to go into work knowing if anything did happen she would be closer to the hospital.

Rose was upstairs in the huge livingroom as the little ones came around in their costumes. Rose thought to herself about how next year her boys would be right there with the rest of the little pups. There was also a shifting ceremony going on as it was the full moon. Dozens of young teenage wolves gathered in the training field for their first time turning into their wolves.

Rose saw all the Omegas ready for the party that would be happening after. She saw everyone take such pride in the fact that this was their pack. Rose headed down stairs to start her shift of folding towels and whatever had been left by the previous shift.

It didn't take long before Rose had all the laundry caught back up. Rose was getting ready to fold the next basket of towels when she felt a sharp pain in her side. The boys were becoming very active and normally when Rose would rub the area with the heel of her hand the pain would stop. This just caused the boys to kick harder. Rose just blamed it on the moon and tried to get back to work.

When she stood up and tried to move the towels into the basket. She felt another really sharp pain. Which was followed by the feeling that she had peed herself. As she looked down she came to the quick realization that her water had broken.

Grabbing her phone immediately, she called Eva. Thank the Goddess she answered on the first ring.

"Aunt Eva." Rose was in pain and panicking.

"What's wrong?" Eva started to freak out and panic.

"I think my water just broke." Rose said, looking back down at the floor.

"Where are you?"

"Down stairs laundry."

"Do you think you can make it to the hospital? Never mind Uncle Tony is there. I'll call him and then meet you there. Don't be afraid everything is going to be alright." Eva hung up the call and called Tony.

"Yes, honey. What's up?" Tony answered

"Rose's water broke. She is in the packhouse downstairs laundry." Eva rattled off.

"I'm on my way." Tony hung up the phone and called over to Alpha Jax. Which was watching the new shifters.

"What's up?" Alpha Jax seeing that Tony was visibly startled.

"Rose's water broke. She's in the laundry room. I gotta go." Tony quickly explained.

"Yeah. GO GO." Alpha Jax basically pushed him toward the packhouse.

Alpha Jax picked up his phone and called Dr. Violet. "Yes, Alpha"

"Rose is in labor and her water broke. Tony is bringing her from the packhouse now."

"Yes Alpha." was all that was said before the line went dead.

Tony rushed right in through the back doors and down the seven or so steps into the laundry room. Rose was braced on a table screaming in pain. Tony wasted no time to scoop her up and run her to the hospital.

It seemed like if someone would have blinked they would have missed Tony rushing into the hospital carrying Rose bridal style. Almost like he was the Flash. Angel was already there waiting with a bed.

Eva came running in about three minutes later. All she had to do was follow the screaming. Tony was right there holding her hand telling her to breathe. Rose was in so much pain it was crazy.

It seemed like slow motion once Dr. Violet came into the room. She checked Rose for dilation but it was already too late. There wasn't even time to give her anything for the pain. The first boy was already crowning.

"Okay Rose you're going to have to push." Dr. Violet said.

Tony on one side and Eva on the other, Rose bared down and with one big push the first boy was free. Contractions came stronger and faster. Two maybe 3 pushes, there was the second little boy.

"Rose, you were a champ darling. You have two healthy boys." Dr. Violet said as the room was already filled with their cries.

Both boys were wiped off and placed on Rose's chest. She was tired and yet felt no pain right then. She was looking into their little faces and was completely in love. Their bright little eyes just stared into her emerald green ones.

"Oh Rose, look at them. You did so good." Eva was crying by this point. "They are so handsome."

"You did so good, little bud." Tony with tears in his eyes kissed the top of Rose's head along with each one of the boys.

They took them over to the waiting bassinets to get them completely cleaned up and weighed and measured. At the same time, they were cleaning up Rose. By the time they had handed them back, Rose noticed each boy had a funny little birthmark. Dylan had a crescent moon on the top of his right foot. Porter had a full moon on the top of his right foot. At least she would be able to tell them apart.

"Dylan is 6 lbs 9 ozs 21 inches. Porter is 6 lbs 8 ozs 21 inches." Angel said.

"They are going to be tall when they get older." Tony said, taking one of the boys to hold. Eva took the other one.

They moved Rose to an actual room and out of the birthing room. Rose just laid in the bed in a euphoric state. Her boys were finally here and they were healthy, safe, and more importantly they were loved.

Chapter 30

It took a few weeks before Rose had the boys down to a routine. Eva came by almost daily to allow Rose to do the basic things like shower and get a few hours of sleep. They wouldn't let her go back to work. The doctor took her off for a complete eight weeks to make sure Rose wasn't pushing herself too hard.

Once she got everything in its place, Rose was good to go. Shortly after they were 6 weeks old, Dylan and Porter were sleeping through the night. Rose had everything scheduled out and she found her groove. Everything was starting to just fall into place.

Eva would come over for breakfast and help get the little things done before she would head to the packhouse. That seemed to be all Rose would allow her to do. Eva knew it made Rose's job easier so she kept doing it.

One morning when Eva came by, Rose was the only one home. This worried Eva a little bit. Rose was always over protective and never let the kids out of her sight. So for Rose to just let the boys go without her was a little unusual.

"Hey where are the boys?" Eva said, looking around.

"Uncle Tony didn't tell you?" Rose looked a little amused.

"Tell me what?" Eva looked a little suspicious.

"He took them to see Santa at the packhouse." Rose smiled.

"All by himself?" Now Eva was worried about him being able to handle both boys.

"Well he had Luna Hazel with him when he showed up. So I thought this was planned." Rose began to panic a little.

"In her condition?" Eva laughed a little.

Right after the boys were born, Luna Hazel had found out that she was pregnant. Everyone has been over the moon. They would finally have an heir for the pack. It was very important not to leave the pack without the next generation.

Eva immediately called her husband. Not one single ring before Tony had just picked up. It was like he knew his wife would be calling him at any moment.

"Yes, my love. How are you this morning?" Tony said, slightly amused.

"You have the boys?" Eva questioned.

"Yes. They are here at the packhouse with all the other pups having cookies with Santa. Well mostly they are just getting passed around by the elves. I thought Rose and you could just use some time." Tony replied.

"But you didn't tell me anything." Eva accused.

"You have been just as stressed as Rose. So, Luna Hazel decided we were going to come and get them to see Santa." Tony picking at his wife.

"Are you at least getting plenty of pictures?" Eva asks.

"Yes. Now spend some time with Rose. I have the boys." With that Tony blew a kiss and hung up the phone.

Rose watched with a little bit of amusement. Eva took her part as Aunt very seriously. Rose and her had spent every minute caring for the boys. They had done little else. Eva thought it might be time to just get out for a little bit.

"You want to go and get some coffee?" Eva finally said exasperatedly about the situation that her husband played her into.

"Thought you'd never ask. Let me grab my jacket." Rose said, walking to the closet for her leather.

Rose was just about back to her pre-baby weight. But due to the boys nursing one thing hadn't gone down. Rose kind of played this to her advantage. She still hated that she couldn't zip her jacket all the way up.

As they headed out the door, Rose noticed that there was another foot of snow on the ground from the night before. Montana weather wasn't forgiving in the winter time. It wouldn't be long before the snow would hinder people from getting anywhere.

Eva had broken out the truck that normally sat in the garage. The big V8 Ford F250 had manual locking hubs, that was helpful in this weather like this. 4 wheel drive was only good if you happened to know how to use it.

Once they got out of the lake side road it wasn't that bad. Someone had already been out clearing the roads. It looked like they had been clearing the road all night. One thing was for sure. They would not cancel the "cookies with Santa". That was a tradition in the Harvest Moon pack.

They drove down to the Lunar Moon Cafe and went to get their coffee. While Rose was still on edge over not having the boys with her, she knew Tony had it under control. They were well protected at the packhouse.

After getting their coffee, they decided to go sit in the greenhouse area that was attached to the square. Thankfully, it was always open to the public. This place had such beautiful flowers all times of the year that people could just walk through and see. With Santa being in town, the place was quiet.

"You know I don't think I can thank you and Uncle Tony enough for what you have done for the boys and me." Rose said, taking a seat on one of the benches.

"It's what family does." Eva smiled sitting next to her.

"Not all families." Rose said, a little bitter.

"Hunny, you gotta just cut that loss. It's their loss not yours. And to be honest do you really want them in your children's lives if this is the way they treat you?" Eva tried to bring some reality checks to her.

"I guess you're right. Plus they kinda got a grandma anyway…" Rose quickly dodged the elbow.

"Oh hush. I'm Aunty Eva and that's that." Eva said, knowing that grandma made her feel old.

"You would have made a great mom." Rose said seeing the bond that they had. She wondered if it would have been the same with Eva's own children.

"Just wasn't in the cards. I mean I thought it was once but it didn't work out." Eva said somberly.

"What happened?" Rose asks.

"It's a long story."

"We got time." Rose said, taking a sip of her coffee.

"I'm not sure you want to know this. It's a lot to deal with and secrets that would be best left in the dark. It's been years and I'm still coming to terms with it." Eva said, trying not to let that wound open again.

"You need to get it off your chest. I'm a big girl. I can handle it, and I'm here to listen." Rose confirmed.

"Okay." Eva took a long breath and began.

"On the eve of your mother's and mine 18th birthday, we found out that the Blue Moon Ball was going to be hosted by our pack. Your grandfather, Goddess rest him, had been lobbying for the ball to be held there for years. See we came from a desert pack called Sand Point, which has now been renamed West Point Water under your Uncle Jimmy as the Alpha.

I still talk to your Uncle from time to time, but he and Kate never really got along. I feel like it was more than just a brother/sister thing. Kate always wanted more, being an Alpha's daughter and all.

The Blue Moon Ball brings together 12 packs. All the unmated females and males into one room. The hope is to have them all mated by the time it's over. Royalty of the Lycans are always included to oversee the ball.

Even though this was our first season, just turning 18, we were required to be there. Our mother had high hopes of us being mated well in the ranks but knew the Goddess would ultimately choose for us. She hoped she would choose well.

Anyway… Your mother had a plan to make sure, under no uncertain terms, that things would go in her favor. So before the ball, she went to see a forest witch. She was convinced that if she had a back up plan going into the ball; the Goddess would have little choice to give her what she wanted.

So when we arrived at the ball, Kate had seen Uncle Tony first. Finding out he was a Beta made him a person of interest and high on Kate's list. There however were six Alpha's at the ball as well. So she was merely just setting her plan in place in case one of them wasn't her mate.

That backfired when Tony had seen me. It was like when lightning strikes sand. Magical. Tony seemed to just glide to me like we were the only two in the room. Without saying a word he led me to the dance floor, kissed me, and we had our first dance. Hell, I didn't even know his name yet.

Kate, on the other hand, was on her way to meet Alpha Kent when she ran into Kyle. Luna Zara was there as well. Kate was furious when she found out Kyle was a Gamma, but she continued with her plan. She slipped the potion into Kyle's drink. We seem to believe that the potion gives Kate complete control. Everyone believes that this was the reason that Kate can do whatever she wants and Kyle will side with her. It also seems to have the effect to make him be completely dumb founded." Eva explained as Rose finally understood.

"Anyway. It wasn't long before Kate and Kyle got pregnant. She was overjoyed when she found out that she was having Delli. Though a couple of years later when Kate found out about you, she was not as pleased.

She almost broke several of our laws to get rid of you. When I found out I offered to take you as my own. She agreed, but just two weeks before she had a change of heart. Kyle had gotten involved and convinced her that having you would be the best thing in her life." Eva remembered the call telling her the deal was off.

"Right before your 7th birthday, I got a call again. By this time I had found out I was pregnant. Now mind you, I would call weekly and write to your parents to find out about you. Kate invited me down to see you. She wanted to discuss something. She, like this, wouldn't do it over the phone. Uncle Tony couldn't stand Kate and decided that it would be best for him to remain here.

So I went alone. Everything was fine the first few days. I played with you and Kate got to find out that at last I was pregnant. When I got the call telling me I was having a boy. I had a blood test done before I left. Kate went off.

She wanted to give you to me, and me to hand over my child. I told her I had no problem taking you back with me, but it was going to be a cold day in Hell before I gave up my pup. I wasn't going to give her what she wanted.

We had a very public fight and I had to almost kill her to get her off me. Kyle would have to jump in to protect her. She told him that I had tried to kidnap you. She was just defending herself. I was the crazy one.

Kyle tried to cuss me, but I put him in his place rather quickly. Had I just agreed and then went back on my word you would have been safe. Maybe Franky would still be here." Eva began to cry a bit.

"Anyway..." Eva brushed away the tears. "I called your Uncle Tony and told him I was coming back early because of problems with Kate. I was driving his old Nova and the brakes went out. I flipped the car six times before it stopped.

By the time they had gotten me to the hospital, I was in really rough shape and unconscious. With how bad the crash was and the fact I rolled six times, I had lost the baby I carried. That was the worst day of my life. Walking up to find out that I almost died and the baby was no more.

When they examined the Nova it was totaled. The brakes were cut and it was rigged that a pone impacted it was supposed to explode. Lucky for me, whoever did it didn't know what they were doing.

When Kate was confronted with it she acted like she was in shock. She couldn't possibly have had anything to do with it. Rumors were that if she could get rid of me, reject your father, and then she could be free to comfort Tony. She figured Tony in his grief of losing his mate and his child would choose and claim her. Kate always reached too high.

Up till now, I haven't had any dealings with Kate whatsoever. By the judge of it, that was for the best. I still prayed everyday for you. " Eva said as Rose sat floored.

Now it all made sense to Rose. Why Kate hated Eva. Why she barely remembered her. Why Kyle, while strong and capable, acted like a complete nitwit. Why Kate was always trying to have what she wanted. Kate believed the Goddess owed her something.

Eva looked at Rose for just a bit. Rose had an arrangement of emotions on her face. While she tried to process everything, Eva wondered if letting the cat out of the bag was actually a good idea but it was a little late now.

"This explains so much." Was all Rose could say.

They sat there quietly just looking at the flowers. Eva did feel better with telling Rose the whole truth. Finally laying it all on the line. Rose deserved to know that everything she had been through at the hands of her mother was in no way Rose's fault. Now they both could deal with healing from the past.

Chapter 31

After that day in the greenhouse, Eva and Rose's relationship had gotten so much closer than just Aunt and niece. Rose always had lunch with Eva at least once a week and coffee a few mornings a week when they both could find the time. Rose and the boy had also made it a point to have dinner at their house a few times a week with Sunday dinners being a must.

Tony had noticed the change but didn't dare try to ask questions that he didn't want answers to. He made that mistake one too many times and didn't care to do it again. He was happy that their family was at peace. He knew that Rose and the boys played a big part in that. They were happy before but they were an actual family now.

By the time spring rolled around the boys were 6 months old. Rose had them in the pack daycare while she got a job working at the local mechanic shop. Rose was happy to finally be back to working on cars. Rose would still keep working at the laundry a few nights a week to make sure she had the money to care for all the boys' needs.

While Rose had completely settled into her life being a mom, some things never changed. She still called and wrote to Mike, Chris and Nathan. They knew it was too risky for them to leave and come see her but they had every picture of the boys. Rose had not come to terms with her parents and felt like that wasn't going to happen. She still wrote and sent pictures. She hoped that a change of heart would happen. No one could say she didn't put in the effort.

One night while working her night shift, Rose heard a commotion up stairs. Rose went up the stairs to figure out what was going on. Alpha Jax was in a state of pure panic running around like he was out of his mind.

"What's wrong?" Rose finally caught his attention.

"Luna Hazel… I think she is in labor." Alpha Jax said looking so concerned.

"Did her water brake or is she just having contractions?" Rose said calmly hoping to get him to calm as well.

"Contractions." Alpha Jax said, still running around.

"Okay. I need you to breathe. I'll call Dr. Violet. Take this to Luna Hazel and I'll be up in just a second." Rose said, handing him a glass of ice chips.

"What's this for?" Alpha Jax looked confused.

"To keep her hydrated. She can't drink anything." Rose explained.

"Oh okay." Alpha Jax rushed back up the stairs.

Rose thought he was too panicked to call the doctor himself right now. Rose grabbed the phone and called. Two rings later.

"Yes, Rose, is something wrong with the boys?" Dr. Violet said in a bit of a panic.

"Nope. Luna Hazel is in labor. Contractions as far as I know her water hasn't broken yet." Rose relayed what she currently knew.

"Okay. I will be there in a few minutes. Tell her not to push." Dr. Violet said scrambling.

"Will do." Rose said, hanging up the phone.

Rose quickly ran down the stairs. She grabbed towels and the basket full of baby clothes that were sent down earlier. Rose rushed upstairs to the screaming of Luna Hazel. Rose understood all too well what she was going through.

As she got to the door, Rose knocked and Alpha Jax opened the door immediately. As she peered into the room, Rose could see Luna Hazel double over in a chair from the pain. Rose thrusted the basket into Alpha Jax's hands and went to Luna Hazel.

"How are you doing?" Rose said, looking for signs of distress.

"Oh my Goddess this hurts." Luna Hazel gasped.

"Yes, I know. But it only hurts for a little while. Then you will have your sweet little boy on your chest wondering how perfect he is." Rose tried to sooth while rubbing on her back.

"Really?" Luna Hazel looked up with tears streaming out of her eyes and sweat beading on her forehead.

"Really. Now let's try to get you to the bed. Has your water broke or is this just contractions?" As the words came out of her mouth almost on cue Luna Hazel's water broke.

They both looked at each other. Luna Hazel's eyes held so much fear on her face. Rose was calm and got her up and walked her to the bed. Alpha Jax climbed in behind her to support her weight.

Thankfully Luna Hazel was wearing a nightgown. Rose got both her knees up to check to make sure there was no baby coming out. Rose was met with the top of a head as Dr. Violet entered the bedroom.

"Luna, Alpha, Rose." Dr. Violet addressed.

"Her water broke. Baby is crowning." Rose explained as Dr. Violet came closer.

Dr. Violet got right to work. Rose slid to the side of Luna Hazel. With just 3 pushes, a baby's cries filled the room. Everyone in the room, who hadn't realized they were holding their breaths, let out a long breath of relief. As Luna Hazel held her son and looked at him in amazement. Rose took this as a sign to take her leave.

Rose knew that it was a private moment for the Alpha and Luna to be with their baby. Rose just smiled. She had gone to the kitchen to get something to drink and just try to calm her adrenaline. Dr. Violet came into the kitchen just a few minutes later.

"You did good, Rose." Dr. Violet praised.

"Well it wasn't that long ago that I was right there. How's she doing?" Rose asked.

"Very good. And our future Alpha is just fine as well. Have you ever thought about becoming a midwife?" Dr. Violet said, putting her travel bag on the counter.

"Oh no." Rose put her hand up. "I just happened to be in the right place at the right time. I don't think I could have kept my cool if it wasn't for that."

"Well if you ever want to talk about it. You know where my office is." Dr. Violet gave Rose a hug and left the room.

Rose calmed herself. She was still flying from being on the other side of the experience of childbirth. Rose went back to her shift of laundry that needed to be washed and folded before morning. She was genuinely pleased with herself.

By the time Alpha Jax had made his way back down to the laundry to thank Rose, She was already gone for the night. He didn't know if he could have made it through that without her. Actually, he was sure he couldn't have done that without her. Rose was someone very special to him and this pack.

Chapter 32

Rose loved the arrangement she had with her Aunt and Uncle. On the nights Rose worked at the laundry, Eva would keep the boys overnight and then drop them off at daycare. Rose would come home and get a couple hours of sleep before going to the garage.

As she got up and got ready for work, Rose got a phone call from Eva. This was nothing new because Eva would call in the mornings to make sure she hadn't over slept. Especially on the mornings she had the boys. Rose's sleep schedule was a bit crazy.

"Good Morning." Rose said, trying to pour a cup of coffee and balance the phone on her shoulder.

"Morning, Rose. How was work?" Eva inquired.

"Oh not bad. How were the boys last night?" Rose asked.

"Angels as usual. Porter and Dylan slept on Uncle Tony." Eva mused.

"Please tell me you got pictures this time." Rose said, taking a sip of coffee.

"Of course. They have him wrapped hard." Eva said.

"I know. Just wait till they are older." Rose is thinking of what they will be able to pull with his help after they're a little older.

"I don't even want to think about it." Eva laughed. "What do you have going on today?"

"I got to go into the garage. Hoping my parts delivery comes in this morning. We have had two that have been taking up space." Rose explained drinking her coffee.

"Oh okay. Is it cool if Keven brings my car in? It's making that noise in the front again." Eva tried to sound nonchalant.

"Yeah that's fine. Should be there in about 20 or so minutes." Rose said, knowing it wouldn't be a big fix.

"Okay I'll flag him down at the packhouse. I would bring it in myself, but I have graduation meetings this morning." Eva knew that Rose understood the responsibilities.

"Oh that's fine. As soon as he gets there I'll get the car on the rack and see what's wrong with it." Rose said, realizing it was almost time for graduation again. She had been there for almost a year. Time had flown without so much as a blink of an eye.

After some more small talk Rose got off the phone and started getting ready for work. Hair braided back, work shirt, black jeans, and her boots, Rose walked out of the house and headed to the van to go to work.

After getting to work, she started her normal routine. Firing up the office coffee pot as well as the one in the bays, No one went without coffee. Rose would open at least two bays to get fresh air in. She would evaluate the projects. Especially ones she was waiting on parts for. By the time she was done hustling and bustling around the bays Jack would come out to talk to her.

Jack was one of the older wolves, but you would never know it to look at him. He stood right about 6'6" and every bit of 250 lbs. Muscular build with a little bit of a belly on him, gave Jack the allusion of being the typical old timer. His graying black hair and smokey brown eyes told a story that not too many knew.

Jack had owned the shop for 30 odd years. Which had been handed down from father to son for generations. Jack's own son helped out in the shop and was going to college currently for paint and body. That would be just one more thing that Jack could add besides the day to day repairs of the current clients.

"Morning Rose." Jack said with a cup of coffee in his hand.

"Morning Jack. Do we have an ETA on the Vet parts or is it still pending?" Rose asked. The 1975 Corvette had been sitting in Bay5 for almost 3 weeks.

"They will be here tomorrow. Keeping fingers crossed. The truck parts should be here by 2." Jack said, reading off the emails he had printed out that morning.

"Okay. Do I still need to run to the parts house for the plugs and wires?" Rose inquired, they were having problems with the delivery guy.

"Nope, they finally got a new delivery driver. So they will be sending them over. By the way, we got three months free on the service. So don't be afraid to make them bring it over. Guess you were right to threaten them on pulling the contract." Jack smiled while sipping his coffee.

"Okay then." Rose was pleased that she was able to help in this situation. "Keven is bringing over Beta Eva's car in a bit. It's making that noise in the front end again. I hope it's just the brakes and not the bearings." Rose informed Jack.

"Okay. So you have everything handled for the moment." Jack said, and started to walk back into the office before turning back to Rose. "You know you work too hard."

Jack knew Rose was putting in her forty hours at the shop and then another three to four nights at the packhouse in the laundry, plus raising two boys. He knew she couldn't have too much time for herself or even to just relax.

"I know, but if I don't put in the time now; then I won't be able to provide for the boys later." Rose tried to explain as she heard Keven pull up with Aunt Eva's car.

"Just think about slowing down just a little bit. You need to take some time to have fun." Jack said concerned about her well-being.

"I will." Rose gave a quirky smile.

Jack went back into the office while Keven was coming through the bay door. Keven looked a little out of place. Rose always had the impression he knew about cars, but not on how to work on them. She always found it a little funny.

"Hey Rose." Keven greeted, looking a little more nervous than normal.

"Hey Keven. Got Eva's car?" Rose said, trying to overlook his awkwardness.

"Yea. She said something about a noise." Keven said, looking back at the car.

"Yea. She called me this morning." Rose stood there a little amused.

"Good thing you know how to fix them. Cars I mean." Keven was starting to stumble over his words.

"Always been a talent." Rose amusement turned to curiosity.

Keven just stood in the bay a little fidgettie. Rose picked up on it right away while they were talking. Keven kept looking around and acting like he wanted to say something but just didn't. Rose, being the person she was, just called him out on it.

"You need to talk about something?" Rose crossed her arms and kept a straight face.

"No... I mean yes but.." Keven started then trailed off.

"Just say it."

"Can I take you to dinner?" Keven just blurted out, hoping that the next words weren't just a straight up NO.

"Well..." Rose began a little shell shocked. "I'm not sure. I would have to get a sitter and there is just a lot going on right now." Rose ball faced lied to him.

"Well I'm pretty sure Beta Eva would watch the boys for you to have one night out. I mean have you even been out since the boys were born?" Keven already knew the answer. Everyone knew the answer to that question.

"Keven, my life is complicated. We know we are not mates. I don't want to lead anyone on." Rose tried to explain her position on the "no dating" thing.

"Rose, it's dinner. I'm not saying let's get married. I'm saying that I find you generally interesting and I want to spend time with you." Keven said, trying not to be offended by her off handed response.

Rose was taken aback for a moment. Was this a set up? Rose had heard Uncle Tony say something when she was pregnant about him always talking about her. Did he actually like her? Rose had a hard time trusting other guys because of her past.

After a few minutes of mentally scolding herself, Rose thought what could the harm be in just dinner. Anything went sideways; she knew Uncle Tony would be right there in a flash. One word to Alpha Jax about his behavior and he would be dealt with. She was safe and needed to just trust.

"Fine. If you can get Beta Eva to agree to watch the boys tonight, then and only then will I go to dinner with you." Rose said, trying to mentally tell Eva to say no. "When?"

"Tonight? 7 work for you?" Keven said with the biggest smile on his face.

"Fine but it's short notice. Beta Tony and her might have plans already." Rose said, knowing that they never had plans. It was sad to say but they were alway telling her that she needed to go out and blow off steam.

"Okay I will talk to her when I get back to the packhouse." Keven said and walked out of the bays.

He shifted into his brown wolf right in the parking lot and ran back in the direction of the packhouse. Rose just shook her head and went to pull her Aunt Eva's car into the shop. After getting it up on the rack, she noticed it was past time to change the brakes and turn the routers. She also noticed that one of the sway bar links had snapped.

Rose, knowing that Eva would want everything fixed at one time, got to work on the car. Within just a few short hours, Rose had everything done, greased, and put back together. She even gave the car a quick oil change, noticing that the sticker in the window had her three thousand miles overdue. Aunt Eva would appreciate the fact that Rose went the extra mile on the car.

Rose was lowering the car off the rack when her phone rang.

"I was just fixing to call you." Rose said as she answered the call from Eva.

"I figured you would have it figured out in a few hours. So what was it?" Eva asked.

"Brakes, your routers, and a broken sway bar link. Also needed an oil change since you were about three thousand overdue." Rose said seeing if she was going to bring up Keven first.

"Okay. So everything is done?" Eva asked like she was deliberately not talking about the elephant in the room.

"Yep. Do you want me to put it on your account or are you going to settle up on pick up?" Rose asked thinking maybe he chickened out and hadn't asked her.

"I'll have Uncle Tony and Keven come and get the car." Eva giggled and Rose knew there was more to the story.

"That'll be fine." Rose said dryly knowing that they were trying to play her.

"So they should be around in an hour or so." Eva said then quickly hung up the phone before Rose could give any response.

Rose knew that everyone seemed to be in on it. Instead of Eva saying anything, she would send Uncle Tony to do the confirmation. Rose knew she had been had and now wishes she had just said No. It's not that she didn't find him attractive. Keven was easy on the eyes. It was just that this was a setup and Rose hated setups.

Rose worked on several more cars as the day stretched on. Tony and Keven showed back up at the shop a few hours later after talking with Eva. Rose was currently under one car doing a front end alignment when she heard their voices. They were both standing at the opening of the bay she was working in. Rose then saw two shadows come across the floor confirming what she was hearing. Rose ignored them at first and finished the car she was working on before then came out.

"No help today?" Uncle Tony said as he watched his niece lower the lift with the car she just finished working on.

"Nope. Just me and Jack today." Rose said being careful not to say or even look at Keven.

"So what time will you be getting off?" Keven said, looking at Rose with a quirky smile.

"Shop will be closing at 5:30. Normally it's 6 but parts haven't arrived yet." Rose tried to keep her tone even.

"So is 7 still going to work for you?" Keven purposely asked right in front of Uncle Tony.

"Well since Aunt Eva hasn't said anything... I guess we will have to rain check it." Rose said hoping that she would escape this very uncomfortable situation.

"7 for what?" Uncle Tony asks, trying to pretend like he didn't know what was going on and not listening in for his cue to chime in.

"Oh I asked Rose to dinner. But she is trying to get out of it due to not having a sitter." Keven smiled while he ratted her out.

Rose knew she would have to kick him hard when she got the chance. She wanted to let him down and just walk away. Even though everyone was telling her she needed to take some time and blow off steam. She just wasn't ready to throw caution to the wind.

Rose wasn't ready to take a chance that could potentially end up in a disaster. Even though she had mentally scolded herself again over this, she trusted once but she also knew she couldn't base everything on another's actions. That wasn't fair to anyone. So for the second time today, she had to make the decision to just push herself forward.

"Well when would this be taking place?" Tony asked Keven.

"I was hoping tonight. I already made the reservations." Keven smiled and then tried to pout. Not a good look for him, Rose mused to herself.

"Yea that should be fine. I'll pick the boys up from daycare on my way back from training." Tony said, working out the schedule in his head.

"You have both forgotten one thing?" Rose said as they turned to her.

"What?" They said in unison.

"I never said yes. I said if I found a sitter." Rose began.

"And you have. So, Keven. 7 tonight and you best be on your best behavior." Tony said smugly smiling and walked into the office by Jack.

Keven stood there smugly smiling. "So I'll pick you up at 7."

"Fine. Are you going to at least tell me where we are going?" Rose inquired exasperated that she was hoodwinked by her uncle and Keven.

"Nope." Keven turned and walked out, getting into Eva's car and driving away.

Tony settled up with Jack for the repairs. Then he left smiling and waving at Rose. Rose finished lowering the car she was previously working on off the rack. Then pulled it out of the garage and into the lot before going into the office to hand over the ticket.

"Here you go. The Accord is ready to go. I would let them know that they are going to need breaks and tires soon." Rose said, flopping onto the couch to take a break.

"Will do. Hey, we don't have anything else. Why don't you cut out early?" Jack said looking over invoices.

"The truck parts will be here in an hour. Don't you want me to handle the delivery?" Rose inquired suspiciously. Jack always had her deal with the deliveries for the shop. Mainly because she put them right in their places ten minutes after they arrived.

"No it's Friday, go take some time to get ready for your date." Jack teased, wiggling his eyebrows.

"It's not a date! It's dinner." Rose went red faced.

"Hunny, that's a date." Jack laughed.

"Oh Goddess. I can't go through with this." Rose mumbled.

"You're 18. You should be going on dates." Jack scolded, knowing she was always working and not taking time for herself.

"I'm a single mom. I have two boys to look after." Rose defended.

"You're also burning yourself out. Quit being stubborn and go have some fun. You know you don't have to prove yourself as the badass 24/7 right? No one will look down on you for just being a woman for one night." Jack tried to convince.

"I have nothing to wear." Rose admitted.

"Well I guess it's a good thing you're getting off 6 hours early then so you can figure something out. And you keep arguing with me young lady and I'll tell you not to come in tomorrow either." Jack played pointing his finger at her.

"Fine. Fine. I give. Uncle." Rose said getting up and going to give Jack a big hug.

Chapter 33

One hour before Keven is supposed to be at the house, Rose is standing in front of her closet with a towel wrapped around her. Rose stares into her closet not knowing what to wear and hoping something will jump out at her.

Rose was getting ready to admit defeat when she heard a knock on the front door. Rose begins to freak out thinking. *SHIT he's early.* She peaks around the door frame and down to the front door. Rose, seeing Eva, instantly takes a long breath. Eva, knowing Rose is probably upstairs getting ready, lets herself in.

"Rose, you home?" Eva shouts up the stairs.

"Yeah. I'm here." Rose shouts from her bedroom.

Eva walks up the stairs to Rose's room. As she walks in she sees Rose in a towel laying on the bed sprawled out. Eva is slightly amused at the sight of her normally very controlled niece looking like she was going to have a meltdown over a date.

"Why aren't you getting ready?" Eva asked with a very amused tone.

"Wow. Why didn't I think of that?" Rose said sarcastically. "Mainly because I have nothing to wear. And I'm going to just tell him I'm not going."

"You are going. A very nice boy asked you to dinner. Which has taken him weeks to ask." Eva began to giggle thinking about how he had asked her and Tony dozens of times on how to do it.

"As I have previously stated, I have nothing to wear." Rose said bring herself to a sitting position.

"Well then I guess it's lucky for you I brought this." Eva said, handing the bag over.

Rose opened it and lit up like the fourth of July. A black knee length denim skirt along with a dark blue poet shirt with flowy sleeves, it was not only just her style but was perfect in every way.

"Oh you shouldn't have." Rose gushed. No one had ever taken Rose shopping or even gone out of their way to buy her anything like this before. Rose was simple and never really needed dress clothes until now.

"Yes, I should have. Now get ready. He should be here anytime." Eva said, hugging Rose and taking her leave. Eva also made a mental note that they would have to schedule a shopping trip for just the girls soon.

Within 20 minutes, Rose was dressed and ready to go. Very light makeup, and lip gloss made her more of a knock out then she already was. Rose left her hair loosely falling in spiral curls with just the front pulled up out of her face. Her black dress boots with just a little bit of a heel made her closer to Keven's height. Maybe even just a little bit taller.

Rose was standing in the kitchen when she heard the knock on the door. Rose thought it was odd she didn't hear him pull up but looking at the clock it was 7 sharp. *Well at least he was on time*, Rose thought to herself.

As she walked out of the kitchen and to the front door to open it, Keven's mouth dropped. It was like night and day with her just being covered in oil just a few hours ago. She looked like a completely different person, and he kind of liked this version as well.

"Well hello there. These are for you." Keven said, handing Rose a bouquet of daisies.

"Oh how sweet." Rose said, taking the flowers. "Let me just put them in some water before we go. Come on in."

Rose walked into the kitchen. More to escape than the task at hand. Keven had his dark brown hair slicked back. He wore a maroon colored button up dress shirt opened to his collarbone, and sleeves rolled to his elbows. He also wore black jeans and black leather boots with a gold chain that hung around his neck with a symbol for the Moon Goddess.

Rose hated to admit it but he looked good. This was not the same guy she had met almost a year ago. Certainly not the guy that came by and fixed things around the house. He was actually, if Rose dared to say it, HOT.

Rose hated to admit she had also never been on a real date before. She had no idea of protocol. This made her even more nervous. She wanted to run back up stairs and hide in her room, but that was not an option at this point.

So, she squared up her shoulders, put on her leather and grabbed her purse. When she walked back into the living room he was just standing there. It was like he had never been in the house once since they met and he was here all the time.

"Ready?" Keven asked.

"As I'll ever be." Rose said and they walked out to Keven's truck.

Rose had noticed that it had been washed, and detailed on the inside. *Was this something he did regularly or just for girls he was taking out?* Rose wondered.

"So, Where are we going?" Rose said, looking over as Keven opened the door for her.

"A surprise." Keven said, helping Rose into the truck.

"I really don't like surprises." Rose admitted.

"Well all I can say is you will like this one." Keven said, closing his door.

When he climbed in, he put his seatbelt on, and started the truck. He smiled at Rose dropping the truck in drive and pulling off. He drove to the other side of the territory. Rose had never been over here before.

He smiled when he pulled up in front of this old Italian restaurant. He had a taste, that was for sure. He parked the truck and quickly jumped out to go and open Rose's door. He led her inside where the tables were covered in red and white table cloths, candles on the tables, and a guy in maybe his 20s was playing violin. Rose thought he had gone all out for this.

"Reservations?" A young blonde walked out from behind a wall that was on the other side of the podium.

"Keven Star." Keven said.

"Yes, sir table for two. Right this way." She said escorting the two to a table by a window.

Keven even pulled out Rose's chair. Then sat across from her. The lady left the menus and walked away. Rose quickly picked up the menu and began to freak out about the prices. This was a fancy fancy kind of place.

"See anything you like?" Keven said when he noticed her attention shifting.

"Little expensive for a first date. I mean dinner." Rose remarked.

"No, Rose, this is a date. And get whatever you want. I will warn you though. That everything can more than likely feed both of us from what I've heard." Keven smirks a little.

"Heard? You have never been here before?" Rose arched an eyebrow.

"Nope. My normal first date is BBQ from Charlies." Keven admitted.

"Then why the change?" Rose was curious.

"I wanted something special since I didn't think you would agree or wouldn't stand me up." Keven laughed. He had a great laugh, Rose thought.

"In all fairness I almost did. But someone said I had to." Rose mused.

"Who?"

"Aunt Eva."

"Remind me to send that woman flowers." Keven still not being able to take his eyes off Rose.

"Not funny."

"So what were you going to use as your excuse?" Keven had to hear this one.

"I had nothing to wear." Rose admitted.

"If you had nothing to wear… what do you call that?" Keven pointed at the cute little number she had worn.

"Again… Aunt Eva. She came by and brought it to me." Rose admitted again.

During their conversation, they had not noticed the waiter had walked up to the table.

"Can I take your drink order?" He said.

"Dr. Pepper." Rose said, knowing in these places it was normally wine but Rose was still technically underage.

"Same."

"Perfect. Can I tell you the chief specials or would you like some more time with the menu?" He said very politely.

"Chief specials please." Keven asked.

"Chief specials tonight are Chicken Parmesan with linguine, a lovely Veal Parmesan, or Chicken Alfredo." He recited.

"Chicken Alfredo?" Keven asked Rose.

"That's perfect."

"Very good, sir. Would you like a bread basket while you wait?" The waiter asked.

"Yes, please." Keven said, knowing that they were both probably starving.

"Very good." The waiter grabbed the menus and walked away.

Keven continues to smile at Rose. Rose, feeling the heat in her cheeks begin to rise, begins to get nervous for the second time. She was trying to think of things to say or not to say. Rose wasn't great at small talk. Rose wanted the date to go well even though this was not her idea in the first place.

"What's wrong?" Keven asked as she fidgeted.

"Why me?" Rose asks in a semi small voice, she wasn't used to hearing come out of her.

"What do you mean?" Keven asked, puzzled.

"I mean that you asked me out. So why me?" Rose looked at him blankly trying hard to hide her emotion.

"Because I believe that you're beautiful, smart, and a bit of a hermit." Keven teased. slightly.

"I'm not a hermit. I'm focused." Rose said, trying not to come off offended.

"No, you're trying to close yourself off." Keven fired back.

"What are you, my shrink?" Rose was feeling like a charity case and started to get upset with the fact that he felt pity for her.

"No. I just felt like you need to be shown that not all guys are like the one that hurt you." Keven said.

"Well I'm perfectly fine dealing with that on my own." Rose said anger rising in her gut.

"No wait. You're miss understanding me. I like you. I like you for all the reasons a guy should like a girl. But I know you're set on not liking anyone right now." Keven said, trying to defuse the situation.

Rose took a minute to fully understand what he was saying. Keven liked her, but she would not hurt him in that way. They knew they were not mates, but Keven still wanted something to be there.

"Keven, it's not a good idea. You get attached to someone that isn't your mate, then you find your mate, and things get messy quickly. In my case, I can't say I had an attachment, but I hoped for the sake of his actions. There was one I didn't see at that time. I dared to hope and love for however brief a time. Well more infatuated than love but you get the picture. Then it was spit back in my face like I was some sort of horny shewolf that was asking for it.

He got what he wanted and thankfully I have no memory of it. All I have that proves his guilt is my boys. Which again he had no problem flipping around on me as well. It wasn't his problem. He wasn't the one knocked up, and according to him how did he know I wasn't whoring around with half the pack." Rose's emotions went high as she had not talked to a soul about what had happened to her outside the ones that needed to know.

Keven sat quietly for a moment and absorbed all the information that was given. How long had she been holding that in and needed to get that out. Keven planned his next move not to upset her any further. Maybe with time, she would change her mind about a relationship with him. He didn't want to push her to the point of never speaking to him again. This first date wasn't going well.

"Okay. So what about just two friends... I can say friends right?" Keven waited for confirmation.

"Yes, we are friends." Rose said, looking skeptical.

"Okay. So two friends that just happen to enjoy each other's company and go out from time to time. If something happens, great. Nothing happens, we have a good time regardless." Keven figured a compromise would do the trick.

"And after you finally find your mate? What then? Still friends and just make a bigger group?" Rose said, taking a breadstick from the basket that was just brought to the table.

"Yes. Simple as that. I care about you. I care about Dylan and Porter. I don't think that is going to change." Keven said, laying all his cards on the table.

They went into lighter conversation for the rest of the night. The story about Rose's car and her friends back at Hollows. Rose hoped that he was a man of his word and would not turn his back on her. Only time would tell, if giving him a chance would backfire.

Chapter 34

*"And suddenly you know: It's time to start something new
and trust the magic of Beginnings."*
-Meister Eckhart.

As the time passed, Keven and Rose found a deep respect for each other. Rose helped him rebuild his first car. Which so happened to be a 1970 Plymouth Duster. That Keven called Dusty. That car turned into his pride and joy.

While their friendship grew stronger, they were never romantically involved. Keven knew Rose was right about not forming that kind of attachment. Things could get messy and he never wanted to lose her. That didn't stop him from taking her out on Friday nights and just enjoying the company.

Rose stood on the porch watching her now 4 year old boys play in the snow. Dylan was skilled with snowballs while Porter was trying to build a snowman. Porter didn't appreciate his brother throwing snowballs at his snowman. Rose just stood there with her coffee looking amused.

The years had been good to them. Rose was asked to join the Harvest Moon pack a few years back and she accepted knowing this would always be their home. The boys thankfully would not have to go through anything like that because Rose had taken the oath for them.

After which, Rose began training again. Her training partner was none other than Keven. Keven realized very early on that Rose was no ordinary warrior. She could use her size and skill to her advantage in a fight.

She was also deadly in either form. Knives were always her weapon of choice. Rose also got into throwing stairs and hatchets. She picked it up pretty easily, being able to always hit her target. Snow, Rose's wolf, was bigger than most. Even with her pure white fur, Snow was very easily hidden in her environment.

Her agile frame made her hard to just grab on to. Rose was able to slip or reverse most holds. Everyone swore she was part cat the way she could easily slink around without being detected. All the leaders wanted her on their patrols.

Rose had quit the laundry but still worked with Jack at the shop. Fixing things would always be her passion. As such, she helped Jack bring the shop from just a daily driver fix it here to a more middle end shop for the classic car guys in the area.

Eva and Tony were always her rock. They were like grandparents to the boys. Spoiling them every chance they got. Dylan and Porter had Tony so wrapped around their figures that all they had to do was poke out their little lips.

Rose smiled thinking of how far they had come. She knew if it wasn't for a lot of people then it could have been a bigger nightmare than it needed to be. Rose was content in her life. Dylan and Porter were happy and healthy and that's all that mattered.

Rose was in the process of calling the boys inside, when she saw the Cougar pull into view. Rose couldn't help but notice that Uncle Tony wasn't alone. Alpha Jax was in the car with him. Rose was a little nervous.

The car came to a stop right behind the van. Tony popped out and Rose got a slightly sick feeling. Tony smiled at her to say they came in peace, but what had gotten her attention was Alpha Jax had never been out to the cabin once.

"There's my boys." Tony said as they giggled and ran to him.

"Hey Uncle Tony." Rose said, taking a sip of her coffee. "Alpha Jax."

"Hello Rose. Might we be able to talk for a minute?" Alpha Jax said.

"Sure can. Uncle Tony, can you grab the boys?" Rose said amused that the boys had him at this point.

Rose opened the door and they all went inside. Rose got the boys coats off and ushered them into the now playroom. She put on a move for them and went to get their snack. After she was sure they were handled, Rose left the playroom keeping the door cracked to be able to hear them.

Tony and Alpha Jax had shown themselves to the kitchen. Alpha Jax had noted how Rose had turned this cabin into a home. There were pictures of her and the boys everywhere. Toys from the playroom seemed to be all over the living room, Alpha Jax laughed because he had the same problem with his little one.

"Can I offer you two some coffee?" Rose asked, coming into the kitchen.

"Yes please." They seemed to speak in unison.

Rose got down the cups and made them both a cup of coffee.

"So is this official or unofficial business." Rose said, getting right to the point while handing off the cups.

They sat at the island and looked at each other. Alpha Jax had asked his Beta to drive him out there to talk to Rose. He had realized he had very few interactions with her since she had come to the pack 4 and a half years ago. While the moments they have shared have been memorable and have led him to have a lot of respect for her, he realized he knew very little about her.

The invitation to join their pack had been relayed through Beta Tony and Eva. Alpha Jax felt bad about that. Everything was handed down to them and relayed back to Rose. Alpha Jax didn't trust himself after their first meeting and his intense blow up. He had his reasons but that didn't excuse his behavior toward her.

"A little bit of both." Alpha Jax finally said, taking a sip of his coffee.

"Well then let's get to it then." Rose said mentally preparing herself for what was to come.

"I want to apologize. With all the new members even before they are, I like to spend time with them. I like to get to know them on a personal level. So, they know they can come to me with anything. I also learn a lot about their strengths and weaknesses in terms of where they will fit into the pack. Since our first meeting, it hasn't been like that. I am sorry for that." Alpha Jax said feeling a little guilty.

"You're a busy man. I don't see it as you didn't. You have done so much for my boys and myself." Rose said just brushing it off.

"Nevertheless, it's a grave oversight that needs to be put right and things put back into place." Alpha Jax explained.

"Well you know everything about me." Rose brushed off the need to repeat the past.

"Also I would like to explain why your situation meant so much to me when you arrived. See, I had an older sister. Lily. Lily was the beauty of the pack and very sweet. She found herself in the same situation of being with child. My father was furious. Lily wouldn't give up the name of the asshole that did this. Which caused more anger. She nor the child made it through the delivery." Alpha Jax's voice was quiet.

"I'm so sorry." Rose said, holding her hand to her mouth in shock.

"You remind me of her. She was someone you didn't mess with. She was deadly. Knew six different ways to rip a guy's throat out. That's why it was so devastating when first she came up pregnant and then when she wouldn't give the name. All we knew was he wasn't her mate and he had rejected her and the child." Alpha Jax was still so upset about that.

"Please tell me this isn't a plea to give up the name." Rose said, looking exasperated by the coming question.

"No. You made it clear that you don't want anyone to know. I just want you to know that I understand. I understand more than anything why." Alpha Jax stated.

"Thank you." Rose said.

"Now as far as the other reason we have come. As a member of this pack there are certain duties we need from you." Alpha Jax said.

"That is? I'm always happy to help in any way." Rose said intrigued by what this could be.

"Our pack has been chosen for this year's Blue Moon Ball. Your Aunt Eva is on the committee and needs volunteers to help set up." Tony pipped up.

"Well of course. When is it going to be?" Rose inquired.

"Second week of December." Alpha Jax said.

"So, in two weeks?" Rose confirmed with amusement.

"Yes. Also there is one other thing." Beta Tony said, looking over at Alpha Jax.

"As an unmated female you're going to be required to be in attendance." Alpha Jax told her.

"Really? Why?" Rose thought her time had come and gone, especially with being a mother.

"It's tradition. All we ask is you make an appearance. One hour max." Tony tried to convince her.

"Fine. If it's necessary I will do it, but I am not doing the stupid Limo ride. I'll drive myself." Rose stated not pleased that she was going to have to do this in the first place.

"In what?" Alpha Jax smirked.

"Is she still in the barn?" Tony asked with a sly smile.

"Yep. Took her out last week before the snow came in." Rose said, sharing the joke with Tony.

Alpha Jax looked at the two of them suspiciously. Rose smiled and checked on the boys before waving the two men to follow her. They walked out in the snow down to the little barn behind the garage.

Rose opened the lock and pulled the double doors open to reveal Princess in all her glory. Anyone could tell she was well taken care of. Not a speck of dust on the presten paint job. The car just sat there like a diamond that was just hidden away.

Alpha Jax's jaw just dropped. Her dark blue paint and black racing stripes looked like it was painted yesterday. He wasn't expecting this. Alpha Jax thought it might have been just some newish muscle car, but Rose had taste and it showed.

"Wow." was Alpha Jax could say.

"Want to hear her run?" Rose asked with a gleam in her eye.

"Oh definitely." Alpha Jax eyes lit up.

Rose grabbed the keys out of the headrest and fired her to life. She sounded mean and looked the part as well. The music pouring from the open door was 5 Finger Death Punch. Alpha Jax just shook his head.

After a few minutes, Rose killed the engine. She then walked to the front of the car to sit on the hood. Rose always got butterflies when she brought her to life. Princess was a big part of her past. Some of her best memories would be building this car.

"Who did the work?" Alpha Jax asked.

"I did from the frame up along with the paint and body." Rose said proudly.

"That's a fine piece of American muscle there. Ever think about selling it?" Alpha Jax tried.

"Not if I can help it. And so far I haven't had to worry about that." Rose shot down the advances on her car quickly.

They talked back and forth for a little while. Rose knew she would have to help set up and she would have to attend the ball. Tony, being her uncle, would have the first dance with her then some pictures, mingling, and done.

Rose had little hope that her mate would be found at this time. If he was found. He would more than likely reject her. That would be that and she was surprisingly fine with that. Rose could get back to her life with no harm being done to her boys.

Chapter 35

For the last two weeks, Rose and Eva have been to each and every dress shop in the territory trying to pick out the perfect dress. Eva wanted something classy. Rose just wanted it to be over already.

Finally, they decided on a strapless black dress. It had a rhinestone bodice that laced up in the back corset style. It also had a long flowy skirt that stopped just above her knees in the front but went almost mid calf in the back. Rose had very defined shoulders and arms that was complimented by a strapless dress.

The ball had one other element. It was a masquerade ball. Why Aunt Eva thought that that would be a great idea. Rose didn't know. Apparently Aunt Eva's Blue Moon Ball was a masquerade and she believed that it would make for a more magical time.

Rose, on the other hand, was trying to figure out a way out of this. Rose knew that wasn't going to be possible though. Eva was overjoyed about Rose being there this year. The Blue Moon Ball was just one of those events that came around maybe once in a pack's history. Since it was held at a different pack each year.

Eva was also happy that Tony was taking part in place of Rose's father. The first dance was held for the fathers of the females. Like the last dance of a daughter coming out of childhood and becoming a woman. Rose had already gone through this transition but it was still an important tradition.

So, in Eva's eyes, there could be not one detail out of place or left to chance. 12 packs from across the United States would be personally invited by Alpha Jax to Harvest Moon for the Ball. They were all extremely careful not to invite Hollows along with several others in or near Hollows territory.

Alpha Jax made sure it looked more like they were broadening the scope of the invitation list to the ball instead of just keeping it for the ones local to the area. Some Alphas did that when it was their turn to host the Ball. That way they had a wider chance to mate as many as the Goddess would allow in one shot. Very few times did the Ball lead to every unmated wolf not to be mated by the time they were done.

All the arrangements were set and the packhouse was booked solid with more than 150 in attendance. Three days before the Ball, werewolves from all over would start arriving. There were mixers and get- togethers to mingle among the different packs.

They were very careful to keep the males and females separate until the Ball.

Rose, on the other hand, stayed as far away from the action as possible until that night. She would come in and help with setting up for the ballroom. She would even check with the Omegas about menus and party details. When it came to the people, Rose kept her distance.

The day before the Ball, the Royalty arrived. The 4 Lycan Kings that were blessed to oversee the Blue Moon Ball arrived at the Harvest Moon pack. They had high hopes for the highest mating in years with such a high number of werewolves in attendance.

Patrols were doubled as the numbers grew at the packhouse. Rose was on double shifts. While most of the leaders tried to take Rose off the rotation because of the Ball, Rose wasn't having it. She knew she would have to be at the Ball, but the days leading up to it she was going to do her job. Rose needed to keep herself far away from the hustle and bustle.

When Rose wasn't on patrols, she would be at the cabin sitting in the backyard watching the boys play in the snow. This was her true bliss. Jack had taken her off the shop until after the Ball because of patrols. Rose understood but she hates losing the money that came with that job.

"You know our lives are fixing to change." Snow came forward to speak with Rose.

"No, I don't think so, Snow." Rose simply said.

"I sense it. Something in the air is different." Snow said.

"Our Mate?" Rose inquired.

"I don't know. I just feel a shift is fixing to take place. I can't see what is fixing to happen." Snow said, trying to look forward but seeing nothing.

"I think we will be just fine as is. Shift or not. I don't want anything to change. We are finally happy and settled." Rose said to Snow.

"We shall see." Snow said fading to the back of Rose's mind once again.

Rose knew what she would do if it was her mate that kept setting Snow off. She would make sure he would reject her and she would finish going about her life alone. After all these years, she didn't want a mate anymore. It wasn't the fairy tales that people made it out to be and Rose knew that.

Eva came by to pick up the boys and drop off the mask Rose would be wearing for the Ball. The pack daycare had arranged a sleepover for all the pups. That way all the parents could attend the Ball. Rose kissed both her boys before helping load them into Eva's car.

"Now you two will be good and Mommy will see you in the morning. Okay?" Rose said to Dylan and Porter.

"Okay mommy." Both Dylan and Porter said getting into their car seats.

"Be careful." Rose said to Eva.

"Always. Go get ready. I'll see you in a few hours." Eva winked and side hugged Rose.

"Yes, ma'am." Rose said watching Eva climb into the car and pull away with the boys.

Rose walked back inside and went to lay everything out on the bed. Rose laughed as the garter she had picked out had a place for at least one of her knives. She thought it would be helpful if someone decided to get handsy.

Rose went and jumped into the shower. After letting the hot water beat on her, she washed her hair and body. Then after turning off the water, she reached for her towels. She wrapped one around her body and the other around her hair before stepping out of the tub.

As she stood in front of the mirror, she wiped the steam from it. Rose no longer saw the young girl that came to Harvest Moon. She was older and wiser. She had become a woman though it would seem she blinked and missed it. She wouldn't let anyone control her or her children's lives.

Rose knew she just had to get through this Ball and go on as she had all this time. One night. Just one night and it wasn't even going to be a whole night if she could help it. She was told at least one hour she would have to stay.

Rose began to do her hair first. She left the curls hanging, pulling just the front back out of her face. Eva had gotten her a lovely hair clip that looked like a silver heart. In all actuality it was white gold. A little gel and hairspray and her hair sat like a cascade of blood red curls falling neatly down her back.

Rose kept her makeup very simple. Light foundation with a hint of blush, black eyeliner and mascara to make her eyes pop a little more green. She didn't want to over do it because of the mask she would be wearing.

Rose then went to get dressed. After everything was laced and fitting just right, Rose put on her dress boots that came up to calf high. A small dagger was placed inside her garter on her upper thigh.

Rose would not back down from trouble no matter if it was a ball or not. She would still be able to protect herself at any and all cost. Rose grabbed a small black satin bag that would act like her purse and headed down the stairs.

Noting the clock time of 6:15pm, Rose knew she would have to get going to have any hope of parking at the packhouse. Rose grabbed her phone, wallet, and leather before heading for the little barn. Rose made sure to have her mask that she wouldn't put on till she got there.

Only two people knew she was coming in her own car tonight. Eva, would be pleasantly surprised to see the beauty out of the garage and on the road once more. Rose had a habit of not letting too many people see her car.

So after walking out to the barn and opening the doors, Rose got in and fired her up. Rose set herself up to pull out of the barn and not hit anything. As she pulled the dark blue beauty out along the garage, she felt like she was sneaking out of the house. Rose headed out of the driveway and toward the packhouse. Rose mused how she missed her car. That she should find more time to just take her out and just drive.

Rose waited in line behind Limo after Limo. When she finally got to the front, a young guy named Tom asked for her keys. Rose merely just laughed. "Just tell me where to park."

The guys looked slightly upset but pointed off to the side of the driveway. Rose smiled and drove over to the side lot and parked her car. Rose put on her mask and made sure she had everything before leaving the car. Rose walked up to the front door of the packhouse and everyone stared.

Rose ignored all the looks and made her way inside. Alpha Jax and Luna Hazel were standing at the entrance of the ballroom. Alpha Jax in his black tux and Luna Hazel in a flowy white gown. They looked like they belonged on top of a wedding cake.

"Rose, is that you?" Luna Hazel said, holding Rose at arms length to get the full view.

"Yes, Luna Hazel. Alpha Jax." Rose said bowing in respect.

"You look amazing." Luna Hazel gushed.

"Thank you. You look absolutely regal. Alpha Jax and you look like you should be standing on top of a wedding cake." Rose complimented.

"I know. Well anyways Beta Tony and Eva are off to the side of the stage if you want to go join them. We should be starting soon." Luna Hazel said pointing the way.

Once inside the grand ballroom, it was a sight to see. Blue, white and silver decorations hung from every inch of the ballroom with white fairy lights illuminating everything its lights could reach. The band was set up on the stage all the way on the far wall. Rose quickly walked over to Beta Tony and Eva.

Eva's eyes went wide seeing Rose all put together. Tony was just as surprised as Eva in the way every element of her outfit complimented her. Tony prayed that the Goddess would grant Rose her mate and they would be happy.

"Uncle Tony." Rose leaned over and kissed his cheek.

"Rose, you look amazing." Tony said, taking Rose's hand and kissing it. Eva just laughed at the old school gesture.

"Rose, do you want me to take your jacket or bag?" Eva asked.

Before another word could be said Alpha Jax was calling for attention to the stage. It was time for the party to start. All the unmated females and their fathers or escorts lined up and as the music began to play each girl was paraded around the outside of the dance floor and then to the center to start the first dance.

Snow kept howling in Rose's head. Rose tried to ignore her as she began the first dance with Uncle Tony. Tony had noticed something was off and had Rose on edge. He quickly mind linked with her.

"What's wrong?" Tony asked.

"Snow is howling. I don't know if it's danger or delight. This is the first time she has ever done this." Rose responded, trying not to step on his feet while dancing.

"Okay. The dance is almost over. Let's try to move to the outside of the circle. So you can go get some air and try to calm her down."

Rose merely nodded. When Rose looked up from Tony's eyes someone caught her attention. The man was 6'7" in a black tux trimmed in red. His long black hair hung to his shoulders. His crystal blue eyes seemed to pierce right into Rose's soul. As soon as the song stopped and everyone turned to clap, while Rose made a beeline for the side door.

Rose ran from the side of the packhouse to the front and ran into something hard while checking if she was being followed. He reached out and caught her before she could even stumble a little bit.

As Rose looked up, the crystal blue eyes were staring back at her. By now, Snow is not only jumping up and down, her howling had become almost deafening. Rose tried to break eye contact to get Snow to stop but the tingles and heat from his touch just made it worse. His scent of fresh pine and chocolate was almost intoxicating.

"Leaving so soon?" He asked. His voice was like honey.

"Indeed I am." Rose said, straightening herself up and trying to walk away.

"Well can I convince you to give me just one dance?" The man said keeping pace as she walked to the parking lot.

"Sorry, I don't dance. But I'm sure there are plenty of females inside that would just puddle to have you lead them around the dance floor." Rose said, grabbing her keys from her purse.

There were three guys that had come out of the front door of the packhouse. That took this man's attention for just long enough for Rose to get in the Cutlass, start it up, and peel away watching him watch her in the rearview mirror.

Chapter 36

"What was that about River?" Axle popped off, amused, never seeing a girl ever act that way toward him before.

"I believe my mate wants to play a little cat and mouse game." River said, taking a cigarette from his jacket pocket and lighting it.

"So it was her?" Sebastian said with a sly smile on his face. "But how is she here? When her scent was there?"

"I don't know but I'm not letting her get away this time. The man that was dancing with her. See if you can locate him and Alpha Jax. I'd like to have a word with them." River said, smiling at the cloud of dust that was just starting to settle.

River did get a good look at the car. So even if he couldn't describe her face because of the mask, he could the car she drove off in. Something about her made him want to run right after her, but River knew he could bide his time.

Within 30 minutes, Alpha Jax and Beta Tony sat in conference with the 4 Lycan Kings. Everyone seemed to have questions and they bet the other had the answers. After everyone was seated but River, they began the meeting.

"You wished to speak to me and my Beta, King River?" Alpha Jax was slightly confused but would handle any problem that managed to arise.

"Well mostly your Beta, but as decorum would allow, you as well." River said cooly.

"What can I help you with?" Tony said, looking to Alpha Jax to ease his concerns.

"You were dancing with a young lady. Red hair, emerald green eyes, black dress, that may or may not be the owner of a dark blue muscle car." River smirked.

"Oh no, she's the owner of that Cutlass." Tony smirked. "That's my niece, Rose. Why do you ask?"

"I believe she is my mate." River said with a sly smile.

"Where does she come from?" Sebastian spoke up.

"She is formally of the Hollows pack in southern Colorado. Since coming here, she has joined Harvest Moon." Alpha Jax answered proudly.

"Who are her parents?" Axel said, trying to put the puzzle pieces together.

"The former Gammas Kyle and Kate Wells. Since Alpha Asher has taken control I have no idea who the current Gammas are.." Alpha Jax answered knowing he purposely had nothing to do with that pack.

"What was the situation that found her here and not there?" Ryder asked.

The two men grew quiet and looked to each other for what should or shouldn't be said. In this case, that was not for them to say. They didn't want to anger the Kings but in the same way it wasn't for them to say.

"I think you need to speak to my mate Beta Eva about that. In all due respect, Rose has been through a lot in almost 5 years. Well May will make it 5 years. And as her Uncle, I can't betray my niece. Beta Eva can give more information then I'm allowed to even know." Beta Tony said looking at the anger and confusion on King Rivers face.

While River was not happy about not getting the information, he was pleased to see that they would protect their own. He did have some information and had no problems reading between the lines. He would find out what he wanted to know; he just had to be patient.

He also had a little information about the girl that was missing from the graduation ceremony party. River had picked up on her scent then and when Sebastian had seen problems and deceit that was being covered up. Which was all he could see because she wasn't there to show which one was the liar. She was the key to unlocking a lot of questions when it came to the Hollows pack.

"Alright then. I understand. I will want to meet with Beta Eva, but let's get back to the Ball before we are missed." King River said and they all stood to leave.

Once down stairs, River and Sebastain went for a walk outside in the garden. They made sure they were out of earshot of the rest of the big ears. They didn't want it announced just yet that River had found his Queen.

"What's troubling you?" Sebastian finally said, when they were far enough away.

"Why would she run from me?" River asked.

"My dear friend, there seems to be more to the story. While I can see what is meant to be and how it came to be. They play it close to the vest when it comes to this Rose. Beta Tony has seemed to take her as his own daughter. Alpha Jax seems to have high respect and admiration for her. There is Beta Eva that more than likely has the whole story, but how much will she tell?" Sebastian said, scratching his own light brown hair.

"Do you think it's vital to find out or just take her as she is?" River asked.

"I believe that would be on you as a King. You have made up your mind on this girl long before you had a face or name." Sebastian remarked.

Sebastian remembered when they had gone for the blessing of Asher and Dallas. River went crazy smelling her everywhere, but she was nowhere to be found. It took days before three boys had said that their friend was the only one out of the graduating class that had left before the King's arrival.

No one would talk about her. He remembered Gamma Kate had made no mention of a daughter, but Gamma Kyle said she had left for school. No name was given which they thought was odd. In fact there wasn't much about the Hollows pack that they didn't find off.

"She has to be mine." River said, taking another cigarette from the pack in his jacket.

"And if the Goddess wishes it, then let nothing stand between you and her." Sebastian said, looking at the full blue moon.

Chapter 37

Rose had raced home as fast as she could in the snow. Backing her car back into the barn, she sat there for a moment trying to control her heart beat. Rose almost expected when she looked up there he would be with his glowing crystal blue eyes.

She felt foolish for running away, but when the fight of flight kicks in its time to grow wings. She would have to call Eva and Tony and tell them something came up and she had to leave. Rose was sure by now they already knew she was gone.

Rose got out of the car and walked inside after locking up the barn doors. Rose thought it was funny that there would be all kinds of creatures looking for that car now. Rose also hoped that no one was looking for her right now either.

Rose got inside and went straight up stairs to take off the dress and wash all the makeup off her face. She knew she would be by herself for a while due to the boys being at the sleepover at the daycare. So after putting on her pajamas, Rose went down to the kitchen to get a glass of wine to calm her nerves.

When it finally dawned on her to look at her phone, Rose had noticed 12 missed calls. They were mostly from Aunt Eva, who would be upset that she didn't say anything before leaving. The fact she didn't get any pictures would probably be brought up as well. The text messages were from Keven. Also probably wondering where she had gotten off to.

Before Rose could put the phone down a call had come in from a private number. Thinking it was probably either a wrong number or someone messing with her, Rose didn't answer it and let it go to voicemail.

The phone rang again with the same private number. Rose wasn't dealing with the childish shit right now. When the phone rang for the fourth time, she finally decided to answer it.

"WHAT!" Rose said as she picked up the phone.

"Well hello, little wolf." Rose knew that voice all too well.

"Fuck off Dallas." Rose began to see red.

"Now is that any way to speak to me?" Dallas said smugly.

"Go To HELL before I send you there." Rose said, hanging up the phone and just watched it ring over and over again.

Rose had been getting calls from private numbers for over two months now. It was always at random and always late at night. Now she knew who was on the other end. And would block the ability to receive calls from private numbers when she had the chance to do so. Why he chose now to start harassing her again was beyond Rose. She didn't belong to Hollows anymore.

When it finally stopped, Rose got the nerve up to call Aunt Eva. Praying she would still be at the party and not out looking for her. It didn't take a few minutes before she answered the phone. Rose was grateful to still hear the music in the background.

"Are you okay?" Eva sounded relieved to see Rose's name come up on her caller ID. She knew not to go look for her. She would call once she was calm enough to do so.

"I'm fine. I just had to get out of there." Rose admitted.

"Are you sure you're okay?" Eva said always reassuring that she was there for her.

"No. But I think I'm going to go for a run to try to blow it off for right now. This wine isn't doing anything for me." Rose explained knowing Eva would know without anything having to be said.

"Okay. I'll come by after the Ball and we will talk then." Eva suggested letting Rose know she understood what she was saying.

"Sure. That will be fine." Rose said and hung up the phone.

Rose went out into the cold crisp night air. As Rose shifted into Snow in the brightest moon light, she felt free for the first time in a long time. While she ran in wolf form on patrols it wasn't the same as just running. She didn't have to answer to anyone right now. It was merely just Snow and her in the fresh powder and bright blue moon.

"Why did you do that to us?" Snow asked after being fully freed.

"I was scared. We don't need a mate. We have other things to worry about." Rose tried to justify her actions.

"You know he's been looking for us for a long time." Snow said, scolding her human counterpart.

"Well he can have another strike his fancy. I don't want our lives, all of our lives, disrupted again." Rose said defiantly.

"What if he just wants us? What if he doesn't want another?" Snow shot back.

"What about the boys?" Rose began. "After all we have been through. Dylan and Porter deserve not to be treated like a mistake or problem. They are my heart and I'll be damned if I let anyone hurt them for not being theirs." Rose angrily said.

"How do you know if you won't give him a chance? I understand we need to be here for the boys, but you need something for yourself too." Snow tried to reason. Snow knew that her very existence after finding out she was pregnant was the boys.

"I need you to trust me to do the right thing for everyone. Even if we don't get what we want. We have to worry about the whole, not just a piece." Rose tried to explain.

While arguing with Snow, Rose hadn't realized where they had run. They were all the way back at the packhouse. They were on the outside of the garden, when Snow saw him. Rose had no control whatsoever. Snow had just pushed her out.

Rose could see and hear but not react. Snow went prancing through the garden as she saw the two men standing there. One she believed was her mate. As Snow approached, she respectfully bowed then flicked her tail and howled.

"I think there is a wolf trying to get your attention." Sebastian said to River looking at the massive white wolf.

"I believe you're right." River walked closer to Snow. Snow hopped and jumped in the air kicking the fresh snow all around her.

River had gotten within one or two steps of Snow. Snow flipped her tail and howled again, taking off like a shot. Snow ran back into the woods just far enough that she could still see and hear what was going on.

"You think your lady decided to go all the way home and change into her wolf to come back and tease you?" Sebastain knew the scent was her.

"Maybe she decided to have a closer look without being so bashful." River said.

"Either way her wolf is impressive." Sebastian said, looking just into the tree line.

"I agree." River said knowing she was still there. He could still smell her scent.

Snow bounced at the words. Snow knew this would try to prove a point to Rose that maybe she should give this man a chance. Rose wasn't happy about being tricked into coming back here but she needed to see that he wasn't with anyone else. At least not someone of the shewolf persuasion.

"Okay, Drama Queen. You have had a closer look now. Let's go home." Rose tried to regain control.

"But I want him to touch me." Snow said seductively.

"NO. He'll think we are just some horny shewolf. Well current wolf. Now come on if he's really interested then he will find us soon enough." Rose convinced Snow to turn around and go home.

She could feel eyes on her as Snow turned toward the cabin and went home. Would he try to follow her? She guessed not. Too many people would have questions on where he went. Especially his friends, which one seemed to be out there with him right now anyway.

Even though Rose was against a mate at this time, Snow wondered if she might be able to change Rose's mind. Maybe even let the mate know that she wants him but she will not be easy to win over. Snow knew that this might take divine intervention. Snow knew that only time would tell what would happen with Rose and her heart.

Chapter 38

Rose got home and shifted back into her human form. She couldn't shake the heat from her skin even though it was freezing outside to a normal person. She went to take a cold shower that seemed to do the trick. She then took herself to bed.

Rose fell asleep long before the Ball was over. As she dreamed, she could feel his breath on her skin just above the nape of her neck. His touch on her back gently rubbing circles with his thumb as he held her. His voice in her ear telling her that she would only ever be his.

Rose woke in a cold sweat and with that feeling of need that she had never felt before. As she absently reached over finding the other side of the bed cold, Rose felt a sadness she had also never felt before. She blamed it on Snow making that run to see him last night.

Rose knew that there was only one cure for this. She knew a cold shower and a hot cup of coffee would put things back the way they should be. So pulling herself up out of bed, Rose headed to the shower. In Rose's eyes, that didn't help one bit. If anything it made her mind wander into scenes of him and her inside a waterfall.

When Rose got out of the shower, she was more pissed off than when she went in. There was no way this should be happening. He had only touched her for less than a minute. There was no way the charge from the electric pulse between them could have caused this to happen so quickly.

Rose knew coffee would put her mind right as rain again. So, she threw on some sweat pants and a tank top and headed down to the kitchen. Rose flipped the switch on the coffee pot and nothing. Rose looked at the coffee pot which was somehow unplugged. Rose plugged it back in and still nothing.

Much to Rose's dismay, the coffee pot she had gotten for a graduation gift, almost five years ago, had finally died. Rose jumped up and down cussing the Goddess forsaken pot when she heard someone laughing behind her. Rose slowly turned around to find Eva holding a very large cup of coffee.

"Rough morning?" Eva laughed.

"You could say that. Rough night, Rough morning. Cold shower and no coffee." Rose very adamantly told Eva.

"Well when I came by last night, I had noticed your coffee pot wasn't letting me set the timer. So, I tried to just run a pot of water through it and noticed it was dead. So, I figured I would stop by and bring you a cup. We both know you can't go without your coffee." Eva mused at the sight in front of her.

"Well I thank you so very kindly." Rose said, taking the coffee cup from Eva.

"You want to talk about it?" Eva asked knowing the events from last night were still bothering her.

"Yes and no." Rose said, taking the first sip of the hot coffee. Rose was finally getting caffeine and she was happy about that.

"Are you sure? Because it seems like a certain someone has you all in a twist this morning." Eva said remembering what it was like when she had found Tony.

"I don't get it. I really don't get it. I mean we locked eyes for less than a minute. Then I was trying to get out of there and ran slap into him. I almost fell and then he caught me. Heat and electricity in the likes of which I have never ever felt ran through my body. Thankfully, I guess his friends came out and got his attention and I jumped into the car and peeled away like I was a getaway driver." Rose spoke while drinking her coffee.

"Then Snow decided, after I decided to go for a run, to run right into the packhouse garden where he happened to be standing with one of the same friends. She flipped her tail at him like a damn bitch in heat. Then I finally got back here and tried to get some sleep and well I found none to say the least." Rose said a little embarrassed to admit to the dreams she was having about this guy.

Eva sat at the island listening. She was trying to hide the growing smile on her face. Rose had found her mate but now was going off the rails. This would happen until they either accepted or rejected each other. Eva desperately hoped she would accept him.

"So why don't you go talk to him?" Eva suggested.

"Because I can't. First he probably thinks I'm some stupid idiot for running away. Second, if he doesn't think that after Snow's performance last night he's gonna think I'm some horny shewolf. The only thing I want is his rejection. So, I can get on with my life." Rose propped on her hands and covered her face in desperation.

"Hunny, I don't think he thinks your stupid or some random shewolf." Eva tried to talk Rose off the ledge she was currently on.

"How do you know?" Rose's eyes pleaded for understanding.

"Mainly because he pulled Alpha Jax and Uncle Tony into a meeting about 30 minutes after you left." Eva admitted.

"Why would Alpha Jax be pulled into a meeting by another Alpha? Wouldn't he just make him find out on his own? I mean I understand decorum and everything but in the middle of the Ball?"

Rose inquired. She knew this guy had to be an Alpha from the power that was coming off of him.

Eva looked at her confused. Then it hit her. Rose didn't know that River was a King not an Alpha. One other thing dawned on Eva. Did Rose even know his name? She kept calling him that guy or man. So it was safe to say No she didn't.

Eva started laughing and it was now Rose's turn to be confused. *What could possibly be so funny?* Rose thought. Rose then started laughing for no other reason than it was hard not to right now. Rose's entire morning had been shot to hell but there they were sitting laughing in the kitchen like a couple of loons.

"Do you even know his name?" Eva finally choked out.

"No, why would I?" Rose said, finally understanding the joke.

"Oh my. Rose, you didn't ask him his name?" Eva couldn't control herself.

"No, I was a little busy trying to get away from him." Rose putting her head back in her hands.

"So what makes you think he's an Alpha then?" Eva finally regained her composure and asked Rose.

"The power that was coming off of him. I could feel it when Uncle Tony and I were dancing. That's what caught my attention." Rose said to Eva.

"Hunny, You can read auras but that wasn't the right read." Eva tried to explain without going back into the giggles.

"Well if he's not an Alpha then what is he?" Rose said, exasperated by this guy as the current topic of conversation.

"He's a Lycan King. More specifically the Lycan King of the South." Eva looked at Rose while her eyes went wide.

"He's a Lycan? How is that possible? I'm just a werewolf, nothing special." Rose began to pace around the kitchen.

"Well the Goddess seems to think you have something very special if she mated you to such a powerful being." Eva said, trying to get Rose to calm down.

Eva got up and wrapped her arms around Rose to keep her still. She knew if she didn't, Rose might explode right where she stood. Rose started to cry, and that broke Eva's heart. Finding your mate is supposed to be a happy time in your life. At this point for Rose, it was anything but.

"I will never let anything happen to you or your boys. If he can't accept them and treat them like his own. Then he is a good for nothing that doesn't deserve you as his mate." Eva tried to calm Rose. Eva knew that her mind immediately jumped to the boys and the fact that most werewolves had a hard time accepting other children as their own. Eva knew that Rose was thinking that a Lycan would probably be worse.

"Hey why don't you and me go and get something to eat. We will work out a plan and then go from there." Eva figured if she could just get Rose to think rationally right now it would be a win in her book.

"Okay." Rose tried to dry her eyes.

Rose went upstairs to get ready. After a few minutes, Rose was dressed in a black tank with a black button up, black jeans, and her black boots. Her hair was pulled back in braids and a bandana was worn across the top of her hair.

Rose slung on her leather and with her bag in hand, Eva and Rose walked out of the house and toward the car.

Chapter 39

Eva and Rose came up with the plan over cheese fries and ice cream sodas at Lunar Moon Cafe. She would set up a meeting with the Lycan King River and explain Rose's side. Then and only then, would Rose have a sit down with him for a formal rejection.

Eva hoped once she did talk to River that she could explain he would have to earn her trust before she would be able to accept him. Give him the same information everyone else has. In case, he starts asking around. This would buy Eva sometime in changing Rose's mind.

After Eva dropped Rose back off at the house, she set off to find the Lycan King. She explained to Rose that she would keep the boys and let Rose have some alone time. Eva knew Rose needed to get her head in the right space.

Eva knew that the Kings were staying at the packhouse. She also knew until they left the territory Tony would be at the packhouse arranging everything with their teams. In Eva's eyes, it was killing two birds with one stone while seeing her husband and tracking down River.

Tony had told Eva early that morning, he would be picking up the boys from the daycare sleepover and bringing them to the packhouse to play with Dom, the Alpha's son. As Eva arrived at the packhouse, she was amused by the sight in the side yard.

Six grown men chasing three little boys through the snow. The funny thing was the little ones looked like they were winning. Snowballs were being thrown and the six men looked to be completely out of breath trying to fight back. Lycans and werewolves don't typically didn't run out of breath but when trying to keep up with the three little ones not a third their size they would lose in the fight at hand.

Dylan and Porter saw Eva pull up and abandoned the fight. They met her in the side yard with red checks and big smiles. They looked around her to see if Rose came with her. Their faces fell a little when they didn't see mommy.

"Where is mommy?" Dylan asked with a little bit of a lip.

"Mommy will be coming in a little bit. She had to do something with Santa for a little bit." Eva said to the boys. They seemed to deem this answer acceptable. Their smiles returned beaming on their little faces.

"We are winning!" Porter announced and took Dylan's hand and ran back to the fight.

Tony walked over as the boys ran back. Like the boys, Tony was looking for Rose to pop around the corner like always ready to throw a snowball. He knew something was up when she was nowhere to be found. Rose never wanted to be away from the boys ever.

"Hey babe." Tony walked over and kissed Eva on the cheek.

"Hey. Hey. How many times do I have to tell you the boys are going to win in a snowball fight? How did this even start?" Eva said as she kissed him back.

"Well the three busted into the office and challenged all of us to a snowball fight, and for the record we are letting them win." Tony said knowing that wasn't really the case. "Rose, okay?"

"In a manner of speaking. She just needs a little bit of time right now. And a new coffee pot." Eva smiled.

"It finally died?" Tony laughed.

"Yes, and I caught the show as she was cussing it out." Eva couldn't help but giggle.

"Does she know what she wants yet?" Tony said, eyeing River chasing the boys.

"Yes, but I think she is wrong. I need to speak with him for a few moments." Eva said, keeping an eye on the boys while she talked to Tony.

"I can probably set something up probably for tomorrow." Tony said, knowing it would have to go through the formalities.

"No. Now! Rose is freaking out and not thinking clearly. I need to know his intentions and hopefully fix this before the Goddess, herself, is the only one that can." Eva said, walking toward the group of men playing with the boys. Tony knew when Eva had something to deal with all bets were off at that moment.

"Beta Eva, so good to see you today." Alpha Jax said, trying to catch his son.

"And you Alpha Jax." Eva said, eyeing the other four men.

"May I introduce King River, King Sebastain, King Axel, and King Ryder." Alpha Jax said, pointing each one of the men out.

"Your Majesties." Eva said bowing.

"Beta Eva, Your Beta Tony's mate, correct?" King Axel said, looking to River.

"I am indeed, and while this is completely out of the normal order." Eva pointed at King River. "I need to have a word with you. Now if at all possible. This won't wait."

"Yes ma'am." King River moved and the others went to move with him.

"Not you three. Just him." Eva said and turned on her heels to walk toward the packhouse.

"You're in trouble." Ryder mused at River.

"You good?" Sebastian asked, looking at the now impatient Eva standing by the side door to the packhouse.

"Yes, I got this." River remarked looking at Beta Tony who had his hands up half in apologies half in this is on you. "I see where Rose gets her fire."

"She gets a lot for her Aunt." Tony mused.

River walked through the door as Eva led the way. She walked over to a room right off the formal living room that ended up being a library. Before going in, Eva waved down an Omega to ask for coffee and cookies to be brought into the library.

As they entered the grand library, Eva found a round table to sit at and checked that no one was currently in there. No one really came in here unless there was research to be done about history or pack guidelines. Hence the reason, Eva chose this room to have this conversation.

"Please sit your Majesty." Eva motioned to the seat on the other side of the table.

"River please. I mean we are about to be family. Titles really don't mean much to us unless we have to use them." River explained. Even though they were Kings, they still saw themselves like any other Lycan, just with a bit more power. They typically didn't abuse the power entrusted to them.

"Well, I'm happy you see the match is favorable. But I have a lot to say and I need you not to react. It would be like shooting the person that is trying to help you." As Eva said this the Omega appeared and brought in the tray of coffee and cookies.

"Thank you, Sky. Can you tell anyone that wants to use the library that it's occupied today?" Eva smiled at the girl.

"Yes, Beta Eva." Sky said leaving the room.

As soon as the door was closed River spoke. "Why wouldn't I find my mate favorable?" River said, taking a cookie from the plate.

"Let's start with something a little more simple. Do you want children?" Eva said getting right to the point.

"Yes, actually I do." River thought it was a weird question but he would play along.

"What do you think of Dylan and Porter?" Eva studied his every movement.

"They are absolutely adorable. You nephews?" River asked.

"Great-nephews. They are Rose's boys." Eva laid it out there and River nearly choked on the cookie.

"Come again?" River said horsley.

"The twins belong to Rose. Rose is their mother." Eva explained trying to understand what he wasn't getting.

"That's impossible." River began but Eva cut him off.

"Now this is where you listen and hear me out, because my niece has been through hell. She has come out stronger for it." Eva waited until River nodded his head before she continued.

"You will not know the whole story. Not by me anyway. That is for Rose to say and no one else. But I will tell you what everyone else knows." Eva began pouring her cup of coffee. "A week, well two weeks before she was supposed to graduate, Rose found out she was pregnant. She had no knowledge of the how but had a suspicion on the who. When that bastard was confronted he didn't deny it. He drugged her with LycanBerry. Thankfully, Rose has no memory of that night.

When she told her mother, hoping for some understanding and support, she was met with outrage. How could Rose have done this to her and all. So, I was called in with no knowledge of what was going till Rose got here.

Since she had the boys she hasn't had any contact with Hollows pack or those within it except for her three friends. Kate was extremely pissed when Rose had told her father of the pregnancy and the fact she wouldn't put the boys up for adoption.

She has been on one date since having the boys. But that was basically friends. He realized Rose was right in not having a romantic attachment with a female that wasn't his mate. Rose and him are still very good friends.

Other than that, Rose lives for her boys. They are the reason she works two jobs to make sure they don't want for anything. She hates asking for help or even admitting she needs it. Hell we have to make up little events from time to time so we know she actually took time to sleep." Eva laid it all out there.

"The Father?" River asked through gritted teeth and glowing eyes.

"Rose won't give up the name to anyone. To add insult to injury, he rejected her and the children. At the time, she didn't know it was twins yet." Eva said.

"So let me see if I got this straight. Rose was slipped LycanBerry without consent, taken advantage of and then tossed away by not only the bastard that did this but her family?" River said, making sure he had all the details correct through all the anger.

"Yes. When she came here, I took care of her. Tony and I were there for everything. Even their births." Eva admitted.

"And her feelings toward me?" River asked knowing that he had to know.

"She wants you to reject her, and find a more suitable mate. While the bond is working on her. She wants to do what's right by her kids. She is more than willing to be alone. I don't believe that is what's best for her. Hence the reason we are having this conversation." Eva said, sipping on her coffee.

River sat there for a moment trying not to fly off the handle. Rose had been through hell. She was strong. She was an amazing mother and was adored by her sons. Now everything made sense. There were more missing pieces but the important ones were present.

"I won't reject her. I swear it before the Goddess right here and now. I, River Easton, Lycan King of the South will never reject or accept the rejection of Rose Wells." River said as his crystal blue eye glowed with a silent promise.

"Then, my dear, we have some work to do." Eva said, looking at him so seriously. "I will say this. If you hurt her, those boys, or don't treat them like they should be... I swear there is not a place for you to hide. Do WE understand each other?"

"Yes ma'am. I know this was not her doing, and even if it was. They came from her. Rose is my mate, which makes those boys mine as well." River said, understanding the load he just put on himself.

They sat and talked for the better part of two hours before Sebastain finally had to come in to make sure River was still in one piece. Eva looked upset and even though River could hold his own against anyone, he would let any female tear his butt up because he would never fight back.

Within a little more time the four Lycan Kings, Beta Tony and Alpha Jax had joined in on the conversation. Luna Hazel took the boys upstairs to get them washed up for nap time. Between the seven of them they hatched a plan to at least get Rose to talk to him.

Hoping he could be a smooth enough talker to turn it into a date. Eva hated to have to go this route, but she knew Rose needed that special person even if she didn't know she needed him. Two, three days tops to get them at least on their first date. Eva prayed to the Goddess this would work.

Chapter 40

Standing on the mountain overlooking the sand and the plains at one time, Rose stood there in a strapless black sundress. She could feel the warm breeze on her skin. Rose could see the sun setting in one direction and the moon rising in the other.

The moon was so full and bright. As twilight set in and the stairs started to appear one by one, Rose felt his strong arms around her waist. Pulling her closer to him, Rose felt safe in his arms.

Rose's hair was pulled up in a bun leaving her neck exposed. She could feel the trail of kisses from her bare shoulder up to her unmarked neck. When he kissed her marking spot, heat and sparks erupted through her body. As she turned around to look him in the eyes, the alarm clock started screaming at her.

As she came out of the heated haze, Rose was thoroughly pissed off. Her body was on fire and she could still feel his touch from the dream. As she wrapped her arms around herself, she knew deep down she wanted to feel his touch for real.

"What could be the harm in giving him a chance? If it makes these dreams go away." Rose thought to herself as she realized the heat from her core was going to drive her mad.

One long cold shower later, Rose was headed out of the house early. She knew she would have to stop by Lunar Moon Cafe to get her coffee. She hadn't replaced the coffee pot yet. As she was headed to the van she looked back at the barn.

"Why the hell not." Rose thought walking past the van and down to the barn.

She opened up the barn doors. With a wicked grin, she got into the Cutlass and fired her up. Princess was reserved for special occasions and Saturday night drives. This morning she was going to go to the shop in style. Why she never drove her during the day was a current mystery.

Rose pulled out just letting her sing. She figured if any one was looking for her then she might as well pull out the big neon sign of here she was in all her glory. Rose always chose to meet problems head on.

The quicker she could nip this in the bud the quicker she could get on with her life. She was set on rejection but the dreams and heat she kept feeling was enough to drive a sane person mad. One way or another this had to be dealt with.

Once she had her coffee in hand, she headed to the shop. Rose was getting plenty of looks and compliments on the car. She merely smiled and thanked them. She tried to keep her tone light if anyone spoke to her. This made her feel better and seemed to let the dreams of the night just fade away.

Once at the shop, Rose opened as normal. She had seen in her absence that things were not handled the way they needed to be. Rose just took off her leather and hung it on the coat rack. She started to put things back into place. Rose kept a tiddy shop and went completely nuts if things were not in their place.

Within three hours, Rose had inventory straightened and put away. Rose had reviewed all incoming and outgoing work orders. She also made two pots of coffee, and called in parts orders for what was either needed or low on for the shop.

She was so engrossed in her work that she hadn't noticed the very large man standing next to the bay door. River was just watching her walk back and forth putting things away and checking her paperwork. He wanted to get her attention but found more amusement in just watching her do her job.

About the time she went to go out of the bay to pull the first car in, Rose jumped and screamed. She was caught completely off guard. He was just standing there with a sly little smile on his face. She had been lost in her own little world, and absently thinking about him. When bam she looked up and he was just standing there watching her.

"Oh my. I'm so sorry. Have you been waiting long?" Rose tried to calm herself and keep it professional.

"Not at all. Just thought I would wait my turn. You looked like a woman on a mission." River said with a slightly seductive smile on his face.

Rose nervously laughed and tried to avoid his direct eye contact. It was something about those crystal blue eyes that would draw Rose in and stop her in her tracks. She knew she would never get out of those pools for mesmerizing seductiveness.

Rose knew being at work in a public place gave her a slight disadvantage. Rose had to keep it professional. She couldn't be rude, overly emotional, or even just run. Rose knew she was going to have to play it cool. Even though Rose just wanted not to.

River was close enough that Rose could smell him. His scent was enough to start her own engine running. Rose knew that she couldn't have that. One because she was at work and two because even though she had come to the decision to give him a chance. She wasn't going to make it easy on him.

"How can I help you?" Rose finally said, trying to distract herself.

"I need an oil change and a tune up." River said, trying his best not to reach out and touch her.

"I can handle that. What kind of vehicle will we be servicing today?" Rose walked out of the shop with a clipboard to check it in and what she saw was just as amazing as seeing him.

Sitting in the parking lot right outside the closed bay door was a 1956 Ford Fairlane Sunliner. It was sky blue with matching blue and white leather seats. Rose couldn't help herself. She walked over and opened the door to pop the hood. The smell of the treated leather made her smile. Someone cared about this car very much.

When she raised the hood, Rose saw the original 312 V8 staring back at her. Her heart just sang with delight. The engine was clean, and when she pulled the dipstick. She noticed that the oil was clean. Maybe had a couple hundred miles on it but looked very recent. The plug wires looked brand new also. Everything on this car looked new down to the belts.

As she closed the hood, she eyed the guy standing there watching her. She did her normal inspection of the car and noticed it was very well kept. No tears in the seats or even a loose drink bottle on the floorboard. The convertible top didn't even have a rip or tear in it. It was a sight to see. Rose swore this guy drove it straight out of a classic car magazine with how clean it was.

"Are you sure you need an oil change and tune up?" Rose said looking at the car and then back at the tall drink of water still propping on the side of the bay door.

"Well she has been sitting for a little while. So I thought she might need it." River said back, watching her every move while examining the car.

"Nope. She's extremely well kept. No tears or holes. Not even a speck of rust." Rose admired running her hand over the hood.

"I appreciate the look over. I was told you were the best in the territory with these older cars. By the way, I never did catch your name the other night." River said, taking a careful step toward her.

"Probably because I didn't throw it." Rose said, trying to figure out if she could get back around him without touching him.

"So, Are you going to throw it now?" River said, taking another careful step toward her.

"Rose Wells." Rose said, pointing to the name tag on her shirt.

"Well it's nice to meet you Ms. Rose." River boldly steps forward this time taking Rose's hand and kissing the back of her knuckles.

Rose felt fire racing through her blood. Not a spark but a blaze running through her body like a wildfire. Rose wanted to just jerk her hand away but something inside her wanted to see what was going to happen next. When he did drop her hand, Rose felt both relieved and regret not wanting him to stop.

"Your name? I gave you mine. Even though I'm pretty sure you already knew it." Rose tried to make her voice sound more steady than it currently could at the moment.

"River Easton, Lycan Kind of the South." River said, bowing a little.

"Well Your Majesty, I love to stay and shoot the breeze but I have work to do." Rose tried to walk around him but ended up brushing right up against him.

This contact was just a little more than Rose could bear. So when he leaned in and kissed her, she didn't stop him. When their lips brushed against each other the blaze in her blood made things ten times worse. She was sure the snow would melt from under feet. Her need for him to touch her was enough to scare her a bit and make her jump back.

Rose could barely breathe and just stared at him with her hands up to stay back. She made a wide circle around him to get back into the shop. As Rose tried to cross the threshold, he caught her by her waist.

"Dinner with me tonight?" River said, just as breathless as she was.

"I can't. I've got to get my boys tonight." Rose said, breaking free.

"Find a sitter. Please?" River knew he needed just one night to try to convince her to be his.

"I can't, I have not seen my boys in two days. You will understand that I am a mother first." Rose said walking back into the shop and far enough away from him.

"Fine. Then tomorrow night?" River would pick everyday of the month if he had to.

"I have a patrol." Rose said, picking up another clipboard.

"Wednesday?" River was starting to want to just walk over and through her over his shoulder and walk out with her. He also knew that there was a right way to earn her.

"Patrol. Here let me help you out. I have patrol every other night, and when I don't I have my sons. So the best thing for you to do is get this over with and let us both get on with our lives." Rose said it but it came out with less conviction than she meant for it to.

River took one step forward and engulfed Rose in his arms. "Look here, you little fireball. I'm not going anywhere and I refuse to ever reject you. So either you let me take you to dinner or I can keep coming back day after day. Your choice." His glowing crystal blue eyes to prove he wasn't playing.

"Fine! You go talk to Beta Tony and Eva. If I don't get a call by 5:30, then you're just shit outta luck." Rose said, breaking his hold and walking away from him.

River stood there for a few minutes. Then merely nodded and walked out of the garage. He got back in the Fairlane and started her up. He knew he was going to have to control himself if he was going to make Rose see that he wasn't going anywhere without her and the boys.

The amount of adrenaline that poured through his veins right that second could make him fly. Her touch, smell, and even the taste of her lips were enough for him to lay down anything for her. Rose still resisted and that made it all that much more fun for him.

Chapter 41

Rose's blood did not stop pulsing even after River left. The need in her grew and the frustration at herself for not allowing herself to have it. To just accept him and let him take away the growing heat in her core.

Rose tried to push the thoughts of him and anything to do with him out of her mind. There was no such luck especially since Snow was now howling and calling for him. Rose finally made the decision to give him one chance to shut Snow up for the time being.

As Rose was pulling the last car for the day off the rack, her phone rang. She looked at the clock seeing it was just after 4pm. She knew who it was. She didn't even have to look when she answered.

"Ello." Rose picked the phone.

"Hey sweetie. How was your day?" Eva said knowing already that River had been there.

"Same as every other day." Rose said, waiting for Eva to bring River up first.

"Well… I heard you have a date tonight?" Eva said cheerfully.

"Only if I have a sitter. Unless this is you calling to tell me you're getting me out of it." Rose already knew the answer to that.

"Nope. Just calling to tell you I dropped something off for you to wear and that Uncle Tony is picking up the boys." Eva said, smiling evilly.

"Why do I need to give in to this? I have been doing fine on my own." Rose blurted out.

"Because the Goddess has given you a match and if she believes he's worthy then you should too!" Eva said always knowing what to say to get Rose's attention.

"Fine. One chance. That's it. Even if I have to reject him myself." Rose finally said.

"That's fine. So, are you going to call him?" Eva said knowing he was literally down stairs, playing with the twins.

"I don't have his number." Rose admitted.

"That's fine. I'll give him yours." Eva giggled.

"Fine. I happen to be done for the day. I'm going to talk to Jack." Rose said, angry and slightly excited about hearing his voice again.

"Okay sweetie. I'll talk to you later." Eva said, hanging up the phone.

Rose pulled the car out of the shop and walked into the office. Jack was sitting at the desk working on invoices. He looked up and smiled when he saw Rose come in. Rose put the ticket for the car on his desk and then plopped onto the couch.

Jack could tell she was more flustered than normal. He knew it had something to do with the scene he had witnessed earlier. Jack had heard through the grapevine that King River had found his mate. Everyone was a little more taken back that it was Rose.

"Rough day?" Jack finally said testing the waters.

"You could say that. We got something else or am I done for the day?" Rose asked knowing it was going to take a minute to get cleaned up.

"It can wait till tomorrow. If you need to go." Jack smiled.

"Jack, why does this keep happening to me?" Rose finally said something serious and Jack was a little surprised.

"Mates find you when the Goddess deems it time. I found mine. I lost her some years back to a car accident. But I will never forget her. Once you find that love that shakes you to the core, can't breathe, can't think, over the moon kind of love. It just does something to you. That young man seems to have it bad." Jack mused.

"Oh no, he doesn't. He just thinks he does." Rose fired back.

"No, he does. I saw the way he couldn't keep his hands off of you." Jack teased at the sight.

"Oh Goddess. I'm leaving now. I'll see you tomorrow." Rose said turning bright red leaving the office.

Once Rose left the shop, she went straight home instead of going by the coffee shop to get her afternoon jolt. As soon as she got to the house, she didn't even put the Cutlass back in the barn. She went straight in and to the shower. She knew there was no way of getting out of this. She, however, would have to make the most of it. When she got to her room, she saw the dress that Eva had brought by and froze in her tracks.

A strapless black dress with a flowy knee length skirt lay on her bed. She knew not to touch it right that second because she had oil and grease on her hands. Rose thought about the dream and wondered if this was fate or otherwise.

She went into the shower trying to put the dream and the dress from her mind for the time being. After twenty minutes of letting the hot water hit her and wash away some of the anxiety, Rose washed herself up and then got a towel to wrap around her.

Rose figured she would play her part well. No reason not to have some fun with it. Rose left her hair loose with her curls falling down over her bare shoulders. She pulled just the front up and out of her face. With just a little bit of gel and hairspray her curls would stay in place for even the strongest winds.

Rose kept her makeup light as always. She put on her black eye liner to make her eyes pop. Rose had noticed that her cheeks already had a pinkish red hue. So, there was no need for blush. A slightly redder than normal lip gloss adorned her look.

Rose stepped back and looked at the finished product. She knew this would probably drive him crazy and Rose was going to play that to her advantage. Rose had no intention of giving in easily. If he wanted her then by the Goddess, he was going to have to work for it.

Rose slipped into her room to finish getting ready. Rose put on the garder from the ball gown. She liked how it neatly hid a knife in case she happened to need it. While she always carried one in her jacket, this one no one knew was there. After slipping into the strapless dress, the phone rang.

Jumping around the bedroom, Rose tried to zip up her dress. As she got the zipper up, she answered the phone.

"Ello?" Rose said finally getting the zipper all the way up.

"Well. Hello Little Wolf." Dallas's voice dripped with honey and acid.

"What part of go to fucking hell did you not understand? Don't call this fucking number again." Rose said and hung up the phone.

Rose cursed herself for not looking at the caller ID before answering the phone. Before she could put the phone back on the dresser, it rang again. Private number on the caller ID once again. Rose thought it might be a trick and almost didn't answer, but Snow started going off in her head.

"WHAT?" Rose answered with a little bite on it.

"Rose?" River's seductive voice turned to confusion and concern.

"Yeah, River?" Rose asked even though she already knew the voice.

"Bad time?" River asked a little more aware that something wasn't right.

"No. Just life. What's up?" Rose said quickly reverting the conversation.

"I was just calling to find out how we were going to work this. I mean, typically, I would come pick you up, but I don't know where you live." River said, trying to see if he could hear any signs of distress in her voice.

"I think it would be better for us to just meet somewhere. Taking separate vechinals would ensure if this doesn't go well we can just leave." Rose said, trying to be real with him.

"What if the date does goes well?" River said cheekily.

"Only one way to find out." Rose challenged.

"Okay then." River would accept any challenge laid at his feet. "There is this little place on the other side of the territory. Dakota's? Know it?"

"Yeah, I know where it is." Rose mused. That was one of the fancier places around these parts.

"30 minutes?" River said.

"I'll be there." Rose said, hanging up the phone.

Rose looked at herself in the mirror. She was giving herself a once over. She was then trying to calm her nerves. Snow began to stir.

"You got this." Snow said.

"I'm not sure this is a good idea." Rose said, trying to breathe.

"I'm right here watching your back. He is our mate. But if I don't like what I see I will let you know." Snow was reassuring.

"One sign of trouble." Rose remarked.

"And I have no problem watching you cut him into little pieces." Snow knew she just needed time with him and what she had seen would play out.

"Alright." Rose said, squaring up her shoulders and walking out of the room to grab her calf high boots.

30 minutes later, Rose was pulling up at Dakota's. She smiled when she saw that River had come in the Fairlane. Rose secretly wondered if he would let her drive it, or if he was one of those guys that didn't let women drive his car.

River saw the blue beast pull into the parking lot and smiled. From what he was told, Rose only brought that car out on special occasions. River believed that meant something that she took it out tonight. That or she thought she would need a quick getaway.

He walked over as soon as she was parked next to his own blue beauty. River opened the door for Rose. He offered his hand to help her out of the car. Both gestures did not go unnoticed by Rose.

"You look amazing." River complimented.

"You clean up nice as well." Rose said, looking at River.

He wore a black button up, black jeans, and a rather nice pair of black and gray cowboy boots. He left the top three buttons undone to reveal a chest tattoo. His hair was slicked back the same way it was the night at the Ball. With River being hot natured, he wore no jacket.

"Shall we?" River escorted Rose to the door.

Once inside the restaurant, Rose could see that it indeed was as fancy as people had said. A man walked around playing a violin. The decorations were mainly dark with a hint of white here and there. This was not her taste but he picked.

"Good evening." A perky young woman greeted them. She was smiling hard at River. "Reservations?"

"Yes, River Easton for two." River said, bringing Rose's hand to his lips to prove a point to any and all onlookers.

"Yes, sir. This way please." The woman remarked.

They were led through the dining room to a door. Apparently, River had booked a private dining room for the two of them. Rose didn't want to act impressed, but deep down she was. River reached over to help Rose with her leather jacket.

River pulled out Rose's chair and hung her jacket on the back. He then walked to his side of the table. The lady merely put the menus down and left the room. It was safe to say she knew she wasn't going to get anywhere with him.

"So should we order wine or do you drink?" River asked.

"I'm driving. Plus I don't think drinking with someone I just met is a wise decision." Rose tried to keep her tone even and not offend.

"That's fair. I would like to thank you for coming out with me tonight." River said, looking over at her.

"Well, in all fairness, I can't have you showing up at my work everyday until I agreed." Rose admitted.

"Yeah, I'm a bit persistent when I want something." River admitted.

"I would say that. So…" Rose began. "So, are we going to get to the point here or just play it out?

River put down the menu and looked Rose in her emerald green eyes. He admired that she was a "to the point" kind of woman. She admitted an aura that was more than just a Gamma's daughter and he didn't need alcohol to be completely intoxicated by her.

"And what point might that be?" River asked, a little amused by her.

"Wine and dine? You think I'm just going to fall all over you?" Rose was a little more defiant than normal.

River started laughing a little bit. He didn't expect that but he knew he should have. Her eyes glowed a little bit greener and River knew the Goddess couldn't have picked a more perfect mate for him.

"Not at all. I like showing the person I'm with my undivided attention. Hence the private room. Wine, some people like a drink with dinner or after a long day. You choose not to. Which tells me you're very safety conscious on all fronts. You're not impressed by all this." River waves his hands around. "Which tells me that you're either really high maintenance and hard to impress. But I'm guessing you're not materialistic at all.

You have a very nice car. From what I'm told you rebuilt it from the frame up. This tells me you appearcate the past and see beauty through it all. You're not afraid of things being hard and that wall you built, would give the Great Wall in China a run for its money." River rattled off.

Rose just sat there perplexed by the man in front of her. He had her number alright, but he never once broke eye contact. This made Rose have a burning in her belly she couldn't explain. How could he read her so well?

"Really you think you know me?" Rose fired back more out of amusement than anger.

"Rose, it would probably take me ten lifetimes and still not know everything about you. But I'm going to do my best to figure it out." River said.

"Well, what do you want to know?" Rose sat back and giggled.

That broke the ice a little bit. The two of them sat there for hours enjoying each other's company. Diner and dessert and a lot of conversation. Likes and dislikes on everything from foods, movies, cars, and a lot about the boys.

River understood she would always be a mother first. He even suggested that they take the boys on the next date. Rose was agreeable to that. She would have to see how they interacted before she made any real decisions.

At the end of the night, River walked Rose to her car. He kissed her lightly on the hand before she got in and drove away. River was sure that he had chipped away at the wall. He would not let her regret that.

Chapter 42

After the first date, Rose's dreams of River had gotten more intense. That led to more cold showers and a whole lot more caffeine due to a lack of rest. Rose found it funny that every morning she would cuss the broken coffee pot and have to leave the house early to go by the Lunar Moon Cafe after dropping the boys off at daycare.

Friday morning, Rose woke up from a particularly steamy dream. River was in nothing but a pair of boxes serving her breakfast in bed with a side of him for dessert. As she woke up to the screaming of her alarm clock, Rose knew she couldn't last much longer like this.

She had never dreamed of a guy before. She could still feel where his hands had been even after waking up. The cold showers weren't really doing anything at this point except reminding her of why she was in there in the first place.

Rose hoped even prayed that River was going through the same relentless toucher at this point. Rose thought if she was going to go through hell. He might as well be too! All is fair in love and war.

Rose didn't even have patrols to take her mind and energy off the situation. Everyone knew she had found her mate and even though they had not accepted or marked each other, Rose was still a Queen.

Pack rules are pack rules. Since Rose was considered Royalty, she no longer did the grunt work as they called it. They couldn't keep her from the shop and that is where she found her solace right now. She had to keep busy or go completely insane right now.

It was half way through her day when Rose smelled his scent flowing through the open bay door. He had been nice enough to keep his distance, while Rose had the boys. A quick text to ask about her day or what she would be doing after work. He watched from afar giving her time and space.

River noticed, since meeting him though, that Princess had not been put back in the barn. Rose practically drove that car everywhere. Almost like she was done trying to blend in where her bright light wouldn't let her. She was also a bit more social from what others had said. Rose always remained a creature of habit but just a little bit more outgoing.

Through all the time and space, he had to see her. Rose wouldn't answer about plans for the weekend so it was time to come face to face. River had gotten smart though. He had found out from Eva that Rose was most definitely a coffee drinker and how she took her coffee. So when he showed up at the shop he was not empty handed.

"Hey." River said, standing at the edge of the bay door.

"Hey. Hey." Rose answered back.

"I got something for you." River said, holding a very large cup of iced coffee.

"Is that a double caramel macchiato from Lunar Moon?" Rose eyed the cup and the dark handsome man holding it.

"Sure is. I also brought you cheese fries. Eva said they are your favorite." River smiled holding the bag of extra cheesy cheese fries.

"Oh my Goddess. You shouldn't have." Rose dropped the clipboard on the workbench and waved him over.

"Sit her. I gotta go wash my hands." Rose motioned to a spot on the workbench that had nothing on it.

"I brought a fork." River laughed when Rose looked at him like he was crazy.

"You don't eat cheese fries, especially Luna Moon's cheese fries, with a fork. We are not classy around this place." Rose explained going over to the sink and trying to get as much gunk off her hands as she could.

Rose wiped her hands on a clean towel and then walked back over and straddled the bench. Opening the container of fries, River watched Rose thoroughly enjoy the first couple of fries. He had never known a girl to have this kind of taste before.

"Thank you so much. I forgot my lunch and sometimes Eva brings me something. With everything going on at the packhouse for Christmas, I know she has her plate full right now." Rose said not even faltering with eating and talking without making it look gross.

She wasn't nervous around him this time. Rose didn't question it all that much. River had food and caffeine. Rose saw this as a middle ground. Rose did smile at the fact of her dream and then him bringing her lunch. But to keep her growing need down, she would not think about it too much.

"Yea, I know. They had the whole packhouse decorated and something about cookies with Santa." River said just to keep her talking.

"Tradition is strong here. The boys have gone every year since they were born. Uncle Tony took them their first year. They were only a few weeks old." Rose remembered the first time she was away form the boys, the conversation with Eva, and how each year they go and drink coffee to mark the occasion.

"So are you taking the boys this year?" River asked.

"Yeah. Then they have a sleepover with Dom. I still have to do the Christmas shopping." Rose thought her days were running together.

"Well, is there anything I can do to help?" River asking, figuring this was his in.

"Oh no, I wouldn't want to impose." Rose tried to take back what she had said out loud.

"Nonsense. Hey I got an idea. You can say no but I really hope you don't. So, please just hear me out." River looked at Rose as she was still devouring the cheese fries. Rose merely nodded and he continued.

"What if I come by tonight and bring some pizzas. I can hang out with you and the boys. After they go to sleep, we can get a battle plan together. I'll come back tomorrow morning and pick everyone up for the cookies with Santa. After which, while they have their sleepover, we can go shopping. I'll even help wrap the presents. Maybe even order in and watch a movie. What do you say?" River laid the plan out hoping she wouldn't just flat out say no.

"Do you know how to wrap presents? You know you can't just stick them in a bag and call them wrapped." Rose teased.

"Is that a yes?" River batted his eyes at Rose.

"Okay. But only because I don't want to cook." Rose had to justify it in some way. Plus it was better for him to meet the boys at the house away from prying eyes and wagging tongues.

Rose would know all she needed to after tonight. The boys had a keen sense about people. If they didn't like someone they didn't like them. That was it. Dylan especially could see right through people. She was grateful he had that gift. Porter was almost like a human lie detector. It didn't always work but on the big stuff it did.

Rose would wait to see what the boys did. She was keeping her word to Snow and everyone else. She was giving River a chance. She wasn't stupid to think he wouldn't mess up just how big would judge her willingness to stay strong and stand beside him.

"What time and where do you live?" River said almost as if she had told him she would accept him right then and there.

River knew this was a huge step. He couldn't wait to tell the others at packhouse. Right now though he had to play it cool. Even though if he could, he would be jumping up and down right now.

"6:30 work for you? Gives me time to get the boys, get home, and get a shower. Possibly clean up a little bit." Rose knew that there were toys everywhere.

"That's perfect. So where?" River pressed for an answer.

"Lakeside drive cut off. The second road. It's a private driveway straight to my house." Rose finally said.

"What kind of pizza?" River asked, trying to keep it going.

"The boys like pepperoni. I will eat just about anything but mushrooms or black olives." Rose explained.

"Okay, I can handle that. What about drinks?" River wanted to make sure he had everything covered.

"Fruit punch for the boys. I have a pretty nice bottle of Abormist if you happen to be interested. If not Dr. Pepper." Rose hated drinking alone. When she did it was because the boys were already asleep.

"Okay. 6:30 pizza at your place. Can I bring anything else?" River wanted to be and appear helpful.

"No, that is it. You're bringing dinner." Rose said, finishing the last fry. "Oh, I'm sorry, did you want some?" Rose realized she ate the whole thing by herself.

"Nope. I went and got those for you." River said, handing Rose a napkin to wipe the extra cheese from her face and fingers.

"Thanks. This was really nice." Rose said, sipping on her iced coffee.

"Not a problem. I'll see you tonight." River got up and went to kiss Rose on the cheek before leaving.

Rose turned about three shades of red when she looked up and Jack was standing in the window in full view. How long had he been standing there? Rose knew she would have to explain later and hope that Jack didn't make kissing noises at her.

"Well... I'll see you tonight. I have to get back to work." Rose said gathering up the garbage and throwing it away.

River left the shop on cloud nine. It took some time but he stayed the course and now he would not only get a second date but also spend time with all of them as a family. He believed that they were meant to be just that, a family.

Rose had finished up her last car around 4pm. Jack didn't say a word when she said she had to cut out early. Just told her to have a nice night and see her Monday. Rose rushed to the daycare and picked up the boys. They were over the moon about mommy picking them up.

After they had gotten home, Rose got the boys settled and ran to take a shower. After which she braided her hair and put on some yoga pants paired with a nice shirt. She didn't want to be overly dressed but it was way too soon for him to see her in sweats.

6:25pm Rose heard a car coming down her driveway. She knew the sound of the Fairlane anywhere. Rose didn't notice but the boys were grinning from ear to ear. Rose opened the door and River was getting out of the car with three very large pizza boxes. The boys jumped up and down in delight.

"Need a hand?" Rose asked while watching River try to balance the boxes.

"No, I got it. Plus, you don't have shoes on." River mused at her.

"Werewolves don't need shoes." Rose laughed back at him taking the boxes while he went back to the car for the rest of the stuff.

"Yes, but you can still get frostbite." River tried to explain.

"Doubtful. We are setting up a kind of casual thing tonight in the living room. Hope you don't mind." Rose said as they all went into the living room.

"This is perfect." River said. River and the guys ate like this all the time.

As they all sat down with pizza boxes open, Rose started a movie for the boys. Normally this would keep their attention and they would eat in peace. Rose should have known better with River being the only guys besides Uncle Tony and Keven to come by the house.

They started with question after question. A couple had Rose almost choke on her pizza. River never hesitated and answered each one as best as he could. After a few minutes, Rose had to cut them off with the "less talking more eating".

"Are you going to be our daddy?" Porter asked while Dylan watched River closely.

"Well yes. Can't do anything without my boys." River said without missing a beat.

While the boys took this as an acceptable answer and went back to eating while watching the movie, Rose nearly died by choking on her pizza. She had to get up and walk into the kitchen to catch her breath.

When she didn't return a few minutes later, River went into the kitchen to check on her. Rose was braced on the island trying not to turn about nine shades of red. River walked over to her and tried to wrap his arms around her.

"Are you okay? Can I get you a drink?" River said, trying to be some kind of help.

"I'm so sorry. You're really the only guy they have ever seen me with. Keven was always a good friend but never came over to eat dinner. They are just little chatterboxes tonight." Rose began to ramble.

River merely put his hands on hers and held her tight. Kissing the top of her head. This seemed to calm Rose but started a fire in a whole different part of her body. She knew that couldn't happen. Not while the boys were awake and hopefully not even when they were home.

Rose just took comfort where normally she would have had none. The boys had started asking certain natural questions as of late. At this time, River was almost a complete stranger to them. That is what freaked her out more than anything. They saw something she wanted in River right now.

"It's fine. They are fine. We are fine." River whispered in her ear. "Let's go finish dinner and we will talk about it later."

Rose knew that trying to discuss this while the boys were awake wasn't going to work. She would bide her time. She would find out if he just said it to say it or was she really up a creek.

Chapter 43

They had watched at least three movies and on the last one the boys had crawled into River's lap and fallen asleep. Rose was so exhausted from the day. She had fallen asleep on the other side of the couch. River smiled as he watched the three of them sleep.

River figured out which room was theirs and put the twin to bed. Then he came back down stairs and effortlessly carried Rose up to bed after turning the T.V. off. As he went to pull the covers up around her, Rose grabbed his arm and pulled him into bed next to her.

Rose laid on his chest for a while. She snuggled into him like a pillow. River merely petted her hair until her breathing leveled once again. She was good and out when he slipped from the bed and kissed her forehead.

River couldn't wait till he wouldn't have to leave her side. Something was troubling her and he noticed it in the way she held onto him in her sleep. Rose wanted to handle everything herself and he could see that was wearing her down in a very drastic way.

River heard her phone go off from the living room. Looking at the alarm clock on her night stand, he saw that it was a little after midnight. While he thought getting a call this late was a little odd, he figured he would still go and get the phone to put it on charge for her. No reason for her to wake up to a dead phone and one less thing for her to worry about in the morning.

The phone had stopped ringing by the time he had found it in the couch. Then it started ringing again as he started to walk into the kitchen. River looked at the caller ID which said Private Number. River again thought it was odd, but even his number came up private. He tried to ignore it but when the phone wouldn't stop he answered it. He would let the caller know she was asleep and to call back tomorrow.

All River heard was. "I know you're there little wolf. I will get what's mine. You will never be able to stop me."

"Excuse me?" River's voice was deep and full of anger.

"Who is this?" the male voice said on the other side of the line.

"Who the fuck is this?" River responded. "Better yet... I don't want to know who this is. The best thing for you to do is leave MY MATE alone before I find you and rip your head off."

The line went dead with no response. River looked at the phone and up the stairs to where Rose lay sleeping. He wouldn't bother her with this. River went into the call logs and went to delete the incoming call. That is when he had seen there were dozens upon dozens of these private number calls. Most of them were never answered.

River knew he would have to get to the bottom of this but right now his Queen was sleeping soundly along with his Princes. They would not be touched by this tonight. River, however, made the decision to go plug Rose's phone up. River also decided he wasn't going back to the packhouse that night.

River slept on the couch in case whoever was calling Rose decided to try to pay a visit in the night. River now thought he knew why she was on edge. Well at least part of it, he was sure. He just hoped she wouldn't get upset for answering her phone.

7:30am came early in the house. Rose knew she would have to get up and get ready for breakfast. Normally she would hear the boys by now. This shocked Rose completely awake since she realized she was in her bed. She was still fully clothed but smelled like River.

She jumped up and ran down the stairs. What she saw stopped her dead in her tracks. A full grown Lycan and two werewolf pups eating donuts and drinking chocolate milk at the kitchen table. Discussing how a Lycan is better than the HULK. Each one weighed in on their side of the debate.

"Good Morning." Rose announced her presence.

"Hey, look who's awake." River said getting up and hanging Rose a hot cup of coffee.

"How did you?" Rose looked at the cup grateful and slightly confused.

"Well… I noticed yours was broken. Why you hadn't thrown it away yet was beyond me. So, I called Sebastain to bring a new one along with some donuts for us. I hope you don't mind." River said as Rose put the cup down on the island and threw her arms around him in a big hug.

"Thank you." Rose said, beginning to cry for reasons she had not yet understood herself.

"Oh, sweetie don't cry. It's only a coffee pot." River didn't understand the weeping woman in his arms.

"I'm sorry. It's silly." Rose said, trying to regain some composure.

Rose knew she had to pull it together. This was not her. When it came to the boys, yes she got emotional but over a coffee pot. Rose saw how ridiculous it seemed to look at the moment. Rose knew she had to pull it together.

Rose walked into the living room with her coffee and just took a minute. She could hear Dylan and Porter talking about a mile a minute about seeing Santa today. They also talked about the sleepover and why mommy didn't have their tree up yet.

Rose knew that it would be just one more thing on her already massive to-do list. She would have to stop by the bank and check her balance to see how much she had to spend on everyone for Christmas. Rose was very careful with the money she made just so she could pull off the little extras this time of the year.

River came into the living room to check on Rose. She was sitting there on the couch with her hands on her head leaning forward. She looked worn out and worried. This among other things pulled at River's heart.

"Everything okay?" River asked cautiously.

"Everything is fine. I'm sorry about that a little bit ago." Rose said calmer and a little more rational. Even though it came out a little cooler than she meant it to be.

"You sure? You look like you're fixing to have a meltdown." River remarked as he carefully came to sit beside her.

"So much to do so little time. I'll pull it off. I always do for them." Rose forced a smile that didn't reach her eyes.

"What do you do for you?" River inquired.

"I gave up worrying about me when the two pink lines showed up. But anyways... I have to get them ready. Santa will be showing up in about an hour." Rose said, drinking down her coffee and hauling her butt off the couch.

River wouldn't press her right now for answers. He already knew she was holding it together with determination and coffee. For Rose, that was working but he knew it wouldn't last for long. She was starting to show cracks in her armor. When the walls finally tumbled down, he was going to be there to put her back together.

A little before thirty minutes were up, Rose had the boys dressed, packed, and ready for their day. Rose was wearing a black off the shoulder blouse with a pair of black ripped up jeans. She had rebraided her hair and put on her eye liner. Slinging her leather on, Rose walked out the door with two little elves and River.

The chatter from the back seat was enough to make anyone giggle over. The topic of conversation was which cookie did Santa like best. The great debate among four year olds. River noted that their child logic was undeniable. He enjoyed it.

Rose remained quiet on the ride to the packhouse. She stared out the window at the trees she passed by everyday, but didn't seem to really pay attention to. River took notice that Rose wasn't really saying anything. He would table that until they were alone.

When they pulled up at the packhouse, the other Kings came out and noticed they were all in the same car. While they spent a great deal of time with the twins, this was the first time since the Ball they had laid eyes on Rose. Sebastian had noticed that she didn't look too happy at the moment.

River parked the car and Rose got out to unbuckle the boys and remove the car seats. Rose had their bag slung over her side and a car seat in each hand as the boys each had one side of her pants pockets.

"Would you like me to grab something?" Axel asked, walking up to them.

"No thanks. I got it. Typical day for me." Rose said, walking with the boys to the front door.

River hung back a moment to talk to the guys as he watched Rose go into the packhouse with the boys. Everything was fine not an hour ago, but the cracks in her wall were rebuilding and he didn't know why. Had he done something that he was unaware of?

"Bad morning?" Axel said walking up.

"I don't know. She was fine, then crying, then freezing out." River said, taking a pack of cigarettes from the sun visor and taping one out of the pack.

"Something is troubling her. I don't think it's you though." Sebastian remarked.

"Everything was going great. We ate pizza. The boys asked me a thousand questions. We watched movies. The boys climbed in my lap and fell asleep. Rose ended up also falling asleep. I put everyone to bed." River recounted the events from the night before. "Something strange did happen around midnight though."

The guys were all ears. Each one of them had a stake in River and Rose's match. When they were blessed into becoming a King they were told by the Oracle of their mates. The order in which they would be found was very clear with River being the first of them. The other three kings knew that the one before and after would play a part in the match. This made them fear if River couldn't seal the deal. They would be doomed.

"So what happened?" Sebastian finally asked.

"Well after I put Rose to bed, she kind of pulled me in with her. Nothing happened except some cuddling." River explained. "But I heard her phone ringing from downstairs. So, I slipped out and went to find it. If anything, just put it on the charger for her. A private number kept calling. So, I answered it to tell whoever she was sleeping.

A threat later and I barked back. They hung up. I deleted the incoming call and found out that the same private number has been calling multiple times a day for the last few months. Most of the time she doesn't answer and when she does it's a short three to five seconds."

"Do you think anyone else knows?" Sebastian asked.

"Rose plays things close to the vest. I would bet if Eva doesn't know then no one does." River said, looking at the guys.

"So what's the plan?" Axel spoke up.

"I'm supposed to help Rose get her Christmas stuff done after this. I will see if I can get her to talk about what is bothering her. I need yall to talk to Eva. Don't mention the phone calls in case she hasn't said anything. Just see if Rose has been feeling some kind of way lately." River said.

"We got this." Ryder said.

The guys headed back inside to help with all the pups. When they visited different packs for whatever reason they tried to be as helpful as possible. They could find out much more about the inner workings and how things were run this way. Plus, they were just four big kids themselves.

Chapter 44

After pictures were taken and cookies were eaten, there were twenty-two sugared up pups chasing the Lycan Kings through the garden. Well three of the four kings were being chased. River was helping Santa with his list.

Rose was standing back watching. She had noticed the shift in herself and didn't like it at all. Rose just felt this funk that wasn't there when she woke up this morning. She was genuinely happy even though it didn't show right then. The man bought her a coffee pot. To Rose, that might as well have been an engagement ring.

"Snow…" Rose called her wolf.

"Yes, my lovely." Snow said as she stretched from her slumber.

"What do you see?" Rose asked her.

"What do you mean?" Snow was a bit confused.

"Do you sense any danger? Do you see anything coming?" Rose asked, praying Snow would have the answers.

"I see you second guessing herself instead of just trusting him. I see that whatever he does is for a good reason." Snow said.

"I mean past him. Do you see anything? I can't shake this funky feeling." Rose said to Snow.

"I see that we can't run from neither the past nor the future and both are about the clyde. Best thing we can do right now is enjoy the peace while it lasts. It will all come to a head soon enough." Snow said her peace and faded to the back once more.

Rose hated when Snow decided to only leave bread crumbs to a question. At least she had a somewhat answer, but what to do with the information? Rose decided to actually listen to Snow, and just let it be for the time being. Which also meant powering through the funk and stop giving River the cold shoulder.

As River walked away from Santa, he noticed that Rose was looking in his direction. River smiled at her and was greeted back with a smile in return. He walked over to her as she offered him a cup of coffee. He didn't dare question the mood shift or the gesture.

"You think it's a good time to head out. So much to do." Rose asked River.

"Yes, of course. If you're ready. I'll let the guys know we are going." River figured whatever had soured her mood was gone now. He would still be careful to not upset the current balance.

Rose went to talk to Eva and let her know she was going to go. Eva was busy helping in the kitchen with the cookies. When

Rose walked in she smiled at the trays upon trays of every kind of cookie imaginable. She knew there would be a debate later among the boys about which cookie was better than the rest.

"How many people are left to eat cookies?" Rose inquired while secretly being glad the boys would be staying at the packhouse tonight.

"Oh these are for later. Going to be doing a movie night for the kids." Eva said covered in flour.

"Oh well. I'm going to go. We have a lot to get done in a very short amount of time." Rose explained.

"We? As in?" Eva looked at Rose wiggling her eyebrows.

"As in, River has offered to help. So I'm not stressing out. Nothing more." Rose said on the defensive side of things.

"Right. Well just let us know if you need us to keep the boys tomorrow. I think Tony misses story time with them." Eva tried to play it off casually but Rose knew what she was getting at.

"Well if you want to keep them tomorrow that would be fine. I'll just pick them up when I come for Sunday dinner." Rose said with a sly smile on her face.

"Okay. Do we set it for five or six people?" Eva said knowing this would earn her a blush from Rose.

"I'll have to see if River has plans and get back to you on that." Rose knew two could play at this game.

"Okay well just let me know then." Eva walked over and carefully kissed Rose on the cheek goodbye.

Rose left the kitchen with a smile. She always wondered why Eva couldn't have been her mom. She knew the Goddess had blessed her with the most amazing Aunt, and that Rose was grateful for.

As Rose walked back into the foyer River was standing there with his three friends. They all seemed pleased about something. Rose knew better than to ask currently. Rose knew if Lycan men were anything like werewolf boys; she didn't want to know.

"Your Majesty." Sebastian greeted Rose with a small bow.

"Awe none of that. None of that. My name is Rose." Rose said to the four of them.

"Well this is Sebastian of the west, Ryder of the East, and Axel of the North." River introduced each of the kings.

"Oh, Your Kings as well." Rose said thinking that they were merely Beta, Gamma, and Delta.

"Yes, we are. And don't worry Queen Rose, we have our own code of conduct. No harm when someone is having a bad day." Sebastian said referencing earlier.

"Can we 86 the Queen part please. I'm not a Queen or at least not yet. And even when that happens it's not going to be easy for me to be addressed that way." Rose said, hoping not to come off rude right then.

"Not a problem, Lady Rose." Axel slickly came off with.

Rose went to say something and stopped herself. She knew these guys probably could go all day with comment after comment. She didn't have time. She had to get a long list taken care of.

So, Rose did something else. She pulled one of her knives from her jacket and began to play with it in her hand. The guys all looked to River whose hands were up and walking backwards toward the door.

They knew right then and there River had not only found his match but they had found their ultimate Queen. She wouldn't just keep River in check. They would be put in their places as well. Finally a female to join their clan.

It also didn't escape their attention when she said when and yet. They knew time would have to be taken. They also knew that Rose was starting to have feelings for River. Sebastian could see past her armor and wall to her heart.

Rose merely put the knife back in her jacket, bowed, and then walked away without saying one word. As soon as she cleared the front door, the men cheered, high fives, and hoots. Lady Rose had fire and they knew River would be in trouble if he crossed her.

Rose could hear the men making a fuss but didn't turn around. She walked right over to a waiting River, who was holding the door, and laid a big kiss on his lips. She figured if they were still watching, which they were, she would put on a show.

River was floored and looked a bit dazed as they both were breathless. What started as a show off quickly turned hot and Rose just got into the car as she could hear the three in the house still cheering and carrying on like a bunch of teenage boys. Rose turned bright red in the confines of the car.

They didn't say a word as River got into the driver's seat and started the car. They were a good thirty miles down the road before either of them broke the silence. Rose had forgotten to go to the bank. As she looked at her watch, she saw it was already closed.

"What's wrong?" River had noticed Rose's mood begin to shift again.

"Nothing. Well actually something. I didn't make it by the bank." Rose admitted.

"Okay. Do you have your debit card?" River asked, looking slightly confused about the big deal she was making about not making it to the bank.

"I do but the money I need is in my savings. I can't access it from my debit card. I purposely set it up that way." Rose explained.

"Okay. So we will use mine." River said still not seeing the big deal.

"No, I couldn't possibly." Rose began but was quickly cut off.

"Yes, you can and will." River said, taking no refusal.

Rose figured it was easier not to fight with him right then and there. She would figure out a way to pay him back even if she had to work till the end of time. For now though, she'd enjoy someone else picking up the bill.

Four hours of braving the mall before River and Rose realized what time it was. They had gotten all the shopping done and a new tree. The boys had told River what happened to the last one. And all the gift wrapping paper needed for the job. The Fairlane was loaded down from the backseat to the trunk.

They had laughed and picked on each other all afternoon. Rose couldn't remember the last time she had had that much fun with another grownup before. She would normally have fun with Eva shopping and girl talk but this was different. Rose was beginning to like different things.

"So, my lady." River started in on Rose yet again. "What are we doing about dinner? Because I'm starving."

"What do you have a taste for?" Rose said, pinching his arm for calling her Lady or Lady Rose for about the hundredth time.

"Ouch. You're going to leave a mark brat." River said, sticking his tongue out at her.

"I'm not a brat. I'm a badass, get it right." Rose went into pinching him again and missed.

"Well I'm hungry. What do you want to eat?" River asked again.

"I asked you first." Rose said.

"Fine Mexican." River snapped out.

"Cool but I get my own cheese dip. I don't share." Rose giggled.

River called in the order as they left the mall. Their plan was to swing by the restaurant, pick up the food, go back to the cabin, eat and wrap gifts. Nothing ever goes as planned. River and Rose ended up under the mistletoe when Rose's phone began to ring.

"Ignore it." River said, slipping his hands up Rose's back.

"I can't." She pulls away and answers the phone without looking at the caller ID.

"Yello." Rose answered.

"Hello Little wolf…"

Chapter 45

Rose froze when she heard the voice on the line. Not because of who it was, but River was now standing from the couch in front of her. She didn't want to have this conversation now. She didn't want him to know about the darkness of her past just yet.

Rose turned and walked into the kitchen with the phone to her ear. "You want me to make good on that promise. Don't you? I will cut your fucking throat if you don't leave me alone."

Rose slammed the phone down on the counter and it shattered the screen. Rose began to cuss as tears flowed down her face. A new phone was half her paycheck and now she would have to replace it. River had heard what she had said. So, he was about ninety-five percent sure that whoever this guy was, when Rose came face to face, she was going to kill him. River was willing to bet that the man was also Dylan and Porter's father.

"Does he know?" River calmly walked into the kitchen.

"Does who know what?" Rose tried to wipe the tears of anger and fury from falling down her cheeks.

"That you had twins. Because I'm willing to bet he doesn't. I'm also willing to bet, while your mother didn't tell him about that, she did tell him that you carried a son." River walked slowly to the island and sat down.

"Rumor has it… While the Goddess blessed me with his seed, his mate for some reason has been barren. They tried to force a pregnancy which she lost as a result. He can't be made a fool even if it is of his own doing. He rejected me and the pups. Whether or not he wasn't my mate is irrelevant." Rose said, walking to the fridge to grab a drink.

"Will you tell me who he is?" River asked, needing answers.

"No. You have to understand. The amount of shit I have gone through. I have always indured. He will not take that from me." Rose said, cracking the bottle of Dr. Pepper open.

"No one is trying to take anything away from you. But I do need to know what we are dealing with." River said, trying to keep his rage under control.

"We are not dealing with anything. I have to deal with this. I have to deal with him. This is my fight." Rose said, turning on River and trying to walk away.

"No it's not. The moment the Goddess blessed me with you as my mate. You had someone else in your corner." River said grabbing Rose by her wasted.

Rose tried to break free of him. The heat and sparks were almost too much to handle for her. While she wanted to give in to him, she knew that this was not the best way. No one was going to fight her battles for her.

River bent down and kissed her to prove his point. He wasn't going anywhere, and he was going to make Rose see that one way or another. River let his hands drift from her waist up to her back. Once his hands reached her hair, he heard Rose let out a barely audible moan against his chest.

After several minutes of invading each other's mouths and hands running up and down the clothed skin, River picked Rose up and brought her into the bedroom. He laid her on the bed and then removed his shirt. His extremely muscular and toned body had Rose's mouth go dry. Rose could feel her need for him grown as her eyes feasted on the site in front of her. She didn't want to think anymore. Rose just wanted to feel his hands all over her body.

As he climbed into the bed beside her, Rose's skin goosebumps. He slid his hand up her shirt and across her bare skin. River could feel the heat coming off her skin as he placed feather light kisses from her bare shoulder up to her neck. River found great satisfaction in her arching up against him guiding his hands to where she wanted to be touched.

As Rose reached up his back to feel the tight muscles under her hand, River was trying to free her from her bra. River just about had the claps completely undone when his phone went off in his back pocket. Cussing and removing himself from her side, he reached for his phone out of his back pocket. The caller ID was read Sebastian. River wondered with all his powers of being able to see why he was calling now of all times.

"YES!" River snapped as he answered the phone.

"Busy?" Sebastian, already knowing by River's tone this wasn't a good time.

"I was. What's up?" River said, running his fingers through his hair. While Rose got up and straightened herself to walk out of the room as swiftly as possible.

"I'm so sorry, but something has come up and I need both you and the Queen back here now." Sebastian said, knowing he was going to get an ear full for this one.

"You couldn't have given me five more minutes. Is it really that pressing?" Rive asked when he noticed Rose didn't come back into the bedroom.

"It really is, I assure you. I tried to mind link you, but you had the block up. When I tried to see it was just a haze. So, I had no choice but to call you." Sebastian explained.

"Fine. We will be there in just a bit." River said and hung up the phone.

Running his hands through his hair, River tried to control his sexual frustration. His inner lycan was spitting fire and was pacing back and forth, which wasn't making him calm down any faster. Argo wanted his mate and River interrupted it. He wasn't happy he broke the connection he was trying to make.

River put his shirt back on and straightened himself. He looked back at the bed and mentally scolded himself for picking up the phone. He knew Rose was in a fragile state and there was no way to handle it. River knew that she needed him and regardless she would figure out a way to be what she needed.

River came down stairs and found Rose sitting on the couch as if it was just any normal Saturday night. She looked slightly embarrassed and her cheeks were still a little flushed. He didn't want her to feel like what just happened was in any way a mistake. It was just poor timing on calls that evening that put them in the current situation.

"We have to go to the packhouse." River said, looking apologetic to Rose.

"Is something wrong with the boys? What happened?" Rose began to panic.

"No, nothing like that. The boys are fine. How they are asleep with that much sugar in their systems is beyond me but they are fine. Sebastian needs us now. Wouldn't talk about what over the phone." River said, trying to calm Rose down.

"Oh okay. Wait, both of us?" Rose asked, confused.

"He said both. So, yes, the both of us." River said, trying to gauge Rose's feelings right that moment.

"Okay." Rose stood, finding her earlier discarded shoes and putting them back on her feet. She wasn't happy about having to go but when a King commands your presents you show up.

Rose put on the leather and checked to make sure her knives hadn't fallen out of her jacket. She walked out of the hallway and looked into the mirror one last time. Her eyes were glowing and this time she didn't know if it was out of frustration or anger.

She didn't know why she was mad. Rose was upset that once she tried to get intimate with River, Dallas broke it up. Then they have a slightly heated discussion that ends with them picking up where they left off. On her bed of all places, which no man has ever been on, only to have Sebastian break it up like throwing ice cold water on a burning fire.

Rose needed a dip in the ice covered lake to kill the heat and need she felt right that moment. As per usual, that wasn't going to happen and might even make her feel worse at the moment. She was pretty sure not even the north pole could put out the flames in her blood.

River could feel the tension like a thick fog. He didn't want to discount her feelings but normally when Sebastian said now it was something major. He was a bit ticked off as well. Argo was fuming, and he could only imagine what Rose's wolf was doing. Duty as a King would always come first though, River wondered if Rose would be able to deal with this in her life.

They left the house and drove in silence. Rose couldn't look at him. Rose didn't know if it was the embarrassment she felt or what. When they had gotten home from Christmas shopping, they brought everything in and on the last trip they brushed up against one another. Rose had leaned into him and kissed his cheek. Rose had taken it a step further and breathed a very husky "Thank you." into his ear. Which led to the make out session on the couch before the phone rang.

Rose wanted to say something but thought it best to keep quiet for the time being. She had a problem with saying the wrong thing at the wrong time. Normally she was spot on and to the point but in these situations it was never as she wanted it to go. Rose did feel like she was falling for him. Rose didn't want to make a fool out of herself though.

They pulled up at the packhouse and River got out to open her door as always. He took her hand and helped her out of the car. River never let go of Rose's hand as they walked to the door where the three other Kings stood. The Kings could feel the power that came off of them and that left them pleased.

No one said a word as the other's led them to the Alpha's office. Alpha Jax, Luna Hazel, Beta Tony, Beta Eva, Gamma Otis, and Gamma Ivy were already there awaiting their arrival. The three Kings walked in ahead of River and Rose. Rose knew this was something very serious if the whole group was here.

"I'm sorry to take everyone from their evenings, but something has reached my attention that couldn't wait for morning." Sebastian said, looking around the room.

Sebastian waited for everyone to take a seat. Rose sat in a chair next to Eva. River stood behind her with his hands possessively on her shoulders. This didn't go unnoticed by the people in the room but no one dared say a word about it right then. This wasn't the time to acknowledge the blossoming romance in the room.

"A report has reached me tonight from Desert Sun and the Hollows pack. Desert Sun has sent information as to the recent fighting and apparent murders in the Hollows pack territory. Hollows is claiming Rogues are aggressively coming into the territory. Alpha Asher and Beta Dallas are swiftly and aggressively executing them. Desert Sun on the other hand says that his scouts are not Rogues and Alpha Asher is trying to start a war over land and power.

Alpha James refused to be allies with them after Alpha Asher took over. Since Alpha James has lost about a dozen men in the last 6 months. Alpha James has requested that we look into the matter at once before any more of his men are found dead. Alpha Asher and Beta Dallas have also requested a meeting to talk about their options. A possible sit down about the blessing to invade and start a war." Sebastian explained to the group the situation at hand.

Everyone knew the importance of nipping this in the bud as soon as possible. If they had a rogue Alpha situation on their hands he could start with one pack then another. If left unchecked this could start a war that the Kings themselves would have to fight in to bring back peace. The last great war caused a lot of damage and brought about the Lycan Kings to become the peacekeepers and makers among the werewolf packs.

"How long can we hold them off?" River said as Rose tensed.

"This needs our immediate attention unfortunately." Sebastian smiled apologetically more at Rose than anyone else in the room.

"What is Asher trying to do? I mean he's not old enough to have experience with this. He's only been Alpha for, what two years, maybe three. He is operating off his father's Allies. Which you have said is dropping him like flies. Because once one breaks with you they all typically start to shun. Desert Sun has always been peaceful. They are a powerhouse for the area but keep their numbers and skills under wraps. I went to spirit camp with a girl that was from Desert Sun. The last year I went it was actually at Desert Sun. Which leads me to believe someone else is pulling the strings." Rose spoke and no one even batted an eye at the fact.

"What do you mean Rose?" Axel said, looking at the standing Queen.

"What I mean is simple. Asher is a spoiled little rich boy. A pup with a spike in his paw and then runs to mommy and daddy at the first sign of trouble. He is spiteful but he isn't smart enough to think of this or pull it off. If someone else is pulling the strings on Asher you can't go in there without a plan. You're going to need at least three from the inside that know the going ons. Asher might very well believe he's entitled to more or it might be someone else advising him. It's always better to air on the side of caution." Rose said, trying to think logically.

"Now what can we do about that?" Ryder asked.

"I have friends that I am still in touch with there. They will let me know what's what." Rose said.

"Can they be trusted?" Ryder asked.

"With my life." Rose said knowing the boys would protect the Kings at all cost.

"So what do we need to do?" Alpha Jax understood that if this got out of hand they would work their way out and the fight would be at his doorstep next.

"We need you to contact every surrounding pack and inquire quietly about if they have heard anything. Allies need to be notified in case Alpha Asher does manage to find someone crazy enough to back him in a war. There wouldn't be many but one is too many." Sebastian said to the group knowing most had friends and families in other packs.

"While the Five of us get ready to travel down to the Hollows pack, we need things to look like business as usual here." River finally spoke up.

Rose looked at River when he said five. This close to Christmas, she couldn't leave the boys. Rose also knew as a Future Queen she would have to handle this at River's side. It would have to be her contacts that got them information. While she swore she would never go back, these were loose ends that had to be handled.

"Okay, we know what we need to do." Sebastian said, looking at the whole of the Harvest Moon pack.

"We do and we will." Alpha Jax said adjuring the meeting.

As everyone left the office all the men stayed behind. Rose and the other women left to go and talk down stairs. River watched after Rose as she smiled and closed the door. River was happy to see her act in her place as Queen.

"So has she?" Axel asked impatiently.

"She hasn't come right out and said it but her actions during this speaks volumes." River grinned.

"I would say it's going to be anytime now." Sebastian chimed in.

"That little fireball is definitely going to make an amazing Queen." Ryder said.

"I don't know what you have done. But Thank you." Tony said and the four Kings stopped in their tracks and just stared at him like he was a ghost that just appeared out of nowhere.

"What do you mean?" River eyed Tony like he knew something he didn't.

"Rose hasn't shown that kind of fire in a long time. Not like that anyways. There always seems to be something weighing on her. Tonight she looked like it didn't matter anymore. The only time I have ever seen her like that is when she was talking about her car. The passion and fire has come back to her finally." Tony tried to explain.

"I understand. By the way may we have a word between us for a moment?"

Tony looked at Alpha Jax with a nod and walked them over to a painting that behind it had a sliding door that led into the Beta's office. Not many people knew about this little trick. They used to use it when they were boys to hide from the then Alpha and Luna.

After everyone was seated in the office Beta Tony waited to find out what was going on. The intense look on their faces was enough to make Tony wish he wasn't in there alone with them. He knew the Kings wouldn't act out of turn but the looks on their faces closely resembled wanting blood.

"What do you know about the strange calls Rose has been getting?" River asked.

Chapter 46

Rose noticed the clock on the wall realizing it was after one in the morning. Rose began pacing and Eva began to worry. The others had already gone home for the night. While they waited for Tony and the Kings to come back down stairs.

Rose knew it was late but she took out her broken phone to send a text to the boys to "Go Fishing" with a 911 attached to the message. They would get it in the morning if not after patrols. Rose knew their loyalty was unwavering. She knew she would have to prove it to the others, but she stood by the boys that had been there for her all her life.

"Staring at the stairs isn't going to make them come down any faster." Eva said to Rose.

"What could possibly be taking them so long?" Rose slightly barked back, not meaning to.

"They are probably trying to figure out what the next move needs to be." Eva said, trying to calm Rose down.

"I know but it's 1:30. I'm fixing to just walk home." Rose said, looking at Eva feeling the unbearable heat that seemed to be coming out of her body.

"I know you're tired and with everything going on things are a little out of sorts right now. But it seems like something more is bothering you than usual. Do you want to talk about it?" Eva always knew what to say when it came to Rose.

"I need coffee for this." Rose said heading towards the kitchen.

Eva got up and followed. Rose skillfully made her cup and Eva one as well. When late night meetings happened the kitchen Omegas always kept a pot of coffee on. Plates of cookies were still on the counter from earlier. Eva grabbed her cup and then a plate of cookies and then headed for the library.

This seemed to be the best hide out in the world. No one really knew anything about this room. So when it came time for a private chat this was Eva's go to spot. It was calming and silent. The books kept the place insulated and sound proof enough to hear nothing outside the walls.

After they settled at the round table, Eva looked at Rose to spill it. Eva was always Rose's most trusted confidant. They had the relationship that most would kill to have. No judgment but also no secrets between them. Good, bad, or otherwise they were there for one another.

Rose took a deep breath and began. "Where to begin at this point. It's been a long time since we have had one of these talks. Well as you know I have always been in contact with the boys back at Hollows."

"Yes, I figured that's who you were talking about upstairs." Eva sat and sipped her coffee.

"Well a rumor is going around the pack. Dallas found his mate not long after I left. He never stopped being a playboy though. Anyways… She is barren. They tried to force a pregnancy about two years ago but it resulted in her losing it not a month or two in. Dallas has gone insane. He has tried the same thing he did to me on not only his mate but also others. Which has not worked out in his favor. Some say this has pushed him over the edge and is now power hungry.

On top of that he has been calling. After I realized he was calling from a private number, I stopped answering the calls. On the off chance I don't look at the caller ID, I never let the call last more than a few seconds. This had been going on for months.

Someone told him I gave birth to a boy. He still doesn't know I had twins. He has made threats which have resulted in me holding down a lot of my own emotions. I will never take the boys there. They will never know about him." Rose looked at Eva with pleading eyes.

"Rose, why didn't you say something sooner?" Eva tried to understand Rose's choice to keep this to herself.

"I can handle Dallas and all the bullshit that comes with him. That's my cross to bear, but with the River situation." Rose ran her hands through her hair.

"I know it's hard to deal with the beginning stages of finding your mate. Especially since you never thought you would. You still need to give him and yourself a chance." Eva said not bringing up Dallas right this moment. Eva would just put a pin in that one.

"You don't get it. I'm falling for him. Not just because he's my mate. He is amazing. He understands that I need my coffee. That I don't like certain things but not afraid to try new things. He loves the boys. He let them crawl into his lap and just fall asleep. He answers every question. There was a debate about superheroes and Lycans. Which I would have found absurd but he sat there and ate donuts and weighed in. I don't want our lives to change but in a blink they have and that scares me." Rose just exploded out with information.

Eva sat there and listened. Rose was in love. She knew it. Everyone could see it. Rose just needed to finally accept it and see the possibilities from it. Finding the other half that makes someone whole was the greatest gift the Goddess could give.

"So what's the problem, sweetie? You're in love with River. Just say it. You're not falling, you fell hard on your butt. You walked into that brick wall. Now what are you going to do about it?" Eva smiled at her niece.

"I want to accept him but with everything hitting the fan. We both need our heads in the game right now. We don't need things clouding our minds dealing with Hollows. Which reminds me. If I can't get out of dealing with this and going down there. I'm going to need you and Uncle Tony to care for the boys." Rose knew she never had to ask but it was always out of respect that she did so. Rose also worried that this was the first time she was going to have to be away from the boys like this.

"We will handle it." Eva said not even blinking.

"I just don't know what we are going to do about Christmas. It's only four days away. There is no way to have this buttoned up in time. Plus, I have never been away from the boys for Christmas." Rose understood her position as not only River's mate but as a Queen.

"We will handle it. You have done the shopping right? I'll have Tony collect the gifts from your house. You do what you have to and get back as quickly as possible." Eva said knowing this would ease a little bit of the anxiety she was feeling right now.

Rose knew Eva and Tony would always be there for her and the boys. She didn't know what she would do when they would have to leave this place. This was home. This is where she had the boys. Rose didn't want to think about that right now though.

KNOCK… KNOCK… KNOCK… came from the door. Rose and Eva both looked at each other before going over to open the library door. River and Tony looked a little worse for the wear at 2:30am. They came into the library followed by the other Kings.

As soon as they saw the cookies, Axel, Ryder, and Sebastian headed for the plate. Eva giggled at the three grown Lycans going nuts over Snickerdoodles and Sugar cookies. Eva left the room to go get another plate of cookies from the kitchen.

River walked up behind Rose to give her a hug and just take in her scent. It had been a long couple of hours and he needed her to calm the beast inside him. They got no new information from Tony on the phone calls but knew somehow Eva might have been told something in their absences. River hoped that one day Rose would hold him in the same confidence as she did Eva. He knew not to push it so soon though. Women needed other women to talk to especially about difficult matters.

Eva returned quickly with the cookies for the Kings. As they closed the door, they began their own meeting. While they held Alpha Jax and the others from the Harvest Moon pack in high regards, Beta Tony and Eva were the Queen's family.

"So…" Sebastian spoke up. "We will need to be leaving no later than tomorrow night. I know it's not ideal but with everything going on… We need to handle this swiftly."

"I already have plans set into motion as soon as I get a text back." Rose said, almost pushing herself more into River's chest.

"What do you mean?" Axel said coming up from the cookie plate.

"I have my three best friends Mike, Chris, and Nathan. Last account that I had, which was just a few months ago. Mike and Chris are warriors. Nathan is a Delta of the Hollows. They are also the biggest busy bodies there are. If something is going down they know about it. Mike's mom, Momma Kay, is also the head of the kitchen Omegas." Rose put the information out there for the group to know.

"How well can they be trusted?" Ryder asked.

Rose merely showed her palm. The only scar on her body was the one that ran down her palm. They cut themselves with a silver blade. The men knew the mark of a blood oath when they saw it.

"They are as loyal as any other that have ever sworn the blood oath." Rose said, touching the scar and remembering the night as if it was yesterday.

"So how are we going to handle this?" Sebastian said, looking to Rose for the answer.

"Carl, Chris's dad, has a house out on the lake. We used to hide out there when we were growing up. Whenever something major goes down we just say we have to "Go Fishing". We all know to meet at the lake house. Carl wont mind us using it. So as soon as they text back there it is." Rose said as they all took pride in Rose commanding the troops.

"We do have one more small problem though. We aren't going to be able to take my car or the Fairlane. My car is too easily recognized, and let's just say the Fairlane is going to draw way too much attention." Rose said, trying to figure out how this was going to play out.

They all looked at each other and laughed. Rose looked at the men like they were crazy. Was it the late hour or the sugar rush from the cookies that had them giggling like little school girls.

"Okay. I'll bite." Eva started. "What is so funny?"

"We don't travel in classic cars. We have them brought to us so we have something nice to drive around in." Axel squeaked out.

"So what do you travel in?" Rose inquired.

"Two blacked out SUVs." River said in Rose's ear.

Rose finally understood. She had heard that the Kings came from very old money. Though they had their hands in a little bit of everything. They could snap their fingers and bring Tech giants to their knees but preferred to stay in the shadows and handle the packs of the territories. Rose understood why River didn't blink an eye when they went Christmas shopping.

Buzz… Buzz… Buzz… Rose's phone went off and she carefully took it out of her pocket. She slid the screen open trying not to cut her figures. Rose saw the message was from the group text.

"10 minutes." was all it said.

Rose knew she would have to get a new phone before they left on this adventure. While waiting, Rose started picking at the cracked screen. Rose knew this was a nervous habit to just pick at things. River picked up on her energy and ran his hands lightly up and down her arms.

The phone began to ring and everyone in the room went silent. Rose saw they had called from Mike's phone.

"Hey Mike." Rose said putting the phone on speaker, but indicated for everyone to stay quiet.

"Rosebud as I live and breathe. What do we owe this honor from the most beautiful girl in the world?" Mike answered.

"How's my nephews?" Chris spoke up.

"You okay Babygirl?" Nathan is always to the point.

"Look guys, I don't have much time. I need a huge favor." Rose said, hoping that they would pick up on the urgency.

"Where is the body?" Mike inquired.

"There is NO body. Why do you always think there is a body?" Rose played back.

"Because we know you. What's going on Rosebud? It's been a minute since there has been a 911 text?" Chris is now getting to the point but also a little worried.

"Can't say much over the phone. I need to come back into town for a few days. Got some friends coming with me. No one can know we are there until we come into the light." Rose gave them all the information she could at the moment.

"Never a problem. What do you need from us?" Mike loved the intrigue.

"The lake house. And yall to "Go Fishing" for tomorrow. I can be there tonight if Carl doesn't mind." Rose said.

"You're his baby girl. Carl won't care and will keep quiet. I have to run the back 12 with Chris tonight. You remember how to come in that way?" Mike said.

"Old 12? Yeah. Come off the pits and run right into 12." Rose remembered.

"Yep. I'll keep it all quiet at the packhouse while the boys sneak you in. We will also stock the lake house with food. Are they boys coming with you?" Nathan asked hoping he was going to get to finally see them.

"No they are staying with Aunt Eva and Uncle Tony." Rose explained.

"Okay so see you in a few hours. Bring pictures." Chris said.

"Bye Little Bud. Be Safe." Nathan said.

"You want me to have momma make something?" Mike asked.

"While I trust your mother with my life. I can't chance it. Even though she has some skill." Rose said remembering how she pulled off graduation.

"I understand the less the better. Key will be in its normal spot." Mike said and then hung up the phone.

Rose looked back at the group. The guys seemed to all have the same look on their faces. Like did that just happen? Did she really pull that off? Rose just arched her eyebrow at them.

"What?" Rose finally said.

"Not a word from us. You heard the Lady. We leave in a few hours. Let's get packed up and ready to ride." River said.

Chapter 47

River drove Rose home to get ready for the trip. So much would have to be done before they left and they both knew it. While River wanted to talk about everything that had happened earlier before Sebastain called. He knew it was best to put a pin in it for now.

The silence was almost deafening in the car as they drove back to the cabin. Rose just stared out the window trying to come to terms with what was going to happen. Rose was worried that coming face to face with everyone in Hollows was going to end in disaster.

Rose knew this was a road that had to be taken. While she was physically free from there, her heart and spirit were tied to the complications that resided there. She needed all to be broken free to move forward with her life.

As they pulled up at the house the sun was starting to break the horizon. While they desperately needed sleep, Rose knew everything they had to get done before they all had to leave in a few hours. Rose would have to get the presents wrapped and find her way to the store to get a new phone.

"What's wrong?" River finally asked helping her out of the car.

"So much to do. I know there is no way out of this. I know I have to be there for more reasons than I care to name at this point. The main one is this started with me, and it will end with me. I am a Queen. Like it or not this is the path the Goddess has set me on." Rose said, sitting on the porch swing looking at the blinding white snow.

River stood there perplexed by the statement Rose just made. She had accepted her place as his Queen. He knew he shouldn't push it but at this time he needed answers. He would feel better going into the next situation knowing where her heart lied.

River bent down in front of her. He took her hands and looked her in the eye. He noticed that there was a heat coming off her skin like pure fire. He wouldn't question that right now, because it didn't seem to be bothering her.

"Are you saying what I think you're saying?" River asked, praying that he was right.

Rose smiled and thought long and hard. If she said it out loud she would never be able to take it back. Not without hurting them both. Words had power and saying them out loud gave them more. Hence the reason Rose would never say Dallas's name to anyone that didn't have to hear it.

"Yes." Rose looked straight into River's now glowing crystal blue eyes. "I, Rose Wells, do hereby accept you, River Easton, Lycan King as my mate, as the father to my children, and your Queen of the South."

River picked Rose up off the swing and spun her around the front porch. He didn't know what tipped the scales in his favor but when it came right down to it he didn't care. He would have to send Eva flowers for the rest of that woman's days. He knew he would have never had a chance if it wasn't for her.

"I, River Easton, do hereby accept you, Rose Wells, as my mate, my Queen, and the mother of my children." River exclaimed.

As soon as they had kissed to seal the deal, River's phone went off like a bomb had just exployed in his back pocket. River broke the kiss knowing he would have to answer the phone. He knew who it was without looking. That was the connection they had as Kings.

"Yes." River said never taking his eyes off Rose.

"We have our Queen." Sebastian said in a way too high pitched voice.

"We do indeed." River said calmly.

"It was just as it was said to be. We all felt the shift. Are you going to mark her now?" Axel chimed in, taking the phone from Sebastian.

"We haven't gotten that far just yet. But it's something we are going to have to talk about." River said, finally breaking eye contact.

Rose left the porch and headed into the house. Rose stood in the middle of her living room seeing things with new eyes. She felt powerful like a new life was being breathed into her. All her worry with the anxiety seemed to melt away.

This seemed to be more than just finding and accepting her mate. It was like something was triggered by the action. Something that stayed dormant inside of her being released from its cage. Rose didn't know whether to say anything or just let it be for right now.

Rose looked at all the presents on the floor. She knew they would all have to be taken care of before she left out in the next few hours. She also had to go get a new phone and pack her bag for the trip.

River finally came into the cabin and Rose was busy wrapping presents and writing out tags. He knew she wouldn't be happy about being away from the boys this close to Christmas, and to tell the truth he wasn't all that thrilled about it under the present events. River also knew certain things had to be buttoned up.

River stood there a moment and admired how carefully she wrapped each and every gift. Rose made sure each name tag was carefully written out as well and placed on the right present. He knew when it would come to the holidays he would just be the man that carried everything to the car. While she did all the important things of shopping and wrapping.

"Need a hand?" River said, taking a seat next to Rose on the couch.

"Not really, only two more shopping bags left. Most of those can be put in bags though. If you want to do that." Rose said not looking up for the gift she was wrapping.

"Okay. That's not hard." River all of a sudden felt very awkward around her.

River wanted to reach out and touch her but knew that if he touched her nothing would get done. That's how this didn't get done last night. River did as he was asked and put the remaining presents into the bags. He put them on the table waiting for their tags.

River could feel something off in the room. He didn't know if she regretted her decision or was just not happy at the timing of having to deal with Hallows. He knew that there was one person there that was going to have to be dealt with. With her accepting him and vice versa along with the boys, the bastard had no claim whatsoever. Not that he had one to begin with.

"Did I do something?" River finally asked not being able to take the tension any longer.

"No, why?" Rose said coming out of her thoughts and back to reality.

"You're quiet. The look on your face says you're not happy right now." River said, watching her very closely.

"Oh, no sweetie. Just running lists through my head and making sure everything is done before we have to go down there. Mind you I don't want to but I also know I have to. Not only to handle my own problems there but also as Queen it's my responsibility to stand beside my King." Rose said, reaching over and sliding her hand down his face.

The sparks from before were ten times stronger and a whole lot more intense at this point of contact. It was seductive and made Rose lean forward to kiss him ever so briefly. The flames that she felt deep in her belly made her blood sing with desire.

River broke the kiss to see Rose's eyes glowing the intense emerald green. While they enchanted him and drew him in he knew they didn't have the proper amount of time for this. That and they desperately needed to talk about other things.

"Your eyes, my love." River said, looking away so he wouldn't get lost in their hold.

"I'm so sorry." Rose blinked to try to regain control.

"No need to be sorry. As you said we have a lot to do and a lot to handle. I want plenty of time to tame that desire but now is not the time." River said, looking back at her.

Rose felt the flames pool in her blood with his words. She was very worried about the first time they would finally be together. Since technically she had never been intimate with a man let alone a Lycan before. That would be interesting to explain, but not now.

"Well…" Rose flushed a little. "We have one thing off the to-do list. On to the next I guess. I have to go to the mall."

"Did we forget something yesterday?" River asked slightly amused remembering all the bags and gifts that were not only bought but currently wrapped all over the living room.

"No, I broke my phone. I need to get a replacement before I can't use it at all. Then I have to pack a bag. I also think we need to get to Hollows between 9 and 10. Should be dark enough to slip in. Plus guard change down there is at 6. So we need to make sure we are there after that. With any luck I will have had a nap before the drive down." Rose explained.

"Drive? Rose, we don't drive. There are people that drive for us." River said as if it were obvious.

"Oh. I thought because I have never seen you with security or guards around you guys didn't roll like that." Rose said, looking slightly puzzled.

"Oh they are there. You just don't see them. We are comfortable enough with everything that they don't need to be right next to us." River explained.

"Okay. So how are we going to work this?" Rose asked.

"More than likely Sebastian, you and I will be in one car. Axel and Ryder will be in the other." River explained thinking of how funny it's going to be soon when there will be a separate car for each King and Queen.

"Okay. So mall, then pack, small nap. Are they meeting us here or at the packhouse?" Rose asked, trying to get all her ducks in a row.

"Packhouse. By the way there is something else we need to discuss." River looked at Rose sheepishly.

"What?" Rose looked a little concerned.

"Your marking." River's mouth went dry when he said it.

"Oh…" Rose freaked out just a little bit while the growing need fanned the flames.

"Normally, there is a ceremony with a Queen and you are marked in front of the Other Kings, the Oracle, and the people of the Kingdom or court. If you want it to be a more private affair, I understand. We can do a ceremony for your crowning." River said, trying to give her options.

"Let's put a pin in it for right now. I mean it's not something we have to decide on this second right? Do we have time for that?"

Rose said, slightly panicking. She was fine with having to do it but this was going to be a bit much to decide right now with everything else on their plates.

"No, nothing we have to decide right now." River explained trying to calm her.

"Okay. Well let's get the show on the road before we run out of time." Rose said, grabbing the keys off River's side and making a run for the Fairlane.

Chapter 48

They were back at the house within a few hours. Rose found a new phone and also refused to give up the keys to the Fairlane. While River wasn't keen on Rose driving his car, he couldn't help but smile at the fact she just did it. Didn't ask, just took the keys and made a run for it.

While they were at the mall to take care of Rose's broken phone, River had something catch his eye. There was a jewelry store next to the phone store and inside was the most beautiful necklace that could be from the boys. River decided to take a chance and buy it, but would show it to the boys later to get their approval. He made sure to have it gift wrapped and in his pocket before going back into the mobile store.

Rose was having a hard time figuring out which phone she wanted. Reality she was trying to figure out which one she could afford at that time. Rose didn't want to spend too much on a phone but needed something sturdy. While Rose was distracted with comparing each phone, River called the salesman over and pointed at the Samsung Galaxy S5 along with the case and screen protector. He handed him his card and the salesman and he knew what to do. Before Rose could make a decision the phone was bagged, paid for, and handed to River with his card.

River walked over and handed Rose the bag with the new phone, the screen protector, and a life proof case. River merely smiled and escorted her out of the store while Rose stood there dumbfounded. River realized that sometimes he would just have to take control of the situation.

He wouldn't let her lift a finger after they got back to the house. Rose was told to sit and set up the new phone, while River handled everything else. Rose had found out that the guys would make sure his stuff was packed at the packhouse. River went up stairs and attempted to pack Rose's things for the trip. Rose had protested in the car but he had a point about needing to just set the phone up and relax.

After about ten minutes of him saying he could handle it, Rose just laughed and told him fine. So, Rose sat on the couch popping her SIMs card out of the old phone and into the new phone. She was about half way through transferring her information to the new phone when she heard River cussing and raising a fuss for her bedroom.

Rose left the phones on the table and went to go see what the problem was. When she got upstairs and looked into the bedroom, she lost it. River had every article of clothing from her closet all over her bed. River was looking at the clothes just dumbfounded.

"What have you done?" Rose said just losing it looking at all the clothes.

"Where are the rest of your clothes?" River said, pointing at the pile on her bed.

"That's pretty much it. Other than a few skirts and the ball gown." Rose was getting heated by the mess she knew she was going to have to clean up.

"You have seven pairs of black jeans, two pairs of ripped up black jeans, twelve black tank tops, six assorted button ups and two or three blouses." River had noticed other than that three work uniforms and assorted sweats.

"And?" Rose was getting highly annoyed at the stating of the obvious right this minute.

"Why don't you have more clothes?" River looked at her perplexed that a woman could have little to nothing.

"One because I don't care to and two there are other things to spend money on like the boys and living expenses. If I happen to need something for an event or occasion I get it then." Rose said having a bit of a battle with herself not to scream at the person in front of her. Here was this pretty boy that didn't have to try while Rose worked her ass off for everything she had.

River, seeing Rose's eye start to glow, took a step back to try to understand. Every other female he had ever been around had closets of clothes and shoes along with matching jewelry and bags.

Rose had her leather jacket and a few styles of leather boots. What dress clothes she did own were probably bought for a particular event or outting. River was overly concerned that she had more sweats than actual regular clothes.

"I'm sorry. I forgot that not every girl has ten tons of things they don't need. But seriously, we need to take you shopping. A Queen needs more than just this." River said looking at the weeks worth of laundry and nothing else but lounging clothes.

Rose calmed down just a little bit. She knew she was slightly over reacting. She just wasn't like other women. Eva had been on her for years to update her wardrobe or lack of one. She was fine being simple and basic, but when it came down to it she wasn't simple anymore. This alarmed her just a little bit and put her one edge.

"I'm sorry too. It's just I have spent a lot of time trying to blend in. I wear things that are functional parts of my day to day. Things with plenty of pockets, black tank tops, and my boots. I'm not trying to impress anyone." Rose said, sitting on the bed with her head in her hands.

"We have a little time if you want to go back to the mall?" River suggested.

"No, let's just get this over with and then I'll deal with it later." Rose said, taking her black duffle bag out of the bottom of the closet and neatly folded everything including her heels and a spare pair of boots along with her toiletry kit.

River noted that it wasn't just her regular clothing that would have to be updated. Some of her under garments were very much thread bare. He knew that she hated spending money on anything that wasn't for the boys or that wasn't for daily living requirements. He noted that was probably the reason she hadn't replaced the coffee pot.

River knew he couldn't do anything right now but maybe while dealing with Hollows he could find the time to take her shopping. He would have to go with her because he knew she wouldn't be a willing participant.

They gathered up the bag and headed back to the packhouse. Rose knew there would be no sleep for her as they were to be leaving so early. So they could take their time getting down there to match up with Chris and Mike as they went on patrol.

When they got to the packhouse the others were already waiting on them. Three not two blacked out SUVs waited for them at the front door. Rose had found out that a small security detail was going with while they rest would remain back for a watchful eye on the boys and any signs of trouble heading this way.

Rose talked to Eva for just a moment before leaving. They both decided that it was better for Rose not to say goodbye to the boys. They would be told that mommy had to go help Santa at the North Pole because she was the only one he trusted to help out with the pups of each pack getting their presents. This would hold them over until she got back from Hollows. Rose was set on them never being tainted by this pack and people within.

As Rose hugged Eva and Tony goodbye, River spoke to the rest of the guys. Rose climbed into the back of the second SUV as per River's request. River put her bag in the back of the first SUV with the rest of everyone's luggage before climbing into the second one with her. When River climbed in and shut the door, Rose was puzzled. Rose noticed they were a Lycan King short in the vechinal.

"Don't tell me that we are riding alone while three are cramped into one of the SUVs." Rose said, knowing while spacious they weren't big enough for maybe two of them comfortably.

"No, Ryder and Axel are in the one behind us. Sebastian is with the security team in the SUV in front of us." River explained.

"Why?" Rose asked curiously.

"Sebastian being a seer will be able to see if something is coming our way. Since now his vision has seemed to clear up with you accepting me. Ryder and Axel will always ride in the last SUV due to their powers. They are a defense incase Sebastian indicates something is coming at us." River explained the order of things.

"What are their powers?" Rose inquired knowing she knew very little about all of them.

"Ryder is a caller of electrical current. So lighting, blackouts, and pulling power from the most unlikely of sources. He does all kinds of things. Axel, on the other hand, can manipulate time. He can freeze it, speed it up, or slow it down." River said, explaining that each one had their own gifts.

"So what's your power?" Rose said realizing she had never known that the Kings were that kind of special.

"I play with the weather. I'm the elemental of the Lycan world." River said knowing his power wasn't as great as his companions.

"Wow. I never realized that being a King came with so many other fascists." Rose said, amazed.

"It's really not that amazing." River said stretching out in the SUV and getting comfortable.

"Well, I can't do anything like that. So whether you believe it or not it is amazing." Rose said looking at him while she noticed him put up the privacy screen between them and the drivers.

Rose looked at him suspiciously. "Why did you do that?"

"I wanted some privacy with my Queen." River said, sliding closer and tried to put his arm around Rose.

"Look, there are a lot of things we need to talk about. And I think now is as good a time as any before things go too far and it is forgotten about." Rose said, turning toward River in the seat.

"And what would that be?" River sat there intrigued by Rose fidgeting.

"What are your plans after this is handled with Hollows?" Rose figured to start off small instead of admitting what she was really wanting to talk about.

"Well, I figured we would have a makeup Christmas with the boys and then plan on packing you all up." River said like it should have been obvious.

"And what after that?" Rose felt like she was slightly out of her league when it came to dealing with this kind of situation.

"Well we typically travel quite a bit. We do have a castle just south of New Orleans. We are there maybe two or three weeks a year for official business." River explained.

"So what are we going to do with the boys? They need stability. I can't be gone all the time. I won't have my boys raised by strangers." Rose began to get upset and her temperature began to rise in her blood.

"Nothing has been decided as of yet. Either we can have our own set of nannies and tutors that come with us on travels. Or we might be able to work something out with Beta Tony and Eva, when we have to travel. Your place is at my side to handle matters of state. No matter how big or small. Like all Queens, you will have to show your dominance and compassion for the people." River tried to explain but knowing this was upsetting her.

"I guess we will have to sit down and figure that out." Rose said, turning in her seat to look out the window.

"Is there anything else you want to talk about?" River said as he slid closer to Rose.

"How are we going to work Hollows? I don't like walking into situations without a plan." Rose said, trying to ease her nerves.

Rose knew what he wanted. He wanted alone time that would lead to something else. Rose felt awkward and a little out of her depth with this. While kissing and some touching was a "Feel as you go" type thing, Rose was not sure about the rest.

Rose thought by keeping him talking he wouldn't realize he got the short end of the stick when it came to her as his mate. She had a little to no experience with anything physical and that made her feel completely awkward and inadequate.

"Well I guess that would depend on what your friends have to say. They are the beginning of the investigation along with names of who was told to commit said acts. If they are the real noisy ones you say they are it shouldn't be hard to get all our information from them. At least a good amount of it to start the formal charges." River said, slipping his hand in hers.

He could feel her heart racing and had no idea why. He could feel the anxiety pick up and that worried him. Was she worried about the trip to Hollows? The boys? River desperately tried to figure it out.

"If Mike, Chris or Nathan know anything they will have no problem in saying it. They hate it there. It wasn't too bad under Alpha Kent. Asher is not his father and has always been more about his title. This is what leads me to someone is pulling his strings." Rose said knowing it was Dallas but couldn't just say it out loud without proof.

"What about the Beta? Is he capable of causing this kind of destruction?" River observed Rose physically stiffen. He would let that go for now but keep it as something to ask about later.

"Dallas is an asshole. Pure and simple. He thinks he is the Goddess's gift not only to every shewolf in the pack but also as a leader. Do I think he is capable of this? I say I wouldn't put it past him. I say if it's not him then there is something I don't know about the Gamma. Hell, who ended up being the Gamma?" Rose said feeling her temperature rising and the flames in her blood growing. She felt almost unbearably hot.

"I think his name is Chase." River said feeling the heat coming off her like a furnace.

"Chase Price? Oh my Goddess. The blind leading the dumb leading the class clown. Chase was one of the not so known underlings in high school. He followed Asher and Dallas around like a puppy. He amused them. So they kept them around." Rose said, shaking her head and removing her jacket.

"Are you alright?" River noticed Rose almost panting.

"Is it hot in here? I feel like my skin is on fire." Rose said putting the window down and having the ice cold air hit her gave Rose some relief.

River wrapped his arms around Rose and she finally felt her internal temp cool down. Rose began to get cold and rolled the window back up. She couldn't understand what was happening to her but she knew the madder she got the worse the fire in her made her blood boil.

"Has that ever happened to you before?" River asked Rose, looking both excited and concerned.

"Here over the last week but not before that I can recall." Rose tried to explain and keep calm at the same time.

"Can you do anything with it or is it just your internal heat?" River began asking questions that sounded absurd to Rose.

"I don't know. I have never felt this kind of fire before." Rose was now beginning to worry something was wrong with her.

River kept Rose embarrassed in his arms to make sure it didn't happen again on the ride. A memory struck him and he wondered if the Orcel was right that each of the Queens would develop a power after they were found. So far everything they had been told was completely on point.

River began to rub Rose's arms and kiss her neck. Rose could feel the fire in her blood sing once again. River had Rose hold her hand out to test to see if his theory was right. As he kissed her neck and even flicked his tongue on her marking spot, he saw smoke come off of Rose's hands.

When he placed his hands on her arms and ran his finger tips up and down, sparks started to dance in her palms. As he nipped at her ears and played with her hair small little flames emerged from her fingertips.

Rose went wide eyed with shock. She had never had this ability before. She wondered why it would show up now. Was it something dormant inside her? She looked at River to say something but all he could do was stare in complete admiration.

"My Phoenix"

Chapter 49

"My Phoenix" was all River would say before quickly getting out his phone and calling Sebastain. It wasn't long after that they pulled off at the rest area that seemed to be completely empty. River got out and then took Rose's hand.

"What's up?" Ryder said not understanding why they had stopped so soon after leaving.

"We have only been on the road less than two hours. No way you have to go to the bathroom already." Axel said looking from River to Rose.

"Will you just shut up? Something truly remarkable just happened and we all need to witness it." Sebastian said.

"What?" Axel and Ryder said and looked at Rose.

Rose was already getting pissed off at the guys for staring at her like she was the problem. How dare they. She didn't ask for this. Before Rose could regain her composure, a fireball bolted to the ground out of her hand.

Everyone including Rose fell silent. Rose merely stared at her hand and each of the men looked as well to see that no burns were on her palm. They were amazed at the sight. Not one hair on her arm was even singed.

"The Orcel was right. I mean nothing she has ever told us was ever untrue but she hit this one dead on the head." Axel said wide eyed and slightly bugging out.

"What do you mean?' Rose said, looking at the four men.

"Sometimes when you are given information it's out of order. So it would seem that what she saw and told us was false. She is always right though and the events did end up happening but not in that order. This time it was not only in the right order but it was actually witnessed." Sebastian said pleased with the events unfolding in front of his eyes.

"Right about what?" Rose looked puzzled and a little frightened at the fact she was not fully understanding what the men were telling her.

"Each Queen has been chosen. When, where, and how are not known to us. Some will have powers. Some won't get their powers until we are with them and they have accepted us." Sebastian explained.

"Okay. So what's that mean for me? I can't just go around shooting fire out of my hands at people. It's dangerous and rude.

And why fire anyway?" Rose began to panic and the flames returned to her figure tips again.

River walked behind Rose and placed his hands once again on her arms. Just his touch and his scent calmed her to the point that the flames extinguished. She knew she would have to control herself if she was going to get through this.

Sebastian continued after seeing that she was under control for the moment. "River was told his mate would be a Phoenix. So your power is fire. Until you're able to completely control it. You're right. You are very very dangerous. River will have to stick to you like glue. He will be the only one that will be able to keep your emotions in check." Sebastian noted.

"Well this isn't alarming at all." Rose said sarcastically.

"It'll be fine. I remember when I got mine. There were a lot of problems at first. But after I learned to control my emotions things seemed to fall into place. You're lucky. You have your mate to keep you grounded." Ryder said, holding out his hand as little sparks danced from tip to tip.

Rose knew that no matter how scary this was going to be at first, she would have to master it quickly. She couldn't risk hurting anyone, especially the boys. After she closed her eyes and breathed deeply the waves of flames in her blood began to cool and calm the raging sea. When she opened her eyes the glowing green had a red circle around the outside of the iris.

Rose had accepted her power as she did her mate. She would have to learn how to deal with both if she was going to fully understand how to control it all. The lack of sleep and caffeine was not helping the situation. Rose was beginning to feel all the exhaustion hit her at once.

"I either need a nap or coffee." Rose finally said, rubbing her temples.

"How much sleep have you had?" Axel asked, seeing the dark circles and the red rims come in darker and more apparent.

"I haven't slept since Friday night. And it's too late in the morning to just nap." Rose said knowing that the next wave would hit her and she would be wide awake once again. For now though, Rose desperately needed something caffeinated to keep her going until it hit.

"Well let's get down the road a little bit and we will stop for lunch. Then we can get some coffee or caffeine of your choice then." River suggested knowing that once she was in the SUV again she would be able to get some sleep.

"Fine. Does anyone have any change?" Rose rummaged through her pockets and realized her wallet was in her bag in the car.

"I got a couple of bucks." Ryder handed her the three one dollar bills.

"Thank you. I'm going to the vending machine." Rose said walking over and looking for something to tide her over for a little while.

Rose managed to find an orange soda. It was the only thing that was still stocked. While she wasn't happy about it. It was something to drink. Rose went over to the SUV and got back in with her drink.

"You know things are moving faster than we expected. The only way she will be able to control her powers is by you marking her." Sebastian said when Rose was completely out of ear shot.

"I know but I don't want to pressure her. She has done enough for one day. I pray that we have time, at least a few days, before I have to convince her." River said to the boys as he smelt the smoke from Rose's aggravation. He knew she was getting more and more upset as we just stood there.

"We have to get down the road." Axel said looking around knowing it was just a matter of time before things were going to get a little more complicated than it should be.

They all climbed into the back of the SUVs and got back on the road. River stayed right at Rose's side. Rose finally felt the heaviness from her eyes become more than she could bear and submitted to sleep. Laying in River's lap, Rose drifted off unsure of what was soon to come.

Chapter 50

The stars shone so bright through the covering of the tops of the trees. When Rose walked into the clearing, she saw a figure she knew had to be the Moon Goddess. They were in a wide open field with trees all around them. The Moon Goddess stood there with her raven colored hair just blowing in the breeze while she looked so intently at Rose.

Rose was not aware of what to do or say and just bowed to the woman dressed all in white. She smiled at Rose and motioned for her to come forward. When Rose got close enough to look upon her flawless porcelain skin, she gasped at her beauty.

"My child, why do you look at me as if you have never seen me before? I gave you life and blessed you with the calling of the wolf." The Moon Goddess said in her angelic voice.

"I never thought in all my life I would ever get to see you face to face. I have heard it could happen but it's not for everyone to see you." Rose said very humbly.

"You are wrestling with something and your wolf can not find a way to help you. She has contacted me and I see it is time for us to talk. You may call me Serna." Serna said, stepping closer to Rose.

"I don't know what I'm doing." Rose merely said more about the situation that was in front of her. Was this real or all in her head? Rose wondered.

"No one ever does my child. There are fates far beyond anyone's comprehension. Sometimes you just have to trust what I put in your path. I have left you clues to make sure you know." Serna said walking over to a stump and sitting down.

"Why a Phoenix? Why grant me powers at all? I am nothing special. What will this do to my wolf? Will I lose Snow forever? I don't think I can handle that. I know she barely talks to me but at least I know I can rely on her when things get hard." Rose began to panic.

"My sweet sweet Rose, you are so much more than you appear to be. I made four amazing she-wolves for four wild and crazy Lycans. Not just any Lycans but Kings. You will each play your part in keeping order and peace. I needed to make each of you strong of will and mind. A little something extra to prove your point from time to time. You need to be the Queen I know you to be. Don't worry about the rest. It will all come in time." Serna said, holding Rose's face in her hands.

"What about Snow?" Rose asked not prepared to lose her wolf.

"You will find her much changed when you have to call her out of her slumber." Serna said looking to the moon and taking note of the hour. "Just know I am always here and watching. You have your clues to make sure you know you're on the right path. It is time for you to go and set things right. Not only for your sake but for others." Serna said, kissing Rose on the forehead and the fog-like haze engulfed her.

Rose laid in River's lap as she slept. Rose was asleep for so long she hadn't realized that the SUV had come to a stop. When she sprang up, she caught River off guard. He was just staring out the window and petting her hair while she slept. Rose was disoriented and trying to push the haze of sleep out of her head to think clearly.

"Whoa whoa little fireball. Easy now." River tried to calm Rose and reassure that she was okay and safe.

"Where are we?" Rose had noticed that it was almost twilight but didn't recognize her surroundings.

"We are about an hour outside Hollows territory. We stopped for dinner. The guys noticed you were still asleep and decided to go in until they knew you were awake. They will be bringing us something back." River explained, still wondering why Rose woke up with such a jolt.

"Oh okay." Rose said, rubbing her face and trying to clear the dream from her mind. She debated with herself to say anything about it but knew it would probably be blown out of proportion if she did. She would leave this little conversation between her and Serna.

"You okay? Come here." Rive said, pulling Rose close to him.

River knew the over excitement or adrenaline rush could cause Rose to release her powers without warning or intent. River rubbed her head and played with Rose's hair. Which seemed to have a more immediate calming effect. River brought Rose to his lap and kissed her deeply.

Rose seemed to melt into him like forming hot wax. River began running his hands up and down Rose's arms while not breaking the kiss. He quickly moved to her back and slowly went under her shirt to touch her bare skin. As River's hands started to climb up to her bra clasp, a knock came at the window.

River cursed the figure of what seemed to be Sebastian standing there with the food. River had told them to bring Rose and him something back, but why was it always when he was finally getting some physical attention that they appeared? Rose merely smiled, pressing her forehead to River's and climbed off his lap.

"Hello." River said opening the window slightly pissed at the growing problem between his legs.

"Well finally you're awake. We have food." Sebastian said, overly energetic holding up a large bag with to-go boxes.

"I'm too hungry to deal with your energy right now." Rose said, digging into the bag that was handed to her.

Sebastian knew something was up. He could feel the Goddess's energy coming from Rose. He believed that had she come to this realm everyone would have seen and would be talking about it. Which led Sebastian to believe, Rose was brought to her. He would have to ask her about it later. He knew this would explain her almost 7 hour nap though.

"Someone's grumpy." Axel teased as River opened the door to stretch his legs.

While the back of the SUV was kind of like a limo, River was really long legged and wasn't used to not getting up and moving around every few hours. He hated long car rides even though he loved road trips. Mainly because on a road trip, he was the one driving. He regretted that he hadn't taken more trips like that in his life.

"Axel, don't mess with her." Sebastian tried to warn.

Rose merely flicked her fingers and shot a small fireball at Axel. Axel dodged it and put a sly smile on his face. Everyone else erupted into laughter. Rose's little fireball wasn't very strong so it barely singed him. The little attitude was there and that's what everyone was growing to love about Rose.

"I'd stop while you're ahead, Axel. She's getting stronger." Ryder punched Axel in the arm.

"I'm just making sure that she can hang with the big boys. Don't want her getting soft on us." Axel said not prepared for the next fireball that hit him right in the stomach.

Rose set his shirt on fire this time. All the men rushed to put him out, while Rose sat there on the floorboard eating her cheese fries. After they put him out, they looked back at Rose with her cheshire grin and the "fuck with me and find out" look on her face.

"Dr. Pepper, Your Majesty." Ryder said, smiling from ear to ear.

"Can we please just go back to Rose? At least while we are down at Hollows or until it's time to come forward with that information." Rose said, taking the large cup from Ryder.

"Why yes, Your Majesty." Ryder said, hiding behind Sebastian while all of them erupted into laughter.

Rose thought it was like having three big brothers. Once they figured out what annoyed her they would keep on until she put them in their place. Axel remained quiet besides the laughter. Rose believed he learned his lesson for now at least. They knew she would be stronger before too long and didn't want to be put in the position of being on her bad side.

"What time is it?" Rose asked once the laughter subsided and she noticed the growing darkness.

"A little after seven." River said, taking his burger from the take out box.

"And we are an hour out from the Hollows territory?" Rose confirmed.

"That's correct." Sebastian said.

"Okay. The boys are already on shift. We have to go down to the pits." Rose looked around trying to gain her barings on where exactly she was.

"So from here where do we go to get to where we need to be?" River asked, taking a bite of his burger.

"We keep heading down the highway. Where we get off at exit 35 to head into Hollows. It is where it's going to get a little tricky. Right as we go to cross into the woods that will lead us to town there is going to be a logging road to the right. Looks like an old dirt road, but it's not. We used to race cars down there through there when we were kids.

On the other side of the pit is Old 12. That will take us to the lake house. I'd say we are about two hours out, give or take. But we need to move if we are not going to be seen. They don't patrol the pits, but they do in front of the access road. Only at the top of the hour is anyone going to be there." Rose explained while using her fries to explain the plan.

"Why do you guys call it the pits?" Ryder asked to know if they would have more problems being this was almost the dead of night.

"Alpha Kent tried logging it out when he took over from his father. It was a giant gravel pit. At one time they wanted to fill it with water for another lake but plans didn't work out on that. Over the years though we had cut a small road down to the bottom of it. That is where most of the parties happen now." Rose said remembering that's where she thought Dallas was taking her that night.

"So are we going to need a distraction?" Ryder asked.

"I would say it would be easier that way. Can you freeze time while we still move or is it only you?" Rose asked Ryder.

"I can make it where everything outside a certain area is in slow motion while we still move freely." Ryder responded.

"Okay. Maybe a lighting strike to take down a tree. A thick fog would also work to hide us. Anything to bait and switch to get past if we happen to get up there when someone else is there." Rose just started throwing out suggestions.

"What about all 3?" River smiled at the fact Rose could think on her feet. "Sebastian will have to see what is going on and signal back. Ryder, you take out a tree a little bit up the road. Axel, you freeze them in time and I'll summon the fog. No one should be able to detect anything."

"Sounds like a plan to me." Sebastian said and went back to talk to the security team that was coming out of the restaurant.

They all knew the plan and it was time to get the party started. They all loaded up and got on the road. Rose and River sat in silence for just a little bit before River finally spoke. He wasn't sure of what to say to her.

"You know you are absolutely amazing." River said, sitting there staring at Rose.

"No, I'm just really good at problem solving. I have always been a critical thinker." Rose said slightly blushing.

"No, it's more than that. You don't take crap from anyone. Not the other Kings or ever other guys. I'm sure I will have my hands full if the boys are anything like you." River smiled thinking of the boys ten years down the road causing all kinds of trouble.

"Honestly, I hope they remember that momma doesn't play. I'm trying to raise them with respect and humility. Goddess knows we have too many entitled little brats out here. Like the one we are headed to deal with now. I won't ever have them look down on anyone." Rose would have them respect their place in the world and that was that.

While Rose knew they would be princes, they would not be too big to get their butts busted for acting out of line. She would not have them out in the world thinking it owed them anything. They would learn to work for their people and understand that with being a prince came certain obligations.

"On another note... we do need to discuss something else." River said, looking at her cautiously.

"And that is?" Rose said.

"You're marking." River eyed her.

Chapter 51

Rose sat in the SUV slightly numb by the turn of the conversation. They briefly talked about her being marked by him back at the house. Most females dreamed of finding their mates and being marked, Rose had so much thrown at her at once that up from down was beginning to be hard to distinguish.

"Why do we have to talk about this now?" Rose said, thinking back to the dream and wondering if this was what Serna was trying to tell her.

"Well for one it will help you control your powers. Secondly, I want everyone to know your mine and vice versa. Normally, you would have a choice on whether to mark me or not but in our position it's something that is more expected." River said looking deep into her eyes.

Rose thought about it hard. She knew what was holding her back but in all actuality she didn't want to cross that bridge and say it out loud. Rose hoped she could buy herself some time until after Hollows was dealt with.

Another thing came to mind while Rose sat there deep in her thoughts, there were others. She knew of a few that were supposed to remain anonymous but were more than willing to give Dallas a child. But how many others were like her? By what she was led to believe there was more than anyone actually knew.

Before Rose could open her mouth about a theory she was playing with in her head, she looked over and saw River's eyes glazed over. He was mindlinking someone and by the amount of time that had passed she knew something was going on. Looking out the window, Rose knew they were close to the access road.

When River came out of the mindlink, he looked at Rose and nodded. She knew it was time to put the plan into action. While no one was seen or even sensed to be in the area, River still called the fog and Axel froze everything in time as they passed onto the access road.

There was no sign of anyone down in the pits either. Rose found this extremely odd, but they kept the fog and everything frozen in place as they quickly traveled down to Old 12. They both heard a howl out of two wolves and Rose grinned from ear to ear.

Rose quickly rolled the window down and answered their call. The woods fell silent again. She knew the call sign of her two friends and smiled that they remembered hers in return. River went back into the mindlink as they hit Old 12.

Within 20 minutes, they were sitting outside the lake house. Rose signaled for everyone to stay in the car while she went out and unlocked the house. When Rose grabbed the ceramic frog that held the key, she could feel someone's eyes on her. Rose immediately went for her knief.

As she came up with the key, her knief was out and the figure that appeared out of the darkness was frozen in fear. "Whoa Whoa."

"Damn it Nathan. How many times do I have to tell you not to sneak up on me. I could have hurt you. Why can't I smell your scent?" Rose said, pulling the knife back from her friend's throat.

"I'm sorry. I was just coming to get the lake house ready when I heard from Mike and Chris. They said they heard your howl. I didn't realize you were so jumpy. My scent well my dear that's what scent block is for. I didn't want anyone following us out here so we started using it." Nathan said as he saw the SUV doors fly open and a bunch of Lycans quickly jump out at Rose's raised voice.

"Whoa guys. Slow your roll. Let's just get inside." Rose said, holding up her hands to the four that were rushing to her side.

Rose unlocked the door and pointed inside the house. They eyed Nathan suspiciously and stood there in spot. Rose just shook her head and walked into the lake house. She started turning on lights and kicking off her boots. Nathan followed after Rose not knowing what was really going on.

The Kings finally came into the house after Nathan followed Rose. Sebastain signaled back for the guards to bring in the bags and set up a primador. Rose sat on the couch thinking it was weird that nothing had changed in the lake house. Almost as if it was frozen in time.

Rose looked around the room at all the pictures of her friends and her. So many memories in the place and she found it odd that she would be led back to here to deal with things once again. The guys all looked around the room as the guard brought in the bags and set them down.

River smiled at the pictures of the young Rose. After he was done surveying the room, River came to sit beside Rose, and Nathan picked up that more was going on than he knew. Nathan sat in the oversized chair where he always sat with just an end table between him and Rose. Nathan noted that there was something very different about this very dear old friend.

"So, do we wait for the others or are you going to lay it out now?" Nathan said, watching not only Rose but the large Lycan next to her.

Nathan knew he had seen him before but where was escaping his attention. So much had happened since Rose left four years ago it was hard for Nathan to keep it all straight in his mind. When it did hit him though, Nathan went wide eyed and completely perplexed.

"King River?" Nathan said, eyeing the man that seemed very protective of Rose. Nathan looked back at the other three that were sorting the bags that the guards had brought in.

"Yes." Rose said, squinting her eyes in the usual "I know I have explaining to do" way.

"Okay spill." Nathan said, trying to regain his composure from the shock.

"Nathan, don't you think we should wait on Mike and Chris?" Rose tried to only have to say this once.

"No, I think you should say something to your friend now?" Sebastian spoke up.

They all looked at Rose like the kid that got caught with her hand in the cookie jar and it was time to let it all out. Rose was always one for only saying things once so when they wanted her to spill now it was a little more than she could handle. Rose felt the heat in her blood start to rise. River tried to subdue it by rubbing her arms and calming her.

"Fine. But not a word to the others when I tell them that you already know. Is that understood?" Rose took a steading breath looking at Nathan.

"Absolutely. Oh before we get started. I have to get the groceries out of the truck." Nathan said, jumping up to go back to the task he meant to do before he found Rose on the doorstep.

"Where is it?" Axel responded, stopping him short of the kitchen.

"Around the back in the bed of the GMC pickup." Nathan said, wondering what was going on.

Axel's eyes glazed over mindlinking the guards outside. Before they knew it four guys came up to the door carrying all the bags of groceries. They put them on the kitchen floor and then walked back out. Nathan stood there amazed.

Rose got up and went into the kitchen to start putting things away. When Ryder stopped her and sent her back to the living room. Rose looked slightly upset but went back to the couch next to River. Nathan's eyes went wider. He had never seen Rose treated with kit gloves before.

"Okay. Since you won't let me put the food away, can you bring me a drink then." Rose looked at Ryder and Axel.

"Yes, your Majesty." Axel said, eyeing Rose. He knew that she couldn't do anything about what he said right that moment.

"Your Majesty?" Nathan repeated staring at Rose for answers.

"Okay. Let's start from the beginning." Rose said, trying to gauge Nathan's response.

"You remember why I left. Oh by the way…" Rose began with pulling out a stack of new pictures for Nathan of the boys. "See I didn't forget. Anyway… I have been in contact so we don't have to go into every detail. Well a week of so ago, we had the Blue Moon Ball. And who presides over the Blue Moon Ball? The Four Kings. That's Sebastian, Ryder, and Axel. This is King River Easton of the South." Rose explained pointing each one out.

"Okay. I'm still not following." Nathan said, waiting for the actual words to come out of Rose's mouth.

"I found my mate that night and it just so happens to be River." Rose said, looking to one of her oldest friends in the world for acceptance.

"You're a Queen? Oh my Goddess YOU'RE A QUEEN!" Nathan kept repeating with his voice almost shouting.

"Yes." Rose just sat there as Nathan kept repeating it over and over.

Nathan got up and bowed. Rose reached over and smacked him on the top of his head. Nathan just looked at her like the same old Rose. When Nathan sat back down, he had the cheesiest smile on his face.

"The guys are going to flip out." Nathan exclaimed.

"Oh don't I know it. Dealing with all this has been fast and I'm still trying to figure things out. So in public, It's Rose. I can't have anyone knowing anything until it's time." Rose looked at all the men as if in a warning.

"Yeah especially with how your mom is." Nathan said.

"Right. So hence the secrecy. Plus, there is something going on here. The Kings would like a word with the three noisest people I know. Let's face it nothing happens around here without one of the three getting a whiff of the action." Rose said plainly as Ryder handed her a bottle of water.

"Any help I can be would be a great honor. I would like it stated for the record though anything I know, witnessed, or heard I could not have stopped. Some of us had to keep our heads down to keep them attracted to our bodies." Nathan stated.

"You will not be held accountable for anything you were ordered to do under this Alpha. We do understand about not rocking the boat while waiting for help to find you." Sebastian said, taking a seat on the bench on the other side of the coffee table.

Nathan looked at Rose. She gave him a reassuring smile. While they settled in to get the questions underway. Nathan knew better than to hold anything back with the King of the West being a seer. That was the reason when they were there at graduation they weren't allowed to say much that didn't revolve around Asher and Dallas.

Rose took note of the time, while they talked. Rose looked at River as if asking if she was needed for anything else. River just nodded and Rose got up off the couch and walked to the room that had always been called hers.

The light blue painted walls and white trim seemed to welcome her back. The queen size bed, that had been moved in there two summers before graduation, still had the same purple bed spread on it. This felt like home to her. It was the one place, on this Goddess forsaken land, Rose felt safe.

She looked in the drawers and some of her old night shirts were still in there. She smiled how the boys never changed anything. She would assume they always hoped she would come back and would want everything to be just as she left it. Rose quickly changed and climbed into bed. It had been a long day and she needed to rest in a non moving area.

Chapter 52

It had seemed like Rose had just closed her eyes when she heard the guys knocking at the door. Rose was trying to get her eyes to focus when she realized she was not alone in her bed. A grumble from the knocking caused River to start stirring on the other side of the bed.

River laid there on his back bare chested in just his jeans and socks. While Rose was enjoying the view, she didn't want the repeated knocking to wake him. Rose had no idea of when he had come to bed and she knew he needed his sleep as well.

Rose quickly got up and dressed with a dark blue tank top and fuzzy blue sleeping pants that she had found in the drawers. When Rose opened the door, she looked pissed. When she was handed a cup of coffee her expression softened mildly.

Mike knew better than to purposely wake Rose this early without coffee in hand and visible. He liked his head attached to his neck and knew she was very capable of being extremely aggressive before coffee. As Rose took the first sip, she smiled letting Mike know the warning light was temporarily disabled.

The smell of bacon and frying potatoes caught her attention and she gravitated toward the kitchen. Ryder was at the stove while Sebastain was sitting at the table with a notebook and his laptop. He looked very upset boarding on distrubed at something. Rose didn't want to interrupt to find out what was doing this to him right now.

Rose knew she was under caffeinated and hungry and this was no time to try to find out the whos or whats of the current situation. Everyone did seem to act a little different when she came into the room. Rose didn't pay it any attention right off and went to sit in her spot on the couch.

Chris was sitting in the chair and Mike sat down on the bench seat on the other side of the table. They both sat and waited while Rose drank her coffee. They knew not to engage in conversation before at least half the cup was gone. The silence in the room was almost deafening and Rose wanted to know what was going on.

"Do I have a booger hanging out of my noise or something?" Rose finally said while everyone looked at each other.

"Why no, your Majesty." Mike and Chris picked at Rose.

"Oh Goddess not y'all too." Rose whipped around being completely outnumbered by the amount of guys in the room. When her eyes landed on Nathan, and he froze.

"Oh don't be mad at him, Rosebud. You know we would have found out at any time." Mike said as the rest of the guys just chuckled.

Rose had found out by the time she had gone to sleep and had been woken up, Mike and Chris showed up. Nathan explained the Kings that were sitting in the living room. Also letting the guys in on the fact that Rose was now a Queen. The Kings had started asking all the questions that would be needed to start a formal investigation.

Of course the boys had answered everything that they knew. Even things that they had overheard that they weren't supposed to know at this time. By the time they were done, River heard Rose fidgeting in her sleep. Therefore, he had taken himself to bed.

They hadn't seen Rose in so long that they had a little catching up to do. Rose realized the amount of things she had missed. Chris had found his mate. A lovely girl named Daisy. They were very happy and were going on two years together. They had met at the annual Harvest Moon Ball.

Daisy was 21 years old and originally from the Desert Sun pack. She had long blonde hair and as Chris described her, she was a polite and shy young woman. As Chris sat there talking about her, Rose now knew why she had more contact with Mike and Nathan.

Rose felt bad though because Chris didn't share the news with her sooner. Rose was also mad but understood why. Rose was nine hours and about five hundred miles away. Rose also understood why when she asked Mike and Nathan about Chris. They just changed the subject.

It was his story to share and they wouldn't betray anyone like that. Rose wanted the best for them. Therefore, she just sat there and listened and let the hurt be short lived about not knowing. She would just have to be happy about knowing now.

It wasn't long before River had woken up and found himself in bed alone. He sat on the side of the bed and tried to shake the cobwebs from his brain. He reached for his bag grabbing a clean sleeveless shirt and his gym shorts. He changed out of his jeans and walked down the hall into the living room.

The conversations were in full swing with each set talking over the other and intertwined into a coherent action. River found it amusing to watch. When he saw Rose sitting in a tank top and fuzzy sleeping pants barefoot on the couch, he walked over and kissed her forehead before going to get a cup of coffee. River found his jacket on the back of one of the dining chairs, took out his cigarettes and lighter then walked outside for his morning cigarette.

When the door closed, the boys began to make kissing noises at Rose. Rose, not thinking, snapped her fingers and a small fireball appeared in her palm. Everyone froze in place. Axel opened the back door and yelled for River.

"Babe!" River said as he came through the door.

"What?" Rose said, closing her hand and making the fireball disappear.

"No playing with fire in the house." River said, still holding his cigarette halfway out the door.

"You can smoke in here if you want." Chris said, pulling his pack out and Rose's eyes went wide.

"When did you start that?" Rose looked at him lighting a cigarette.

"About three years ago." Chris responded by taking a drag and blowing out the smoke.

"And you got on to me when I tried it one time." Rose scolded.

"That's you." Chris stuck his tongue out at Rose.

"Wow, Butthead." Rose said, walking over and popped him in the arm.

They all laughed again as Rose walked over to the kitchen to get another cup of coffee. So much had changed and yet everything was still the same. She knew that one day all she would have is these memories of them being like this. Four friends picking on each other. That would have to be enough.

River wrapped his arms around her as she came into the kitchen. He knew she was feeling sad. He also knew she would never show it. She was a strong woman and never wanted people to see the pain she felt.

Chris sat there smoking his cigarette and as he took the next drag, he looked at Rose in River's arms and began to speak. "So do we get to do this now or do we wait?"

Rose knew what he meant and smiled. One of two things was going to happen. They were either in the "Big brother and best friend" fashion and going to threaten him. Or they were going to start asking questions about what they had just seen with the fireball. Rose knew it was going to be both, but in what order had her turning slightly flushed.

"Do what you do. Ryder, I'm stealing a piece of bacon." Rose slipped River's hold and grabbed a piece off the plate.

"Rose, breakfast isn't done yet. Stop stealing the bacon." Ryder playfully scolded.

"I know but I'm going to take a shower. So y'all can talk without me here." Rose walked over and kissed River on the cheek and smiled.

All eyes were on her as she grabbed the duffle bag and walked into the bathroom. They all waited till the door was shut when they began to look at one another. The three boys knew they were no match for the Kings in a fight but when it came to their Rosebud all bets were off.

"Now, first someone want to explain the fire bit?" Mike said, trying to keep his voice down until he heard the shower turn on.

"Rose is a phoenix. She can control fire. A somewhat dangerous power for someone with a short temper." Sebastian admired.

"No way. When did that happen?" Chris asked.

"When she found me." River explained taking a drink of his coffee while putting out his cigarette.

"And we thought she was dangerous before." Nathan remarked.

"What do you mean?" Axel asked curious of what the men knew about Rose.

"Rose has always been a skilled fighter. Knives are her weapon of choice. She is very much into hand to hand combat." Nathan explained as the other smiled.

"From what she told me over the last two years, she is also skilled with battle axes, throwing stars, and swords. She is a hell of a marksman when it comes to a bow as well." Mike said, relaying the information he knew.

"I wouldn't be surprised if she didn't have at least three to four on her at any time. She really is the ultimate threat. Beauty and brains with the face of an angel and the fearlessness of a killer. Not to mention, she can rebuild anything with her eyes closed." Chris said, taking the last drag off his cigarette and putting it out.

"Looks like the Goddess found you a match in every way." Sebastian mused at River.

"I believe so." River smiled.

River was the more skilled fighter of the Kings. While the others were more in the defensive nature, Ryder with his lighting was the only one that could match his strength in a fight. They were all strong but others had more brains that were involved with their powers instead of brute strength.

"Now that we have given you a little insight on your beloved Queen." Nathan slyly smiled. "We need some answers ourselves."

"Such as?" River arched an eyebrow at the three men.

"What are your intentions for our best friend and our nephews?" Mike said calmly.

"You mean my boys and my mate? I will do whatever is needed to make sure they don't want for anything. And I do mean anything." River said, putting his cup down and looking at all of them seriously.

"I know you probably know more about this than us at this point, but Rose is very special. She keeps everything in order. She has to its just her way. She doesn't show emotion the way the rest do. She is very much the "I'll handle it." kind of woman. So, we would never know if anything happened." Chris began. "If anything happens to her or the boys... We don't care if you're a King or the Goddess, herself, there is no where you will be able to hide. We might die, but we won't go down without a fight."

"We swore and we stand behind that whole heartedly. The sameway Rose would be with us, we are with her. Not that she needs the Knight in shining armor, but she does need someone that can show her she doesn't need the armor herself." Nathan said, looking at the group.

River realized at that moment Rose had more than just her Aunt Eva and Uncle Tony that cared about her. How special was this red haired beauty that the Goddess had made for him? There was a lot that the others thought he knew but didn't.

"I swear to you all, she and the boys will always be held in the highest regard and be taken care of. I do have one question though." River said, hoping they might have the answer.

"That is?" Nathan asked.

"Who's the boys' biological father?" River inquired.

"No one knows. Rose won't say." Mike said sadly.

Chapter 53

Rose let the hot water beat down on her back while standing in the shower. She didn't want to be a part of the conversation that was being held about her. She knew the boys all too well and it was something that had to be done in their eyes.

When Rose stepped out of the shower, she could hear some mild chattering with the men about Chris' El Camino. Old stories about her and how close they were once. She was happy that they were getting along for now.

While looking in the mirror, Rose called Snow forward. She hadn't heard from her wolf and it was beginning to unnerve her. She felt Snow stretch up and come forward to see what was going on.

"Yes, my sweet." Snow said, looking around.

"I missed you. I thought something was wrong. I haven't heard from you in a little bit." Rose said looking into the mirror seeing Snow's eyes looking back.

"No, everything is fine. All this transformation can wear a wolf out." Snow said.

"It happened so quickly. All of this." Rose said, slightly exasperated.

"And more is coming. We will need to handle it. Some extra help wouldn't be too out of line right now." Snow said, trying to hint.

"What extra help?" Rose asked, confused.

"It's time for our mate to mark us. The transformation is not complete yet." Snow gave an almost duh answer.

"Not you too." Rose said.

"Look without his and yours being bound things will quickly turn upside down. You need to bring to light what has only seen dark. Bind not only powers but your hearts and minds." Snow flicked her tail exasperated at Rose and went back to her corner of Rose's mind.

Why did she have to get a wolf that spoke in riddles? Rose went over it again and again. While she got dried off, dressed, and handled her hair. While it seemed simple, it never was what she wanted. This would blow everything out of the water.

As Rose grabbed up her dirty clothes and grabbed her duffle bag, a knock came to the door. She could smell River on the other side of the door. As she opened the door they locked eyes. He was slightly stoopid down. So he would be eye to eye with her.

"Can I help you?" Rose said, almost breathless.

"Breakfast is done. I thought I'd tell you before the animals tore it apart." River said, almost tasting her scent.

To him it was always something new, but since the phoenix gave her fire, she started smelling like campfires and marshmallows. Smokey and sweet. He tried not to reach out to touch her but it was too late his hand was already halfway to her face.

The electric sparks that still exhilarated her seemed to intensify. Which caused the fire to blaze not only in her blood but in the core of her stomach. Rose was getting lost in his eyes that were normally a calm blue but now were like a raging storm.

Rose knew she had to break this up or she would never hear the end of it later. Rose looked up and River took his opportunity to kiss her on the neck right on her marking spot. He knew that they couldn't keep dancing around this much longer. Avoiding the inevitable, would cause them both to go mad.

Rose slid her hand down his face to his chest to feel his heart racing like an over-revving engine. She knew he was feeling the same thing but this was not the time to handle it. It was unfortunately time to put the breaks on. Soon was all she could think. This would have to be handled soon if either one of them were going to keep what little sanity they had left intact.

From behind them, they could hear seval of the guys clearing their throats. Apparently they were sending out enough pheromones, that everyone knew what was going on down the hall. Rose turned red and went around River to put her things in her room.

Thankfully he didn't follow her as she tried to calm her hormones back into place before facing a room full of men that would act like teenage boys once she showed her face. As she was trying to breath through the blaze of heat and desire that was racing through her blood, she could hear Snow howling with delight. This made Rose roll her eyes at the very much losing battle.

Rose grabbed the necessary things she needed from her bag and pants pockets before going to face the music. No one would make eye contact with her, not even River, who was still trying to calm his raging hormones. That was probably for the best at the moment. Rose walked over to her refilled cup of coffee that sat on the counter. She grabbed it and headed for the deck door.

As soon as the door to the deck was closed, she could hear the entire room erupt into fits of laughter. Stupid boys was all Rose could think as she sat down on the deck chairs with her back to the windows looking out at the frozen lake. It was peaceful out here with just the faint sound of birds chirping in the trees off in the distance.

Rose breathed in the cold clean air and remembered what it was like being here as a teenager. Now it was so different, she wasn't hiding from her mother like then. She was there to hopefully bring justice and peace to what was their kingdom.

After some time had passed, River had gone outside to check on Rose. He knew this was all too much right now but unfortunately it would not slow down even if Axel froze it in time. They knew when River found Rose it would only be a matter of time before the rest of the King's mates were found as well.

"You Okay?" River said, taking a seat next to Rose.

"Yeah, I'll be fine. Looks like my boys aren't boys anymore." Rose said, looking over her shoulder through the bay windows at the three playing on the couch.

"They still care about you, my love." River said, taking Rose's hand and bringing it to his lips.

"I know. We each hold a piece of each other's past." Rose said thinking back to all the good and bad they had gone through together.

"They threatened me." River snickered.

"As they should. Right of passage among our little group." Rose said secretly proud of the three and the men they had become.

"Well we have a somewhat plan. But it's going to involve you being seen." River said, trying to gauge Rose's response.

"Well I didn't come to play on the sidelines. What's the plan?" Rose smiled knowing she would have to just endure and be prepared for what was to happen.

"We don't need them to know we are here yet asking questions. Sebastian has some contacts inside the pack right now doing that and will be reporting back within the next few hours. Enough of the rumor mill is going to be raised when you just happen to show up. Especially with Daisy.

Chris is going to be heavily watched to see what will happen when he comes back from... How do you guys put it "Fishing"? Daisy was really close to some girls that have been recently attacked and apparently busted up pretty badly. She was also the sister-in-law to one of the men that were killed from Desert Sun." River explained.

"So while I'm playing bait, I will also be getting information?" Rose repeated making sure she understood the assignment.

"Basically, yes. Chris has indicated that she was being harassed but wouldn't give anyone information. We are hoping as a female, she might talk to you about it." River explained.

"So, what am I supposed to be doing while I'm being seen?" Rose didn't like she wasn't the real part of the action but she knew it was a matter of time. She had been gone so long that it was only a matter of time before things got around about her being in town.

"Shopping?" River cringed away to keep from getting hit by whatever she might throw his way.

"I hate shopping." Rose whined, knowing that the mall was the place that everyone could get a good eye on her and start the gears rolling. Even on a Monday afternoon this closes to Christmas, the mall was the place for every busy body in the pack.

"I know, but it's a girl thing. It won't look out of place." River said and Rose knew he was right.

"It would be for me to be there. Unless that's the point. You would have the rumor mill working overtime." Rose realized she really was bait.

"Exactly. Plus, you'll be using my card. Spend some money. We need something to happen. Look at it this way. Either nothing happens and in that case you got to shop for the afternoon for whatever you want. OR someone makes a move and in that case I will be not five steps behind you." River tried to reassure Rose.

"Fine, set it up. But I'm getting a new knife, jacket, and boots." Rose said laughing because the last real leather dealer and her favorite knife store was in that mall.

"Buy whatever you like. Just know I want something sexy for later." River said walking behind her chair and nipping at her ear.

The plan was simple according to the guys. Rose would appear in town to go out with Daisy. Rose would hopefully get Daisy to talk about things that were going on. Which would give the Kings one more piece to the puzzle for their case against Hollows. One thing Rose wasn't aware of, they were going to see if they could trap the mystery man that was leaving harassing comments on Rose's phone.

Chapter 54

Rose left out with two guards to pick up Daisy. Chris had called and told her that Rose was in town. She was overjoyed about finally meeting the famous Rose. Daisy had gotten to hear all the stories about the four of them growing up.

As they pulled up outside of Chris and Daisy's house, Rose was aware that they were being watched. She signaled to the driver to be on the watch. The second guard got out and opened the door for Daisy.

Daisy had long blonde hair with sky blue eyes. She stood around 5'7" and a slender 120 pounds. While Rose was told she was shy, the bubbly girl next to her in the SUV didn't seem to fit the description.

"I'm so glad we finally got to meet. I have heard so much about you." Daisy said after the door was closed.

"I'm sorry it wasn't sooner, but Chris had been tight lipped about finding his mate." Rose said trying to apologize.

"Oh no matter. You're here now. Chris can be a very reserved kind of guy. I think after two years, he still can't believe it himself." Daisy said sporting what looked like an engagement ring.

"So when is the date?" Rose said, looking at the ring.

"Oh there isn't one as of yet." Daisy said, slightly sad. "It was supposed to be this Spring but when things started happening we thought it was responsible to postpone it."

"Well let's see if we still can't make that happen." Rose gave Daisy a conspiratory smile.

"Really?" Daisy lit up like the sun.

"Of course. Anything I can do to help?" Rose knew that girl talk was her way in.

"Convince Chris." Daisy said hopeful.

"That's an easy one. Do you have a dress picked out yet?" Rose asked.

"I have a couple in mind. I want something simple." Daisy said with a dreamy look on her face.

"We can, if you want, go look and see what we can find. We have the whole day to just hang out." Rose said, trying to keep her talking.

"You would go dress shopping with me? Are you serious? Oh my Goddess. You are the best!" Daisy basically bounced in her seat.

"Of course, I know it's a very important decision. While I don't have much fashion sense, I will try to be as much help as possible." Rose said, really wanting her best friend and his mate to be completely happy.

"Just the fact you offered..." Daisy started to cry. "Means so much to me."

"Hey no. It's okay. Everything is fine. Don't cry." Rose reached over like a mother hen and started drying her tears.

"It's been so hard around here lately. I miss home. Chris isn't happy. We had one bright spot which was the wedding and it was put off. Then you come into town. Chris is starting to really smile again." Daisy began to unload the burden she was carrying. "I'm just really happy you are here."

"Oh sweety. I know how it feels to just have things feel like they are just out of reach. We will get it handled. If I have anything to do with it, you will be the spring bride you hoped to be." Rose said, hugging Daisy to get her to calm down and stop crying.

"Thank you. You really are the glue." Daisy said, whipping her eyes.

"The glue?" Rose smirked.

"That's what Mike and Nathan call you. You were there glue that held them together." Daisy said remembering them talk about her as if she was some sort of super shewolf.

"I knew I kept them in line, but not the glue." Rose laughed.

They had chatted about everything. While it was a secret from the rest of the pack, Chris did tell Daisy about the boys. They all had pictures of Rose and the two little boys that always seemed to be doing something silly. Daisy had seen every picture. She always remarked on how Rose looked so happy.

By the time they had pulled up at the mall, Rose had gotten Daisy to open up to her. Rose knew that the girls in question were from both the Desert Sun and Hollows packs. As far as Daisy knew, the only contact that Alpha Asher and Beta Dallas had with the Desert Sun was when they hand delivered the invitation to the Harvest Moon Ball. As the hosting Alpha, Alpha Asher took this opportunity to personally invite what he thought was an alley pack.

Six of the girls, who weren't of age yet, disappeared three days before the ball from Desert Sun. Three of them, two months later, turned up not far from Chris and Daisy's house. They were busted up and in really bad shape. One of them was Daisy's cousin and she would confide in her what had happened.

Daisy would hide the three girls out for almost a week before making her way to the territory line and handing the girls over to patrol members. At that time, no one had been killed as of yet. Daisy said she kept an eye out for anything after she had found the first three.

The other three had not been found to date. Daisy feared the worst due to one of them being her niece and the daughter of the brother-in-law that had died at the hands of the current Alpha. Alpha Asher had announced after the men were killed that they were Rogues and they should all be on the lookout.

Daisy had recognized her brother-in-law along with several others that had been killed. When she brought it to Chris's attention, he had told her not to say anything to anyone. That he was trying to get intouch with the proper people to come handle it.

Rose had also found out that Chris was so worried about his mate and himself that he had started staying on and off at the shop or the lake house. On the nights he would have patrol, Daisy would stay at the shop with Carl and that's when the phone calls started.

Rose decided to store this information for later. Sebastian would need to know this information for his investigation. For now though, Rose was going to try to do what she was asked and make herself seen. Maybe even have a little fun even though shopping wasn't her thing. She did however have a very nice black credit card in her back pocket that she was sure was going to get some action today.

The girls agreed to pace themselves. After all it was a very busy time of the year, and there was so much to look at. They had no real plan going into this, but they were going to do some shopping.

The two guards accompanied them to every store. They would stand outside if it was just too much to handle while they looked around. The girls headed to the bridal boutique first which was at the other end of the mall. Daisy started trying on dresses. She had even convinced Rose to try on a few just for fun.

Daisy ended up finding the perfect dress. Simple and elegant with just a hint of sassiness. It was an off white strapless gown with a corset style lace up back and a moderately length skirt. It seemed to hug all the right spots. Rose thought she looked like a princess.

When Rose put on the last dress that Daisy had picked out, everyone in the store gasped as she came out of the dressing room. It was an off the shoulder bodice with a built in corset. A semi short front with a long flowing train in the back that could be pinned up for dancing. It was done in the most beautiful shade of ivory and blush.

As the two of them stood in the mirror admiring the dresses, Rose's phone began to buzz. She was pleased to see it was a text from River.

"Well don't you look like the most beautiful bride." River wrote.

"You're not supposed to see the dress, it's bad luck." Rose smiled as she responded.

"I'm only looking at the back." River wrote cheekily.

"OMG. Go somewhere!" Rose wrote while turning slightly red.

Rose put her phone down and looked at Daisy with a wink. They went back into the dressing rooms to change back into their regular clothes. Daisy had convinced Rose to buy the dress even though she was not the one getting married. Rose smiled at the fact that at least Daisy had her dress and that was one step closer.

They did agree not to pick out bridesmaids dresses until they knew what was going to happen with the weather for the spring. Rose wanted to make sure whatever venue they ended up with would have the appropriate attire. Everyone needed to be comfortable, which was one of the things the girls had talked about while trying on dresses.

Chris had told Daisy that Rose didn't have much of a wardrobe and needed some help finding some clothes. By the time they had stopped for a snack, they had been to no less than fifteen different stores. Rose had gotten so many different outfits, shoes, boots, a new leather jacket and matching vest, and five new knives.

There was also a lengthy visit to a lingerie store that happened to be having a sale. This resulted in Rose not only turning as red as her hair but about three thousand dollars being spent on new everything. Rose hated to admit when she needed anything. When Daisy had seen the condition of her current under garments, she took no chance making sure everything was taken care of.

They had one more stop for the guys' Christmas gift, which led them to the food court with the store they needed being just on the other side. The guards were taking turns running bags back and forth to the SUV. Everything seemed fine until Rose caught the scent of something foul.

"You know we can probably come back tomorrow and pick up their gifts if you want. I'm kind of all walked out for the moment." Rose tried to signal to Daisy that they needed to leave and leave now.

The guards saw Rose starting to tap her fingers on her cellphone, which was a sign something was up. As the guards scanned the room, the girls stood up and were getting ready to walk toward the opening of the mall. Rose locked eyes with Dallas from across the way. Rose knew she knew that scent of cheap cologne anywhere.

Dallas started to approach them, when River had come out of nowhere. River bent down and kissed Rose square on the lips and Dallas had stopped dead in his tracks. When Dallas finally did move forward coming face to face with Rose, she tensed but relaxed under River's touch.

"I thought I would surprise you. Did you have fun today?" River said, snaking his arm around Rose's waist.

"Always. I love surprises." Rose said, giving River alarm bells going off in his head.

River knew enough about his mate to know she hated surprises. This was her code to let him know that there was danger afoot. When Rose smugly smiled at Dallas, she could see the fury in his eyes. This please Rose immensely.

"King River Easton, I had no idea you were in town." Dallas said cooly, reaching to shake River's hand.

"We came in early for the meeting. Christmas traffic and all." River said, shaking Dallas' hand a little harder than needed.

"Awe yes, it can be bad this time of the year." Dallas said never taking his eyes off Rose.

"I believe you know my mate, Rose Wells." River said, gauging more Rose's reaction than Dallas.

"Yes, we graduated high school together. Does your parents know you're in town yet?" Dallas said almost dripping with glee at being able to put this out there.

"No not yet, but I'm sure with the way news travels. They will know before I ever have a chance to call." Rose said dryly as the fire built in her blood.

"Well we would love for you to stay at the packhouse. As always you are more than welcome there." Dallas said with a venomous smile.

"We have made other arrangements for lodging this time around." River said, trying to stay as level headed as he could with another wolf staring at his mate.

"Well then you should all join us tonight for dinner at the packhouse." Dallas extended this invite.

"We would love to. I'll tell the other Kings to change our plans so we can join you. We can go to Desert Sun tomorrow night, my sweet." River played it up as he kissed Rose's neck.

"Well I guess we will see you all tonight then. Come Daisy, we have to get ready. Oh by the way Chris, Mike, and Nathan will be our personal liaisons while we happen to be in town. So, someone will need to cover them for their duties." Rose said, looking back at Dallas.

"I don't think that's going to happen. You have..." Dallas started but was quickly cut off by River.

"You heard the Queen, Beta. I suggest you make it known an order from her is like an order from anyone of the Kings." River snapped back, putting an arm around each woman and walking them to the entrance of the mall.

By the time Daisy and Rose were safely in the SUV, Rose began to shake uncontrollable. They had barely made it out of the parking lot when the guard had to pull over and signal River to get out of the other SUV. When he got in the back and saw the state of Rose, he immediately engulfed her in his arms and began to rock her like a child. River had never seen Rose like this before, and didn't want her phoenix to react to the stress.

"It's okay sweetie just breathe." River said.

Daisy just took her hand and tried to calm her the best way she could. From what she was told by Chris, Rose was the strongest woman he had ever known. Daisy was not happy to see Rose in this state. It sickened her to think that someone would willingly do this to her.

Chapter 55

By the time they had gotten back to the lake house, Rose was sitting between River and Daisy stone cold calm. Daisy had been ordered not to go back to the house without Chris or the guards. Therefore, she was going to get ready for dinner at the lake house with the others.

Between the two women, they had bought more than enough clothes to be set for a month or so. So while the guys and guards unloaded the two packed SUVs, Daisy was telling them which bag was hers and which was Rose's.

Rose got out of the SUV and went around the back of the lake house. She needed to clear her head without being asked a thousand questions. River let her be for a moment, but did end up following her to make sure she was going to be okay.

Daisy was instructed to tell the Kings about what happened. River also urged her to tell them everything she happened to know about the current situation. That would keep her busy while River tried to figure out what sent Rose off the deep end.

Rose stood there just staring out over the water. She was aware of River's presence since he was only standing a few feet from her. Rose knew that she was going to have to pull it together to complete the mission at hand. She would have to table her well needed breakdown until after everything was handled. For now though, Rose had to be the strong Queen.

"You okay, baby?" River wrapped his arms around her from behind.

"Yeah, I'm sorry about that. I know I must have freaked Daisy out." Rose said feeling a little foolish for letting Dallas get to her.

"No, she's worried about you though." River said, still feeling her blood boiling.

"No need. I'm fine." Rose said, pulling away from River.

"Why are you being like that?" River asked a little hurt that she didn't want to be in his arms.

"Like what?" Rose said knowing good and well what she was doing. It was her way of dealing with things.

"Like something didn't just rattle the hell out of you. Like you haven't just reached the end of your rope and you're just grasping at strings. Like you haven't just reached your breaking point." River said, taking Rose by the arms and making her look at him.

Rose struggled to get away from his grip to create distance between them. It was all in vain as River didn't break his hold on her. He wasn't sure what she would do if she was let just stand on her own.

"Because, per usual, I don't have the luxury to break down and show the emotional wounds. That can and will be used against me. I have to be the wall. I have to be the unmovable force that protects and keeps everyone else moving forward. I am a Queen now and with that I have to hold face whether I like it or not. One crack in my composure will be looked at as a sign of weakness. I can't have that. WE can't have that." Rose spit venom in each and every word knowing what she was to do.

"Why? Why won't you let anyone help you carry that load? You know you're not alone in this. You never were. Eva and Tony have always been there. Chris, Mike, and Nathan before that were there. Sebastian, Axel, Ryder, and me are here now.

You're not a one woman wrecking crew anymore. You have proven yourself time and time again. You don't have to anymore. You're a badass little fireball, but you're also a woman that needs to desperately take care of herself.

Yes, we all need you. We will always need you. Dylan and Porter will always need you. I need you. But my love, you need to let some shit go, and get it off your chest. It's slowly killing you." River tried desperately to get Rose to understand she was wearing herself too thin by being so strong for everyone else.

The tears from her glowing green eyes began to flow as she looked back into River's eyes. He just held her until there were no more tears left. River picked her up and carried her bridal style up the stairs to the deck. When they got up to the deck doors, Axel was there to open the doors. Axel looked concerned at the sight before his eyes.

River didn't say a word, but one look said that someone was going to pay with their life. River took her down the hall to the bedroom. River made it through the sea of shopping bags to the bed. He laid her on the bed and climbed in next to her. He wouldn't leave her side regardless if the world had come to an end.

It took about an hour of the on and off crying to stop before Rose finally passed out on River's chest. River knew she was emotionally spent. He ran his hands through her hair keeping her as comfortable as possible while she slept.

River felt a tug at the corner of his mind. It wasn't the Kings or the guards alerting to something. River hesitated answering but eventually did answer the knocking in his mind. He smiled when he found Snow trying to make contact. She was a powerful wolf indeed.

"How can I help you Ms. Snow?" River said, smiling.

"Thank you. I just wanted to say thank you. I know your intention was not to make her cry. My lovely stubborn other half has some issues. I see soon they will be known, but until then please be gentle with her. Our transformation is not yet complete and I need her to willingly do this." Snow said bowing her head and began to take her leave.

Argo didn't want her to go, but as Snow passed him on her way out she flicked her tail at him. As she faded into the darkness, her action sent howls a plenty through River's head. Argo was trying to call Snow back with no luck. He eventually gave up and went to his corner and sulked.

River stared at his mate. She lay sleeping like the porcelain doll she was. Her strength was the only thing that kept her from busting into a million pieces. River gently kissed her head and removed himself from under her.

River quickly and quietly left the room to go to the bathroom. His poor bladder was screaming at him in need of relief. After coming out of the bathroom he headed to the kitchen for something cold to drink. River knew he had to be quick. He didn't want her to wake up alone.

When the guys heard him come out of the bathroom, they sat at attention for some sort of explanation. Ryder had already pulled two cold water bottles from the fridge by the time River had made it to the living room.

"Is she going to be okay?" Ryder asked.

"I believe so. It's just going to take some time." River said, keeping an ear out.

"What happened? Daisy said something about a certain Beta setting Rose off. That one minute she was fine and the next she was shaking like a leaf." Axel said ready to start busting some heads together.

"She was calm by the time we had gotten back here. She went down by the water. I might have pushed her too far. But it wasn't anything she didn't need to hear right now." River said forever etched in his mind would be the tear stained face of Rose and how it about killed him to see her like that.

"What did you say to her?" Sebastian inquired.

"Why was she acting like nothing was bothering her? That she is loved, wanted, needed, and always will be. That she needed to take care of herself and stop shouldering everything on her own." River cringed at how it sounded at that moment.

"You cracked her armor." Nathan said coming through the deck door.

The others were outside as Daisy had told them what had happened. Mike and Chris had gone to check on Carl and the shop. Nathan was at the packhouse when word had reached him that the Kings were in town with Rose. Nathan was given instructions by

Alpha Asher, which he was going to be relaying to the Kings when he found out that Rose had had a break in her normally steady and steel composure.

None of them at this point had ever seen Rose cry. Not even when she broke her hand putting the engine in Princess. The hoist had malfunctioned and Rose's hand had been pinned for almost thirty minutes between the engine and her steel fender. So to find out that she was bawling her eyes out, each one of the men wondered who was going to be set on fire for this.

They all closed their eyes and cringed. Sebastian knew this could go one of two ways and he couldn't see which. Either she would trust River and finally let him in or the walls were going to be thicker and taller than before. They knew they had to play this all very carefully when she woke up. No one would be allowed to mention anything about earlier.

They all agreed not a word. As River grabbed the cold waters and headed back to the room, he prayed she was still asleep. Thankfully, she was. River carefully put the bottles on the nightstand and climbed back into bed beside her.

River laid next to her for about an hour before he noticed her eyelids start to flutter. She was trying to fight waking up by snuggling in closer to River. River lightly touched her face to try to wake her up gently.

Rose's eyes opened and looked up at River. He smiled down at her. She leaned up and kissed him on the lips. Then rested her head back on his chest. She needed this right now. Even though she hated to admit it. She needed him like air to breathe.

Rose was lightly tracing one of his tattoos on his forearm, when a light knock came at the door. Rose knew the moment was over. River got up a little aggravated and answered the door. Mike was on the other side checking on Rose.

"She is just waking up. By the way, when is dinner at the packhouse?" River asked before Mike could get a word out.

"7pm. So in about an hour or so. Why?" Mike said looking at his watch and eyeing River suspiciously.

"Time to put on a show. Everyone in their best casual wear. We leave in forty-five minutes. We are going to be casually late." River said with a sly smile on his face.

It was time for all of them to be in the same room. Sebastian needed all the pieces of the puzzle. While every piece of evidence collected thus far had been true, it was time to put the puzzle together fully. If everything worked out with Rose and Daisy front and center, Sebastian would be able to make formal allegations by as early as tomorrow night.

Chapter 56

Three fully loaded SUVs pulled up at the Hollows packhouse at exactly 7:30 pm. Rose was surprised at how much the packhouse had actually changed in the four and half years she had been gone. Rose assumed that under Asher and Dallas a lot of modern changes had been made. It looked more like a fraternity house than the landmark of the pack.

Sebastian, Ryder, and Nathan took the lead in the first SUV. River, Rose, Daisy and Chris took the second SUV making sure that the girls were surrounded if something broke loose. Axel and Mike rounded out in the back in the last SUV. None of them were too happy about being there, but they knew they had strength in numbers.

As they unloaded, Rose stayed close to River. Rose took a deep breath as they approached the packhouse doors. When the doors opened, Alpha Asher and Beta Dallas along with two other females stood there to greet them. Rose gritted her teeth and reminded herself that they needed to handle this.

"Awe King River Easton, so good of you to join us. It's been too long since you visited." Alpha Asher exclaimed.

"Yes, it has." River said politely. "May I introduce my mate Queen Rose Wells."

"Awe yes. I remember Rose from high school." Alpha Asher reached out to shake Rose's hand.

"Alpha Asher." Rose said cooley. "The packhouse looks different after being gone so long."

"We have tried to bring it up to date. So many plans for it, everything is still a work in progress." Alpha Asher said with his eyes glinting at the rising moon.

"Well come in. I'm Luna Bethany." She said bowing to the group. "And this is Beta Lizzy."

River did not take the fact that Alpha Asher had not introduced his Luna well. There was protocol in these situations and they were acting like this was any other day. River put his arm around Rose's waist and led her inside.

If anyone thought the outside looked like a party house, the inside would confirm it. The once elegant and well put together packhouse, now smelt of beer and looked like there was a rave going on inside. The formal dining room was set up as a party.

People were dancing and the stage area that normally held the long table for high ranking wolves was now covered with speakers and a live band. Rose was truly disgusted at the site. *This is how they welcomed the Kings?* Rose thought to herself.

The large group was led over to the tables close to the dance floor. While the group sat down at the large round table in the middle of one side of the room, the guards surrounded them sitting at a few of the smaller tables. Everyone stopped and stared at the group while they were taking their seats. It didn't escape anyone's attention that Rose was being escorted by King River.

Rumors had already circulated about Beta Dallas seeing them at the mall earlier that day. When Dallas got back to the packhouse, he had told everyone that not only was Rose back in town but she was mated to the King. The impromptu party was for them even though it looked more like a regular Saturday night kegger.

As the waitress came around to get drink orders people were starting to slowly come by the table to get a closer look at the couple while paying their respects to the Kings and group. Rose felt the hair on the back of her neck rise and Snow began to howl fiercely in her head. As she looked up to scan the room, she came face to face with her parents. Rose cut her eyes to River when he noticed her tense up.

"King River, what an immense pleasure to have you back in the territory. Rose, you look well." Kate said with her usual overly polite attitude.

Kate reached out to hug Rose and the guards all stood. Rose merely raised her hand to call them off. With the events that had unfolded earlier, everyone was on their guard with Rose. The guards were just as over protective of the Queen as River was at that point.

"Mother. Father." Rose said dryly.

"So, how is school going?" Klye said, playing along with the original lie they had told everyone.

"Your grandchildren are fine. Thanks for asking." Rose said, cutting her eyes at them.

"Don't you dare." Kate began to raise her voice.

"The best thing for both of you to do is what the fuck away. Stay out of my sight or so help me. I do have the power to make your lives more of a hell than you ever made mine." Rose said, rising from her seat to make her point.

Rose was trying hard to control the fire that was building in her blood. She had no intention of playing their game. Rose was not ashamed of her children or the fact that she decided to bring them up on her own. She was however extremely ashamed of the two people that were in front of her.

"My Queen." River stood next to Rose. "Grace me with a dance?"

"I would love to." Rose took River's hand and walked right past Kate and Kyle to the dance floor.

Everyone's eyes were on them as River led Rose around each corner of the dance floor. River noted for someone that didn't dance she was very light on her feet. Rose slightly stiffened when River had gotten a tap on the shoulder.

"May I cut in?" Dallas said with a sickening sly smile that was a little more enthusiastic than he needed to be.

River looked to Rose for approval before giving up his dance. They needed information and with Dallas and Rose side by side, Sebastian would have all the puzzle pieces aligned. Rose knew she would just have to endure for a few minutes for Sebastian to be able to see everything he needed. Rose just prayed she could hold out.

"I would be delighted." Rose said with a wink letting River know the clock was ticking.

River kissed Rose and handed her over to Dallas. All eyes were now on them as Dallas led Rose around the dance floor. Rose tried to remain straight faced as ever with Snow trying to claw her way out. Rose was counting the minutes for the song to be over and she could escape.

Dallas tried to pull Rose close and whisper in her ear. As the fire in her blood began to boil, she knew it was time to end this anyway possible. Unlucky for her, Dallas decided to pull an old trick slipping his hand down from her lower back to her butt. Rose pulled away and decked him so hard that the sound of his breaking noise could be heard over the bass guitar.

"You fucking Bitch. You'll pay for that." Dallas said, trying to control the bleeding from his nose.

"No, I won't. Keep your fucking paws to yourself you worthless mutt or next time I will do far worse." Rose said, walking away.

Dallas stood up with blood pouring and reached out to grab Rose by the arm. "Look here you little Whore."

Rose turned around, eyes glowing an iridescent green and her hand were already starting to shoot sparks. When she raised her hands up the sparks had turned to fireballs that she was now playing within her hand. Those that were minding their own business and not paying attention to the drama unfolding were now completely paralyzed by the sight of Rose playing with two fireballs one in each hand.

River walked up behind Rose and kissed her neck ever so gently on the marking spot. The fireballs dissipated and Rose's eyes went back to her normal emerald green. Everyone stared in shock as they couldn't take their eyes away from what was happening.

Even Dallas stood there looking white as a ghost with so much fury in his eyes. Rose would not back down this time. If he came at her again, he would pay with his life for his general stupidity. River was the only one keeping him alive at this time.

"I believe it is time for us to go. Since you have already offended my Queen, I see no reason for us to have any further dealings here tonight. We will be in touch soon." River said as the rest of the party had already gotten up and proceeded to gather their things.

"Wait, King River. There must be some misunderstanding." Alpha Asher rushed over.

"No, I don't believe so. Your Beta has insulted my Queen. You're lucky he is still alive for now. We will be in touch." River said, taking Rose's hand and leaving with the rest of the group in tow.

Before they could get out the front door, Kate had grabbed Rose by the arm and tried to pull her out of River's hold. Kate looked infuriated. Rose just shook her off and looked at her like a stranger.

"What do you think you're doing?" Kate said to Rose.

"I'm leaving." Rose responded with disgust.

"Go in there and apologize to the Beta NOW." Kate demanded.

"Or what Mother? I will not waste one single breath on an apology to anyone that did that to me." Rose said, trying to walk away.

"You little WHORE. You do what I SAY." Kate said, trying again to grab for Rose's arm.

Rose came up with a fist as she spun around breaking Kate's nose and knocking her flat on her ass. Kyle came out of the ballroom to find Kate on the floor pouring blood out of her nose as Rose stood over the top of her. Kyle was furious with his daughter as he came to Kate's aid.

"What has gotten into you? First the Beta and now your mother? Have you lost what sense the Goddess gave you?" Kyle said, helping the squalling Kate off the ground.

"I believe you lost your damn mind long before I was born. After all she has done to me, she deserves so much worse than just a broken nose that will be healed in a day or so. Now I'm leaving with my Mate. I'm done with this and with you. You want her sorry ass then there she is." Rose said, taking River's arm and walking out of the packhouse.

Rose knew it took a lot for River not to jump into the situation. She hoped through it all he knew that she could handle herself. Rose proved it that night. When they headed back to the lake house everyone was silent.

They had decided that until things were handled with Hollows that none of the boys would return home. Sleeping arrangements were being made when they pulled back up at the lake house. Each of them would take their old rooms except for Nathan and Mike, who offered to bunk together to let the Kings have something more than the couch.

While the guys and Daisy headed inside to straighten out the bedroom situations, Rose headed for the lake to try and cool off with the brisk night air. River followed remembering earlier and knew she was less stable now than before. She handled herself well with everything being considered. He wanted to rip Dallas's head off right then and there. Even though he would have been in his right to do so, he knew it wasn't time for that just yet.

"Baby? Are you okay?" River said, wrapping his arms around her and pulling her tightly to his chest.

"Yes, I'm fine." Rose said as the moonlight shimmered over the snow covered lake.

"You know if you want. I can have them gone. Disappeared to the ends of the world without a trace of their whereabouts." River tried to make her smile.

"That's too good for them. Will I always be treated this way? I'm a Queen and yet I'm treated like some sort of leach. Like I'm worse than what Kate did to my father. Like I tricked or trapped you." Rose turned to face River.

"What do you mean?" River eyed her with curiosity.

"Do you know why I'm so hesitant to have you mark me? Do you know why I wanted you to reject me? Why do I believe, until proven otherwise, that I'm nothing to anyone but something to play with like a piece of meat. Very few have proven I'm worth more than that to them. Harvest Moon proved I belonged somewhere that wasn't here. That my boys belonged." Rose tried not to lose control of her emotions again but it wasn't going to be easy to not tell him now.

"My love, you are so much more than that. I know it will take me a hundred lifetimes to understand you. I will do whatever I have to for you to see that I'm never going to do anything to betray your trust in all areas of our lives together." River looked deep into her eyes.

"You might feel differently when you know everything. So, I'm going to give you this one chance. I'm going to tell you everything. If when I'm done you don't want me no harm. I go back to my boys and you go do you." Rose said.

"And if I do accept everything the way it is?" River eyed her knowing there was nothing she could say that would change his mind.

"I'll let you mark me." Rose looked at him so determined.

"Deal." River said walking over and sitting on a stump.

Chapter 57

Rose took a hard breath. She had not said any of this to anyone but Eva in almost five years. Now it was time to test the validity of the bond between them and hope that it was as strong as iron that would not break.

"I was 17 when Asher and Dallas came sniffing around. I knew cars. I was and still am a grease monkey. They saw me race down at the pits a few times. They decided to start coming by the house when I would be outside working on the car. It got to the point where Dallas would chat me up after class or even training." Rose began.

"It had become an everyday thing. Lunch. Between classes. Training. Hell he would even wait up the road from work and pretend that there was something wrong with his car so I would stop and help. At first I thought he was one of those big mouth jocks that didn't actually know how to ask someone out on a date. So when he finally got around to it, it was like okay whatever. I didn't have anything going on that night.

Shit got really weird really quick. I don't remember much more than Dallas picking me up and me thinking we were going to the pits for the party and ended up out in the backwoods. I don't know how I got home. I don't remember the party or anything that was done to me. He slipped LycanBerry into my drink not long after we got there.

Two weeks after the fact I found out I was pregnant. I had never been with a guy in any way prior to going out with Dallas. So, I knew the who but not the rest. When I confronted him, he confirmed everything. Said if I ever opened my mouth about what happened he would see that everyone would know I was just a whore. I asked him if he was my mate, because he was 19 and would know. It was confirmed he was not my mate and to add insult to injury he rejected me and my child. I, regretfully, told my mother in hopes that for once in my life she would be on my side.

She beat the hell out of me for the last week I was here. I was sent to Eva with the instruction to have the baby, put it up for adoption, and after losing some weight return back to marry a man of Kate's choosing. I had other plans.

Eva told me after the boys were born that my mother had more than just my blood on her hands. And how she did something that was against the Goddess. My mother has always reached too high and in such manor she wanted to be a Luna. Eva and her are Alpha's daughters and believed it was only right that she got what she wanted. Of course all she got was a Gamma.

She did try to get Uncle Tony with a potion from a witch, but when Eva turned out to be Tony's mate, it didn't go well. Kate gave Kyle the potion and now the man can only half think for himself. No one seems to know if she is still giving it to him or if it's just the lasting effects. When I was little though, Eva found out she was pregnant with a boy. Kate wanted her to trade children. When Eva refused, Kate made a big public fight and Eva went to leave to go back home to Harvest Moon.

She ended up flipping Uncle Tony's Nova six times and almost died. When they looked at the car after the accident they had found that the car was supposed to explode on contact. Whoever did it thankfully didn't know what they were doing. While Eva lived the child didn't. She knew it was Kate but with no evidence and she got away with it.

Personally, I'm glad I left. I'm glad my children will not be brought up in this environment. I can't stand the fact that shit has become so vile around here that toxic waste seems like an upside." Rose watched River's reaction the whole time, never leaving eye contact.

River's eyes were glowing with such anger and fury, Rose was unsure of what to do next. None of this was on her and she knew that. It was such a relief to finally have this off her chest that she began to cry which River couldn't stand to see her cry.

Rose braced herself for what was to come next. She had said her peace and River now knew that Dallas was the boys' father. If he wanted to take that information and run then he was within his rights according to Rose to do so. If he wanted to reject her then she would take the pain and live with it. At this point, what was one more shattered piece of her heart.

"So none of this was in any way was your doing?" River spoke as calmly as he could right now.

"No, but a lot would see me as tainted by their actions. That I'm not worthy of you or to be Queen." Rose spoke honestly even though she had accepted him and her place the ball was in his court on what the next actions would be.

River went and touched her face. Small streams of tears had started flowing down her cheeks. He couldn't stand to see her cry. Rose was the strongest and most delinquent object that had ever been placed in his care. He would not see her break for anything in the world.

River had no way of telling her, where she would believe him, that he was a virgin also. If they did happen to have a companion before finding their mates they were never allowed to go all the way. Something the Orcel made very clear. So at most they had rounded the bases but never got a home run.

"Rose, my love, nothing could change the way I feel about you. Not the Goddess herself. You're my Queen and that is that." River said, cupping her face in his hands. "Now onto the business at hand."

"The business at hand?" Rose blinked the tears away and tried hard to understand what was going on.

"Your marking." River said getting dangerously close to Rose sending hot sweet shivers rolling down her spine.

Rose's need for him grew down in the bundle of nerves in her belly. After everything that happened that day, she just wanted to have him alone with her. She no longer wanted to think. She just wanted to feel his strong capable hands all over her and make her forget all that wasn't him right now.

Rose flashed her glowing green eyes daring him to do something. River knew the gauntlet had been laid at his feet to see what he would do next. River slyly smiled at her and in one quick movement he slung her up over shoulder. River then proceeded up the stairs into the deck doors.

All conversation had come to a halt when they entered in such a fashion. River merely smiled and walked down the hall to their room. There were all kinds of hoops and hollers once they cleared the living room. Rose was holding her face in embarrassment for being carried into the room like a cavewoman.

Once they entered the room, River smacked her on the ass and dropped her on the bed. Rose looked at him in defiance. A carefully placed challenge with no words actually being said. River stood over her propped on the bed with her elbows when a slight knock came at the door. River never took his eyes off her as he moved to see whose head would be on a platter for interrupting.

When River opened the door, Sebastian stood there slightly embarrassed by having to talk to him right then and there. River looked at Rose putting up just one finger letting her know he would be right back. River stepped out into the hallway with glowing red eyes.

"You keep on and I'm going to make sure your mate gives you blue balls before you ever get to first base with her." River growled.

"I was just letting you know we are leaving the house to give you two some privacy. Do you want us to bring you back anything to eat?" Sebastian said, trying not to turn red.

"Yes, that's fine. You could have just left a note." River said with a growing need for the lovely redhead laying on the bed.

"Also. We have all the information that we need. They left themselves open for everything and I do mean everything."

Sebastian said, trying to get the last bit of business handled before leaving for the evening.

"Fine. We will discuss this in the morning. Now can I please get back to what I need to handle right now?" River said shooting daggers at Sebastian.

"Yes, your majesty. Just a word of caution. Be careful with our Queen. She might as well be a virgin with her lack of experience in this area." Sebastain said in a slightly embarrassed tone.

"Don't worry, I'll handle her with care." River understood the statement without Sebastian having to go into any kind of detail.

When River re-entered the bedroom, Rose was laying on the bed in a black lace babydoll negligee. The bedside light was casting an orange hue over Rose's ivory skin. River stood there with his mouth open and it had gone dry at the sight of her. As he approached the bed, River kicked off his boots.

River climbed onto the bed beside her and ran his hand down her face and into her hair keeping complete eye contact. He admired her body, all muscle and curves that the fabric hugged every possible curve of her body. River kisses her lips so gently that it sends sparks and fire through every possible area in Rose's body.

Rose brought her hand up to his face and ran her fingers through his hair weaving her fingering in the locks bringing him closer to deepen the kiss. With River's tongue licking her lips begging for entry, Rose parted with permission. As River's tongue began to invade Rose's mouth, Rose arched and her body begged for his touch.

River ran his hands over the fabric and down her side where her thighs lay bare and exposed. River ran his hand up the exposed thigh to the apex of her hip and Rose felt a flash of heat run through her blood which excited her. Rose released River's hair and her hands made their way down to the buttons of his shirt.

While Rose's lips never left his, her hands were busy making quick work of each and every button and pulling his shirt free from the waistband of his jeans. Once his massive chest was free from the shirt, Rose began running her hands all over tracing every muscle with her finger.

River brought his hand from her thigh to her breast cupping it though the fabric and making her peaks harden to his touch. He took down one strap exposing the milky white flesh and then broke the kiss to tease the nipples with his tongue. Rose moaned and began digging her nails into his back in pleasure. Which caused River to nip and suckel harder.

The bundle of nerves began to harden in Rose's core and she arched against him again this time feeling his growing member against her thigh. This made the fire coursing through her blood almost boil over and she silently begged for a release that she didn't know would ever come at this point.

River took down the other strap and began assaulting the other milky white mound of flesh. As all the sensations began to build, River slipped his hand down between her moist thighs to the treasure trove of nerves. He knew he wanted to play with her and build her to the point of no return before the consummation of penetration.

As he ever so gently moved around the outside of the treasure trove, River brought his lips to her neck and began to rhythmically play in two spots to drive Rose wild. River laid kisses from her collarbone to the marking spot and down again. Rose arched and bucked as River just took his sweet slow time.

As River began to slowly explore with his fingers the tight, hot, wet area, Rose began to lose her mind and the rollercoaster of sensations building to its peak. River knew it wouldn't take much to push her right over the edge so he would stop and start teasing her and making her cry out for him not to stop.

River wanted to taste her first explosion and kissed his way down from her marking spot across the mountains down past her belly and to the apex of her thighs. He was getting lost in her hot scent when he flicked his tongue and in the most sensitive area and watched as she arched up for more. He was certainly going to give her everything she could handle and more.

It didn't take long at all as he nipped, sucked, and teased. Rose felt the climb and the nerves began to tighten to the point of driving her mad. River began to explore the treasure trove with his tongue and as he began to lick the quivering jar, Rose was sent over the edge clamping her thighs around his head and grabbing his hair and she let go and found her release.

River could feel her body singing to his touch and licked up every drop making the area more sensitive and Rose moaned harder and she unclamped her thighs from around his head. River let her legs fall around him as he came back up to kiss her with her taste still on his lips.

Rose laid there perplexed at the emotions and sensations running through her body and above all she wanted and needed more. To feel his hands all over her body and his breath on her skin, she wanted every last bit of him to be melted and mageled into her.

Rose reached for his belt buckle and began to pull his belt free. Unbuttoning his pants and using her heels of her feet to move them off her waist as she felt his weight on her body. When she felt the enlarged member against her thigh, Rose went wet again in anticipation of having him inside her.

Rose used all her strength and flipped him on his back. She climbed on top of him teasing the opening of her treasure trove with the thick head of his member. River pushed himself up til his back was against the headboard. River pulled the babydoll nighty over her head so he could see every inch of her sweat sheened body.

Rose looked deep into River's eyes as she lowered herself onto him. She felt everything stretch and mold around him as she felt full with him inside her. Rose slowly began to rock her hips as River ran his hands down her back and across every curve. As they built agonizingly slow deep thrust into faster paces, Rose bent her head down to River's marking spot and licked it. She felt the twitches of pleasure he was feeling.

As Rose began to climb higher and higher, she ascended one of her canines and as she felt herself go over the edge she bit down on his marking spot. River, feeling himself start to go over the edge with her bite, came up and marked her as he emptied himself into her. Both moaned, shaking the room with the deafening sounds and Rose seemed to be glowing from an eternal flame.

They collapsed into each other's arms. As the moon came into view casting shadows across their bodies, Rose knew there was no other place in the world she would ever want to be. She had given everything to him in that moment and she prayed to the Goddess that it wasn't a mistake to do so.

River laid there with Rose on his chest running his fingers up and down her bare back. He understood more now on why they were told they had to wait. This was an incredible moment that would only be shared with one woman and that was his mate.

Chapter 58

The light was bright and almost blinding in Rose's eyes as she lay on River's chest trying to hold her eyes shut not wanting to greet the day. Rose's body was still singing from the activities from the night before. She was surprised at the aggressive nature they both put forth. Rose knew that no matter what came or went this is where she wanted to be and who she wanted to be with.

River began to stir underneath her and it caused Rose to have to shift off of him. This made Rose upset because she knew at any moment she would have to get up out of this bed, and in the process the moment would be gone. She knew there would be more but she didn't want this first one to end.

River's eyes opened and he looked at her pouty lip. He thought she looked adorable and knew this was only the beginning of a very long life with her. He took his hand and brushed her check and leaned up to kiss her nose.

"Good Morning, my Queen." River said looking deep into her eyes knowing this would make her smile.

"Good morning, my King." Rose said, putting a sly smile behind her words.

After the marking last night, Rose truly was the Queen. They had officially marked each other and now nothing could tear them apart. River did notice not so subtle changes to Rose. Her hair was brighter in the sunlight and her emerald green eyes had a red ring around the outside. River wondered if the transformation that Snow had talked about was complete.

River had no idea what other things had changed. Rose seemed more at ease and comfortable around him. Though it was a little hard not to be when they were both lying there naked. While River did stare and admire every inch of her body, he knew certain things had to be handled today and the briefing of what Sebastain found out was unfortunately high on the priority list at the moment.

"I need coffee." Rose said leaning up to kiss River knowing it was time for them to climb out of bed and deal with the events that brought them to this awful pack.

"Do you want me to bring you some or should we go out there together?" River responded knowing that everyone would have to be briefed to go forward with the issues of the Hollows pack.

"No, we might as well get dressed. Just know I'm not putting on real clothes until we have to leave this house." Rose said stretching and River noticed the definition of her muscles in her back.

"That's fine. I think I smell food." River said, smiling at the tall red head that was currently pulling on a hoodie and fuzzy sweatpants with nothing on underneath.

River's heart skipped a few beats with the knowledge that he could bend her over and have his way with her with little to no issues. River tried to shake the images out of his head while getting dressed to walk into the living room. River pulled on a muscle shirt with a pair of black gym shorts.

Rose pulled her hair back in a simple braid and began to walk out of the room with River right behind her. As they walked down the hallway, they could hear the conversations going on in the room. Rose didn't even blush when they crossed over to be within view of the others.

The room went bone silent. Rose walked over to the now waiting cup of coffee and took her first few sips. The other Kings bowed their heads and Rose merely nodded as she went to the living room. River was looking at the others as laughter erupted in the room.

Boys was all Rose could think rolling her eyes at the group. She knew they would be discussing the conquests of the evening when she wasn't around but for now it was time to get down to business. Rose merely cleared her throat and the silence returned. Some would think that the King was the highest rank but in all actuality it was the Queen that held everything together.

"Your Majesty?" Axel brought over a biskit and some jelly.

"Thank you." Rose thought it would be best not to argue about the title thing this morning.

"How are you doing this morning?" Daisy came over and sat next to Rose on the couch as the boys were all around the table talking with Sabastian.

"Surprisingly okay. How are you doing after last night's trash fiasco?" Rose responded by sipping her coffee.

"Actually that's what I wanted to talk to you about." Daisy said, looking around to make sure they couldn't be heard.

"Yes?" Rose looked at her curiously.

"Is it true?" Daisy looked at Rose seriously.

"Is what true?"

"Dallas?" Daisy said in the lowest voice possible.

"And the boys?" Rose said, looking surprisingly unfazed by the question.

"Yes, that he is the father." Daisy finally spit it out and hoped that she would not be offended by her asking.

"He might have helped in the genetics department. But..." Rose sat up and looked at River from across the room. "That man right there is their father."

"I'm sorry. I didn't mean to offend you. It's just a few people were talking about it last night. Chris shut them up quickly but I just thought I would ask." Daisy said knowing that she had probably upset Rose which was not her current intention.

Rose stood up and smiled at Daisy. Rose knew she meant no harm but it was finally time to let the cat out of the bag since this was all going to come out at any time anyway. When Rose stood from the couch, everyone turned and looked.

"May I have everyone's attention please." Rose said and everyone stopped what they were doing to look at her. "I would like to say this one time and one time only. No I will not be taking any kind of questions or do I care what anyone besides my mate has to think of the situation. I am laying one item of business to rest right this second so listen up.

I, Rose Wells, was raped. I do not remember anything but I did find out the who after I found out I was pregnant. When the slimmy SOB was confronted he told me to keep my mouth shut or my reputation would be ruined. I left and chose to raise my boys on my own. I stand her and tell you that River Easton is their father from this day forward and if anyone values their life that will be all they ever know.

Dallas Ellis, on the other hand, is the one that perpetrated this heinous crime on me. Now if you all will excuse me. I am going to take my coffee outside and get some fresh air. I will also be on the phone to check on my boys." Rose flung her hair off the side of her neck showing her mark proudly as she went to the room to retrieve her phone and shoes.

Daisy sat there slightly embarrassed as she was the reason Rose just decided to announce to the whole room the secret she had been caring for so long. This was no skin off Rose's nose at this point. Rose knew that Dallas had no claim over her or the boys and by the time she was done she would have his head.

When Rose came through the living room and kitchen, she had her head held high and the red in her hair seemed to pulse. All the Kings looked at the River, he shook his head as not to say a word until she was outside. River handed Rose the coffee cup and kissed her on her mark.

Rose smiled and walked out the doors to sit on the porch to look out over the lake. Rose picked up the phone and called Eva to check on the boys. She was happy to hear that they were being good and couldn't wait for Santa to show up in just two whole days.

Back inside everyone looked at River to see what they should do with this new information, River was in just as much shock as the rest with Rose finally standing up and releasing this information after five years of keeping it silent. It was absolutely absurd that no one knew anything about the current situation.

"Did she at least tell you first?" Sebastian asked, knowing the truth all night and not being able to say anything.

"She did." River said comfortably at the decision Rose decided on.

"So what do we do with this now? I mean we have enough just with her to bring Beta Dallas up on charges." Ryder said, looking outside at the strong woman. Ryder hoped his mate was just as strong as Rose.

"But she isn't the only one." Mike said standing at the counter.

"What do you mean, Rose isn't the only one?" Axel arched an eyebrow.

"She is the only one to have children by Dallas. None of the others given the LycanBerry have resulted in a to term pregnancy. Dallas's own mate is barren. So is the Luna." Sebastian piped up.

They began discussing everything that Sebastain had found out the night before. How there were too many beyond count that had been given the LycanBerry by not only by the Beta but also the Alpha. They had girls that were being hidden somewhere but Sebastain couldn't see where since they were not there long enough to get that information.

All of a sudden something outside caught their attention, Rose was levitating off the deck. By the time they tried to move to the outside, Rose had touched down and looked at all of them with fiery red eyes. River made it to Rose's side in a flash.

"Baby, what happened? What's wrong?" River repeated to get her to look at him.

"We have to go now. Right now." Rose said in a stern but commanding voice.

"Where?" River still did not understand what was going on.

"The packhouse." Rose said, looking at him so seriously.

"You heard her. We leave out in 10 mins." River yelled back through the open door.

Chapter 59

Rose and River went to their room to get ready. River couldn't get the fiery red eyes to subside. Rose merely put on her black cargo pants, black tank top, and her new leather vest. Rose had bought a new chain for her wallet that had three at different lengths that went down her left leg that she hung each one of the new throwing knives on.

Rose didn't say a word, she just merely got ready and walked back out of the bedroom into the living room. River watched her carefully but didn't know what to do. He had never seen Rose in this kind of state before. He knew she was heavily armed for reasons he had no knowledge of at this time.

Within ten minutes, they were all loaded up and headed toward the packhouse. All the guys and Rose. Daisy was ordered by Rose to stay there and lock the doors. Three guards were left with her in case this did not go as it was intended. Rose didn't want Daisy to get hurt or become a liability to the current mission.

When they pulled up at the packhouse, Rose immediately jumped out and the Kings along with Chris, Mike, and Nathan followed closely. Rose held out her hand and blew the doors open and watched as Alpha Asher and Beta Dallas looked at her in shock. When they went to say something to her all she did was look at the guards and point to them. They immediately restrained them and took them to the ballroom to be held out of the way.

Rose walked to the side door that led down a long hallway to the basement. After walking to the other side of the basement, she was met by three guards. She indicated for them to open the door and move out of the way but they stood fast in their position. Rose looked at Axel and Ryder to remove the men that blocked the door.

Without so much as a blink of an eye, they both held the men out of Rose's way. When Rose opened the door the smell hit her like a jab to the stomach. Blood, urine, and just general body odor filled the area. This was the dungen and during the other Alpha"s reigns was hardly ever used.

Rose drew a fireball to her hand to light the way in the darkly lit area. There were ten to twelve cells down there and each one had a female chained to the wall. Everyone, including Sebastian, looked at Rose in surprise. Not even Sebastian saw this coming.

Rose looked at the men to start releasing the woman. They were all worse for the wear but they were alive. The three missing girls that were now women from the Desert Sun pack were among the over 20 packed down there chained to walls and bars like animals. Rose grew more angry by the second.

Each one of the females were marched up the stairs and out of the packhouse. The guards were instructed to take them back to the Lake house and to make sure each one was cleaned up with fresh clothes and food. They would be questioned when they returned but no one was to leave until they returned.

They nodded at Rose and loaded everyone into the three SUVs and took off like a bat out of hell. No one dared to question Rose's orders once they were given. Rose walked into the ballroom where the two men were being held. Rose looked directly at Dallas in disgust and the fire of a thousand flames coming out of her eyes.

Dallas just sat there with his usual smirk on his face. Rose walked straight over and belted him so hard across the face that blood and teeth came out. Growls from the others that were also being held in the room erupted echoing off the walls. Dallas just spit the blood and began to laugh.

"What you fucking whore is that all you got?" Dallas spit blood at Rose's feet.

"No, I have so much more. I can kill you without ever laying a hand on you. But I told you if you ever called me a whore again. You even breathed wrong in my direction. I would make sure you paid. Now it's time to pay up." Rose got about an inch from his face with River pulling Rose back and tried to calm her down.

"That's right, comfort your whore." Dallas was now taunting King River. "You know I had that sorry piece first. How's it feel to not get that trophy?"

"Asher and Dallas, you are brought up on crimes against the Goddess and all wolf kinds. How do you plead?" Sebastian stepped forward to get the trial started.

"You have no right to ask us anything." Dallas spit back.

"Oh you're wrong there. We are the Kings. See that lovely redhead right there, she is a Queen." About the time Sebastian said the words Dallas saw not only River's mark but Rose's as well. This infuriated him to the point of jumping up and trying to go after Rose.

Rose just brought her hand up with a fireball in her palm. Dallas froze in his tracks wondering how she could be doing this. As she walked closer to him, Dallas backed up and went back to his chair. Dallas couldn't tell if he was more amazed or scared at the site he was currently seeing.

"You heard him. How do you plead?" Rose said, looking right at the pair.

Rose was too distracted looking at the pair and didn't notice standing off to the side was Chase Price. When Rose locked eyes,

Chase freaked out. He went running from the room when one of the guards caught him and sat him down with the rest.

"Chase, I'll give you one chance to tell me the truth and your punishment will not be as harsh as these two. Did you have anything to do with the girls in the dungeon or the drugging of unsuspecting females?" Rose's eyes intensified looking at him.

"I didn't want to do it, they made me." Chase began to sing like a canary. "They figured if they could produce pups they could keep the males and sell the rest off. Some of the girls didn't make it. The others were locked up down stairs. I swear I had no part in what they did. Even though I knew about it and didn't stop it." Chase rambled and began to cry.

"Chase Price, you are stripped of your title as Gamma. You will receive one hundred lashings and set loose on the far end of the territory to live out as a rogue. You will never come back here and if you do you will be killed on site." River handed down the punishment swiftly and without mercy.

Two guards grabbed Chase and took him from the room to the dungeon to await his punishment. Everyone could hear him screaming and crying while he was being escorted to the room where so many had already suffered. It was only right that he went there to suffer as well.

"Asher, How do you plead?" Rose looked at the sniveling little weasel that still looked like he was going to get away with what he had done.

"Not guilty. This is my pack and I will do with it as I see fit. Dallas as my Beta also has every right to do with the pack as he sees fit. You have no right to tell me what I can and can't do Whore." Asher grew a set since the last time they had come face to face.

"I will take that as guilty of all charges. Now you have this opportunity to explain yourself or let the charges stand." Ryder glared at the two men.

"You will get nothing from us." Asher said some would say half expecting his father to come in the room and stop what was about to happen.

"River call the Pack to the garden. This is going to need to be public." Sebastian said.

River let out a growl that anyone within a ten mile ear shot could hear. The two men were dragged out with their hands bound behind them. As the pack members started to arrive, most of them were too scared to make eye contact with the Kings or Rose. They all lined up to see what was going on.

After every single member including the former Alpha Kent and Luna Zara, the Kings began to address the group. The current Luna Bethany and female Beta Lizzy were crying loudly at the site of their mates being accused of such heinous crimes.

"We the Four Lycan Kings of the sacred Orcel mother of power by the Goddess of the moon do hear by bringing formal charges against Alpha Asher and Beta Dallas. Gamma Chase has already admitted to his crimes and is being dealt with swiftly and with haste. Your Alpha refuses to see what he has done to unsuspecting women of this pack and others as a crime. Beta Dallas refuses to do the same. King Sebastian being a seer has seen their acts and now put them into formal charges.

We now demand you, Alpha Asher and Beta Dallas to speak now or remain silent with and suffer your consequences. It would be best for you to see the error in your ways and speak to your people for they may be your last words they ever hear." King River addressed the group and hoped that the humiliation would cause them to ease their tongues.

They remained silent holding their heads high as if they had done nothing wrong in the matter. The rules of the Goddess that were passed down to every high ranking member of the pack were sacred and the punishment for even a shred of proof was death. They were willing to take their pride to the grave as they knew they would be publicly executed.

"No words on your behalf? Not even for the members of this pack that followed you blindly to this demise?" King Axel spoke to the worthless men before them.

"Your charges are as such. Alpha Asher and Beta Dallas, you are charged with giving LycanBerry to under age shewolves. You are charged with the rape of said shewolves for not only your own personal gain but gain for profit. You are charged with the kidnaping and imprisonment of six under age shewolves of the Desert Sun pack. You are charged with the wrongful death of no less than twelve Desert Sun pack members. You are also charged with the withholding of information to willfully start a war. Dallas Ellis, you are charged with the rape and harrassment of Queen Rose Wells. How do you plead?" King River rattled off the charges.

"We aren't guilty of any of this. We are the leaders of this pack and as such we will do what we wish." Asher spat at the Kings while looking out over the people of Hollows.

"I didn't do anything to any of those bitches that they didn't want." Dallas said so arrogantly.

"King Sebastian?" King River brought forth the seer.

"They are past guilty of all charges." King Sebastian looked out over the crowd. "Will anyone speak for them?"

The crowd remained silent. Even their parents knew better than to speak up when it came to the Kings. While it broke their hearts to watch their sons stand there like that, they knew if they had broken the law then they had to pay the price. Though everyone looked to Queen Rose to try to save the boys. Rose would not say a word in their defense.

"Then by the power of the Goddess, you will be executed for your crimes. You and your families will be forthwith stripped of your titles. Your mates are also stripped of the titles that bind them to this pack and We hope that the Goddess has mercy on them if they themselves have no dealings with the situation." King Ryder said moving in front of Asher and Dallas.

In less than a heartbeat, King River moved first to Asher and ripped his throat out while King Sebastian reached right into his chest and pulled out his beating heart. King Axel removed his head while King Ryder held Dallas's head and made him watch the fall of a corrupt Alpha.

As they moved to Dallas, he cried and begged for his life. So different then just moments ago when he decided not to plead for his life. Now his best friend was dead and he knew he had moments left on earth. While Rose was disgusted by this blubbering figure in front of her, the sight did pull on her heart strings ever so slightly.

"Wait." Queen Rose said as they got into position to start his execution.

"Yes, Your Majesty." King River said, watching her every move.

"I believe he needs to be punished, but death is too good for him. He learns nothing if he doesn't live in the same pain and misery that each one of those women will have to go through for the rest of their lives. Even if by chance they were to find their mates. There is a high probability that they will be rejected and left in pain for the rest of their lives. If by chance they don't take their own lives.

He needs to feel that pain. He needs to be rejected and disfigured and made to live as an outcast rogue. He needs to look like the things nightmares or made of so anyone that looks upon him will know the consequences to breaking the laws of the Goddess." Rose said in not so many ways begging for Dallas's life even though he didn't deserve it.

"As you wish, your Majesty." River bowed before his Queen knowing it would be far worse to make him live looking like a monster then letting him off with death. "Grab the wolfsbane and silver wipes. Someone hang him by his wrists from the tree."

As River was shouting out orders Dallas stupidly opened his mouth where only the ones standing close to him could hear him. Unfortunately for Dallas, Rose was still in ear shot. When she turned around River had already had him by the hair of his head showing him something on his phone. Rose recognized the picture, just taken days ago, of the boys with him and Santa.

Rose walked over and placed her hand on River's arm. When he looked back at her, there was an unspoken understanding. River would always be Dylan and Porter's father.

Dallas might have been the genetic material but it was going to be River that would be there through it all.

"Get everything ready. We have our sons to get back to." Rose quietly said to him.

As River nodded and turned away, Dallas began spitting more insults at not only at River but anyone that dared follow the whore Queen. "You all are a bunch of pussies. That bitch wasn't even a good piece of ass. And those bastards will never be more than just that."

Before anyone could stop her, Rose had fired a fireball right at his genitals. She then waved her hand and made his whole body burst into flames. Everyone just watched in shock and horror as he screamed and writhed in pain. The crowd began to get sick when they could smell his cooking flesh. As the screams stopped, Rose waved her hands and the flames were gone.

She looked to the men and told them to behead him as she began to walk away. Rose was stone faced as she walked through the crowd and no one dared make eye contact. When she got to the outer edge, a familiar hand was beginning to pull her back to reality right then and there.

"What the hell have you done?" Kate's voice screeched.

"I'm handling official business. I would kindly ask you to remove your hand before I have you brought up on charges as well mother." Rose's eye glowed red and some would take that as a warning and back the hell away. Then again Kate had just witnessed her daughter turn Dallas into a rotisserie chicken and was still trying her patients.

"You aren't shit. Queen or not, you still serve your mother and father." Kate was going wild.

"You have about two seconds and your fate will match Dallas's. So I suggest you take your hands off of me NOW." Rose looked at the Four Kings walking towards her.

"Your Majesties. This woman is a fraud and I can not believe you would trust her judgment against the former Alpha and Beta. I implore you now to see her for what she is and have her stand trial." Kate looked like a crazy woman talking nonsense all wild eyed and such.

"I would suggest you take your hands off the Queen or you can suffer the same fate as the rest." King Sebastian said looking to the others who with just a twitch would have your head removed from this woman's body.

"Now now. She is just overly excited by the actions of the day. Maybe she should go lie down and regain her senses." Rose said, walking away.

Rose barely made it around the side of the packhouse when Kate tried to pull her by the hair. Snow at this time had had enough and overrides Rose's control. Standing bigger than before the snow white wolf had changed. She had bright Red fur and white tips with four pure white paws.

Snow went straight after Kate. Kate didn't even have time to react let alone shift at that point in time. Snow had Kate by the throat and was beginning to bite down when Kyle tried to stop her. Snow did not take kindly to anyone, father or otherwise, interrupting her fun. The low growl that came out of Snow rattled the ground and caused Kyle not only to bow but show his neck in submission.

Snow knew that now matter what was to happen, Kate needed to be tried for the crimes she had committed. While the vast majority of them would have her put to death, Snow knew there were far greater punishments that would last a whole lot longer. She grabbed Kate by the hair of her head and dropped her at Sebastian's feet. She knew she couldn't say anything but with the look in his eye he knew what to do.

"While our Queen has shown you mercy and has not wished you death even though your crimes show otherwise. You and your mate are banished from this place. You have 24hrs to remove yourself or you will be put to death. This will be your only kindness." King Sebastian said as Kyle came to rush to Kate's aid.

"Where are we to go?" Kyle said as this was the only home he had ever known.

"Not our problem. Your clock has already started." King River spoke.

"From here on out you will be known to this pack as a rogue and will be treated as such if you ever return." King Ryder explained.

Kyle quickly gathered his mate off the ground and ran toward their car to escape the Kings and the oversized red wolf. While it hurt both Snow and Rose to see her father look at her this way, they knew he was too trapped by her spell to ever see reason on his own. They did hope that one day he would come to terms with the issues and see Kate for what she was.

Snow walked up to River and began to rub her head against his arm. River understood that with the quick transformation Rose would not be able to turn back without proper attire. River just ran his hand through the soft fluffy fur. Snow began to howl and wag her tail.

Snow merely winked at him and took off running in the direction of the lake house. The kings had instructed the guards to handle the bodies and make sure that Kate and Kyle were out of the territory in the amount of time they were given. The rest of the pack were instructed to return to their homes until more information could be given to them about the pack's fate.

As of right now, one of the three SUVs had returned back to the packhouse. So all the men had piled into it and headed back to the lake house to regroup. They knew either the pack would have to be disbanded and in such the word would have to be put out to the other packs. The only other option was for the Kings and Queen to come up with an appointed Alpha and Beta.

There would need to be heavy discussion among their options. There were also calls that needed to be made to the families of the females, and Alpha's of their packs to let them know that they were not only found but were in fact alive. This was going to be a long evening and too much was up in the air to know what was going to happen next.

Chapter 60

A quiet hush fell over the Hollows pack that night. Chase had received his punishment and was turned loose. They took compassion and treated his wounds before being sent on his way. The widows of the former Alpha and Beta could be heard howling at the moon in their loss.

Alpha James and the other Alpha's of the missing girls quickly came to retrieve the girls after they were questioned by the Kings and Queen Rose. They didn't simply just turn them back over to their packs though. Rose made sure to make sure everything would be in place to help with any and all problems that would arise from the trauma.

Kyle took the words of the Kings seriously. While Kate demanded he do something, Kyle knew this was not the time or place to challenge the ruling. Kyle and Kate packed up everything of worth and intended to leave at first light. Kate tried and failed at getting anyone inside the pack to help them.

Kate even called Eva which refused to even answer the phone. Rose got a call from Eva later that night to find out what was going on that would warrant a call from Kate. Rose explained what she could over the phone saying she would give her the play by play when they got back into town.

Chris and Daisy took peace in knowing all the hell was over. Chris admitted since it all started that he was put on double patrols to keep him away from home. On those nights, Daisy would get strange and threatening phone calls. They were happy they finally could go home and breathe easy.

Nathan and Mike took the opportunity to just visit with family. They knew something big would be happening soon and they wanted to make sure they were all prepared for what the Kings would decide. Mike knew more than anything it would be Rose calling the shots when it came to this because of her being the Queen.

The Kings and Rose were left at the lake house to decide Hollows fate. They knew they had two options. They could disband the pack and make sure everyone found better homes elsewhere. Or option number two was to name a new court for the pack. While everyone was going back and forth about it for hours, Rose finally stood her ground and put her two cents into the men's decision.

"Okay… Okay… Enough. We can not send these people from this place. Most of them have been here since birth and it's not fair. Carl, Chris' Dad, has owned that shop since we were all pups. It's not fair to expect him to just give up everything and leave." Rose finally said in a huff.

"Well then what do we do then?" Axel asked, getting more aggravated.

"We name a new Alpha, Beta, and Gamma." Rose said simply.

"And how do we know Who to name? It's not like we have time to interview and sort through every man or woman in the pack." Ryder said, taking a cigarette from River.

"Well see, you're looking at it all wrong. We already know three that have gone above and beyond to help. They would hold up tradition and put things back the way they are needed. It would take some time but it would take less if we were to call in some help from other packs." Rose said with a sly smile.

"Well your Majesty, do enlighten us." Sebastian smiled knowing which way Rose was going with this.

"Mike is the strongest and more dominant one of the three. I would say for him to be Alpha. Chris has always been a good second and while quiet he is level headed. Nathan moves up from Delta to Gamma. We leave the Delta position open for them to be either named at a later date or to eliminate the position all together. As I believe, there are not many packs that have a Delta anymore." Rose said, pouring herself a glass of wine and going to sit on the couch.

River looked around the room at the men that couldn't make a decision not two hours ago and looked at Rose like some sort of miracle worker. Really Rose was. She was thinking of the people as a whole, not just a pack that happened to be led astray for the moment. River was in awe at his mate and her settling into her role as the Queen.

As the room sat in silence while the Kings were mauling it over, they realized there really was no other way. These three had proven their worth and would also be loyal to the Queen herself. Anything managed to break out, they would be the first to know.

"I believe you are absolutely right." River said, shaking his head at the fact that the answer was staring them right in the face but it took Rose to put the big neon sign around it.

"Agreed." the other three said at once.

"Okay. Then if that is all the pressing business of the evening may we please discuss dinner? I'm starving." Rose said cheekily.

"Do you have any good places around here?" River asks.

"Rocky's but he is already closed for the night. There used to be a decent pizza place that delivered. Hold on, let me see if I can find the number. They have amazing cheesy bread." Rose said, hunting for the phone book.

A knock came at the door and Rose grinned when she saw Mike standing there with a very large bag. Rose ran over and opened the door with two of the guards in tow carrying bags. Rose just began to laugh as everything was laid out on the counters.

"Momma Kay, sends her regards to the Queen. A little bit of everything and all your favorites. She does request you stop by if you can before you leave. She also wants to know when you will be bringing her grandsons to see her." Mike said as he unpacked everything.

"Well please tell her thank you from all of us. I will see what I can do. Tomorrow is Christmas Eve and I need to pull off a miracle and get home fast for the boys." Rose said, looking at enough food to feed an army.

"She understands. You know she can't send you off without feeding you." Mike giggled.

"It's been her way since we were kids and she found out what Kate was doing to me." Rose leaned over and gave Mike a hug.

"Speaking of which. They were supposed to be leaving at first light. Two of the guards have reported they left under the dead of night. They were headed south. So I believe Delli is fixing to get a visit from the wicked witch." Mike said, relaying back the information.

"I almost feel like I should call and warn him but you remember that one time he laid that scratch on my fresh paint job. I said I would get him back and Kate told me to stop being so sensitive?" Rose smiled evilly.

"I remember." Mike was damn near in tears holding back the laughter.

"Payback's a bitch." Rose said, digging into a casserole dish of mac-and-cheese.

"That's so cold. Funny but cold." Ryder said, peeking under the tinfoil.

"Look I had just painted Princess. Delli was trying to impress this girl, which would end up being the cousin to his mate that happened to be visiting family. He leaned up against my car with his chain on his wallet. As he moved down my car trying to get her attention, he scratched my paint job. I told him one day I would get even. Looks like that day has come." Rose smiled, taking a heaping forkful of cheesy chicken and rice.

"Note to self: Don't mess with Majesty's princess." Axel said as the whole room erupted into laughter.

"Bet your ass." Rose said, waving her fork at the men.

"I have to confess. The food isn't the only reason I came by tonight." Mike looked around to see if he could read the room. "Have you come to a decision?"

They looked around trying to decide whether to be tight lipped or let what would soon be known out. Rose knew that a little information wouldn't hurt. It would be just a few hours before they would all know what was really going on anyway. She didn't see the harm in it and the rest of the men seemed to feel the same way at that moment.

"We have." Rose said.

"Good, bad, or indifferent?" Mike looked at Rose.

"I would say good. But that would depend on the rest involved." Rose said, taking the next forkful.

"Just give it to me straight." Mike said.

"The pack will have a new high court named and the world will go on spilling once again." Rose noticed that Mike let out a breath that he wasn't prepared to hold for long.

"Can you say who as of yet?" Mike pressed for more information.

"All will be revealed in just a few hours." Rose said, winking at Mike.

"That's fair. I will have everyone at the packhouse first thing in the morning." Mike said. "Oh and Momma Kay has already started the clean up and such."

"Goddess, I love that woman." Rose said knowing that the last time she had to leave and say goodbye they had come here first.

Rose quickly texted the rest of the guys telling them there was food that Momma Kay had sent over. She wanted to spend as much time with the guys as she could before she would have to leave and go back to her own little family. She had these last few hours as even then she has that last perfect day.

Within minutes, the house was filled with so many people, laughter, and really bad stories of when Rose and the guys were younger. Nothing was off limits. Therefore, before the end of the night, River and the others knew all kinds of things about the red headed Queen. While most would die from embarrassment, Rose owned all the crazy things she did.

Hours later, they all made their way to bed and tried to get some shut eye before the announcement and the long drive home. If they were lucky they would get back to Harvest Moon before Santa. They wouldn't dare tell anyone in case something happened and they ended up being later than expected.

When they got up the next morning, bags were packed and loaded into the cars before heading to the packhouse. Rose was certain this was the best course of action since the three men in front of her believed in the old ways and would bring peace to the Hollows pack. She would get regular reports to make sure things were running smoothly.

Once everyone was gathered into the ballroom, Rose looked out over the crowd not seeing Bethany or Lizzy. Someone told her that they left for their grieving period and to seek counsel from the Orcel. Since they were marked, they would have to plead their case to the Orcel and have her plead to the Goddess on their behalf.

"Settle… Settle…" King River was drawing all attention to the stage where the group was standing. "We understand that everyone is very concerned with the situation as of late. We are here to put your mind at ease."

"Hollows will not be disbanded. We have come to the conclusion that most if not all would like a chance at building back a better pack. And with that being said." King Sebastian said looking over to Queen Rose.

"Mike, Chris, and Nathan, will you please come up here?" Rose said trying to keep a straight face when it came to her friends. "Do the three of you promise to uphold all the responsibilities of this pack. To renew the old ways and always to hold these peoples' safety in the highest regard?"

"We always have and always will." Mike said, looking at Rose curiously.

"Then with the Power vested in me as the Queen of the south Mike you will be the Alpha of this pack and may you rule it well. Chris, you will be the Beta. I hope you always keep a level head in all situations. Nathan, you will be Gamma. Your head for business and conflict resolution will serve well here. We leave Hollows in your capable hands." Queen Rose walked over and kissed each man on their cheek as her final blessing.

Rose gracefully bowed and walked out of the room toward the front door and the three blacked out SUVs that waited outside. She held herself well through it all but this leaving again to start the next chapter in her life was still going to be hard for her to do.

The Kings shook hands and followed after Rose. It was going to be on the three young men to see what they could make of this pack. As for now, they would leave some help behind cleaning up the mess and help in forming new bonds with the surrounding packs. They had no doubt that Rose made the right decision in making and holding the men in such high regard.

One last look back, Rose smiled and loaded up. They had an even more important mission than this, and that was beating Santa to the Harvest Moon pack.

Epilogue

Standing in the bridal room with a nervous Daisy was not how Rose saw her morning going. It was a bright sunny May 15th. Everyone stood there sweating in the dry heat. Daisy was sure that her hair was going to fall or she was going to be tripping over her dress.

Rose had promised that Daisy would be a spring bride and by the Goddess she had pulled everything off with class and style. The two wanted a very traditional wedding but small with just close pack members from both Desert Sun and Hollows. The event was heavily guarded and it was meant to be a peaceful day.

The boys were playing with River and the others. Rose kept sticking her head out the door to ensure they were not getting dirty. Daisy, Chris, and all the guys insisted that the boys be in the wedding as the ring bears. Since they were doing the traditional wedding they would need two. One to walk with Daisy and one to stand with Chris. They looked adorable in their little tuxedos and top hats.

Mike's mom, Momma Kay, had even made all the food and helped with every piece of the event. She was also currently sneaking the twins cookies when Rose had told them NO. Momma Kay had told her to hush and see to the bride. Which is code for "I will do with my babies as I see fit."

Daisy's mom stuck her head into the room in complete awe at the blushing bride-to-be. She knew that it was going to be an amazing day but she went through the motions of fluffing Daisy's dress and making sure her jewelry wasn't hung up in the vail.

There was a sadness that hung in the air that they tried to overlook. Daisy's dad had died two months prior on a southern patrol run. Axel and Ryder stepped up to walk Daisy down the aisle. They knew how important this moment was and tried their best to do the honor proud.

"It's time ladies." River called into the small room.

Chris and Daisy were keeping up with the old traditions when it came to their ceremony. Daisy was formerly of Desert Sun and became the Beta Female of the Hollows. So in this tradition she would walk toward the line and cross over once the "I Dos" are done. Binding both packs together in a sign of love and peace.

It was a lovely ceremony. With the sun clearing the mountain behind the bride as she walked toward the archway that was built for their ceremony. As River stood there saying the speech and going through the motions, Rose even thought she saw the Kings shed a few tears. Dylan and Porter made adorable ring bears. Rose even wondered if this was what her wedding would be like. Rose always wanted something simple if she was ever to actually walk down the aisle.

The kiss was made and there were immediate hoops and howls from the crowd. The happy couple walked over to the big tent and little by little everyone followed. Rose hung back looking out over the mountain where the sand touched the plains. As River walked up behind her and wrapped his arms around her waist, he knew what she was thinking.

River wanted to wait to pop that very special question when he had more time to have a sit down with Uncle Tony. He respected that Rose looked at him like a father and knew it was only right to ask his permission. He thought using the boys to help would also be a nice touch.

While Rose was standing there looking out over the clear sky and plains, she was remembering the dream from what seemed like forever ago. Her body stiffened and she began to levitate. Thankfully, everyone was too busy with the current celebration and pictures to take notice. When Rose touched back down her eyes were glowing red and she looked stoned face.

"Baby, what is it?" River looked at Rose concerned.

"Sebastian is next, isn't he?" Rose looked amused.

"Next? You mean for his mate?"

"Of course."

"Yes, why?" River looked confused.

"The raven-haired beauty's name is Star." Rose said, looking up at her mate with a wicked grin.

www.ingramcontent.com/pod-product-compliance
Lightning Source LLC
Chambersburg PA
CBHW070848260626
47170CB00007B/2540